WAR

LAVABROOK PUBLISHING

Published in the United States by Lavabrook Publishing, LLC.

Cover by Regina Wamba
www.maeidesign.com

In loving memory of Robert H.

Forever your "little sister."

When He broke the second seal, I heard the second living creature saying, "Come." And another, a red horse, went out; and to him who sat on it, it was granted to take peace from the earth, and that men would slay one another; and a great sword was given to him.

—*Revelation 6:3-4 NASB*

Cry 'Havoc,' and let slip the dogs of war;
That this foul deed shall smell above the earth
With carrion men, groaning for burial.

—Shakespeare

Chapter 1

Year 13 of the Horsemen

Jerusalem, New Palestine

THE DAY STARTS off like most others. With a nightmare.

The explosion roars through my ears, the force of it knocking me into the water.

Darkness. Nothing. Then–

I gasp in a breath. There's water and fire and ... and ... and God the pain–the pain, the pain, the pain. The sharp bite of it nearly steals my breath.

"Mom, Mom, Mom!"

Can't see her. Can't see anyone.

"Mom!"

The sky bobs above me. I cough in the smoke. My bag is wrapped around my ankle and it's dragging me down, down, down.

No. I try to kick my way back up to the surface, but despite my efforts it moves farther and farther from reach.

My lungs pound. The sunlight above me grows dim even as I struggle.

I open my mouth to cry for help.

The water rushes in–

I sit up in bed with a gasp.

I can hear my wall clock clicking away, the pendulum swinging back and forth, back and forth.

I touch the scar at the base of my throat as I steady my breathing. My sheets are twisted around my ankles. I disentangle myself and roll out of bed.

Grabbing a nearby box of matches, I light an oil lamp. Briefly, it illuminates a picture of my family before I raise it high enough to see the time on the clock.

3:18 AM.

Ugh. I rub my face.

I set the lamp down on my workbench, shoving aside the feathers, glass arrowheads, and scraps of plastic that litter its surface.

I glance longingly at my bed. There's no way I'm falling back asleep, which means I can work on my latest commission or I can go scavenging. I glance at the walls, where some of my finished products hang—the oiled bows and painted arrows barely visible in the darkness.

Salvage-chic weaponry sells for a pretty penny these days.

It's too dark to make out the photos hanging alongside them, but my throat tightens at the thought of the images anyway.

Right now, on the wings of my dream, I don't want to keep company with the memories that haunt my flat.

So scavenging it is.

MY BOOTS CRUNCH along loose gravel as I wind my way through the streets of Jerusalem, outfitted with my bow, quiver, and the canvas bag I'll use to store my finds. I have a dagger at my hip and a small axe in my bag.

I pass by a darkened mosque, which will be filled with people by the time I return. The synagogue down the street is dark and ominous, several of its windows boarded up. It looks meek and repentant, like it didn't once proudly own that space.

No one else is out, save for the occasional Palestinian guard. They eye me grimly but leave me alone.

Life wasn't always this way.

I can vaguely remember my childhood. I had a happy one—or rather, I used to lack worries, and that's almost the same thing. Now, worries stack like stones on my shoulders.

But that life is less real to me than even the dream I woke to.

I touch the hamsa charm on my wrist as I glance around me. The moment I get a little too comfortable with my surroundings is the moment I get attacked.

No, life wasn't always this way, but this has been my reality ever since the Horsemen arrived.

I can see Day One in my mind's eye like it's happening all over again.

How the lights in my fourth grade classroom popped as they burned out, one after the other. My ears still ring from the sounds of my classmates' screaming.

I had the misfortune of sitting near a window, so I saw firsthand how the cars lost power, their metal bodies crashing into whatever—or whoever—was nearest them.

I saw a woman mowed down by a car, her eyes wide for that single second before impact. Sometimes, when I remember it, it's my father I see and not the woman.

I wonder sometimes, if that's how it played out. I never saw his mangled body—I just heard that he'd been hit by a bus—so all that's left is wonder.

People around here are fond of saying that life can change in an instant, and it's true. Birth, death, four strange men showing up one day with plans to destroy the world—all instant life changes.

But sometimes, the most insidious change happens over time. Because Day One ended and Day Two began. We were all expected to just continue to exist even when cars couldn't drive and phones couldn't call, and computers couldn't compute, and so many beloved lives were lost. Eventually this terrible new existence had to become normal. And that's how life's been for most of my twenty-two years.

I move west through the city, past an aviary, the birds inside quiet at this hour. Once, you could get news almost instantaneously. Now carrier pigeon is the fastest way of sending messages ... and there's no guarantee that an outgoing message will get where it needs to go on one try. Birds, after all, are only so obedient and intelligent.

The night is quiet. It's been like this for the last month. Not that it's ever particularly rowdy here at night, but this feels different. You can sense people's worry in the still air.

It must be the rumors.

There were ... strange stories from the east, stories meant to scare you when you're huddled over a fire and the night seems especially terrifying.

Stories about entire cities going to the grave. About streets scattered with bones and cemeteries tilled like fields. And through it all, War, riding on his blood red steed, his sword brandished.

I don't know how true they are—these days, so many things are hearsay—but Jerusalem has been more subdued than usual. A few people have even packed up and left.

I might've been one of those people, if I had enough money to get where I wanted to go. But I don't, so Jerusalem it remains.

As I get close to the Judaean Mountains that lie on the outskirts of the city, I hear the echoing footfalls of someone walking behind me. Could be the Muslim Brotherhood, could be the Palestinian police force, it could be a raider like me or a prostitute looking to fill the last of her quota for the night.

It's probably nothing. Still it doesn't stop me from going over my survival code, otherwise known as *Miriam Elmahdy's*

Guide to Staying the Fuck Alive:

(1) Bend the rules—but don't break them.

(2) Stick to the truth.

(3) Avoid notice.

(4) Listen to your instincts.

(5) Be brave.

Five simple rules that, while not always being easy to follow, have kept me alive for the last seven years.

I pick up my pace, hoping to put distance between me and the stranger. Less than a minute later, I hear the footsteps behind me quicken.

I sigh out a breath.

Sliding my bow off my shoulder, I remove an arrow from my quiver and nock it into place. Spinning around, I take aim at the dark shape.

"Move along," I say.

The shadowy figure is maybe ten meters away. They raise their hands, stepping forward a little.

"I just wanted to know what a girl like you was doing out this late," the man calls out.

So, the individual's not a prostitute and probably not the police either. That leaves the Muslim Brotherhood, a local gang member, or an ordinary civilian willing to pay for a woman's company. Of course, he could also be a fellow raider looking to poach my finds off of me.

"I'm not a prostitute," I call out.

"I didn't think you were."

So, not a confused customer.

"If you're with the Brotherhood," I say, "I've paid my dues for the month." It's the cost of moving about the city with impunity.

"It's alright," the man says. "I'm not with the Brotherhood."

A raider then?

He takes a step towards me. Then another.

I pull my bowstring back, the wood of my bow groaning.

"I'm not going to hurt you." He says it so kindly that I *want* to believe him. But I've learned to trust what people do rather than what they say, and he's *not* backing off.

A criminal then. Honest people don't just sweet talk their way into getting closer unless they want something from you.

And whatever he wants, I doubt I'm going to like it.

"If you come any closer, I will shoot," I warn.

His footfalls pause, and the two of us stand there for several seconds at an impasse.

He's standing in the shadows between the gaslit streetlamps, so it's hard to make out what he's doing, but I think he's going to leave. It would be the wise thing to do.

His footfalls resume—one, two, three—

I close my brown eyes briefly. This is no way to start a day.

The man begins to pick up his pace as he gains more confidence that I won't shoot. He's completely unaware that I've done this before.

Forgive me.

I release the arrow.

I don't see quite where it lands in the darkness, but I do hear the man's choked gasp, and then I see him collapse.

For several seconds I stay where I am. Only reluctantly do I lower my bow and walk over to him, a hand hovering near the dagger at my hip.

As I get close, I see my arrow protruding from the man's throat, his blood darkening his skin and the ground beneath him. His breathing is wheezy and labored.

I stare at his face for several seconds as he grasps at the projectile. I don't recognize him, not that I assumed I would. I guess that's a relief. My eyes go to the bag he was carrying.

Crouching down, I open it up and rifle through his things. Rope, a crowbar, and a knife. A murder's starter pack.

Unease skitters through me. Most people who do bad things have their motives—greed, power, lust, self-preservation.

It's unnerving to cross paths with someone who plans on hurting you not as a means to an end, but as the end itself.

The man's choking breaths slow, then stop altogether, his chest going still.

Once I'm sure he's gone, I remove my arrow from his body, wiping it off on his trousers before I slip it back into my quiver.

No one will bother to investigate what happened. No one will be punished, and by the time the sun is high in the sky, the body will be moved and the city will soon forget there was ever a corpse in the road to begin with.

Giving the man one final glance, I touch the hamsa on my bracelet and walk away.

I HEAD OUT of the city and into the hills that lay to the west, trying not to think about the man I killed and what he wanted. Or that I barely paused before killing him.

I rub my forehead and then my mouth. Death is getting easier for me to dole out. That's ... worrisome.

Once I've made my way into the rolling mountains, I veer off the road and towards the trees. The sky is just starting to lighten, turning from navy to ash as the sun gets closer to the horizon. Farther up the hill I see the bones of a half-complete house, the cinderblock and corrugated iron frame only partially complete before its owner abandoned the project.

I move towards it, the shell of a house a familiar sight. But it's not the building I was seeking so much as the trees around it.

Heading over to a pine tree, I pull out my axe and begin to chop away at a thick branch. The wood here makes for good bows and arrow shafts.

Fifteen minutes into my work I hear ... something.

I pause, my eyes going to the road. I strain my ears, but the wooded hills are quiet—

Wait.

There it is again. The sound is barely audible. I can't tell what it is, only that it's steady.

Probably a traveler.

I move to the nearby house, quietly slipping inside. I'd rather not get into a skirmish twice in one night.

Inside the abandoned structure, dirt, old leaves, and several cigarette butts litter the ground. By the looks of the place, it was built after the Arrival—there are no electrical outlets, nor are there any pipes that might carry running water. Those luxuries we lost shortly after the horsemen came, and try as we might, we haven't been able to get them back.

I move over to an open framed window, keeping mostly to shadows. I feel like a coward, hiding behind a wall because I *might've* heard something, but after my earlier run-in today, better a coward than a dead woman.

Ever so slowly the sound gets louder, until I can make it out distinctly.

Clop. Clop. Clop.

A mounted traveler.

I peer out the window, the sky now a rosy hue. There's trees and brush that partially obscure my view of the road, so I don't see the individual right away. But when I do—

I suck in a breath.

A monster of a man sits on his blood-red steed, a massive sword strapped to his back. There are gold rings in his dark hair and kohl thickly lines his eyes. His cheekbones are high and the scowl he wears makes him look absolutely *petrifying*.

For a moment, none of what I'm seeing really registers. Because what I'm seeing is *wrong*. No horse has a coat that red, and no man has that impressive a stature, even in the saddle.

Well, if the rumors are true, then maybe *one* person does ...

I feel myself start to shake.

No.

Dear God above, no.

Because if the rumors about his description are true, then it means that the man I'm staring at might actually be War.

My lungs seize up at just the thought.

And if the rumors *are* true—

Then Jerusalem is fucked.

A small noise leaves my lips, and War—if that is, in fact, War—turns my way.

I duck back down.

Oh my God, oh my God, *ohmyGod*.

A horseman of the apocalypse might actually be standing twenty meters from me.

The hoof beats pause, then leave the main road. Suddenly, I hear the clop—clop—clop of them heading up the hill towards me.

I cover my mouth, muffling the sound of my breathing, and I squeeze my eyes shut. I can hear the crunch of dry brush and the horse's noisy exhalations.

I don't know how close the horseman gets before he stops. It *seems* as though he's right outside the building, that if I stood and reached out the window, I could pet his steed. The hair on my arms rises.

I wait for its rider to dismount.

Could that really be War?

But why *wouldn't* it be him? Jerusalem has been the epicenter of several religions for centuries. It's a good place to bring about the end of the world—it's even been foretold that this *is* where the world ends on the Day of Judgment.

I shouldn't be surprised.

I still am.

After one long minute, I hear the retreating footfalls of War's—shit, I guess I'm assuming it really is War—horse.

I wait until the footfalls are sufficiently far away before I gasp, a fearful tear slipping out.

Oh my God.

I don't move. Not until I'm sure War has moved along.

But just when I think he's gone, I hear more hoof beats. *Several* more hoof beats.

Who else could possibly be following the horseman?

The hoof beats seem to multiply on themselves until it starts to sound like thunder.

I peer from that shell of a window. What I see takes my breath away.

There must be *hundreds* of riders all squeezed onto the road, armed with knives and bows and swords and all other manner of weaponry.

My heart begins to pound faster and faster, and yet I keep still, so still, afraid to even breathe too loudly.

I wait for them to pass, but they keep coming, the riders followed by what look like foot soldiers, and those followed by horse-drawn carts.

The longer I watch, the more riders pass me by, until it becomes clear that there aren't merely hundreds of men, but *thousands* of them, all who follow in War's wake.

There's only one reason this many armed men are traveling together.

War isn't simply riding into Jerusalem.

He's invading it.

Chapter 2

I WAIT UNTIL the entire army has passed through before I leave my hiding spot. I step out of the building on shaky feet, unsure what to do.

I'm no saint. I'm no hero.

I stare at that road heading west, in the direction *opposite* the army, and it looks awfully enticing.

I glance in the other direction, towards where the army headed.

My home.

Leave, my mother's voice says in my head, *leave with the clothes on your back and never come back. Leave and save yourself.*

I make my way to the road, leaving behind the branches I chopped down. I glance both ways—west, away from the city, and east, back to Jerusalem.

I rub my forehead. Goddamn but what should I do?

I go over my survival code again: Bend the rules—but don't break them. Stick to the truth. Avoid notice. Listen to your instincts. Be brave.

Always be brave.

Of course, these are the rules to staying alive. I don't need the rules to know that going west will increase my survival odds while going east will lower them. It shouldn't be a question at all—I should go west.

But when I turn and start down the road, my feet don't take me west.

Instead I march back towards Jerusalem. Back to my house and the army and the horseman.

Maybe it's stupidity, or morbid curiosity.

Or maybe the apocalypse hasn't beaten the last bit of selflessness out of me after all.

I'm still no saint.

BY THE TIME I arrive in the city, the streets are already running red with blood.

I press the back of my hand to my mouth, trying to cover up the sick smell of meat that tinges the air. I have to step around the bloody bodies that litter the streets. Many of the buildings are burning, and smoke and ash billow about me.

In the distance I can hear people screaming, but right here, right where I'm walking, the people have already been killed off, and the silence seems to be a thing itself.

Before New Palestine was New Palestine, Israel's military drafted most of its citizens. Since my country's civil war, there's been no mandatory conscription, but most youths here learned to fight anyway. As I glance around at all the dead bodies, I realize none of that matters.

For all the knowledge they may have on fighting and warfare, they're still dead.

Truly, what was I thinking, coming back here?

My grip on my bow now tightens. I pull out an arrow and nock it.

I shouldn't even care to save these people. After everything the Muslims did to the Jews and the Jews did to the Muslims, and what everyone did to the Christians and the Druze and every other minority religious sect, you'd think I'd be happy to just let it all burn to the ground.

All religions want the same thing–salvation. I can hear my father's voice like an echo from the past. *We're all the same.*

I walk faster and faster through the streets, my weapon at the ready. The place has been swept through. More structures are on fire, more dead bodies lay scattered in the streets.

I came too late. Too late for the city, and too late for the people.

A few blocks more, and I start to see living people. People who are fleeing. A woman runs with her son in her arms. Ten meters behind her, a mounted man chases her down.

I don't even think before I raise my bow and fire off the arrow.

It hits him square in the chest, the force of it knocking him off his horse.

I glance over my shoulder in time to see the woman and her son duck into a building.

At least they're safe. But then, there are so many others who are fighting for their lives. I grab an arrow, nock it, and shoot. Grab, nock, shoot. Over and over. Some of my shots miss, but I feel a flush of satisfaction that I'm managing to pick off any of these invaders at all.

I have to duck as I continue through the streets. People are leaning out their windows, throwing whatever items they can at this strange army. As I move I see a man get pushed off his balcony. He lands on a burning awning below. The last I hear of him are his screams.

At some point, a few of the invading soldiers recognize that I'm a threat. One of them aims his own bow and arrow at me, but he's on a horse, and his shot goes wide.

Grab, nock, shoot.

I hit him in the shoulder. Grab, nock, shoot. This time my arrow gets him in the eye.

Need more arrows. And other weapons, for that matter.

I make a break for my flat, which is several blocks away,

whispering a prayer under my breath that I don't run out of arrows before I get there. I have a dagger on me, but I'm no match for a bigger opponent, and most of these soldiers are just that—big opponents.

It takes about thirty minutes to get to my place. I live in a condemned building—not that anyone's going to tear it down anytime soon. It sustained some damage during the fighting a few years ago and most people moved as a result. I didn't. Call me sentimental, but it's where I grew up.

When I get to it now, the entryway is on fire.

Crap, why hadn't I thought of this?

I eye the structure. It's mostly made out of stone, and besides the entrance, it looks alright. I chew the side of my lip.

Making a decision, I dash inside. Not three seconds after I do, the overhang collapses, closing me in.

Well shit. I'm going to have to either hop out of a window or else hope the ancient fire escape works.

Once I'm inside, I dash up the stairs to my flat, coughing against the smoke.

I slow when I catch sight of my apartment. The front door hangs ajar.

Motherfucker. Someone else must've already had the same idea I had. People around here know I make weapons.

I step inside, and the place is a mess. My workstation has been overturned. Along the shelves, the knives and swords and daggers, bows and quivers and maces and arrows I'd carefully stored have almost all been removed.

I don't pause to scavenge through them. Rushing to my bedroom, I lift up my mattress. Beneath it are dozens upon dozens of arrows and a spare dagger.

Dropping my canvas bag to the floor, I scoop up the arrows and shove as many as I can into my quiver. Then I grab a sheathed dagger and quickly strap it to me.

After I've armed myself, I head downstairs. Kicking in a door to one of the apartments I know is abandoned, I step inside. The windows here are mostly intact, and I have to grab a discarded chair and smash it against the glass for it to shatter.

Knocking out the last shards, I step outside and run into the fray once more.

IT'S NOT UNTIL I'm just outside the Old City that I catch sight of War.

And it's him alright. I didn't believe my eyes when I first saw him, but now, bathed in the blood of his victims, his eyes gleaming like onyx, there's no way he could possibly be anyone else.

He sits astride his horse in the middle of the road, his steed pawing the ground. The creature is just as fearsome as all the stories promised it would be.

War surveys the carnage around him, looking far too pleased with the results.

Nocking an arrow into my bow, I line the horseman up in my sights.

Aim for the chest. Anything else is too likely to miss altogether.

War's head snaps to me, almost as though he heard my intentions whispered on the wind.

Shit.

He takes in my weapon, then my face. War kicks his horse forward.

I let the arrow fly, but it veers off, missing him entirely.

Slinging my bow across my chest, I turn on my heel and take off, my arrows jiggling at my back.

I glance over my shoulder. War is driving his steed forward, the horseman's cruel gaze locked on me.

I cut across the rubble where a building used to stand and head into the Old City.

Please don't twist an ankle, please don't twist an ankle.

Behind me I can hear the pounding of hooves, and I can

practically feel the horseman's menacing stare boring into my back.

There are a dozen other people fighting and fleeing around me, but the horseman disregards all of them. I'm the only one he seems to have eyes for.

Fuck. Fuck. Fuck.

It's fitting, I suppose, that I would meet the horseman here, in this place that has seen millennia of strife and war. Jerusalem is full of just as much blood as it is soil.

The hoof beats grow louder, closer.

I don't dare look back.

Normally, there are always a few people who linger in the Old City, but right now, the place is utterly abandoned.

Why did I think to come here? God can't save me. Not when his spawn is too busy running me down.

I hook a left and suddenly the Western Wall is looming next to me. I run alongside it, my eyes locking on the Dome of the Rock.

If ever there was a time to believe in salvation, now would be it.

I push my arms and legs, snaking back and forth so that the horseman can't cut me down from behind.

The mosque is so close I can make out the finer detailing along its walls, and—

The entrance is shut.

No.

I keep running for it.

Maybe it's not locked. Maybe ...

I close the last few meters between me and it, grabbing the door handle.

Locked.

I want to scream. I can see the Foundation Stone in my mind's eye, I can see the small hole that leads to the Well of Souls below. If there was ever a place that a horseman would need to respect the sanctity of, that would be it.

I back away from the locked door and the columned archway. I back into the blinding sun.

Behind me, the hoof beats come to a stop. The hairs along my forearms rise.

I swivel around.

War swings off his mount, and I stagger back at the sight of him.

He's *huge*. Taller than a normal man, and every centimeter of him is built like a warrior—broad shoulders, thick arms, lean waist and powerful legs. Even his face has the look of some tragic hero, his feral, masculine beauty only serving to make him appear more lethal.

Almost casually, War pulls his sword out of the scabbard on his back. My eyes go to the massive blade. It gleams silver in the sunlight.

How many deaths has that weapon delivered?

But then another sight catches my eye. My gaze travels up War's weapon to his hand. On each knuckle is a strange glyph that *glows* crimson.

War begins to stride towards me, his red leather armor making soft noises as it rubs together, his golden hair adornments glinting in the sun. He looks less like a heavenly messenger and more like some pagan god of battle.

Grabbing my bow, I nock an arrow.

"Stay back," I warn.

The horseman ignores the command.

God save me.

I release it.

It hits War in the shoulder, embedding into his leather armor. Without looking away from me, he grabs the arrowhead and yanks it out. It comes away bloody, and I have a moment of pride, knowing that my weapon made it past his armor.

I reach behind me for another arrow, nock it, and let it fly. This one bounces harmlessly off of him, the angle of the hit all wrong.

And now I'm out of distance.

I only have time for one more shot before I need to switch weapons. I grab a final arrow, aim it, and release.

It goes hopelessly wide.

I drop my bow and quiver, my carefully collected arrows now spilling across the ground. My hand goes for one of my daggers.

No match for that beast of a sword. I take another look at War's enormous muscles, and there's just no chance of me winning this.

I swallow.

I'm going to die.

My hand tightens on my blade. I have to at least *try* to stop him.

I begin to move, trying to place my back to the sun. War closes the last of the distance between us, not bothering to outmaneuver me. He doesn't need any sort of advantage to cut me down, we both know it. And if the sun is irritating to him, he shows no sign of it.

That's about the moment when I realize that this isn't actually going to *be* a fight. This is a lion swatting a mouse aside.

Must've really pissed him off earlier.

War lifts his sword, the sun making the blade shine blindingly bright.

With one pounding sweep of his arm, War's terrifying blade connects with my own much smaller one, knocking it out of my hand. I cry out at the impact; the force of the blow numbs my arms and drives me to my knees.

I reach for my other blade, unholstering it. When the horseman steps forward, I swipe out at him, catching him in the calf.

A line of blood wells from the wound. For an instant, I stare at it dumbly.

Holy balls, I actually clipped him.

War glances at the wound then his eyes move to me, and he laughs low and deep, the sound drawing out goosebumps along my skin.

This fucker is downright *terrifying*.

I scramble backwards, dagger clutched in hand, trying to get away from him as fast as possible. The horseman leisurely strolls after me, looking mildly entertained.

I manage to get my feet under me and pull myself up.

Run, my mother's voice commands, but I'm petrified of turning my back on this man. I'd like to look death in the eye when it's delivered.

War steps forward and swings his blade again and I raise my dagger to meet the blow. Even knowing what's coming, the numbing force of his hit is still a shock. I cry out at the impact, my weapon thrown once again from my hand. It clatters to the ground a meter away.

I stumble back. The heel of my boot catches one of the arrows scattered across the ground, and I slip, falling hard on my ass.

The horseman steps up to me, the sun illuminating his olive skin and lightening his eyes. He stares down at me, our gazes locking.

I raise my chin defiantly, even though I'm afraid. My body trembles with my fear.

The horseman lifts his blade.

But he doesn't end me right away. He stares at my face for a long time, long enough for me to wonder why he's hesitating. War's eyes drop to the hollow of my throat, and his sword wavers.

What is he *doing*?

My hand twitches with the need to touch my throat and feel the grisly scar that decorates it.

War's eyes travel back up to me. Now there's something different about his expression, something that terrifies me in a whole new way.

"*Netet wāneterwej.*"

You are the one He sent me.

I start at his voice. His words aren't Hebrew or Arabic or Yiddish or English. He doesn't speak *any* language I recognize ... and yet I understand him as though he does.

"*Netet tayj ḥmet.*"

You are my wife.

Chapter 3

YOU ARE MY *wife.*

That statement doesn't process. Nor does the fact that I can actually understand him.

The horseman sheaths his sword, giving me a strange, fierce look.

He's not going to kill me.

That *does* process. I lay in place for about two more seconds, and then I scuttle back again.

I force myself to my feet as War prowls after me, and now I do run.

I bolt back the way I came, heading towards an exit out of the Old City. I don't hear the horseman behind me, and foolishly I think that maybe he's going to let me go.

My hopes are dashed a minute later when I hear the menacing clack of his horse's hooves against the stone pavement.

Oh man, step one is some asshole claiming you're his wife, and step two, shit suddenly gets *real.*

The hoof beats close in on me just as they had earlier. Only this time I don't think I can outrun them. My adrenaline is nearly spent.

War's horse is nearly upon me, and I swear I can feel its hot breath against my skin. Just when I think it's going to trample me, something slams into my back.

The air leaves my lungs as I pitch forward. But I don't hit the ground. Instead, I'm scooped up and cleanly deposited onto the horse's saddle.

For several seconds I sit there, getting my bearings. Then I glance behind me, into the monster's eyes.

War is staring down at me, that strange expression still on his face. I feel myself quake under his gaze.

This is a man made to be feared.

And for several long moments, I am afraid. I am thoroughly terrified of this grim creature.

But then good ol' self-preservation kicks in.

I begin struggling against him. "Let me go."

His response is to tighten the arm he has around my waist, his gaze moving to our surroundings.

"Seriously," I say, trying and failing to shake his ironclad hold. "I'm not your *wife*."

War's eyes snap back to mine, and for a split second, he appears surprised.

Maybe he doesn't like the fact that I didn't agree to this wife business, or maybe he didn't realize I could understand him.

Whatever it is, he recovers quickly enough, his surprise draining away from his features. He doesn't respond to me, and he doesn't release me, instead driving his horse onwards through the city.

I struggle a little more against him, but it's useless. His arm is like a manacle, shackling me to him.

"What are you going to do with me?" I demand. I sound shockingly calm. I don't feel calm. I feel frazzled and freaked out.

Again, War doesn't respond, though his grip tightens just a

smidgen. Just enough to know exactly where his mind is.

I pinch my eyes shut, trying to keep out all the horrible images of what happens to women in war.

"*Neṯet ṯar*," he says.

You are safe.

I nearly guffaw at that.

"From your blade, maybe." Not from other things.

Maybe the horseman has eighty wives, each one a war prize he's plucked from a different conquered city.

Oh God, that actually sounds plausible.

A wave of nausea rolls through me.

War unsheathes his sword as he rides through Jerusalem. The buildings are on fire, and the streets swarm with people—fighting, fleeing, dying.

I've seen my share of fights, but my home has never looked like *this*, like a steaming heap of human savagery.

I stare at it all, dazed. I think shock might be setting in.

I can feel dozens of eyes on me as they take in me and War. Their fear is plain—no one expects to come face to face with one of these mythical, deadly horsemen—but I also sense a deeper terror. No one had realized that War might take prisoners, not until this moment when they see the proof sitting in his saddle. The sight of me must spawn a whole new set of fears.

Around here we know that sometimes a quick death is a better way to go.

The horseman begins to drive his steed forward at a punishing pace. His sword is still brandished and he steers his mount towards fleeing humans. Anytime he closes in on one, he takes a great swing of that mighty sword.

I have to close my eyes against the sight, but even still, I sometimes feel the sick spray of blood.

For a long time, I simply focus on not retching. It's all I can manage. Escape is impossible with War's viselike grip on me, and fighting—well, I already exhausted that avenue.

We move west through the city, back towards the hills I so recently visited. The horseman takes the same route out that we both took in.

City gives way to forest, and eventually the sounds of battle fade away. Out here, you'd never know an entire town was getting slaughtered.

The two of us ride past the shell of a house I hid in, moving deeper and deeper into the mountains.

Once we're well and truly far from civilization, War's hold on me loosens.

"Where are you taking me?" I ask.

No answer.

"Why did you leave the fight?" I start again.

I feel War's terrible eyes on me, and I glance behind me to meet them.

He holds my gaze for several seconds, then moves his attention back to the road.

Okaaaay.

Maybe he doesn't understand me like I understand him?

The rest of the trip we ride in silence.

At some random point, War veers off the road. The plants here have been pulverized by the horseman's army. He follows the tracks that his horde left, winding us through the mountains.

Eventually we round a bend, and I suck in a breath.

Nestled in a relatively flat section of land is a camp as big as a small city. Thousands of tents lie nestled among the trees and brush, covering a huge portion of the mountainside.

Who knows how long they've been camped out here, completely out of sight from the main road.

War rides past several makeshift horse corrals and rows upon rows of tents. Now that we're moving through the place, I notice that even right now there are people here. Most of them are women and children, but there are a few muscle-y soldier types as well.

The horseman stops his steed. Dismounting off of the creature, he then turns around and lifts me from his horse.

I have no idea what the fuck is going on, but I really wish I still had my weapons.

The horseman sets me on the ground. He stares at me for several moments, then tucks a strand of hair behind my ear.

What in the ever-loving hell is going *on*?

"*Odi acheve devechingigive denu vasvovore memsuse. Svusi sveanukenorde vaoge misvodo sveanudovore vani vemdi. Odedu gocheteare sveveri, mamsomeo.*" War says.

You will be safe here until I get back. All you must do is swear fealty with the others. Then we will speak again, wife.

"I am *not* your wife."

Again, I catch an echo of his earlier surprise.

I don't think I'm supposed to understand him.

One of the soldier-types comes over, a red sash around his upper arm. War leans in to him and says something so low I can't hear it. Once he's finished, the horseman gives me a long look, then remounts his horse.

With a jerk of his reins, War turns around and rides out of the camp, and I'm left to figure out the situation alone.

BY THE TIME the sun is setting, my wrists are bound behind my back and I'm forced to wait in a line alongside other similarly bound individuals.

I don't know if this is what War had envisioned for his *wife* when he dropped me off, but it feels about right.

The other captives have trickled in throughout the day. There's maybe a hundred of us; we probably amount to a fraction of a fraction of the city's total population. And the rest of the city ...

When I close my eyes, I see them. All of those people who breathed only a day ago now lay dead in the street, food for scavengers.

For a long time the line of us just stands there. A huge

man a couple meters in front of me is trembling uncontrollably, probably from shock. I can see blood splatter across his back.

Who did he lose?

Stupid question. The answer must be *everyone*. The only difference these days is who *everyone* includes. A wife? Parents? Children? Siblings? Friends?

One of my clients once told me that there were over fifty members of his extended family. Did they all die today?

The thought brings bile to the back of my throat.

My attention sweeps over our surroundings. Most of the other captives in line are male. Male and noticeably athletic. I search for another female amongst us. There are a few. *Too* few for my taste. And all of them are young and pretty, the best I can tell. A couple of the women cling to children, and that is another shock to my system. I don't know what sickens me more—that these small families are now at the mercy of these savages, or that there must be countless more left behind in Jerusalem ...

I close my eyes.

Always knew this day would come. The day when the Four Horsemen finished what they started.

But knowing couldn't prepare me for the reality of it. The bodies, the blood, the violence.

This is some sick nightmare.

"I'm going to enjoy *you* later."

I blink my eyes open just in time to see a man pointing his blade at me, his free hand moving to his crotch.

It takes a mountain of effort not to react.

My mind flashes to all the pretty women in line.

What is this camp planning on doing with them?

With *us*?

A chorus of screams interrupt the thought. The crude man's attention is drawn away, towards the front of the line where the screams are coming from.

The man flashes me a mean smile, backing away. "I'll have you soon enough," he promises.

I stare at him a long time, memorizing his features. Long face, the beginnings of a beard, and dark, receding hair.

My gaze moves over the other men guarding us. They all have a mean look to them, like they'd rob you and rape you if the opportunity arose.

"Move! Move!" one of the soldiers shouts.

The line of us shuffles forward.

A ways in front of me, another prisoner leans over and vomits. A couple of the soldiers laugh at him. And the screams, those piercing, terrible screams, they continue intermittently, followed by the camp's boisterous heckling.

I can't see ahead to whatever's going on; there's too many people and tents in the way, but it turns my stomach nonetheless. There's a peculiar agony to waiting when you know something bad is coming for you at the end of it.

It's not until I move around a bend in the line that I get a view of what that bad thing is.

Ahead of me, there's a large clearing free of tents and shrubbery. Standing in the middle of it is a man holding a bloody sword. A captive kneels in front of him. They're talking, but I can't quite make out what they're saying. All around them, men and women ring the space, watching with hungry, avid eyes.

Sitting on a dais a short distance away and overseeing it all is War.

My heart lurches at the sight of him. This is the first time I've seen him since he captured me.

The man with the sword grabs the captive's hair, dragging my attention back to the two of them. Now I can hear the captive's cries.

They seem to fall on deaf ears. The man with the sword pulls his blade back, and with one clean swing of the weapon, he beheads the captive.

I turn my face into my shoulder, breathing against the cloth of my shirt to keep my rising sickness at bay.

Now I understand the screams and the nausea.

The prisoners are being culled.

IT TAKES AN agonizing thirty minutes for me to move near the front of the line. In that thirty minutes I've seen several more captives die, though many have walked free.

The huge man I saw earlier, the one who trembled uncontrollably, is now at the front of the line.

Someone grabs him roughly, leading him to the center of the clearing before pushing him to his knees. He's no longer shaking, but you can practically smell his fear tinging the air.

For the first time, I make out the executioner's words over the noise and distance.

"Death or allegiance?" he asks the kneeling man.

Suddenly I understand. We're being given the option to join this army ... or to die.

My eyes swing over all the people standing around. They must've all chosen allegiance. Even though they might've watched the horseman kill their loved ones and burn down their towns.

It's unfathomable.

I won't become the very thing I fought against today.

In front of me, I don't hear the kneeling man's answer, but then the executioner grabs him by the hair.

That's answer enough.

The captive takes one look at the sword. "No-no-no—"

With the sweep of the blade, the executioner cuts his cries short.

Saliva rushes into my mouth, and I force down my nausea.

That's what will happen to me if I don't agree to this camp's terms. It's nearly enough to make me change my mind.

I close my eyes.

Be brave. Be brave. I probably shouldn't be using Rule Five of *Miriam Elmahdy's Guide to Staying the Fuck Alive* to convince myself that death is the better option. The whole point of my rules was to *stay the fuck alive.*

The handful of prisoners that follow all choose allegiance. They're pulled from the arena and swallowed up into the crowd.

Someone pushes me forward, and now it's my turn to face judgment.

A SOLDIER ROUGHLY drags me to the center of the clearing, where the executioner waits. Puddles of blood soil the area, and the liquid splatters beneath my boots as I walk up to the man with the blade. Here, the air smells like meat and excrement.

Death is messy. You forget that until you cut a man open.

The camp's eyes are now all on me. They look sickly fascinated by this, like it's some sort of macabre show.

But all of their faces fade when I gaze up at War.

As soon as the horseman sees me, he sits forward in his seat. His face is placid, but his dark eyes are intense.

All you must do is swear fealty with the others. Then we will speak again, wife.

One of his hands squeezes his armrest; the other rests beneath his chin, those odd glyphs glittering from his knuckles.

Now that he's not on the battlefield, War's removed his armor and his shirt, leaving him bare chested. No wounds mar that skin even though I know that at least one of my arrows embedded itself in his shoulder. There are, however, more of those strange glowing glyphs on his chest, the two crimson lines of them arcing from his shoulders to his pecs before curving back towards his ribcage. The markings look just as dangerous as the rest of him.

He no longer wears his giant sword. In fact, the only

weapon he *is* wearing is a needle-like dagger that's strapped to his upper arm.

The executioner moves in front of me, forcing me to tear my gaze away from War. The man's blade is so close that I could reach out and touch it, the steel thickly coated in blood.

Behind me, a soldier shoves me to my knees. Blood splashes as my knees hit the soaked earth. I cringe at the warm feel of the liquid.

I close my eyes and swallow.

"Death or allegiance?" the executioner demands.

It should be an easy answer, but I can't force myself to say the words.

Despite everything, I don't want to die. I really, really don't want to die, and I don't want to feel the bite of that blade.

Right now anything, even the thought of turning on my own brethren, is more tempting.

I open my eyes and look to the executioner. The man has dead eyes. Too much killing and not enough living. That's what'll happen to me if I choose to live.

Inadvertently my gaze moves to the horseman sitting on his throne.

The horseman, who caught me and spared me. Who called me his wife. He watches me now with captivated eyes. I know which answer he wants from me, and he seems almost certain I'll give it.

The longer I look at him, the more unnerved I become. A shiver runs over my skin. There's a whole unexplored world in his eyes, one that promises me dark and forbidden things.

I tear my gaze away from him and my wandering thoughts, my attention returning to that bloody sword in front of me.

Death or allegiance?

Be brave, be brave, be brave.

I glance up at the executioner and force out the one word I couldn't only moments before.

"Death."

30

Chapter 4

THE EXECUTIONER FORCES my head down, so that the back of my neck is bared for him. I don't see him lift his sword, but I feel the warm drip of blood from it.

I bite my lip at the sensation.

This is not how I imagined my life ending ...

"*No.*" War's voice fills the camp. The sound of it is like a lover's breath against my skin. It's sinister, deep—so very, very deep—and the weight of it seems to echo across the clearing. Or maybe it's simply the silence that falls in its wake.

Every rowdy, beady-eyed soldier goes quiet.

I glance up. The crowd seems to shrink back into itself, and their fear is a physical thing.

My eyes move to War, where he reclines on his throne. His gaze locks with mine, and suddenly, it's as though we're back on holy ground and he's declaring me his wife all over again.

War's eyes aren't anything like the executioner's. They are so very, very *alive*. They burn bright. And yet, for all the life that fills them, I cannot say what the man behind them is thinking. If he were a human and I defied him, I'd expect anger, but I'm not sure that's what he feels at all.

War lifts a hand and beckons me forward.

A soldier grabs me by the arm and leads me towards the horseman, only halting me a couple meters from his dais.

With a nod to War, the soldier backs away.

The horseman's gaze rakes over me, and not for the first time, I register just how unnaturally handsome he is. It's a vicious sort of beauty, one that only dangerous men have.

His upper lip curls just the slightest, and it makes me think that he's disgusted at the sight of me.

The feeling's mutual.

All of a sudden, he gets up. I swallow delicately as I crane my neck to look up at him.

He's not human.

There's no mistaking it now. His shoulders are too wide, his muscles are too thick; his limbs are too long, his torso too massive. His features too ... complicated.

He pulls the needle-thin dagger from the holster encircling his bicep. At the sight of it, a bolt of adrenaline rushes through me, which is ridiculous considering that I asked for death moments ago.

"*San suni ötümdön satnap tulgun, virot ezır unı itdep? Sanin ıravım tılgun san mugu uyuk muzutnaga tunnip, mun uç tuçun vulgilüü,*" he says, circling me.

I spared you from death, and yet now you seek it out? How you insult me wife, I who have never been known for my mercy.

Each word is gravelly, resonate.

Under his scrutiny my throat bobs. "I'm not going to keep my life just so that you can make me kill others," I say, my voice hoarse with fear.

At my back, I sense the horseman stop.

Is he once again surprised I can understand him?

Before I can turn around, he takes one of my hands. It's only now, when he's touching me, his calloused hands swallowing mine up, that I realize I'm trembling.

I take a few deep breaths to settle my mounting anxiety.

War leans in close, his mouth brushing my ear. "*San suni sunen teken dup esne dup uynıkut? Uger dugı vir sakdun üçüt?*"

Is that what you think I want with you? To make you another soldier?

He laughs against my hair, the sound making my skin prick. I flush, unnerved at his words.

I feel the cool metal of War's blade as he inserts it between the bound hands at my back. There's a brief pressure as his dagger presses against my bindings. A second later I hear a rip as, in one clean stroke, War cuts the twine and frees my wrists.

My arms sting as blood flows back into them.

"I know what you want from me," I say quietly, beginning to rub out my wrists.

"*Uger uzır vurvı? San vakdum tunduy uçıt-uytın.*"

Do you now? How transparent I have become.

War comes back to my front. He's still grimacing at me, like I've offended his delicate sensibilities.

"*A hafa neu a nuhue inu io upuho eu ha ia a fu nuhueu a fu Ihe,*" he says. His tone and the language he speaks seem to change and soften.

There are many things I can give you that Death cannot.

"I don't want your things," I say.

The corner of War's mouth lifts. I can't tell if his smile is mocking or amused. "*Ua i fu ua nuou peu e fuhio.*"

And yet you'll still get them.

He eyes me over. "*Huununu ia lupu, upu. I fu ua fu ipe huy.*"

Clean yourself off, wife. You will not die today.

He throws his dagger at my feet, the thin blade sinking into the earth, and then he walks away.

AFTER WAR LEAVES, no one seems to know what to do.

I react first. Kneeling down, I grab the hilt of War's discarded weapon and yank it out of the earth. On the horseman's arm, it had looked more like a hairpin than a dagger, but in my hand, it's heavy and big. Quite big.

Spinning, I point the blade at anyone and everyone. Someone laughs.

Time to get the fuck out of here.

Clutching the blade, I stride out of the clearing, elbowing my way through the crowd. I expect someone to attack me, but it never comes.

I only manage to walk a short distance before a woman grabs my arm.

"This way," she says, beginning to direct me through the maze of the camp.

I glance down at her. "What are you doing?"

"Leading you to your new accommodations," she says, not missing a beat. "I'm Tamar."

Tamar is a petite thing, with greying hair, tan skin, and olive green eyes.

"I'm not planning on staying."

She sighs. "You know, most people I greet here say that to me. I'm tired of having to tell you all the brutal truth."

"And what's that," I say as she winds us through rows of tents.

"Everyone who leaves, dies."

TAMAR LEADS ME to a dust-stained tent that looks identical to the dozens of tents erected to either side of it.

"Here we are," she says, gazing up at it. "Your new h—wait." She calls out to another woman four tents down. "This is one of the one's we're giving out, right?"

The other woman nods.

Tamar turns back to me. "This is where you'll be staying from now on."

"I already told you, I'm not staying."

"Oh, hush," she says, shrugging off my words. "You've had a harrowing day. Tomorrow will be better."

I bite back a response. I don't need to convince her of my

intentions.

She pulls the tent flaps back and gestures for me to peer inside. Reluctantly, I do so.

It's a small space, hardly big enough for the rumpled pallet that lays the length of it. In one corner rests a dog-eared book and a Turkish coffee set. In another corner rests a comb and some costume jewelry.

It's clearly someone else's home.

"What happened to the last person who stayed here?" I ask.

Tamar shrugs. "She left on her horse this morning ... but she never came back."

"She never came back," I repeat dumbly.

My eyes sweep over the furnishings again. Whoever this woman was, she'll never pick up that book again. She'll never sleep on this bed, wear this jewelry, or drink from those cups.

"They weren't all hers," Tamar says, staring at the items alongside me. "Some belonged to others who passed on before her."

If that explanation was meant to give me any comfort, it missed its mark.

So I've inherited the dead's possessions. And when I die, someone will inherit what few items of mine remain.

That is, of course, assuming I'll stay. Which I won't.

Everyone who leaves, dies.

I swallow a little at that. The thing is, I really *don't* want to die. And I'm still bent on figuring out how to leave this place, but I can already tell that's not going to happen just yet.

My eyes sweep over the sparse furnishings. So I guess this is home for now.

Tamar turns to me. "What can you do?" she asks.

My brows furrow before she adds. "Can you fight, cook, sew, ... ?"

"I make bows and arrows for a living—or I used to anyway."

"Wonderful," she says, like I gave her the answer she was seeking. "We could always use more craftsmen. Very well, I'll tell the administrative staff to keep that in mind when they assign you your duties.

"My duties?" I ask, raising my eyebrows.

Our conversation is interrupted by several women who come over carrying a basin full of water.

"Ah," Tamar says, perfect timing. "Go ahead and put it inside the tent," she says to the women, who then proceed to march the basin into my new home.

To me, she says, "Enjoy the bath. We'll be back in fifteen minutes with clothes and food."

Before I can say anything else, Tamar and the rest of the women are gone, presumably to situate other newcomers.

I turn back to the tent. After a moment, I take a deep breath and step inside.

I chew on the side of my lip as I stare at the bath water. It's reddish brown and murky. Next to it, one of the women left a wet bar of soap and a towel.

Dare I actually get in?

I almost don't. It's not that this is anything unfamiliar. We have to hand-pump most of our water these days, so I'm used to sponge baths and sharing bath water. It's just usually not this filthy.

Still, I can feel the drying blood on my jeans, fusing the material to my legs, and that, in the end, is enough to drive me into the bath, murky water and all.

I wash myself quickly and towel off. Once I'm done, I go to work on my clothes, using the bathwater to wash the blood from them.

You can never fully get bloodstains out ...

Midway through, one of the tent flaps pulls back and Tamar and the other women cram inside, bringing with them several items—most notably a plate of food.

My stomach cramps at the sight of it. I haven't eaten for most of the day. Up until now, I've been too wired to feel much hunger, but now that I've had time to rest, my hunger has swarmed in.

Tamar takes one look at me, wrapped up in the towel they left me. She holds up the items draped over her arm. "Your clothing—and some shoes," she says, handing me the gauzy clothing and a pair of sandals.

The outfit is a two piece ensemble, and all I can say about the top and skirt is that both are flimsy, the black and gold material gauzy and transparent in most places.

I shift a little in my towel. I want clean clothes badly, but I'm also not too eager to prance around this camp in that filmy outfit.

"Um,"—How to not be a dick about this?—"do you have anything more substantial to wear?"

Tamar frowns at me, clearly feeling unappreciated for helping out. "The horseman likes his women to dress up," she says.

The horseman?

His women?

The fuck?

"I am *not* his woman," I say defensively.

You are my wife.

This is the first time Tamar has even brought the horseman up to me. I set aside the fact that she just confirmed that War is in fact War and focus on the fact that Tamar has been grooming me for the horseman.

"Better his woman than someone else's," one of the other girls says. Some of the other women murmur their agreement.

I'm going to enjoy you later, that soldier had said to me only hours ago.

I suppress a shiver.

Is that how this place works?

Reluctantly, I take the silks from Tamar, the material seeming to slide through my fingers.

Do I put them on?

My only other option is to slip back into my wet clothing

and shoes.

I eye the items again.

I'm no more War's woman than I am anyone else's, and wearing these items doesn't change that. But the horseman's interest in me is another matter.

There are things he wants from me, things that have nothing to do with my fighting abilities and everything to do with the fact that he calls me *wife*.

My grip tightens on the silks.

There are things *I* want too. Answers, information, a solution to this monstrous apocalypse.

Who knows, maybe tonight I'll get some of them.

I just have to put on the damn outfit.

Chapter 5

BATTLE DRUMS FILL the night air. Outside my tent, torches blaze, their smoke curling into the inky sky.

I spin my hamsa bracelet round and round my wrist as I follow the women back to the clearing, my dark skirt rustling about my legs.

In the time since my near death, the place has been transformed. I can smell meat sizzling, and there are tankards of some sort of alcohol already set out. The sight of all that liquor is somewhat shocking. Most people in New Palestine don't drink.

Around me, people are talking, laughing, and enjoying each other's company. It's strange to think that earlier today, they were raiding and slaughtering a city. There's no sign of all that depravity now.

My eyes move from person to person, trying to read their sins in their eyes—until I catch sight of War.

He sits on his dais just as he did earlier. He watches me, the smoke and firelight making his brutal features mesmerizing. I don't know how long he's been staring, only that I should have noticed. Those eyes of his feel like the touch of a hand against my skin; it's hard to ignore the sensation.

Some part of me reacts to the sight of him. My stomach tightens as fear twists my gut. Beneath that, there's another sensation ... one I can't put my finger on, only that it makes me feel vaguely ashamed.

One of the women next to me catches my hand. Fatimah is her name. "He cannot die," she tells me conspiratorially, leaning in close.

I glance at her. "What?"

"I saw it myself, two cities back," she says, her eyes bright as she retells the story. "A man had gotten angry over something—who knows what. He pulled out his sword and approached the horseman.

"War let the man drive his blade straight through his torso—right between those tattoos of his. And then he laughed."

An unbidden chill slides down my spine.

"The horseman pulled the weapon out of himself, and then he snapped the man's neck like it was tinder. It was awful." Fatimah doesn't look all that distressed by the story. She looks eager.

I glance at War again, who's still watching me.

"He doesn't die?" What sort of creature is deathless?

Fatimah leans in and gives my hand a squeeze. "Just do as he wants and you'll be treated well."

Yeah, that's not going to happen.

"What about the others?" I ask her. Someone has come up to the horseman with a platter of food, dragging his attention away from me.

Fatimah's brow crinkles. "What others?"

"His other wives." There must be others.

"*Wives?*" Fatimah's forehead creases. "War doesn't marry the women he's with." Now she gives me a weird look. "How *did* he find you?" she asks. "I heard he rode straight out of battle with you on his horse."

I'm picking my words when War's attention returns to me. For the second time today, he gestures for me, the scarlet markings on his knuckles glowing menacingly in the gathering darkness.

Guess someone got tired of waiting.

For a moment, I stay rooted in place. My stubborn side kicks in, and I'm having dark fantasies about what the horseman would do if I simply ignored his command.

But then Fatimah notices and nudges me forward, and I begin to walk, feeling the weight of the crowd's mounting gazes.

I move through the throng of people, only stopping once I'm a short distance away from the horseman.

He rises from his seat, and a ripple goes through the crowd. The drums are still pounding, but it seems as though we have the whole camp's attention.

War steps forward one, two, three steps, leaving his makeshift throne and closing the distance between us until he's right in front of me.

He studies my features for several seconds and his gaze is so intense I want look away.

Torchlight burns deep in his eyes. Torchlight—and interest.

He doesn't say anything for so long that I finally break the silence between us. "What do you want?"

"*Meokange vago odi degusove.*"

I thought you already knew.

He throws my earlier words back at me.

And yeah, I still think I do.

War's eyes drink in my face. He's wearing the same strange expression he gave me back in Jerusalem.

After several seconds, he reaches out and brushes a knuckle over my cheekbone, like he just can't help himself.

I bat his hand away. "You don't get to touch me," I say softly.

His eyes narrow.

"*Sonu moamsi, mamsomeo, monuinme zio vavabege odi?*"

Then tell me, wife, how do I get to touch you?

"You don't."

He smiles at me, like I'm charming and quaint and extremely ridiculous in the most endearing way.

"*Gocheune dekasuru desvu.*"

We'll see about that.

I back away from the horseman then. He watches me avidly but doesn't try to call me back to his side. At some point, I turn on my heel, my filmy skirt swishing around my ankles, and melt into the crowd.

I'm almost disappointed. After all that fanfare the women made about presenting me to the horseman, I would've thought the mighty War would've done more than mutter a few words and gaze at me.

But it's that gaze that I can still feel against my back like a brand.

I glance over my shoulder and meet those inquisitive, violent eyes. The corner of his mouth curls into a challenging smile.

That's all it takes for me to do the one thing I hate the most: flee.

I SIT LIKE a fool in the near darkness of my tent for several hours. Even from here I can hear the party raging on, and I can smell food cooking.

I would slip out and grab a bite to eat, except that I would then have to show my face. It's bad enough that I ran, but at least it was some sort of exit. To show back up as though nothing happened ...

I can see War's challenging, taunting gaze. He would enjoy that. He'd think of it as another opening. That's really what stops me.

The world might be coming to a bloody end, but damn it if

I don't skip a meal just to save face.

So I ignore the smell of meat, and after lighting the small oil lamp Tamar gave me, I read the dog-eared romance novel left in my tent and idly debate how horrible of an idea it would be to burn the camp down.

Amongst all the distant conversation, I hear footsteps approach. Instinctively, I feel my muscles tense.

After everything War said to me, I expect to be carted away to his tent, so I'm not surprised when the flaps to my own tent rustle, and Tamar enters my borrowed residence.

"I'm not going," I say.

"Going where?" she asks.

I frown. "You're not taking me to his tent?"

"War's?" she says, raising her eyebrows. "There are plenty of willing women the horseman can choose from if he wants to enjoy a warm body tonight. He doesn't need for it to be *you.*"

Other women? I imagine those heavy, assertive hands settling on other flesh, and I scowl.

"That's not why I'm here," Tamar says, changing the subject.

She sits down next to me. "I heard you two talking earlier," she says, her words hushed. She leans in close. "How do you know the horseman's language?" she asks, her voice hushed.

I shake my head.

I'm about to deny it when she says, "We all saw you communicate with him," she insists.

I hadn't realized anyone was watching the exchange that closely.

I take Tamar in. "I don't know what I heard," I admit, "or why he spoke with me at all. I'm sorry, but that's the best I've got. I don't understand any of this."

Tamar searches my face. Eventually she nods and reaches out to squeeze my hand. "War goes through women." She says this like it's some sort of confession, and I feel a little sick. I really don't want to know about War's personal relationships.

"If you want to be over and done with him," she continues, "just give in for a night or two."

What is *with* the women here and giving me unsolicited sex advice?

"It'll gain you some measure of protection," she adds.

Last I checked, a blade protected me just fine.

"And if I don't give in?" I say.

There's a long pause, then Tamar grabs my chin. "This is a dangerous place to be a woman—particularly a pretty one." Her eyes drop to where War's blade rests next to my oil lamp. "Keep that knife close. You'll probably need it."

Chapter 6

I TAKE TAMAR'S final piece of advice—I sleep with War's dagger beneath my head.

It's a good thing I do, too.

"*Wake, Miriam.*" A deep voice drags me from sleep.

My eyes snap open.

Sitting next to my pallet, his arms loosely slung over his knees, is War.

My hand goes for my blade, and I sit up, brandishing my weapon.

War's eyes gleam as he takes me in, blade and all.

"Enjoying my dagger?" he asks.

I start at his words. He's speaking fluent Hebrew.

"You can talk," I state. *And you know my name*, I realize.

He grunts.

"I mean, I *understand* you." I'm used to hearing him speak in tongues, his meaning overlaying the words. It's unnerving to actually hear him speak the same language as me.

Which means this entire time, he's been able to understand *me*.

I keep my blade pointed at him. "Why do you speak in

tongues?" I ask.

Wrong question, Miriam. The correct question is: What the fuck are you doing in my tent?

The horseman gets up and comes closer. In response, I lift my weapon.

He utterly ignores the threat. War sits down on the edge of my pallet, even as the tip of my blade presses into his skin of his throat.

War's black eyes drop to the blade, and the corner of his mouth curves up. He looks darkly amused.

There's obviously no point threatening him. If anything, I'm getting the impression that he finds the whole thing endearing.

"How is it that *I* can understand *you* when you're speaking in tongues?" I ask.

"You are my wife," he responds smoothly. "You understand my nature and my gifts."

There's one problem with that. "I'm not your wife."

War smirks, his expression mocking me again. "Would you like me to prove my claim? I'd be *more* than happy to." His words full of sexual undertones.

I readjust my grip on the dagger. "Get out of my tent."

War studies me, his eyes gleaming in the darkness. "Is this tent really yours though?" he asks.

No. Doesn't change the fact that I want him out.

"Get out of *this* tent," I correct.

"Or else?" He raises an eyebrow.

Isn't that obvious enough?

I press the tip of his dagger a little deeper into his flesh. A dark line of blood drips down his throat.

War leans forward. "Brave little warrior, threatening me in my own camp." His eyes search my face.

"How did you even find me?" I demand. There are thousands of residences in this place.

"I thought you wanted me gone from your tent," he says. I

sense his amusement.

"And yet you're still here. So."

"I can't answer your question if you slit my throat." He looks pointedly at the dagger.

I hesitate. Waking up to any man in my tent is what I would consider an open threat. Yet I have to admit that if War wanted to harm me in any manner, he probably would've done so by now, and no blade of mine would be able to stop him.

Finally, I lower the dagger.

He touches the blood at his throat, and I swear I see a whisper of a smile on his face. "This is my camp. There are no secrets here that can be kept from me."

I eye him some more, my grip tightening on my dagger. "I've heard you can't die," I say.

"Is that why you haven't tried to kill me yet?" That mocking tone is back in his voice.

Yes.

My silence is answer enough.

"Can you?" I press.

"Die?" War clarifies. "Of course I can."

Damnit. Just when I lowered my blade too.

"I just have a tendency to not *stay* dead."

I scrutinize him. "What's that supposed to mean?"

He grabs a lit oil lamp I didn't notice, then stands. "You'll understand, eventually—along with everything else, *aššatu.*" *Wife.* "All you have to do is surrender."

Casting me one final enigmatic look, War blows out the lamp, and then he's gone like a phantom in the night.

EVEN THOUGH MY city is gone and I've been captured, I'm expected to just go on with my life.

That's clear enough the next morning when I wake up to the sound of general chatter outside my tent.

I guess I shouldn't be all that surprised. The same thing

was expected of me the day after the horsemen's Arrival. By now I'm an old hand at this.

I dress in my stained clothes. They're still damp from yesterday, but God, it's a lot more practical than the outfit I was given. Pulling on my boots, I step outside.

People lounge around their tents, chatting, laughing, drinking tea or coffee. This section of camp is filled mostly with women and children, and I'm shocked to see that several of them have their heads covered. I would've assumed that War would want us all to forsake our religion for his, but apparently not.

The air is still full of the smell of meat, and for a moment, all I can think of are the dead bodies that littered the ground when I entered Jerusalem yesterday. It smelled like meat then, too.

I follow the scent back to the clearing. This terrifying place seems to be where breakfast is served. My eyes move over the sheep being turned on a spit and the trays of fruit and nuts and bread that are spread out before me.

I wander over to the line for breakfast and try not to think about where all this food came from. Armies need to be fed, and one as big as this one ... well, raiding cities would be the lesser of the atrocities they've committed.

By the time I'm at the front of the line, I spot a familiar face. The man from yesterday, the one who grabbed his crotch and pointed his blade at me, stands on the other side of the clearing, wearing a keffiyeh and smoking a hand-rolled cigarette. He runs his fingers through his short beard as he chats with the men around him. But his eyes are on me, and no matter how long I stare back at him, he won't look away.

The weight of the dagger at my side is some small comfort.

I break eye contact first, grabbing my food and leaving the clearing.

I head to the edge of camp, finding a relatively quiet place to sit down and eat. As I do so, my eyes drift over the mountains that surround us.

It would be so easy to slip away unnoticed.

I pause, mid-chew, surreptitiously glancing along the outskirts of camp for any patrolling guards.

I don't see any.

Setting my plate aside, I stand up. I have to fight the urge to look around me and check that no one's noticed my behavior. That's the quickest way to alert people you're up to no good.

Casually, I begin walking away from camp, holding my breath as I do so. The seconds tick by, and the general buzz of camp life continues on, gradually fading away behind me.

I'm actually doing it.

It's only when I've passed half a dozen trees, however, that I exhale my relief.

I did it.

That was easier than I thought it would—

"On pain of death, stop!"

Damnit.

I come to a halt, positive there's an arrow aimed at my back.

Sure enough, when I turn around, a man is striding over to me, an arrow trained on my chest.

"All deserters face the executioner's block," he informs me.

I've been in a tight position more times than I'd like to admit. With the Muslim Brotherhood, with the Palestinian guard, with other raiders who caught me off guard. The key to getting out of these situations relatively unscathed was to have a convincing story and to follow Rule Two—stick to the truth.

"I make weapons," I say quickly. Tamar had mentioned that the camp could use a weapons maker.

The soldier squints at me. "What the fuck does that have to do with anything?"

"I use the wood from trees in this area to make bows and arrows," I say slowly, like this whole situation should be obvious.

"You expect me to believe you're out here collecting some goddamn wood for *weapons?*"

To be fair, he has a point. I have no bag to collect branches, and my holstered dagger is hardly useful for chopping wood. I look like an escapee, not a worker.

"I cleared it with War." The lie rushes out of me.

Immediate regret.

So much for sticking to the truth—I just threw that rule right out the window.

The soldier eyes me up and down, probably weighing the pros and cons of believing me versus not.

Finally, he comes to some sort of decision. "I don't care who you cleared your activities with, if you want to live, you better get the fuck back to camp. Now."

Giving the trees around me a final, parting look, I leave the brush, heading back to camp, an arrow trained on me the entire way there.

So much for escape.

THERE'S AN ORDER to this maze of a camp. It takes me the rest of the day to figure it out, but eventually I do.

The layout is broken into four quadrants. I live amongst the women and children in one of them. Another is cordoned off for the men and women who choose to live together. By far the biggest quadrant is the one dedicated to the men.

Then, of course, there's War's area.

All these quadrants of camp ring the clearing, which appears to be the heart of this place. And it's a blackened heart at that.

Throughout the day, the drums pound intermittently, and I come to learn that these noises precede executions. Some are for petty theft, some are for captured deserters, one man was even sentenced to death for pissing into a comrade's drink. Apparently that joke didn't go over so well. And then there are some executions that have no stated cause. I guess it doesn't really matter in the end; War wants us all dead, he'll just keep enough of us alive to help him achieve that goal.

You'd think that the sheer quantity of executions would make for a somber atmosphere—and maybe it does affect people on a more private level—but everywhere I look, men and women are moving about, chatting and carrying clothes or weaving sleeping pallets and baskets, and on and on.

Everyone seems to have tasks to complete. I can't figure out if they've been given these duties or if they simply volunteer to help out, but there are people to cook, people to clean, people to guard, people to care for the horses, people to dig out latrines, and a hundred other tasks that are needed to keep this camp running like a well-oiled machine—not that any machines run smoothly anymore, oiled or not. But whatever. My point still stands.

I take it all in.

It seems so hopelessly normal. I don't know how War does it. How he manages to get people to work together after they've lost everything at the hands of his army.

But not everything is normal. After all, there's no indication that religion exists here. Granted, I've only been at camp for a day, so maybe I just need to be patient. However, so far there have been no calls for prayer and no public sermons. I haven't seen anything that indicates which god—if any—these people believe in. The only signs of religion that I have seen are the few religious items that people wear on themselves. Other than that, it's as though God doesn't exist.

Which is so very ironic, considering our circumstances.

Eventually, I return to my tent. No one visits me or gives me any duties to perform around camp, and I only leave when food or nature calls.

The thunderous sound of hoof beats eventually draws me back outside. By then the sun is sinking in the sky, the heat from the day gradually cooling. Around me, other women leave their tents, glancing towards the sound.

"They're coming," I hear one of them murmur.

Around me, most of the people make their way towards the clearing. Curiosity pulls me along with them. I've barely arrived when dozens of mounted men cut through camp, kicking up dust and mowing down the shrubs in their way. Riding at the front is War himself. He and the rest of the riders are all drenched in blood.

Back from another invasion.

I hadn't realized there were more people *to* kill; the army seemed to do a good enough job of it yesterday. It makes sense though. Jerusalem is large, and then there are the nearby satellite communities. I guess even a supernatural force like the horseman needs more than a day to wipe us all out.

The war drums start up again, the beat of them stirring the blood in my veins.

War charges into the clearing as people scramble to get out of his way, and I swallow at the sight of the blood-red beast he rides. His horse has barely slowed when War swings himself off his mount.

Behind him, other riders gallop into the clearing, each one wearing a red tie on their upper arm.

"Who are those men?" I ask a woman next to me.

"Phobos riders," she says, briefly tearing her gaze away from them. "They're War's best soldiers."

Which means they're his best killers. I stare at them with new eyes as they circle the horseman before fanning out around him. When the last one has fallen into place, the drums cut out.

I have no idea what's going on until the dust has settled a bit. Laying on the ground in front of them all is a bloody man.

He looks dead, the way he lays there, but after a minute or so, he picks himself up.

War doesn't speak, just watches him rise to his feet. Once

the man is standing on shaky legs, the horseman prowls towards him.

The crowd goes quiet as a phobos rider hops off his horse and steps forward. "This man, Elijah," he says, gesturing to the nearly dead man, "was one of the *Phobos*, the warlord's inner elite. Our warlord fed him, gave him shelter, *trusted* him. And what did he do to repay that kindness?" He pauses, his gaze sweeping the crowd. "He turned on our horseman and he turned on his fellow warriors!"

As if on cue, the people around me shout their outrage. I glance at them, shocked to see that many look legitimately angry. If they're acting, they're doing a very good job of it.

"As soon as battle began, Elijah started slaughtering his brothers-in-arms," the speaker continues, all while War stares down Elijah, his eyes sharp as blades. "We lost many good men today."

Still staring at Elijah, War reaches over his back and grasps the hilt of his enormous blade. The steel zings as it's pulled from its scabbard.

I cringe at the sight of it, remembering my own close encounter. But instead of swinging it down on the man, War tosses the blade in front of him.

"*Sunu uk. San suni, adas Susturu tıtuu üçüt huniŞüü nunıtnuu utenin dukikdep nurun.*" he says.

Take it. Prove that you are worthy enough to defy me, human.

Elijah is shaking, either from fear or from exhaustion, but he doesn't look like he regrets his actions.

War backs away slowly. "*San Tuduygu uturun teknirip, nik niygiziŞüçüt hutiŞüü nunıtnuu utenin dukikdep nurun.*"

Prove that you are worthy enough to defy God Himself.

With that, the horseman turns, giving Elijah his back.

The bloody phobos rider waits a second or two, then scrambles for War's blade. He hits his first snag when he picks up the sword. The weapon is clearly too heavy for him to wield; even with both hands on its hilt the sword sways in his grip.

My heart plummets at the sight. Here is a man who decided to kill the killers. I *want* him to stop this horseman once and for all. The realistic part of me knows there's no chance of that. I've seen War's strength. There is no beating him.

The horseman turns around, his hands bare. His red leather armor is splattered with blood, and his kohl-lined eyes are ferocious. He wears another blade on him, but even when his opponent begins to approach him, he doesn't reach for it.

Elijah approaches, his face full of righteous anger. "You expected me to just watch as you slaughtered us?"

"*Tuz utırtı juni Şuur üçüt önüt dup atna üçüt ıtuuzı vokgon.*"

You were content to do that for the last seventeen cities we passed through.

Seventeen? *Seventeen?*

Not sure I should be cheering this man on anymore ...

He stumbles forward, his grip shaky, his body obviously exhausted from the day. He must know fighting is a lost cause, but that doesn't stop him from running at War, hatred in his eyes.

The man is almost upon the horseman, the latter who stands very still. Elijah fights to lift the sword high enough to strike. War still doesn't move.

"*San sunin nupŞrsunı suksugın tönörö ukvuyn.*"

You cannot carry the weight of my task.

As if in challenge to War's words, the phobos rider swings the blade. The horseman easily ducks under the blow, the gold coils in his hair glinting as they swing in the light.

Elijah stumbles forward, kicking up dust as he tries to regain control of the heavy weapon. It takes an agonizing several seconds for the phobos rider to turn around and face War once more.

The horseman is completely at ease, and yet I sense so much bridled power behind his relaxed stance.

"San Tuduydın urtin nüşitüü süstün eses," he taunts.

You cannot understand God's will.

With a yell, Elijah comes at him again, swinging War's sword wildly. And again, the horseman sidesteps the attack. His opponent is panting, his arms shaking at the effort it takes to hold the horseman's blade.

It's almost painful to watch, and what makes it worse is that I'm rooting for Elijah. I might be the only one here who is.

War steps in close and grabs one of his opponent's wrists. The move forces Elijah to lose the two-handed grip he had on the giant sword, and without that grip, the weapon sags in his hand.

The horseman leans in close, his next words barely audible. *"Sani övütün urtin nüşitügö süstün eses, vurok San senin öç nüşinön."*

You cannot understand His will, but you will understand my vengeance.

It happens almost too fast to follow. I hear something snap, then a scream. The man drops War's sword, cradling his arm against his chest.

The warlord catches the massive weapon as it falls. He unsheathes his other smaller sword. For a split second the two men stare at each other. Then War scissors his blades across his opponent's body.

Blood sprays, and part of the man's body goes one way, the rest, another. It takes everything in me not to sick myself at the sight.

Around me, a cheer rises up from the crowd.

The world has gone mad.

Sheathing his swords, the horseman walks away, letting the rest of the camp close in and defile the body.

NOT AN HOUR later I'm called to the horseman's tent.

I walk alongside several solemn-faced phobos riders, the

men bracketing me in. For the first time since I arrived, I enter War's section of camp.

Now that the raiding is over for the day, the phobos riders meander about the tents here, smoking hand rolled cigarettes and playing cards. A few of them watch me with interest, but most of them simply ignore the woman being brought to War's tent.

It's unmistakable which tent is the horseman's. War's home is set apart from the rest, and though the phobos riders' accommodations are much larger than mine, War's tent dwarves theirs. He's made a canvas palace for himself, the place illuminated on the outside by smoking torchlights.

About a meter away from the tent flaps, the phobos riders break away from me to stand guard, leaving me alone at the threshold to War's tent.

My heart beats fast in my chest. I've faced a decent amount of scary shit since the Arrival. You'd think I'd have some tolerance to it by now. But I don't. I'm still afraid. I'm afraid of this place and what it does to people. I'm afraid of what the future holds. Most of all, I'm afraid of the horseman and what he wants with me, especially after watching him mercilessly butcher a man.

"Go in," one of the phobos riders calls out.

Blowing out a breath, I step forward and enter.

The first thing I see is War's massive frame sitting on a bench. He's still clad in his red leather armor, still covered in dust and blood. His eyes catch sight of me just as he begins to remove an arm guard.

"Miriam," he says by way of greeting.

I swallow.

War's tent is filled with a table and chairs, a bed and several chests that must contain all of his spoils of war. Brightly woven rugs and pillows are scattered throughout the space, and then there are the weapons. Swords and daggers, double-headed axes and bows and arrows sit on various surfaces. He's clearly fond of sharp objects.

It's all so very lethal and luxurious, but it's hard to take in when I can barely stand to look away from War himself.

"Why am I here?" I ask, lingering near the doorway.

War pauses in his work. Setting aside his loosened piece of armor, he stands, his kohl-darkened eyes moving to mine.

My knees go a little weak, having the full force of War's focus on me.

God, but he's handsome—handsome the way deadly things are. He has no soft edges, from his sharp jaw to his full, wicked lips. And then there's his violent, violent eyes.

"How are you, wife?" he says, not bothering to speak in tongues. "Enjoying yourself?"

No, not fucking really.

I have to fight myself from taking a step back, especially when he takes a step forward. There's still meters and meters between us.

"I heard you were adventurous this morning," he says.

He's been keeping tabs on me?

I swallow delicately. "And?"

He removes his back holster, his sword and sheath coming loose. I stare at the blade that so recently slaughtered a man.

"I was told that you make weapons," he says casually.

I close my eyes for a moment.

That soldier must've told War everything, including the fact that the horseman supposedly okayed my being in those woods.

I don't mean to start shaking, but I do. I just saw this man turn a person into a human kabob for betraying him, and now he knows that I tried to defy him too.

"Apparently, I approved these plans of yours."

This is why I have a rule against lying. It's so easy to get caught.

I open my eyes and defiantly raise my chin.

He walks up to me, each footfall ominous. War steps in

close—far too close. "Don't ever use me in a lie again," he says, his voice low.

I hear the unspoken threat in his words.

Or else I will punish you.

And I've now seen War's justice. It's every bit as terrifying as I could imagine.

The horseman's eyes search my face. "You're going to be trouble, aren't you, wife?" He studies me some more. "Yes, definitely trouble," he says to himself.

War removes the last of the space between us, his leather armor brushing against my chest. He's close enough for me to see the gold flecks in his eyes. Those eyes are *terrifying*. Beautiful and terrifying.

"You're wrong if you think that angers me." His smile is menacing. "Everything you are has been made for *me*."

This arrogant bastard. I bet he thinks all humans were created for his entertainment. To fight, to fuck, to kill.

The horseman reaches out and draws a finger over my collarbone, his gaze never leaving mine.

"I saw you, and for the first time, I *wanted*."

His words pucker my flesh.

"And so, I took."

Chapter 7

WAR'S TOUCH PAUSES on my skin. "To think you almost got away." He backs away then, reaching for his vambrace, his fingers unlacing the arm guard. "It's a good thing you didn't."

He's well and truly inhuman. Nothing of this earth could frighten me the way he does.

I've now tried to escape the horseman twice within that many days—once through death and once through desertion. If he's just as merciless as he's made himself seem, then my actions will have consequences.

"Can you really make weapons?" he asks.

I pause, unsure where he's going with this.

"I'm not very good at it," I say after a moment.

He glances up. "Is that a yes?"

Reluctantly, I nod.

War's gaze drops to my lips. "Good. Then you will make my army these weapons I commissioned."

Another fucking reason why I should never, ever break Rule Two and lie. Because now I have the job I made up only hours ago.

"I can't make anything without my tools," I say. "And

those are back in my flat."

War stares at me for several moments, perhaps trying to figure out whether I'm lying again. "Where did you live?"

Did. Past tense.

I stare at the horseman as that sinks in. As far as he's concerned, my house is a thing of the past; this tented city is my home now.

After a moment's hesitation, I rattle off my address. I normally wouldn't give it out, but ... if War's seriously suggesting that he'll get my tools for me, then I'll take him up on it. After all, I'm being watched too closely to escape this place anytime soon.

"Can I go now?"

War's searching gaze is back on me. He takes me in for several seconds, then redirects his attention to removing his armor.

"You don't believe in God, do you?" he says.

Guess I don't get to leave yet.

In spite of myself I raise my eyebrows. "Why do you ask?"

The corner of his mouth lifts, like the answer is some inside joke that I wouldn't get. "It's curious."

"Why is it curious?"

War's eyes move back to mine. "Come closer and I'll tell you."

He dangles the answer like bait.

I take a single step towards him.

Again, that smile, only this time it appears a little less humorous, a little more dangerous.

"Cowardice doesn't suit you, wife."

"I am *not* a coward," I say from my safe distance away from him.

His dark gaze is weighty on mine. "Then prove it."

Be brave.

I haltingly close the distance between us, until I can smell the sweat and dust clinging to him.

60

"Not a coward after all." The horseman scrutinizes me. "As for your question—it's curious that you don't believe in God when *I* exist."

"Why should that be strange? *You* aren't God."

I believe War is a supernatural entity. It's everything else that I find hard to believe.

The horseman is completely unfazed by my words and the challenge in them.

"I'm not," he agrees.

The horseman breaks eye contact to remove a greave, and I exhale sharply at the loss of that gaze on me. I don't know why it feels like a loss; every time his eyes fall on me, I tremble like a leaf.

"I believe in God," I say. "I just don't believe in *your* God."

My mother was Jewish, my father was Muslim. I grew up believing in everything and nothing all at once.

"That's too bad," War says, eyeing me, "because He seems to have taken an interest in you."

THERE ARE MORE days of raids, days where the pounding of hoof beats marks the beginning of the day, and the bloody parade that returns marks its end.

It's only on the fourth day when the sounds change.

I blink my eyes open and stare at the worn wood poles above me. Outside, I can hear women chatting.

I rub my eyes, stifling a yawn as I sit up. My knee knocks into a pile of branches that take up most of the room in my tent.

War made good on his end of the deal—I've been *allowed* to gather wood for weapon-making. With a chaperon, of course.

I give the pile an extra deliberate kick.

Rolling off my pallet, I grab my boots and begin to shove them on. Once I'm finished, I run my hands through my dark brown hair. These days I sleep in my clothes—I'm not brave enough to risk anything else in a city with no true doors—so I simply smooth down my shirt before I head outside.

All around me, tents are being broken down and packed up. I glance about in confusion. A woman bustles by.

"Excuse me," I say to her, "what's going on?"

She gives me a look like it should be obvious. "We're moving."

MOVING.

Even now, when my tent is nothing more than a pile of sticks and cloth at my feet, the idea tightens my gut.

I hadn't anticipated moving. But naturally that's what a terrorizing horde does. They move and raid, move and raid.

"Miriam."

I nearly jump at the voice behind me. When I swivel around, two men wearing red arm bands stand at my back. War's phobos riders.

"The warlord wants to see you."

My gut clenches again. It's been half a week since I last spoke to the horseman, and I can't decide whether I'm now terrified or exhilarated at the thought of meeting with him again. I had convinced myself that whatever interest he initially had in me had passed. That perhaps he'd found another woman to pester and call *wife* for seemingly no reason at all.

War's palatial tent is still up. It's one of the last structures left standing. And when I step inside, the man himself is in there, wearing black pants and a black shirt, a knife strapped to his waist. He kneels in front of an open chest, his back to me and my escorts.

"My Lord," announces one of the phobos riders next to me, "we've brought her."

War doesn't react immediately, choosing instead to settle whatever item he's holding into the chest. He closes the piece of furniture, running his hands along the lid.

"You may go," he says, not bothering to speak in tongues. I

guess he saves his gibberish for the general announcements he makes to camp.

On either side of me, War's phobos riders retreat. I begin to leave with them.

"Not you, Miriam."

I pause mid-step, the hairs along my arms rising. I want to say it's because I'm spooked, but there's a note to his voice ... it makes me think of soft sheets and warm skin.

I swallow, swiveling back around.

War stands and faces me then, looking giant and magnificent and frightening all at once. The menace that rolls off of him in waves has nothing to do with his armor or his weaponry. There is something intrinsic about him that incites fear.

He takes me in for several seconds. Long enough for me to think he definitely hasn't replaced me with another wife. My heart rate ratchets up at the thought.

"I have something for you," he says.

I raise my eyebrows. I don't think I want anything that the horseman has to offer.

When he just continues to stare at me, my eyebrows nudge up a little higher. "Are you going to go get this gift?" I ask.

"I want to gaze at you first, wife. Will you deny me even this?" His eyes hold a heaviness to them, and I'm not sure what to make of it. Every time I think he's going to go left, he goes right. For four days the horseman kept his distance. Now he's making it sound like he's been starved to see me.

I can't make sense of him.

But I *can* deny him.

Unfortunately, before I get the chance to do exactly that, War moves to the corner of his tent, grabbing a sack that rests there. He saunters over to me, his black shirt hugging his frame as he does so. He dumps the bag at my feet.

It only takes a moment for me to recognize my old canvas satchel.

But I'd left that back at …

My eyes snap to War. "You saw my flat?"

I try to imagine the horseman filling up my home, his sharp eyes moving over my space. He would've seen all the mementos I've kept of my family. He would've seen my messy workbench—made even messier by whoever raided the place—he would've seen the pictures hanging on the walls and the wall clock and the cluttered kitchen and my dirty clothes and my rumpled bed and a dozen other personal details.

What must he have thought, looking at my things?

When he doesn't respond, I turn my attention back to my satchel. Kneeling in front of the bag, I open it.

My eyes first land on my leather roll. I pull the case out and unravel it. My various wood-working tools are tucked into its soft pockets. I set it aside and return to my satchel.

I catch sight of sandpaper and a couple clamps; it looks like he might've even packed one of my smaller saws and my axe.

War really did it. He brought me my tools from my house. I didn't expect him to.

I still can't believe he saw my place. It makes me feel oddly exposed, like he's peered into my mind and seen its contents.

The tent flaps rustle then, and a phobos rider enters. "My Lord, we need to begin packing your things."

War nods, and the rider moves to grab one of the smaller chests before leaving the tent.

Once the soldier is gone, the horseman closes the distance between us, his body eclipsing all our surroundings.

"You are to ride next to me."

"Do you order around all your 'wives'?" I ask.

War's eyebrow arches. "You think there are others?" War gives me that smile of his, the one that's fucking *terrifying*.

More of the horseman's men enter the tent, immediately getting to work packing his things.

"Someone will see to your horse," War says, backing away from me. "I look forward to our ride."

I DON'T UNDERSTAND why we have to ride horses when bikes exist. Bikes don't get hungry or tired, they don't shit, and they definitely don't try to kick you because they're temperamental bastards.

Though, to be fair, an army of soldiers on bikes doesn't exactly strike fear into the hearts of men.

I stare down at Thunder, the horse I'm sitting on. I only barely managed to avoid getting punted by this beast, and now I have to ride him.

Pretty sure the horse senses my inadequacy as a human being.

It takes an eternity for camp to ready itself. By the time everything is packed up, the horde is now gathered into one giant procession made up of mounted soldiers, hitched wagons, and many, many individuals loaded with packs.

The horseman is the last one to come riding out, looking portentous on his steed. He's clad once more in his leather armor, his gigantic sword strapped to his back and his gold hair pieces glinting in the sunlight. He doesn't look like anything that belongs to this century.

War rides up to my side. "Ready?"

Not like I have much of a choice. I nod anyway.

"Follow me."

He rides off, his horse racing to the front of the line that's formed. People cheer as he passes them by, like he's their savior rather than some supernatural menace. I watch him for several seconds before I coax Thunder to follow the horseman.

People don't cheer when I ride by, but I feel their curious, questioning gazes.

Who is she?

Why is she following War?

I make my way to the front of the procession, and then past it altogether.

There, War waits. His eyes seem to dance as I get closer to

him. Once I come to his side, he wordlessly begins to ride, setting the pace for us.

No *hi*, no *how are you?* Just a quiet confidence that I'll fall into line.

I glance back at the horde, which is beginning to move. It's clear from their pace that they're not going to catch up to us. Never have I wanted such a faithless mass of people to save me as I do now.

They follow behind us for half a kilometer before the horseman and I pass a bend in the road, and then the two of us are alone.

The silence swarms in. I wait for War to break it—surely he's going to break it—but he just rides on, those dangerous eyes of his fixed on the road ahead.

I clear my throat. "Why did you want me to ride next to you?" I ask, finally breaking the silence.

"You're my wife."

I'm not your wife, I want to insist. *Not in any way that matters.*

The words are right there on the tip of my tongue, but then I study War's profile, and there's something so ... *certain* about the way he handles me. I take him in for a bit longer, from his dark, shoulder-length hair to his curving lips and sharp jaw.

"Why do you think I'm your wife?" I say.

War's eyes flick to just beneath my chin.

"I don't 'think' it," he says. "I *know* it."

Chills. There it is, that certainty. You'd think that if I was supposed to make a husband out of War, I'd *know* it too.

"If I'm your wife, why don't I sleep in the same tent as you?" I say. "And why don't—" I stop myself before I can say more.

The horseman glances at me. Now I've caught his interest.

"Go on," he says. "Tell me, Miriam, all about the rest."

I don't.

"Why don't I fuck you raw and feast on your pussy and

keep you chained to my bed like a proper husband?" he finishes for me.

Chained to the bed like a proper husband?

I glance over at him. "Who the *hell* educated you on marriage?"

Seriously, what the fuck?

Forget God. This dude has to be a demon.

War takes one look at my face and laughs. "Is that not what proper husbands do?"

I have no clue if he's actually kidding.

Holy fucking balls.

"Who says I'm not already married?" I don't know why I say it. It's certainly not true.

For a moment, War doesn't react. Then, ever so calmly, he glances over.

"Are you?" he asks softly. "Do you have a husband, Miriam?"

His voice, those frightening eyes ... it sends a chill down my spine, and I remember all over again that this isn't a man; War is some preternatural creature who kills without remorse.

"No." I couldn't lie under that gaze even if I wanted to.

War nods. "That's fortunate for you—and for him."

Another chill.

I suddenly have no doubt that if I were married, this horseman wouldn't think twice about ending it. I sway unsteadily in my saddle at the thought.

War is most *definitely* a demon.

It's quiet for a few moments, then while he takes in our surroundings, War asks, "Do you have any family?"

"*Did.*" I have to force the word out. "But then you already knew that, didn't you?" The horseman had been inside my flat—or at least I assume he was the one who went there to retrieve my tools. He would've seen the pictures of my parents and the childhood photos of me and my sister.

"What happened?" he asks.

You happened, you crazy bastard.

I glance down at the hamsa bracelet I wear. It's nothing more than a single metal charm shoved onto a leather cord—the red string it was originally threaded around has long since broken. But that simple metal charm was the last gift my father gave me.

To protect me from harm.

"My father died the day you and the other horsemen arrived." He'd been crossing the street, on his way back to the university after having lunch with another professor. The bus hit him and his colleague, and neither had survived.

"My mother and sister—"

The gunfire is deafening. The three of us run out of the city with nothing more than a backpack each. We're the lucky ones. But then, that boat, that ominous boat—

"There was war in New Palestine long before you came around." For as long as people have lived in this corner of the world, there's been war. "We were escaping it ..."

I can feel the horseman's eyes on me, waiting for me to finish, but I can't talk about the rest of it. This loss is fresher than the other one.

I shake my head. "They're gone too."

WE RIDE WEST, away from Jerusalem, along the lonely road. It's shockingly quiet, like the very earth doesn't have words for what's happened to this land.

I glance over my shoulder, looking for some sign of the horde traveling behind us, but for the last twenty minutes I haven't been able to see any sign of them.

"They're back there," War says.

I'm not sure if he's reassuring me or warning me—probably both.

"How do you get them to follow you?" I ask. "Not just right now, but in battle?"

One small oath of allegiance cannot possibly be enough to

earn an army's devotion, especially not after the atrocities we've all witnessed.

"I don't *get* them to do anything," the horseman says. "My job isn't to earn their loyalty, it's to judge their hearts."

That response sounds ... biblical. Biblical and worrisome.

"And what about my heart?" I ask. "Have you judged it?"

War stares at me for a beat before he says softly, "Your heart is largely an enigma to me. But we shall find out the truth of it soon enough."

Chapter 8

WE DON'T PASS a single soul while riding along the mountain road, and after a while the lack of people becomes alarming.

My skin pricks.

Are they all dead? And if so, *how?*

How could War and a few thousand men at most take out an entire *region?* Not just cities, but everything in between as well? Something about that doesn't add up.

I glance at the horseman, and his calmness only further unnerves me. None of this bothers him. It *should* bother him.

Not human, I remind myself.

And whatever beast War truly is, I have the pleasure of being his plaything for the moment.

You'll get through this, Miriam, just as you have everything else.

The problem is that for the first time in a very long time, I don't think just getting through this is good enough.

I just don't know what *is* good enough.

Not yet.

We pass by the burnt remains of a large structure that could've once been a mosque or a Jewish temple.

I've heard of the horrors that happened in some other

areas of New Palestine during our civil war, but this is the first time I might be seeing evidence of it outside of Jerusalem proper. No one and no religion was spared.

That was my first lesson in war: everyone loses, even the victors.

One mountain leads to another, which leads to another. It's beautiful and all, but—

"Where are we going?" I ask War.

"Towards the ocean."

The ocean. My heart skips a beat.

There's water and fire and ... and ... and God the pain—the pain, the pain, the pain. The sharp bite of it nearly steals my breath.

I haven't seen the ocean in seven years.

War glances at me. "Is everything alright?"

I nod a little too quickly. "I'm fine."

He stares at me for a beat longer, then faces forward again. "Over the course of human existence, your kind has come up with hundreds of thousands of words for everything imaginable, yet somehow none of you have figured out how to actually speak your mind."

"I'm *fine*." No way am I sharing my true thoughts on the ocean.

Overhead, the full brunt of the midday sun is frying my skin to a crisp. My face feels tight, and I can see the dusty red flush of my forearms.

I'm also sweating like a cow.

I glance over at the horseman, eyeing the maroon armor that he wears over his clothing.

"Aren't you hot?" I ask him, changing the subject.

If I were him, I'd be effing *miserable*.

All that leather just locks the heat in. If I were him, I'd be bathing in sweat. Instead he appears irritatingly unaffected.

"Is my wife concerned for my wellbeing?"

I fix my gaze on a horse stall up ahead. "I forgot—you're used to hotter climates," I say. "I hear hell is *particularly* warm this time of year."

I can feel the weight of the horseman's eyes on me. "You think I'm a demon?" he asks skeptically.

"I haven't ruled it out ..." My words fall away as I squint a little more closely at another structure ahead of us.

These days you can find newly erected stables and inns and general stores speckled along roadways. They're the sorts of places you stop at to refuel and rest. It looks like we're coming up to one such place.

But as we get closer, something appears ... *off*.

Birds circle overhead and there must be more on the ground because I can hear them calling out to one another.

I stare at those birds. Despite the heat, a chill slides over my skin.

It's not until we pass the general store and the abandoned horse stalls that I see *what's* caught the birds' attention.

Close to a dozen birds—eagles, vultures, crows—all swarm and fight over some unmoving *thing* on the ground.

A few moments later, it registers that the thing on the ground is a human.

I stare and stare and stare and then I'm halting my horse and hopping off.

The birds take flight as I near the body. I use the corner of my shirt to cover my mouth as I peer down at the corpse. I can't make sense of exactly what I'm seeing, and I don't try to. The individual is dead. That's all that matters. Anything else is just nightmare fodder. About a stone's throw away rests a pile of discolored bones, the grinning mouth of the skull smeared with blood.

I furrow my brows. This looks less like a mass murder and more like some ritual sacrifice.

"Miriam."

I turn and face War. He hasn't dismounted. In his hand he holds Thunder's reins.

"You killed even all the way out here?" I ask. It seems

excessive. We're in the middle of nowhere. This is no bastion of humankind; there can't be more than a handful of people who live in this particular patch of hills.

"I kill everyone," War responds smoothly.

Everyone except for me.

I glance at that body again, the body that was once a person with hopes and dreams and friends and family.

"Remount your steed, Miriam," War says, completely unfazed by our surroundings. "We have a long way to ride."

It's not personal. I can tell it's not personal. None of the suffering War's inflicting is personal.

My gaze flicks back to the corpse.

Only it *is* personal.

I take all of this very, *very* personally.

I don't want to get back on that horse, and I don't want to ride next to the horseman. I don't want to pass more horse stalls with more fresh corpses.

The horseman narrows his eyes, like he can hear my thoughts.

Be brave, Miriam.

I force myself to take that first step forward. The second one comes easier. I take another step and another and another until I'm taking the reins back from War and staring into his wicked eyes as I pull myself onto my horse.

He doesn't try to offer an explanation, and I don't tell him my thoughts. I mount, and we resume. That's all.

BY THE TIME the sun is setting, we've passed more dead bodies and circling birds than I care to admit. It's clear that those raids War went on were more than a little successful.

There's no one left.

I frown at the thought, the movement pulling at my tight skin. After a day of riding, my face is more than a little sunburnt. I'm beginning to feel feverish, and my exposed skin is painful to the touch. There's not much I can do about it at the moment. I don't have a hat or a headscarf to shield my skin with.

The horseman glances at me and frowns. "You do not look well, wife."

"I don't feel so good," I admit.

He curses under his breath. "We're stopping for the evening."

I glance behind me at the empty road. "What about the rest of your army?"

"They'll be fine. We're not camping with them," he says.

"We're ... not?" That takes a minute to filter its way in.

My gaze moves back to the setting sun.

Oh dear God.

It's one thing to ride alone with War, another to spend the night next to him and *only* him. And now that I've been reminded of what he can do, I'm doubly nervous.

About a hundred meters ahead there's a water pump, a basin, and a pile of hay. We stop long enough for Thunder to drink his fill from the basin and eat a little of the hay before War steers us down one of the sloping hills.

War smoothly dismounts his steed, grabbing the horse's reins.

Gingerly, I slide off Thunder, wincing as my inner thigh muscles scream in protest. God's left nutsack, that *hurts*.

I take a shaky step, then another, cringing at all my aches and pains. It's not just my legs. My skin feels too hot, my stomach is churning, and I'm a little too lightheaded.

"I don't feel so good," I say again. Maybe it was the cured meat someone had packed for me; maybe the water I drank earlier was contaminated.

Or maybe this is heatstroke.

I stumble a little, then sit down hard.

I don't hear War approach—the fucker is quiet—but he crouches in front of me, his brow pinched just a touch. I think that's about as much concern as hardened War ever shows. He reaches out.

"You touch me, and I'll cut you with your own blade," I say.

War cups my face anyway. He's such a bastard.

I go for my dagger, but my hand has barely grasped its hilt when the horseman's free hand closes around mine. He twists the blade out of my grip and tosses it aside.

"Miriam, leave the battle on the battlefield."

"Oh, that's rich of you to say."

His eyes meet mine, and my breath catches. God is he annoyingly attractive. And the longer I stare at him, the more I notice every single inconvenient detail that makes him that way—like the fullness of his lips and his tiger's eye irises, and the sharp, high cheekbones that make him look so exotic.

"You should've said something about the sunburn," he says.

"I didn't think you'd care."

He studies me. "I do."

"Why?" I say.

"We've been over this," he responds.

Because I'm his wife, he means.

We stare at each other for a little longer.

After a moment I take a deep breath and tear my gaze away. "I feel better."

I really do. Now that I've sat down, I don't feel so feverish anymore, and I swear my skin doesn't throb nearly so much as it did a few minutes ago.

Now that I've had enough time to regroup, I want the horseman to stop touching me. A few kind words, a gentle touch, and I'll start to believe he's not a heinous demon spawn.

War drops his hand and gets up, heading over to his horse, who tosses his head about as his master approaches.

"Steady, Deimos," he says to his steed, placing a hand on the beast's dark red coat.

Deimos? He's actually named his horse?

He reaches into the creature's saddle bags, withdrawing water and food. The horseman heads back over to me and hands the items over to me.

I take them from War and give him a brief smile. His eyes linger on my mouth for just a moment, then he moves away again to deal with the horses—or maybe to unpack.

I take in his form. He's been oddly kind to me today, and I have to remind myself that I've seen him cut down many, many people—I was almost one of them. I can't let his concern and a few gentle touches overshadow that.

"Do you feel anything?" I call out to him. "When you kill?"

It's time for my hourly reminder that War is a bad dude.

He pauses, his back to me. "Yes."

I wait for him to say more. The silence stretches out.

"I feel bloodlust and excitement, and a deep satisfaction at a job well done." The horseman says this like he's talking about something mundane, like the weather and not the wholesale slaughter of innocents.

He turns to face me. "I am yours and you are mine, Miriam—"

I quake at those words.

"—but I am not like you, and you should *never* forget that."

Chapter 9

THE STARS TWINKLE above us when War lays out our pallets. One is just a mat and a thin quilt, but the one he's working on now is lavished with blankets.

Which one is his, and which one is mine? I sort of hate the fact that he made them so obviously unequal. If he takes the pimped out pallet, I'm going to know that on top of being depraved, the horseman is also kind of a dick. But if he gives that one to me …

I squirm a little uncomfortably at the possibility. I don't like excessive kindness; it makes me feel like I owe someone something in return. And I really don't want to think about what War might think I owe him.

At least he made two beds to begin with. I guess I should be glad we don't have to share one.

After the horseman finishes, he comes over to where I sit by the fire we made a little while ago. He unfastens his armor piece by piece, setting them at his side. There's something terribly confident and unhurried about his movements, like the world and everyone in it waits on him.

I am not like you.

I watch the horseman for a bit, trying not to focus on the fact that beneath all that armor is a wicked, wicked body.

"Your bed is the one with the blankets," he says, unfastening his leather breastplate.

Damnit. Definitely going to feel like I owe him something now.

"Your accommodations seem a bit rough," I say, nodding to his pallet.

War takes off the last bit of his armor. "I wouldn't be a proper husband if I couldn't make my wife comfortable."

Him and this *proper husband* business.

I glance around. "Where are the chains you're supposed to shackle me with?"

Pretty sure that was on the list of things a proper husband should have.

"Packed with the rest of my tent, unfortunately." War says it so calmly that I think he may not be kidding—until a sly smile creeps up on his face.

"Next time then," I say.

"I'll hold you to that, wife."

The two of us actually get along when I want us to. How troubling ...

War removes his shirt, his markings glowing in the night. They give off eerie red glow.

Definitely a demon.

"Earlier," he says, "you wanted to know why I don't speak the languages of men when I can," he says.

I had asked him about this when he invaded my tent several nights ago; I'm still curious about it, especially since he can speak perfect Hebrew with me.

"I speak every language that has ever existed. Even the ones that left no record. They have long faded from mortal memory, but not mine. Never mine."

War is quiet for another moment. "What people don't understand frightens them."

How many times had I seen proof of that fear? Dozens, at least. And now War has weaponized that terror.

"So I speak dead languages, and I let the humans piece together from it what they will," War finishes.

"But you don't always speak in tongues," I say. There have been a number of times where he spoke Hebrew or Arabic to me and his riders.

"I don't. There are times when it serves me to be understood."

"And when you speak in dead languages," I say, "why is it that I can still understand you?"

War gives me a patient look. "I told you, you are my wife. You will know me and my heart, whether you want that or not."

Unease coils low in my stomach.

Again, he says it with such certainty that I wonder ...

But no. I refuse to believe I'm supposed to be with this monster.

"What do you want with me?" I ask, toeing a nearby pebble.

I sense rather than see War's eyes draw down my face. "Isn't it obvious?"

My gaze moves to his. "No." It's not.

From the few stories I've heard, this man has bagged himself a city's worth of women—a *big* fucking city's worth—and yet he hasn't done more than touched my cheek and claimed that I'm his wife.

"Would you like me to tell you then?" he asks, his voice deceptively soft.

My pulse picks up. "Yes."

"I want you to surrender."

A beat of silence passes.

I have no clue what that actually *means*, but I note that chaining me to a bed and feasting on my pussy were not mentioned. Shame. Under the right circumstances (a.k.a., lots and lots of booze), I could actually get behind that one.

"Surrender?" I echo. "I already have."

"You haven't," he insists.

Are you *kidding* me? He's forced me to leave my life behind because it suited him. If that's not surrender then I don't know what is.

The more I stew on my thoughts, the more indignant I become.

"We've talked about how different you are and how difficult you are to understand, but we haven't talked about me," I finally say. "I don't want you as a husband, and I don't accept you, and whatever your god thinks he wants to do with me and the rest of the world, I will fight it with my every last breath.

"Oh, and I'm not surrendering *anything* to you, motherfucker."

War gives a malevolent laugh, and despite myself, it raises the hairs on the back of my neck. "Fight all you want, wife. Battle is what I'm best at—and I assure you, you won't win this one."

THE SECOND DAY of riding is both more and less miserable than the first. More, because I still have to ride alongside War, and less, because Thunder has only tried to kick me once so far, and that's an improvement from the three attempts he made yesterday.

My terrible sunburn also seems to be much better today— the skin only slightly tight and tender—and my saddle-sore thighs don't ache nearly as much as I expected them to. I don't know what witchcraft is responsible for this, but I'm not going to complain.

Today we leave the arid mountain range behind us, moving towards the flatter ground near the coast. The moment those rolling hills fall away, I feel bare. I've lived with the mountains my entire life. The wide, flat expanse of land that stretches out in front of me now is foreign and it makes me painfully homesick.

I'm really not going back. My heart squeezes a little at the thought, even as a strange sort of exhilaration takes hold. For years I had been trying to save up enough money to leave Jerusalem. And now I've truly left it.

Not that this part of New Palestine is much to look at. It's nothing but swaths and swaths of yellowed grass, interrupted every now and then by a struggling patch of farmland. Every so often we pass a dilapidated building or a seemingly empty town, and maybe there are still people living here. It doesn't look like War has laid waste to these places, but it's all so very quiet.

"Are the people here already dead?" I ask.

It *feels* like they're dead. Everything's too still. Not even the wind stirs, like it's already abandoned this place.

"Not yet," he says ominously.

How is it feasible for War to stretch his reach this far? The cities he lays siege to, those I understand, but the houses that speckle these forgotten places—how does he get those?

He doesn't say anything further, and I'm left with a horrible, gnawing worry that he and the other horsemen are truly unstoppable.

But they *can* be stopped, right? After all, another horseman came before War, and then, at some later time, he vanished.

"What happened to Pestilence?" I ask.

Quiet fear had settled into Jerusalem after the news came that a horseman of the apocalypse was spreading plague through North America. But then a short while later rumors erupted that Pestilence had disappeared. I don't know if anyone truly believed that—that he'd disappeared, I mean. We'd been fooled by that explanation once before, when the horsemen first arrived.

But Pestilence hadn't returned after all; War had come instead.

"The conqueror was vanquished," War says.

"The conqueror?" I repeat. "You mean Pestilence?"

War inclines his head a little.

"I thought you were all immortal," I say.

"I didn't say my brother was *dead*."

I narrow my eyes, studying War's profile. How could a horseman be both alive *and* vanquished?

He glances over at me. "You carry trouble in your eyes, wife. Whatever you're thinking, *un*think it."

"Tell me about him," I say. "Pestilence."

War is quiet for a long time. His kohl-lined eyes far too aware. "You want to know how Pestilence was stopped?"

Of course I do. I had no idea a horsemen *could* be stopped. A second later, War's words truly register.

"So he *was* stopped?" I try to imagine Pestilence chained and immobilized, thwarted from his deadly task.

War settles himself deeper into his saddle. "That's a story for another day, I'm afraid." His words are final. "But wife," he adds, "there is something you should know now."

I raise my brows. Oh?

War flashes me a fierce look. "My brother failed. I will not."

I think I'm supposed to be frightened by War's words, but all I can think is that Pestilence *failed*. He failed at whatever he was supposed to do.

Shit. The horsemen really can be stopped.

War continues on, unaware of my thoughts. "Pestilence might've been a conqueror, but I don't seek to conquer, savage woman, I seek to *destroy*."

IT'S LATE BY the time we eventually stop. We're not at the ocean, but from the few words War's said on the subject, this expanse of land is where the entire army will set up camp when they arrive tomorrow.

Which means I only have to endure one more night of

one-on-one time with War. The thought isn't nearly so daunting as it was yesterday. Aside from cupping my face, he hasn't so much as tried to touch me.

However, tonight War lays the pallets noticeably closer to each other. Close enough for us to reach out and hold hands from our respective beds—if we wanted to.

Like yesterday, War still gives me all the blankets, and I still feel guilty about it. I shouldn't feel guilty. Going cold for one night is the least of what this fucker deserves.

But even once I slip under those blankets, the guilt still trickles its way in. Maybe especially then because the evening air already has a bite to it.

Don't offer him a blanket, Miriam. Don't do it. You extend that olive branch and you open the door to being something more than distant travel companions.

I bite my tongue until I no longer feel the urge to share my blankets.

War, for his part, looks completely at home on his threadbare pallet. He lays on his back, his hands behind his head and his legs crossed at the ankles as he stares up at the stars. Again I envy his ease. He seems perfectly at home here, on this random patch of dirt—more at home than I feel, and I've lived on this earth a helluva lot longer than he has.

"So," I begin.

He turns his head to me. "Yes?"

God, that deep voice. My core clenches at the sound of it.

"What were you doing before you were raiding cities?" I ask.

War glances back up at the stars. "I slept."

Uh ... "Where?"

"Here, on earth."

His answer doesn't make much sense to me, but then, not much else about him makes sense either—so far, what I've learned about him is that he can't be killed, he doesn't need food or water, and he doesn't shit or piss like the rest of us.

I repeat: the horseman doesn't shit or piss.

I'm telling you, he makes no sense.

War's voice cuts through the night air. "While I slept, I dreamed. I could hear so many voices. So many things," he murmurs.

I study his profile. So far, War has been haughty, possessive, silver-tongued, and terrifying. But this is the first time I've seen him like *this*. Full of his otherness. An eerie feeling creeps over me, like he might've just been about to spill the secrets of the universe.

He seems to shake himself. "But that is no matter."

I stare at him for a little longer.

"Tomorrow my army will arrive here."

"And things will go back to the way they were," I say.

I imagine my tiny tent. I should feel relief that I'll be able to put distance between us once more. Instead my stomach twists. I hadn't realized how lonely I've been. You don't really focus on things like loneliness when you're just trying to survive each day like I'd been in Jerusalem. But I *had* felt lonely. I'd felt it every night I fell asleep without my family and woke to silence.

And then War swept into my town and I stopped trying to survive. I opened my arms to death, and it was the horseman who kept me from that fate.

"Things don't have to go back to the way they were, wife."

Wife.

The horseman knows exactly how to bait me. I don't *want* to be with him, but now I've remembered just what it's like to be with someone. To have open, unvarnished conversations.

My throat works. "They must."

Chapter 10

I WAKE IN War's arms.

I know it before I open my eyes—even before I fully shake off sleep. I'm far too warm, and I can feel his heavy limbs draped all over me as I lay on my side. Still, when I blink my eyes open, I'm not prepared for the reality of it.

My face is all but buried against his naked chest. I pull my head away a little. This close to him, all I can see is the crimson glow of his markings and endless olive skin.

How did this happen?

I glance down between us and—damnit, we're on his pallet, not mine, which means *I* scooched over to *him* at some point in the night, sacrificing my blankets for his thin mat and thick muscles.

My eyes travel up, past the column of his throat, to what I can see of his face.

In sleep, War looks angelic—or, more appropriate, angelically demonic. All his sharp features have been blunted just a bit. He almost looks ... at peace. His jaw isn't so firm, his lips seem a touch more inviting, and now that I can't see his dagger-like eyes, he's not nearly so intimidating.

I stare at him for a long time before I remember myself.

Stop ogling a horseman of the apocalypse, Miriam.

I also need to get out from under him, stat. The last thing I want is for him to wake up to this, too.

War's leg is thrown over mine, and his arm is draped over my side, hugging me to him. With a little effort, I manage to slip one leg, then the other, out from under his own. When I get to his arm, I try to push it off of me—*try* being the operative word.

My God, his arm weighs five billion kilos, and it is not giving up its hold on me.

I twist a little with the effort. This ogre.

"Wife."

I take a steadying breath, staring at his chest. This is really what I didn't want.

Slowly, my eyes move up to War's. He's so close I can see those flecks of gold in them. There's a hint of a smile on his lips and a deep look of satisfaction.

"This is your fault," I say.

He raises his eyebrows. "Is it?"

The horseman doesn't bother pointing out that we're on his flimsy excuse of a bed. He also doesn't bother removing his arm from where it's draped over me. Instead, his hand slides from my back to my ribcage, settling into the dip of my waist. I can tell he's mapping out the contours of my body. He must like what he's discovering because he looks annoyingly pleased.

His eyes are like honey when he says, "Stay with me, Miriam." His hand flexes against my side. "Sleep in my tent. Make your weapons. Argue with me."

I search his face. If only he knew just how tempting his words are to a lonely girl like me. And he asks it right as I'm guiltily basking in his arms. Touch is a luxury I've gone too long without.

But that's what it is—a luxury. One I cannot afford,

especially with this creature.

"No," I say. Now that War's awake, he's back to looking fierce. It makes it easier to turn him down. "I'll play along and let you call me your wife, but I'm *never* going to choose you of my own free will."

War's grip tightens against my waist. He pulls me in close. "Do you want to know a truth, Miriam? Humans make proclamations like that all the time. But their oaths are brittle and break with age. I'm not afraid of yours, but you should be afraid of mine for I will tell you this: you are my wife, you will surrender to me, and you will be mine in every sense of the word before I've destroyed the last of this world."

THINGS HAVE GONE back to the way they were.

War is in his tent, I'm in mine, and there are now five thousand people that separate us.

We haven't spoken since the horseman's army arrived yesterday. He was swept away into talks with his phobos riders, undoubtedly strategizing the best way to kill off the next city they've set their sights on.

As for the rest of us, we're all settling into this place like it's a new pair of shoes. In my case, a very ill-fitting pair of shoes. But I guess that's a personal problem at this point.

My tent and my things were returned to me yesterday, right down to the tattered romance novel and coffee set I inherited from the last poor soul who lived here.

Even my wood was returned to me. My *wood*. I thought for sure that would disappear.

I run my hands over a branch now. I've been putting off making weapons, but the itch to create has returned to my fingers.

I grab the canvas bag War gave me several days ago. Unceremoniously I turn it over and dump everything out.

I sift through my tools, looking for one to shave away bark. As I do so, my hand brushes against something that doesn't belong. Pausing, I push away the tools and uncover a familiar metal frame.

Inside it is a picture of my mother, my father, my sister, and me.

A small sound slips out.

Grabbing the photo, I lift it reverently. *There's my family.* My throat works as I run my thumb over my sister Lia's dimpled face. She and my mother are younger here than I remember them—as am I. But this was the last family photo of all *four* of us. In it, my mother is alive, my father is alive, my sister is alive, and I am sitting amongst them all.

Getting this back is like getting a piece of myself back. Without it, I might've forgotten their faces.

I don't realize I'm crying until a drop of water hits the glass.

Why would War pack this? Was it an accident? He doesn't seem like the sentimental type. Or was it meant to be cruel? If it was, it missed its mark.

Outside my tent, I hear the rhythmic pounding of a drum— one, two, three times. I've started understanding the noises well enough to distinguish execution drumbeats from celebratory or battle drumbeats. This one heralds in some sort of announcement.

I take a stuttering breath, then carefully I set my family photo aside and leave my tent. Following the growing crowd of people, I make my way to the center of camp.

The layout here is just like it was at the last campsite, so I know exactly where to go; the setting may change, but the spaces don't.

War is already in the clearing with his riders, standing on a makeshift dais so he can be seen. My breath catches at the sight of him. I don't know what I feel, only that I feel *something* when I look at him.

He retrieved the photo of my family. That couldn't have been anything other than intentional. I want to thank him, but the distance between us and the fearsome look on his face make him seem farther away from me than ever.

Once most of the camp has arrived, War steps forward, and the crowd quiets. He gives us all a long look, then he opens his mouth and speaks in that guttural tongue of his. "*Etso, peo aduno vle vegki.*"

The hairs along my arms rise.

Tomorrow, we head into battle.

Chapter 11

I SIT IN my tent, flipping War's dagger over and over in my hands.

Surviving isn't good enough.

It once was, hence my rules for surviving the apocalypse. But now the game is no longer just about survival. It can't be. It's about remaining decent during the true end of the world.

War wants us to fight—well, to be fair, he doesn't give a rat's ass whether *I* fight. He made that plain the day he took me. But most of the camp's occupants *are* supposed to go into battle and kill just as their family and friends were killed. I don't know how many people here can stomach that, but I can't. I can't just stand by as innocent people get slaughtered.

I glance over at where I've propped up the photo of my family.

My hands still.

What if I spent my time in battle killing off this ungodly army?

Killing is a horrible, messy business. And killing War's army is akin to a death sentence—if I get caught doing so. My idea isn't all that wise or decent.

I also know I can't simply sit around and watch the world

burn.

My tent flaps are thrown open, and a phobos rider peers inside. "The warlord wishes to see you."

My stomach clenches.

Re-holstering War's dagger, I follow the rider out of the women's quarter, the two of us making our way towards the horseman's tent.

As we move through camp, I notice that weapons have been set out, and people are picking through them, finding which ones best suit them. I even see a child checking out a dagger. I shudder at the sight.

Among the cluster of people, I see the man from the first night who grabbed his crotch and pointed his dagger at me. He chats with a few other men, but their eyes follow me as I pass by. The crotch-grabber runs his tongue across his lower lip as he takes me in.

He hasn't forgotten about me, which isn't good.

This is one of the reasons why Rule Three—avoid notice—has made my list of guidelines to live by. When people notice you these days, it's often for the wrong reasons. Too pretty, too wealthy, too vulnerable, too wounded, too sick, too stupid. You can become easy pickings for the wrong person.

I frown at the man and move on.

When War's tent comes into sight, my heart begins to pound.

This is the first time the two of us will have talked since we traveled together, and my emotions are conflicted. The War I rode alongside was a halfway normal person. The War who manages this camp is a fearsome, conscienceless being.

And the truth is, I don't even *know* the full extent of his power and cruelty, only that it's capable of wiping out entire cities.

How much of New Palestine is gone? For that matter, how much of the lands east of New Palestine is gone?

Nausea rolls through me. That's the man I'm dealing with.

A horseman who has already killed off countless. A horseman who *enjoys* the carnage.

As soon as we near the opening of War's tent, the phobos rider steps aside, leaving me to enter alone.

Inside, War sits on a chair, his fingers steepled and pressed to his mouth.

When he sees me, the horseman's eyes come alive. My heart stutters a little at the sight.

Out of fear, not flattery. At least, that's what I tell myself.

The horseman stands and comes up to me, and he's just as intimidating as ever. He reaches out to touch me, but I flinch away before he can.

Things are different now.

War frowns. "You slept in my arms only two days ago, and now you can't bear my touch?"

If I didn't know better, I'd say that the horseman sounded a tad wounded.

"I didn't *mean* to sleep next to you," I say.

"Didn't you though?" he throws back at me. "I lavished your bed as best as I could, and still you came for me."

"Stop rewriting what happened," I snap.

He steps in close. "Am I?"

"I wouldn't knowingly sleep with you," I say. "Not while you're butchering my kind."

"I am doing what I must, just as you are," he says. "Can you fault me for it?"

"*Yes.*" I damn well can.

"If you knew what lay on the other side of death," he says, "you would know it is nothing to fear."

"And what about pain?" I add.

"What about it?"

"If you don't care about the fact that you're killing us, what about the pain you're causing us?"

"Your kind only feel it for a short while."

I stare at him. He doesn't get it. Pain is pain, and death is the end—maybe we go on in some other form, but it is *an* end. Our bodies die, and all those earthly hopes and dreams die along with it. He's overlooking the fact that there's worth in life itself.

I step back. "Why did you call me to your tent?"

"The fight tomorrow is not for you," he says. "You are to stay here, in my tent. I will have all the amenities you might need.

Ah, so he is happy to kill people, but when it comes to me, he doesn't want me touched by his violence.

Surviving is no longer good enough.

"What if I want to come along?"

War's eyes narrow. He stares at me for a beat too long, and I have to fight the urge to fidget.

"What mischief are you up to?" he says.

"Why are you worried?" I say a tad defensively. "What could I possibly do?"

"You could die."

"If you're so confident God sent me to you, then surely you know He will spare me—or are you unsure after all?"

The horseman's mouth curves up. "Challenging me will get you nowhere, wife."

"Let me come." *So that I might kill all your loyal killers.*

When he doesn't respond, my gaze moves to his lips.

There are other ways of convincing the horseman ...

Adrenaline spikes my bloodstream at just the thought. I know the horseman wants to kiss me. He wants that and undoubtedly more.

"Please," I insist, trying again to coax the horseman with my words. "It's only fitting that"—I hesitate over my next words—"your *wife* should be out there fighting alongside you."

He scrutinizes me, but I swear he looks a touch convinced. His eyes drop to my lips, gazing at my mouth the same way I was gazing at his just moments ago.

Victory is within reach; all I have to do is—

Before I can think twice about it, I wrap my hand around the back of War's neck, my fingers brushing against that dark, wavy hair of his. I was sure it would feel coarse—like the rest of him—but it's soft. So soft.

War's eyes widen almost imperceptibly at my touch.

Standing up on my tiptoes, I press my lips to his. The kiss is over before it's barely begun—I'm not even sure something this brief could be *called* a kiss. Nonetheless, the horseman looks thunderstruck from it. Thunderstruck and hungry.

My hand slides from his neck and my heels touch the ground. "You'll get another one if you agree to let me fight."

War's eyes are alight with want as he studies me. "I knew you were going to be trouble." He looks away and runs a hand down his jaw. "This makes me *twice* as reluctant to let you go tomorrow. And yet ..."

He turns back to me, a fierce edge to his features.

"*Paruv Eziel ratowejiwa we, pei auwep ror.*"

God's hand protects you, but mine cannot.

My entire body shivers as the words pass through me, my knees weakening from the sound of them. The affect lingers for several seconds before dissipating away.

"What was that?" I say, rubbing my arm.

"Angelic—my native tongue." He gives me an intense look. "Tomorrow I will not be able to shield you from battle. You will have to keep yourself safe."

Holy crap, is he really going for this? Only minutes ago he seemed convinced I should stay out of the fray. Who would've known some cajoling and an itsy bitsy kiss could change all that carefully calculated consideration?

"So is that a yes?"

Instead of answering me, War reels me in, tilting my face up. Before I fully know what he's doing, his mouth is back on mine.

His kiss isn't anything like the one I gave him. I know it the moment our lips crash together. This kiss is raw desire, and it cuts me wide open. I haven't been truly kissed in over a year, and even that experience pales to this one. War's lips burn against mine as he crushes me to him.

My knees were already weak from his earlier words, but now they completely give out, and it's his grip alone that keeps me standing.

The horseman smiles against my mouth, more than aware of his effect on me.

His need is sparking my own. I kiss him back—I don't think I could do anything *but* kiss him back in this moment.

I'm going to pay for this later ... but right now I don't really give two shits. I've forgotten what self-control feels like.

War parts my lips with his own, and suddenly his tongue is pressing against mine. His body feels like sin, but he tastes like heaven.

My hands move back into that soft hair of his, and my core is on fire. If this is what his kiss does to me, I can't imagine what everything else would feel like.

I don't know who ends the kiss, but eventually our lips part.

I stagger out of War's arms. Now I'm the one who's gobsmacked. I stare at his mouth.

My God, I've *never* so badly wanted someone I disliked. But then again, here's another side of War I'm only beginning to see—the reckless, passionate warlord.

War breathes heavily, that overwhelming body of his heaving with the action. I thought he might flash me one of his mocking smiles; he knows exactly what he did to me. Instead, he steps towards me, his expression determined, clearly ready to resume that kiss.

I take a halting step back. "I can't."

The correct response should've been *no*, but the truth is, I want to kiss the horseman back. It's embarrassing how *much* I want that.

His gaze is fixed back on my lips.

"Why," he says. It's hardly a question.

I take a deep breath, beating back my lust. One day my vagina might stage a coup and overpower my brain—but that day won't be today.

My eyes meet War's. "Because tomorrow you're still going to ride out with your army, and it's going to break my heart."

Chapter 12

WE ASSEMBLE BEFORE dawn.

It's a quiet, somber thing. I'd like to think that the soldiers around me are just as pained at the thought of killing innocents as I am, but I don't know.

I'm one of several hundred who's given a horse. The rest of the army is heading in on foot—well except for the few men and women who are manning the giant carts they'll bring into the city, carts that will eventually return to camp stacked with stolen goods.

The soldiers have me wait off to the side of the army procession, just like last time I left camp. And like last time, I hear the pounding hoof beats of War's horse cut through the early morning air. War rides out of the darkness, the torchlight making him look particularly menacing.

I stare at his blood red horse. Deimos, he called the creature.

War stops when he gets to me.

"Stay safe," he says, his voice as serious as I've ever heard it.

"Try not to kill too many people," I respond.

A smile curves his lips. "There's no such thing as too

many."

Ugh.

"Farewell, wife. We'll meet again on the battlefield."

With that, War rides to the head of the procession. The soldiers who can see him lift their weapons and torches and whoop.

Idiots.

Slowly, the entire army begins to move. I slip into line along with the rest of them, my nerves ratcheting up. The lot of us are heading into Ashdod, a city nestled along the coast of New Palestine. Home to many, many people.

The ride in is unnaturally quiet. No one speaks with each other, so the only sound is the fall of hoof beats and footsteps. Dozens of soldiers carry torches, and the firelight illuminates their somber faces.

On one side of my waist is War's sheathed dagger and on the other is a sword I lifted earlier. It's a bit too heavy and the edge is fairly dull, but I'm going to need to use it anyway if I'm going to throw myself into the fray.

I feel my resolve hardening into place.

Rule One has always been: bend the rules—but don't break them. But if the rules are wrong, then they need to be broken. They need to be smashed to fucking pieces.

And today I'm going to do just that.

WAR'S ARMY TAKES out the aviaries first.

As soon as I enter the town, I can hear the birds' shrill cries. Fire already engulfs several buildings, and in one of them, there are birds trapped inside. All around me people are fighting and screaming and fleeing and dying, but it's the sound of those birds' cries that truly chills me.

To attack the aviaries is akin to cutting off any and all warnings that could be passed along to the outside world.

I assumed War met with his men to talk about battle strategy, but I hadn't actually thought about what that strategy might look like.

A lone bird soars through the air, its form partially obscured by the plumes of smoke rising from the burning city. I dare to hope that it escaped the fire, that it's carrying a warning someone managed to scribble out before it was too late. I hope that it's heading somewhere that hasn't already been hit by War.

And I hope that the bird actually gets there.

Go, I silently cheer it on.

It has a fighting chance, it really does.

But then I see a few archers on a nearby roof. I see those soldiers cock their bows and aim. And then I see them release their arrows. There must be a dozen of them arcing through the sky.

Most miss the bird, but one hits the creature square in the chest. It tumbles out of the sky, and I feel my hope plunge with that bird.

There will be no warnings to pass along, just as we weren't warned. We'll all just fight and die and War will move on to destroy more cities until the entire world is gone.

We're facing a mass extinction, and we're not going to survive it.

Chapter 13

IT'S AWFUL. THE things I see.

The bodies, the blood, the needless violence. But the worst, the absolute worst, are the faces of the civilians as they lose everything all at once.

Some of them don't even run. They see the lives they built for themselves torn down, and they stand in the streets and simply weep. All of these people survived a civil war. They've seen destruction and violence sweep through once already. And for a second time, they have to endure it. Some of them simply give up. If the world is this hard to live in, it's not *worth* living in.

I ride through the city on my horse, my heart in my throat.

Buildings are utterly engulfed in flame. Worse yet, Ashdod happens to be a city that people flocked to *after* the Arrival, and the shantytowns I ride past appear to be even more flammable than the older buildings. It's nothing but a wall of red-orange flame; even the ground seems to burn in these newer, more desperate neighborhoods, and I can hear the horrible dying screams of those trapped inside.

I stop my horse, my eyes scouring the landscape. I've been

so set on fighting War's army that I've forgotten that I can still help people *live*. Isn't that the ultimate goal? To survive this apocalypse?

I catch sight of a mother and the two children she presses close to her, and I can't not react. That could've been me and my family. It once *was* me and my family.

I guide my horse to them and hop off, keeping the steed's reins in my fist.

The woman's eyes are pinched shut, like that can shut out the nightmare, and she's shushing her crying children.

"You need to get out of the city," I tell her. When she doesn't react, I grab her upper arm. She screams and flinches away. "Listen to me," I snap, shaking her a little.

Her eyes open at the tone of my voice.

"Take your kids, get on this horse, and ride as far and as fast from the city as you can. I think the army is heading down the coast, so ride in any direction but that one."

She gives me a shaky nod.

"There should be some food and water in the saddle bags. Not much, but enough to keep you going for a little while. Don't stop, not until you're far, far away."

When she doesn't move immediately, I jerk my head to the horse, who's growing more and more agitated at the violence around us. "Hurry, before they kill us all."

The woman seems to snap out of whatever spell she was under, bustling herself and her children towards the horse. Quickly I help her and her children up onto it, and then I hand her the reins.

"Stay safe," I say, echoing War's earlier words.

With that, she taps the horse's sides and Thunder—or whoever that horse is—takes off. I stare at them for several seconds, watching them ride away. I have a terrible feeling in my gut that they are no better off than that bird that escaped the aviaries. That within a mile or two, they too will be shot down.

I hope not. I can't bear the thought of that family getting torn apart like mine was.

The sounds of war drift in—the screaming, the shouting, the weeping, and amongst it all, the wet slap of bodies being sliced open.

I pull out my sword.

Be brave.

I turn just as a man aims a long-barreled gun at me. At the sight of it, I freeze.

My heart is in my throat.

I haven't seen one of those in months. But I remember guns, and I know what flesh looks like when a bullet tears through it.

I take in the man's white shirt and pajama bottoms. He was probably sleeping when we came riding through—and now he's fighting for his life. There's blood splatter on his shirt, and shit, I really don't want to fight him, I want to help him.

"Please," I say raising a hand to placate him. "I'm not going to—"

I don't see the man's finger move, but I hear the gun blast. Metal shrieks as part of the gun explodes, blowing away the owner's face.

At the sight of him, I cover my mouth with the back of my hand, forcing down my nausea.

This is why people stopped using guns. These days, firearms had a nasty habit of jamming. You were more likely to kill yourself than you were to end an enemy.

I only have a few seconds to process the fact that the man's dead and I'm not before I'm swept along on the tide of the fight.

Over the next couple hours, there are others who I help in the melee. I'm not entirely sure it makes much of a difference. I want to keep saving innocent people—and I will—but it's hard to see the point when they are so overwhelmed by soldiers. It's War's army that truly needs to be stopped.

The army's wagons roll through the town, and marauding soldiers load them up with goods. Sacks of grain, jugs of water and whatever spirits they can get their hands on. Dried fruit, nuts, farm animals—which they will promptly butcher because chickens and goats don't travel well.

What isn't being sacked is being burned to the ground. The entire city seems to be on fire.

Ahead of me, my eyes fall on a dead soldier, a bow and a mostly full quiver still strapped to his back.

I stare at the items for several seconds. The bow is big—made for a man of stature—and the grip will be unfamiliar, but there it is. I'm far better with a bow and arrow than I am with a blade. And a weapon like that would give me the ability to injure enemies rather covertly.

Without another moment's hesitation, I run for it, ducking and swerving to avoid the battles raging in the street.

I slide to my knees at the side of the fallen man. His blood is running like a river from a head wound. I try not to look at him any more closely as I begin to pry the bow and quiver from his body.

I have the bow over my shoulder when a woman on horseback charges down the street, and I have to roll out of the way so that her steed doesn't trample me. A moment later, I'm back at the man's side, lugging his quiver away from his body, the arrows rattling within it.

I've got it!

The quiver is fitted for a much bigger torso and the bow is heavy and strange in my hand, but I have them both!

Now I run, my eyes scanning the streets for a good building to perch myself inside. There's not much to choose from, considering that most of the city is burning, but I spot a few buildings that are resisting the flames.

I sprint for one of them, a three story structure that must've once held offices or apartments. Finding the stairwell,

I take the stairs two at a time. Sweat drips down my skin, and I cough as I breathe in the smoky air.

On the third floor I head into one of the rooms, which are not offices after all, but apartments. The family inside screams, and an older woman tries to bash my head in with a pot.

"Whoa! I'm leaving!"

Hot damn.

I slip back out and close the door behind me. "Lock your door next time!" I yell through the walls.

Door probably doesn't have a lock, you numbskull.

Jogging to the next door, I enter the apartment, this time a little more wary. But the place is empty. I make my way to the window, and grabbing a nearby pitcher, I smash out the glass pane.

Knocking out the remaining shards, I grab an arrow and settle it against the bow. And then I hunt.

In the streets beneath me, War's soldiers are causing chaos. I aim my arrow at a woman driving her knife through another woman's belly.

Please don't miss.

I take a steadying breath then release the arrow.

It goes wide by a meter.

Nocking another arrow into the bow, I aim again, this time correcting for the distance. Pulling the bowstring back, I release the arrow.

I don't hear the sickening thump of it hitting the woman's stomach, but I see the arrow skewer her. It's a wound she might survive, but I don't bother following up with her because ten meters down the street, a man is trying to pull down a woman's pants.

I might hit her ...

The thought doesn't stop me from aiming and firing. The man's body recoils as the arrow strikes him just beneath the heart. He staggers forward, onto the screaming woman. She pushes his body away from her and runs, not looking back to see where deliverance came from.

On and on I shoot from the perch until I run out of arrows.

I leave my vantage point, heading back down the building. I've just walked out the front entrance when War rides down the street, his sword bloody. People are screaming and scattering.

Another gun goes off. I don't have time to see the shooter or wonder at the fact that the firearm actually works. I'm too busy watching War as the shot blasts into him. His body jerks back, the force of the hit throwing that mountain of a man off his steed. His mount continues to charge forward, leaving him behind.

The horseman lies unmoving on the ground, those golden hair pieces dull in the hazy light.

Is he dead? He said he *could* die.

My skin tingles strangely at the thought. Whatever it is I feel, the emotion is more conflicted than it should be.

War begins to move, and my thoughts banish themselves. He pushes himself off the ground, rising to his feet once more. A malicious smile spreads across his face.

Now I turn to look at the woman holding the gun. Her hand is steady, though her eyes are wide. She's a little older than me, and the hijab she wears billows in the breeze as she trains her weapon on War. And then she resumes pulling the trigger.

The bullets light up his body, jerking his frame left and right as he strides forward. He spreads his arms and laughs like a crazy fucking bastard as the shots pierce his armor and sink into skin. His blood drips in thick rivulets from the wounds, sliding down his body.

I stare at him in horror.

Dear God, he really can't die.

The woman shoots until her gun clicks. War gives a low

laugh, and his eyes are so, so violent.

Without thinking, I cut across the street, dashing in front of the woman, blocking her from the horseman.

War's eyes settle on me. There's a moment of surprise; this is the first time since battle began that we've run into each other. But his surprise quickly withers away, and his eyes narrow.

"Don't come between us, wife," he says, not bothering to speak in tongues. His guttural voice cuts through me like a cold wind.

"I'm not going to let you kill her." I don't know what the woman was thinking, but she better make herself scarce *fast*.

"Miriam." War's voice is as serious as I've ever heard it. "Move."

Be brave.

"No."

The horseman scrutinizes me, his wounds still weeping blood. "There are thousands of innocents in this town. She is not one of them. Don't waste your mercy."

I square my shoulders. "I'm not moving."

War steps up to me, and I'm reminded of why he's so goddamn frightening. He's over two meters tall, and nearly every square centimeter of him is coated in blood.

"You are playing a dangerous game, wife," he says, his voice pitched low.

I think it's supposed to be a threat, but I feel that voice low in my belly, and I'm reminded all over again of the horseman's kiss.

"I don't consider life and death to be a game. Spare her."

"And have her attempt to kill me again?" he says. "That's madness, woman."

As he says this, I hear a dull clink. I glance down just in time to see a bloody, spent bullet roll along the road.

That ... came out of him.

Holy balls.

"What harm would it do? Spare her," I urge again.

"You like her simply because she tried to kill me," he says, giving me a look.

Maybe.

"She's brave."

He stares over my shoulder at the woman, a grimace on his face. "She'll cause trouble."

But he's actually considering this.

I press my advantage. "Give her a useful task—make her cook things or manage stuff."

The battle is still brewing around us, and every second that passes the odds of this woman surviving grow smaller and smaller.

War stares at her for an impossibly long time. His upper lip curls.

"This is a waste of my time," he says. "For the sake of your soft heart, I will let her live—*for now*."

He whistles to a nearby soldier and beckons him over. The man jogs to War's side. Leaning in close, the horseman whispers something to the soldier. The man nods in response, then breaks away.

I glance behind me. The woman is still standing in the middle of the road, though at some point she procured a knife.

Why didn't you run when you had the chance? I want to ask her.

She shifts her weight from foot to foot, her eyes going to me, then to War and the soldier. She has an angry, desperate look about her.

The man breaks away from War, striding over to the woman.

"What is he doing?" I ask War, alarmed.

The horseman's upper lip curls. "Sparing her," he says, a note of disgust in his voice.

The woman raises her weapon as the soldier comes in

close, but the man easily knocks away the blade, grabbing her by the shoulder. As soon as the soldier touches her, she goes berserk, scratching and kicking and screaming.

Gritting his teeth, the soldier begins to explain himself to her, gesturing first to the horseman and me, and then to a nearby horse. Whatever the soldier is telling her, it's causing her to slowly, reluctantly cooperate.

A minute later, he takes the woman to a nearby horse and helps her onto the saddle, murmuring quietly to her.

"Are you sure he's not just going to slit her throat the moment we're out of sight?" I ask War while I stare at the two of them. I don't even know why I'm so invested in this. Maybe it *is* simply because the woman hurt War.

"No," he responds as the soldier and the woman ride off, "I'm not. The hearts of men are fickle and cruel."

I give him a look just as another bullet wiggles its way out of his armor, clinking to the ground.

The horseman steps in close, and without warning, he cups the back of my head and pulls me in for a savage kiss. The world is spinning on its head, but the moment War's lips touch mine, the cyclone seems to stop.

There's no more battle, no more death and violence, no more heaven pitted against earth. It's just him and me.

He tastes like smoke and steel, and my lips respond to his, just as they did last night. It seems I can't *not* kiss him, even when he represents everything I'm fighting against.

His mouth scours mine over and over and—

War breaks away from the kiss, and the world rushes back in.

I stare at the horseman, dazed, as he backs away, his kohl-lined eyes fixed to mine.

"Deimos!" he calls out, not looking away from me.

War's steed comes galloping to him like it had been just waiting for the order.

The horseman mounts the beast while I stand there,

wondering what the fuck I was thinking just now when I kissed him back.

War doesn't say anything else. With a final look at me, he rides back into the fray.

BY THE TIME the fighting is done, no one is left.

The streets are filled with the dead and dying. The buildings are ashes and rubble. The once blue sky is now a hazy red-brown and ash drifts down like snow.

The captives have been taken away, and the rest of us are filtering back out the way we came.

My hands shake from pain and exhaustion and hunger and a deep sense of *wrongness*. What happened today wasn't right.

I stumble across the horseman again on my way out of the city.

War is standing at a crossroads, his back to me, a field of bodies spread around him. He's splashed with blood, calmly surveying the destruction.

He can't be something holy. He *can't*. Nothing pure can be responsible for pain like this.

But then he turns, and his eyes meet mine. Beneath the bloodlust, there's a weight and a resolve in his gaze. And if I stare long enough, I might even say that he looks a bit burdened.

I glance away before that can happen.

I continue walking on, skirting around the bodies and strolling right past him as though he were invisible.

Not two minutes later, I hear galloping behind me. I swivel around just in time to see the horseman astride his warhorse, Deimos, the two of them heading straight for me.

War leans out of his saddle, his arm outstretched. I begin to move out of the way, but War simply adjusts his trajectory so that he's still closing in on me. The distance closes between us—ten meters, five, *two*.

His arm slams into my midsection, sweeping me off the

ground. My breath leaves me all at once as I'm dragged onto his horse. I gasp for air as War secures my back to his front.

"Next time, you'll wait for me," he says into my ear.

Unlikely.

I scowl at him over my shoulder as he carries me out of town, hating that I'm pressed so close to him.

Once I've taken in a few deep breaths, I say, "You made me kill today." They were his soldiers, but still.

It wasn't right, none of it was right.

War doesn't respond.

Of course he doesn't.

The horseman's steed slows as we rejoin the last of the army, who has gathered at the edge of Ashdod. I don't know why War's soldiers have stopped here, rather than back at camp, or why War is stopping with them.

Deimos comes to a halt, and as soon as he does I slide off the steed. War lets me go, and that in and of itself should've tipped me off that something strange was going on.

I feel the horseman's gaze burning into my back as I make my way into the gathered crowd of soldiers. The people around me look to their warlord like they've been waiting for an announcement.

War's phobos riders fan out around him, the group of them still on their steeds. I stare at these stoic, mounted men, each one wearing a red band on his bicep. Like War, many of them have taken to wearing kohl to darken their eyes.

A hush falls over the crowd, and my skin pricks at the silence. All eyes are still on War.

What is going on?

Wordlessly, the horseman reaches towards the ruins of Ashdod, his palm upturned. His arm begins to shake, his muscles tense beneath his armor. Slowly, he raises his arm, higher and higher as though lifting a great burden.

I glance around me again at all the rapt faces.

Okay, seriously, what the *fuck* is going on?

For a long minute, all is quiet, all is still.

Then, I feel it at my feet.

The earth begins to tremble. It's subtle at first—I almost think it's my imagination—but it continues to intensify until my legs are vibrating from it. Pebbles skitter along the ground and the earth. All the while War sits on his steed, arm uplifted, his features placid.

A shiver runs down my spine. Something is happening, something ...

Around us, the earth begins to split open. People either jump or stumble away as the ground around them parts.

And then—

The ground is *moving*. Not just opening, but *moving*. It looks, alive and I can't make sense of what I'm seeing—until, that is, a desiccated hand rises from the ground.

"Dear God," I breathe.

From the earth, the dead rise.

Chapter 14

THE STORIES WERE true. The ones from the east. The ones *about* the east.

My eyes sweep over the flat landscape. Everywhere my eyes land, the dead are rising. There are dozens and dozens of them. The ground beneath my feet was unknowingly speckled with unmarked graves, and from them, the long gone are coming back to life.

Some of them are nothing more than skeletons; others still have bits of flesh clinging to their desiccated bodies.

As soon as they rise, the dead turn towards Ashdod.

It takes less than a minute for us to hear the distant screams start up.

Dear God. There were still people alive in the city. Only now, hearing those screams ...

The horrible, haunting truth sinks in, and it's *paralyzing.*

The dead are killing the last of the living. This is why I heard nothing but rumors about those cities gone to the grave. War left no survivors, and without survivors, there was no way to warn the rest of the world that the horseman was coming.

I push my way to the front of the group, just off to the side of the phobos riders. Ahead of me I can see the road into Ashdod. My legs nearly fold as I stare out at the burning city now riddled with zombies.

My gaze moves back to War, with his arm extended.

He's doing this. Singlehandedly.

Without thinking, my feet are moving me forward, towards him.

A mounted phobos rider blocks my way. "No one disturbs the warlord."

War turns then, his eyes filled with dark intent. He lowers his arm, though the screams don't stop.

"*Jehareh se hib'wa*," he says.

Let her through.

I push past the rider, feeling the horseman's gaze on me.

"Stop this," I say when I get to him.

He stares at me for a long time, his face unreadable. Then, very deliberately, he turns from me, back towards the city.

There is my answer. It's written in every line of his body.

No.

"Stop it," I say louder. "Please. This isn't *war*."

This is eradication.

The horseman's voice rumbles. "This is God's will."

I'M FORCED TO wait until it's over. It's depressingly quick. From the sounds of it, there is no winning against the dead. If your opponent can't die, then they can't truly be stopped.

At some point, the screams begin to lessen. It's no longer a distant chorus of cries but a whisper. And then that, too, is gone.

Shortly after the screams die away, something around me ... *changes*. I can't say exactly what it is, only that the air seems easier to breathe. Maybe it's everyone's collective tension. The crowd seems to be rousing itself now that the entertainment is over.

War lowers his hand and turns his steed away from the

city, steering him over to me.

He stops at my side, extending a hand to me. It's the same hand he used to raise the dead.

"*Aššatu*," he says.

Wife.

It's clear he means to load me back onto his horse and return me to camp.

I step away from his hand, my eyes rising to meet the horseman's.

"I hate you," I say softly, my pulse pounding in my veins. "I think I hate you more than I have ever hated anything."

War's confident demeanor slips a little at my words. I swear for a moment he looks almost ... *uncertain.*

I back away from him then, and he gets the message loud and clear, withdrawing his hand. He lingers for several seconds longer, and again, I sense his deep doubt. For all he supposedly knows of humans, he doesn't appear to know how to handle our moods.

Eventually, War gives me a heavy, final glance, then steers his horse towards the front of the crowd. I guess he figured I'd follow him back on foot alongside the rest of the soldiers, who are now trailing after him.

I don't.

I stay rooted in place, watching them all retreat back the way they came.

I swivel around and face the burning remains of Ashdod. My heart aches at the sight of it. Was this what Jerusalem looked like? If I could stand on the Mount of Olives at this very moment and look out over my hometown, would it appear as silent and still as Ashdod?

I take a few steps towards the city, the thought giving me shivers.

This might be my chance at escape. There are undoubtedly bikes and boats and food and all other sorts of resources left in the city. I could arm and equip myself and I could *leave.*

Throwing a brief glance over my shoulder, I check to make sure that no soldiers are storming back for me. But none of the men and women so much as throw a glance behind them.

Why isn't anyone stopping me? The worrying thought flitters through my mind only for a second or two before I face Ashdod again.

I take a few more steps forward. It doesn't matter, I decide, it's me who needs to stop lingering if I want to actually do this.

Because War will likely come for me, and I can only imagine his wrath.

With that chilling thought, I begin jogging towards the city.

Chapter 15

ASH SWIRLS ALONG the roads of Ashdod, and the air smells like smoke and charred flesh.

It's just like the stories said it would be. Bones in the streets, cemeteries tilled like fields. Only now do I fully understand.

I crouch down and pick up a femur, leaving the rest of the skeleton where it lays in the road.

The dead came and razed the last living remnants of the city, and then by the looks of it, they went back to being dead. A chill crawls over me when I see the bodies, some who clearly died today, and others, like the skeleton in front of me, long gone.

Now to find a bike.

I begin to scour the streets for any bicycles left lying about, trying not to be spooked by the unnatural silence.

I'm so lost in my own quest that I nearly miss the soft footfalls at my back.

It's almost too late by the time I turn around.

An enormous man is only a couple meters from me, and he's sprinting at full speed, a sword in hand. I have only seconds to unsheathe my own weapon.

He swings his sword overhead, bringing it down upon me, and I grunt as I hastily block his attack, his blade meeting my shorter one. I have to hold my borrowed sword with both hands to keep him at bay.

I stare into the man's eyes.

Holy shit.

They're glassy like a doll's and slightly clouded over. But worst of all, there's nothing behind them. No intelligence, no curiosity, no personality.

We really do have souls. We must because that spark of life is *gone* from this man's gaze.

Bringing my foot up between us, I kick him away, buying myself a few precious seconds.

Now that I get a good look at him, his eyes aren't the only thing wrong about him. His torso is drenched in blood from a stomach wound he received, and his skin is an ashy color.

He might be moving and fighting, but there's no doubt in my mind that this man is well and truly dead.

I manage to drop my bow before he attacks again. My arrows jiggle in their quiver as I deflect another hit, and then another.

I feel like an idiot. I came here assuming that whatever magic War used on his dead, it was over. I deserve the death I'm probably going to get for this sort of fuck up.

The dead man keeps coming at me, and it's all I can do to deflect his blows.

I really hope my sword is sharp enough for the butchery I need to do. And it *will* need to be butchery. A lethal blow won't stop this corpse.

I grab the man's wrist, then nearly drop it out of shock. His skin is just a touch too cool, and there's some other element to it, like maybe the flesh is too hard, or it gives when it shouldn't—I don't know, *something*—that's distinctly abnormal about it.

A second later, I draw my sword down and begin sawing through his wrist. My assailant jerks his arm away, sending me stumbling into him.

In a fit of panic I unsheathe my dagger and stab him in the eyes, grimacing as I do so.

If he cannot see me, I might live.

I try to remember that the man is gone, that this thing is just a puppet that can't feel pain. And I'm pretty sure the creature really can't feel anything because rather than fending me off, he drops his sword and reaches for my throat.

And now my blind attacker doesn't need to see me to kill my dumb ass. He can squeeze the life out of me perfectly fine without his eyes.

So I desperately begin to saw at his wrist again, and when that makes no notable difference I wedge one of my feet against his chest, then the other.

Black dots fill my vision.

Choking.

The water rushes in–

No, no, no. That's not going to happen again.

With one massive thrust, I shove my feet against the dead man's chest, leaning back against his hold.

My neck rips free from his hands, and I fall hard onto the ground, choking for air. When he dives after me, I manage to roll away just in time, my weapons miraculously still in hand.

Heaving, I drag myself off the ground.

The dead man is scrambling to get back on his feet.

Can't let that happen.

I squeeze my eyes shut against what I'm about to do, and then I bring my blade down on his neck.

My sword hacks away at his flesh, and it really isn't as sharp as it needs to be. It takes a few too many swings to sever his head from his body, and I'm ashamed to say that all the while I'm biting my lip to keep from screaming–just in case there are more dead around.

Fuck this day and all its atrocities.

Even after I manage to remove the man's head from his shoulders, his body still moves. His arms still flail, his legs still kick; he hasn't lost any of his motivation.

I stagger away from him, then trip, landing hard on my ass. I press the back of my hand to my mouth, holding back a lingering sob that wants to claw its way out. The corpse picks itself up, swaying a little now that its head is gone.

Get up, Miriam. Get up before another creature finds you.

I force myself to my feet and back up, sheathing my sword and my dagger. My eyes keep returning to that abomination, even as I move away from it.

And then I run.

I DON'T KNOW how the next zombie finds me, only that I'm not out of the city before another one is tearing towards me, a sword in hand.

Fuck.

I'd always imagined revenants dragged and limped themselves about. I never imagined they'd be this agile.

Then again, judging by the massive man heading my way, I'm guessing that War chose only the freshest, most equipped dead to linger on while the rest rotted away.

These final few zombies must patrol the area for any last living people who dare to move through the city.

I pump my arms and force my legs to move faster, though the weight of my weaponry is slowing me down. I don't dare drop any of it. I fear I'm going to need it again soon.

The thought of escape seems like a dream. I've abandoned all hope of fleeing War and his army. All I want now is to return to camp with my life.

I make it barely a block before the corpse has nearly caught up to me. I swivel around, unsheathing my sword.

The man comes at me like a freight train, swinging his weapon with unearthly expertise. The left side of his body is awash in blood. Other than that, he looks almost completely untouched.

I fend him off the best I can, but he's relentless, untiring. He swings his sword over and over again, and with every blow I block, I feel myself weakening. Despite my earlier adrenaline, weariness is setting in. I've been fighting too long, and I've just about spent the last of my energy.

The sound of hooves thunder at my back.

"*Cease!*" War's deep voice rings out.

At once, my attacker falls to the ground, inanimate once more.

The hoof beats at my back don't slow.

"*Miriam!*" War roars.

I turn to face him, my entire body rising and falling with my labored breathing.

The unflinching warlord is stoic no longer. His face is a mask of fury.

The horseman is off his mount in one fluid movement. And then he's running to me. "*What in God's name are you doing?*" he bellows. When he gets to me, he grasps my upper arms. He obviously doesn't care that I'm still holding a sword.

I heave in and out, gasping for air. I glance down at the dead man at my feet, and an unbidden shiver racks my body.

Dear God, I've never seen anything so frightening and unnatural in my entire life. And it couldn't be stopped.

"This morning I asked you to be safe, and *this* is what you do?" War demands. "Did you come out here seeking death?"

I'm still trying to catch my breath. All I manage is a shake of my head. I didn't even *know* there were still zombies patrolling these streets for survivors. Of course I wouldn't have come if I'd known.

"You could've been killed!" he says, his eyes wild.

I almost *was* killed.

War releases me to curse, running a hand down his mouth and jaw.

I take a shaky breath and pace away from him, trying to regain my composure and, more importantly, not to piss myself.

"Where do you think you're going?" The horseman's voice is calmer now, more under control.

Still, I don't respond.

In front of me, one of the dead begins to twitch. Then, like a marionette, the man rises. He's one of the grotesque dead, half of his face bashed in. He approaches me, and now I stop, my hand instinctively tightening on my sword.

But the creature doesn't attack. Not that he needs to. All he has to do is walk towards me, and now I'm backing up, backing up until I bump into hard, warm flesh.

War's hands close over my upper arms, shackling me in place once again.

In front of me, the dead man collapses to the ground.

"You will answer me," the horseman says. "And you will not leave."

My anger rises, filling me like poison in my veins. I rotate around in War's arms so that I can face him.

I mean to tell him again how much I hate him, how repulsed I am by him, but one look into the horseman's eyes, and he knows. I don't know if he cares, but at least he knows.

"Why?" I say instead. "Why did you have to kill *everyone*?"

Now it's his turn not to answer.

"Why?" I say again, more insistent.

War's upper lip is curled, his face grim. He doesn't respond.

He still holds my upper arms captive, but that doesn't stop me from pushing him.

"Why?" I repeat. Another push. "Why?" Another. And another. "Why why why?"

I'm asking it like a chant and pushing him over and over. The horseman doesn't so much as sway. I might as well be pushing a boulder.

Now the tears are coming and I'm angry and sad and I feel so, so helpless.

War pulls me to him, gathering me in his arms. And I just let him. My body sags against his, stupidly soothed by the embrace. I cry against his shoulder and he lets me and somehow that makes this whole ordeal even more awful.

His hand runs over my hair again and again.

At some point he sheaths my sword for me, then picks me up. I don't bother fighting him. It would be about as useful as my earlier pushes were.

Silently, War settles me onto Deimos, swinging on a moment later.

He holds me close to him as we ride out of that city.

"I feel you slipping through my fingers like grains of sand, Miriam," War says into my ear. "Tell me what I've done wrong."

"Everything," I say wearily.

He forces me to look at him.

"Human hearts can be fixed," he says, like *I'm* the one whose perspective needs altering.

"Can yours?" I ask.

He searches my face. "Will that make you hate me less?"

I don't know.

"I won't lose you," War says, a promise in his voice. "I spared you that day in Jerusalem because you were mine. And I intend to keep it that way, no matter the cost."

BY THE TIME we return to camp, night has fallen. The smoke from the last fires in Ashdod obscures the stars. It's better that way. I'd hate for the heavens to see all the horrible things we've done to each other.

As soon as War stops his horse, I hop off Deimos.

Once my feet hit the ground, I pause.

I'm ready to walk away and write War off completely, but there *is* something he should know.

Turning back to him, I say, "I found the picture of my family. The one inside my tool bag."

The horseman stares down at me, emotionless.

"I was absurdly grateful to you, you know," I continue. "For a moment there, when I held that picture, I wanted to go back to those two nights we were together. I wanted to relive them differently. *Better.*"

I leave him with that.

I can feel War's intense gaze on me as I walk away, but here there aren't any dead for him to stop me with. Or maybe he's done caging me in. Either way, he lets me go, and I'm left to deal with my grief and horror alone.

Chapter 16

I'M DISTRACTED FROM the walk to my tent when I pass by a cluster of women, Tamar and Fatimah amongst them. At the center of the group is the woman I saved earlier, the one who repeatedly shot War.

She stands in front of one of the tents, surrounded by the same faces who welcomed me. Her pants are stained with blood, and her hijab is slightly askew, revealing the smallest sliver of black hair. She hugs herself, looking completely miserable.

I cut over to the group of them, drawn in by curiosity and a deep sense of shared purpose.

The woman's eyes meet mine as I join the group; recognition sparks in them.

"You're the one who spared me," she says. I can't tell if she's thankful for that, or if she wants to gut me alive for it.

"How are you doing?" I ask carefully.

She swallows, her eyes flicking away.

Right.

I give her a brief smile. "I'm Miriam."

"Zara," she says.

My eyes move to the women clustered around her. "I can help her from here," I say to them.

They're happy enough to move on. There are other new recruits who need their attention.

Once we're alone, my gaze returns to Zara. "So you swore allegiance."

She's not like me, I realize.

Earlier, all I saw were our similarities, but after the battle in Jerusalem, the fight had gone out of me. Had I not been spared by War, my body would be food for scavengers right now.

But not Zara.

She fought against the horseman and maybe then she wanted to die, but when the soldiers lined her up and asked for her allegiance, she gave it. She wanted to live.

She sighs. "*Yeah.*" She kicks the earth with the toe of her boot.

When she looks at me again, I see all those deaths she witnessed. She had to watch, just like I did, as her neighbors and her friends were cut down. And then she had to stand in line and watch them get cut down all over again.

"And this is your tent?" I ask, nodding to the home at her back.

"It's not *mine*."

Right. It's some dead woman's tent.

I raise my eyebrows. "What did you inherit?"

"What do you mean?" she asks.

Moving around her, I pull back a flap and peer into her tent. "Bracelets, a toothbrush, a journal, and some eye makeup." I list off the items I see. At least the folded blanket resting on her pallet looks new.

"I don't want any of those things," Zara says vehemently.

I don't fucking blame you.

"You don't have to keep any of them."

She looks at me forlornly. "What happens now?"

Dropping the tent flaps, I meet her gaze reluctantly. "Do you want me to tell you what you'd like to hear, or do you want me to tell you the truth?"

She works her jaw. "The truth."

I give her a sad look. "You'll be forced to celebrate the slaughter of your city with the rest of the camp." Already I can hear the horde gathering in the central clearing. The drums haven't started up yet, but they will soon.

I exhale. "After the celebration, you go to bed and you'll wake up in that tent tomorrow and you'll realize it wasn't just a nightmare after all. That this is your life. It'll be up to you what you make of it. But the pain won't stop. War and his best fighters will hit all the surrounding communities in the next few days, and they'll kill everyone, and you'll be helpless to stop it."

"Bastards," she swears.

"And then you'll be given a job—either as a soldier or as a cook or something else, and that'll be what you do here."

"And if I don't?" she challenges.

We both already know the answer to this question.

"Then you'll probably die."

Zara glances at me. "*You* haven't yet."

I can tell she's remembering earlier, when I stopped War from killing her, but all I'm remembering is the feel of that zombie's hands on my throat, choking the life out of me.

I give Zara a long look. "Yet."

BY THE TIME the sun is setting, the war drums have started up. I can smell someone's prized animals sizzling over a spit, and people are steadily streaming towards the center of camp, chatting idly like we didn't just massacre a town. Torches have already been lit and people have changed into festival attire.

I head towards the clearing, driven by my hunger. Now that the adrenaline has worn off, my empty stomach is cramping.

I slip into line for food, and while I wait, I study the crowd. Tonight, I see something I hadn't before. So many faces hold a desperate edge to them. They smile and act normal but there's a haunted, hollow look in their eyes that I hadn't taken the time to notice before.

It was a shit move for me to assume that these people aren't just as scared and witless as I am. They're petrified. We're all petrified—me, Zara, and everyone else.

And we have good reason to be.

Through the haze of the crowd, I see War sitting on his throne, leaning to one side as a phobos rider chats with him.

All of my earlier emotions rise up. He sacked a city, then raised the dead to feast off the scraps of it.

And then he saved me from his ungodly abominations.

The horseman rubs his lower lip as he listens to the rider, his kohl-lined eyes looking as dark as pits.

Swiveling away from him, I grab two plates of food and two drinks and head back to the women's quarters. The torches burn low here.

"Knock, knock," I say when I arrive at Zara's tent.

I don't bother waiting for her to answer before I duck inside. I remember how little energy I had for manners or anything else the day I arrived.

Zara is using what's left of the previous owner's eye makeup to draw images on the dirt floor, though in the fading light, it's hard to make out exactly what those images are.

I hand a plate of food to her.

She stops drawing to take it from me. "Thank you," she says. "This was kind of you."

"I also grabbed you some wine, but ..." I give her headscarf a meaningful look. "I don't know if you want it.

She takes it from me anyway and sets it aside with her plate. Her gaze moves from the food back to my face. She studies me a little. "Why *are* you being kind to me?"

Why indeed.

I take a sip from my own glass of wine and sit down next to her. I don't bother asking her if I should leave. I probably should, and I also know the two of us would be all the more miserable for it.

"Because you're worthy of it. Also, you managed to shoot War, and I'm a little jealous of you for it."

Zara gives me a small smile, but it quickly falls away when cheering rises from the festivities.

"Why are they happy?" she asks, listening to the sounds.

"The fuck if I know." I take another sip from my cup.

I can feel her staring at me, weighing my words.

"What?" I finally say.

"If you hate them so much why were you fighting with them?"

I glance at her, lowering my drink. "Why did you choose allegiance over death?" I ask.

She doesn't say anything to that. There isn't anything *to* say. It's all so very complicated.

I slosh around the liquid in my cup. "I *have* been fighting," I admit, "but I've been targeting the horseman's army, not the civilians."

Zara gives me a sharp look. "You can do that?" She looks intrigued.

"Not with impunity, no." Eventually someone will catch me and I'll have to face the consequences of killing War's army. They don't really like traitors here.

"But you haven't gotten punished for it?" Zara presses.

I hesitate. "Not *yet*." There it is again, that word—*yet*. Because it's inevitable that something bad will happen to all of us.

The two of us are silent for a bit, but eventually, I have to ask—

"Where in God's name did you find the courage to fire a *gun*?"

I can't tell if Zara's smiling or frowning at the reminder. "I didn't have a lot left to lose, and I was *so* mad. So, so mad. I'm still mad. I just grabbed my family's gun and hunted that asshole down.

Family.

Oh God. I feel my horror spread through me. Of course she had family. And now I'm left to wonder what she saw before she picked up that firearm and decided that *fuck it, I'll take my chances.*

"How *did* you stop the horseman from killing me?" Zara asks then.

It's such a reasonable question, but there is so much to that question that I don't want to answer.

"I asked him to spare you," I say, glad that the darkness shadows my face.

There's a pause. Then Zara says, "That's not really what I'm asking."

I know. What she wants to know is why would War listen to me at all.

I bring my drink to my lips and swallow almost all of it, wincing at the taste.

Just tell her.

"He thinks I'm his wife."

More silence.

"What is that supposed to mean?" Zara eventually says.

"I think it might eventually mean"—my mouth dries—"*sex,* but for now, it's an empty title."

I think of the times the horseman and I have kissed, and I am so conflicted. So, so conflicted.

Zara's silent, undoubtedly because I'm making no sense. One should either be married or not married, having sex or not having sex. Anything else deserves a larger explanation.

One that I'm not really ready to give, partially because I don't understand the situation much myself.

"So you have some sway over him," Zara eventually says.

Sway?

I mull that over. "Maybe for isolated incidents—like sparing your life—but no, he's pretty unbending when it comes to killing us all off."

"Have you tried to convince him to stop?"

I give Zara a look that I'm sure she can't see in the darkness. "Of course I've tried."

It's not good enough, that annoying little voice says in my head. *Try again. And again. And try harder.*

Zara exhales. "Why is he doing this?"

"Because his god told him to, or some bullshit like that."

"You don't believe in his God?" she asks, sounding surprised.

My eyes move to Zara's headscarf. "Do you?" I ask.

We're both quiet.

Like I said, it's all so *very* complicated.

Chapter 17

THAT NIGHT IT takes longer than usual to fall asleep. Between the battle today, the revelation that War can raise the dead, and the exciting possibility that I might've actually made a friend in Zara, my brain won't shut off.

It doesn't help that following the camp's festivities this evening, people are loud and obnoxious and *they won't go to sleep*. I can hear several groups of women talking about this or that.

Just go the fuck to bed and put us all out of our misery.

Eventually, the voices do quiet down and I slip off to sleep.

I feel like I've only been asleep for an instant when I wake to a tingling sensation on the back of my neck that something isn't right.

Rule Four of my survival guide: *listen to your instincts*. I've lived on the edge long enough to know they're rarely wrong.

Reaching under my pallet, I grab War's dagger. My eyes scour the darkness, searching for the horseman, sure that he's the one responsible for waking me. But my little home is horseman-free.

I'm almost disappointed at the thought.

Outside my tent, I hear several male voices whispering.

This late at night, men shouldn't be in this section of camp, especially after a day fighting and an evening drinking.

For a split second I think that maybe some woman brought them here, or they made plans to meet up with someone here.

I hear those voices again—there's at least three of them—and they don't sound confused, they sound devious.

Listen to your instincts.

I move to the back of the tent. The canvas wall is too taut to slip under, so I lift War's dagger, pressing the tip to the sturdy material.

If I'm wrong about this, and I cut a hole in my tent for no reason, I'm going to feel like a fool.

Better a fool than anything else …

With that, I pierce the canvas. As quietly as I can, begin to saw through the coarse fabric, creating an opening.

I grit my teeth at the *riiiiiiip* of material as I part the canvas.

Outside, the whispers have gone silent.

I bite my inner cheek so hard I taste blood.

Faster! Faster!

It's the most agonizing sort of situation, trying to cut that tent as quickly and as quietly as possible. What sound I am making seems deafening to me.

Finally, the hole is big enough. Clutching my dagger in my fist, I plunge through the opening headfirst—

Behind me, I hear the slap of my tent flaps being thrown open.

Dear God dear God dear God.

I claw my way forward, forcing my torso out of the tent.

A hand latches onto my leg. "She's trying to escape!" one of the men whispers as loudly as he dares.

I let out a shriek, not bothering to stay quiet. Hopefully that'll wake up the entire camp.

That hand drags me back inside my tent, and I feel more

than see the group of men who have squeezed themselves inside.

Now I'm trapped in here with them.

I continue screaming like a banshee. Fuck if I'll silently let this happen.

"Shut the fuck up, you stupid slut," another male voice says.

I kick out, and I hear something crunch. One of my assailants cries out, releasing my ankle.

I scramble once more for the opening I made, screaming the entire time.

More hands catch my ankles and they drag me back in.

One of them flips me onto my back, and another set of hands rips open my shirt. This time, when the material tears, it sounds like a gunshot.

Oh God oh God oh God. This isn't happening.

Where is everyone?

Why is no one helping?

I scream and swipe my dagger in front of me, the blade catching someone's chest. I feel their hot blood hit me, and the sensation only makes me scream louder.

My attacker cries out in pain.

Another hisses, "She's got a weapon!"

I'm kicking at them and fighting off their hands, which are busy trying to pin me down and immobilize me.

I feel knees on my thighs, hands on the bare flesh of my stomach.

Oh God, please God, *no*.

I scream louder.

Where the *fuck* is everyone? We live in a city without true walls, and we are camping in a country that has a strong military background. There has to be at least one other person sober and brave enough to stop this.

One of my assailants goes for my dagger, leaning in close to grab my wrist. With one last burst of energy, I plunge my blade into the man's throat.

I feel his blood spurt out from the wound, and even in the dark and even with the confusion, I'm pretty sure the injury is lethal.

Now it's the men who are shouting, panicking.

"The bitch got Sayid!"

"You filthy whore!"

Someone kicks me in the ribs so hard my scream cuts off. Another booted foot kicks me again, this one just above my ear.

I curl in on myself, covering my head as the men shift from immobilizing me to beating me. I feel the blows everywhere—my arms, legs, torso, head. The pain—

The pain the pain the pain—I can't breathe around it. It's exploding from a hundred different places. I'm losing all my other senses to it.

It's blinding, screaming, choking agony.

Suddenly, I hear a voice like thunder, speaking words I don't recognize but still understand.

"Jinsoi mohirsitmon dumu mo mohirsitum!"

You cross God when you cross me!

I would recognize that voice if I heard it in hell itself.

War.

The beating stops at once. Then there are more screams—high-pitched, horrible noises that animals make as they're slaughtered—but they don't come from me.

I try to open my eyes to see what's going on, but my eyelids won't obey my commands.

A minute later, hands are back on me, slipping under my body. I attempt to shout, to fight against those hands, but my mouth is full of blood and when I try to move one of my arms—*blinding pain.*

"Miriam—*Miriam.*" War's voice ... I've never heard it sound like this. Soothing and agonized all at once. "It's only me."

I cry out as he lifts me. "*No.*" The word comes out garbled as I try to push his hands away.

"Ssssh. You're safe." War's voice is deep and rough and terrible and—*shaken*. Or maybe my ringing ears are playing tricks on me.

I still can't see and I can barely move. I'm frightened of my own vulnerability, but I feel ... I feel protected. For the moment. In his arms. It's all so fucked up.

War barks orders at someone, and I flinch at the wrath in his voice.

"My wife, my wife," he says, his voice soothing and shaken once again, "you are safe, you are safe."

Everything hurts. God, but everything hurts. As we begin to move, the pain goes from blinding to unimaginable.

I'm helpless.

Where is my mind going ... ?

I mean, where am I going ... going ... what was I thinking? Things are moving and fading so fast ... so, so fast ...

And then that voice cutting through the darkness like a blade.

"*I vow to you, they will pay.*"

Chapter 18

I WAKE TO the feel of hands on me, and the touch is terrible and unwelcome.

I gasp, beginning to struggle.

Where is my dagger?

Why can't I open my eyes?

The pain returns like an unwelcome admirer, and I sob at the blinding intensity of it.

"Steady, wife," War's voice rumbles.

It's his hands that are on me, I realize. What is he doing?

"Stop stop stop," I moan, trying to push his hands away. "It *hurts*." Everywhere. It hurts *everywhere*.

"I'm sorry, Miriam," he says, but a moment later, his touch returns.

"*No, no, no.*" I begin to fight against him.

Why the fuck can't I see?

These hands are not like the others. They hold me fast, and nothing I do seems to dislodge them.

"I'm not going to harm you, Miriam. Please, I need you to hold still."

I don't hold still. All I can remember is the sound of my

shirt ripping and the feel of those unwanted hands against my skin, and then the pain. All the pain.

I'm struggling, panting. And then my senses fade away ...

This time, when I wake, War's blurry form fills my vision. He leans over me, his brow creased and his dark eyes heavy. I feel the warm press of his palms against my skin.

"What's going on?" I murmur.

He frowns, his body close. Alarmingly close. I reach out to push him away. Instead my hand slides uselessly against his cheek.

"Sleep, Miriam."

"No," I say almost petulantly as War's form shifts in and out of focus.

When his features sharpen, I see him give me a whisper of a smile. "You have a fighting spirit, wife, and I am pleased beyond measure by it, but you don't need to battle me. You are safe now."

Am I safe with a horseman looming above me?

My head hurts too much for me to decide one way or another.

I try to focus on him, but my eyelids are heavy and they keep closing.

I don't want to sleep. I really, really don't. But the pain has worn me out.

My eyelids settle shut and every last worry fades away.

THE FIRST THING I notice is the warm touch against my brow. By now I recognize *that* touch. The horseman's hands are defter and kinder than those that attacked me last night.

War brushes my hair back, murmuring things too low for me to understand.

I sigh at the feel of his hands on my skin. There's no more pain with the sensation; if anything, it's oddly *soothing* at the moment.

In response to my sigh, his hand pauses, his fingers

pressing into my flesh.

I don't yet open my eyes. I'm not ready to deal with the fallout from last night. Already the aches and pains are resurfacing. I'm not sure I want to face my current situation.

But I'm not falling back to sleep, and I can only pretend for so long.

I open my eyes.

War sits next to where I lay, his thigh nearly pressed to my side. He stares down at me, his eyes looking light this close to me.

"You're awake." His gaze searches mine. "How do you feel?"

"Like shit," I croak out.

My lips are split and swollen, a headache is starting to pound behind one of my eyes, my torso feels like one throbbing ache, and my throat is raw—though that last one was probably from being throttled by a zombie, not my would-be rapists.

This bitch just can't catch a break.

War's hand flexes against my skin, but he doesn't move it away from where it rests against my forehead.

"How long have I been out?" I ask.

"Just for the evening." Slowly, he begins to brush my hair back again with his fingers, watching me like he's sure I'm going to push his hand away the moment I get the chance.

I think I was doing that a lot last night.

Now for the harder questions. "My injuries—how bad are they?" Damn, but it hurts to speak. My teeth feel loose and my jaw aches.

The horseman gets a dark look on his face. "They were ... significant."

Were?

"Can you tell me more than that?" I ask him softly. I'm scared to move and feel the pain ripple down my body.

A muscle in his jaw flexes. "Wife, I am used to breaking

138

things, not repairing them. I cannot tell you precisely what injuries you sustained, only that there were many of them. Your body was swollen and bruised and broken when I took you from your tent."

I shiver at the reminder.

Now the hardest question of all. "My attackers ..." I'm supposed to say more—there's a question I need to get out, but I can't seem to voice it.

A look comes over War's face, like he's some wrathful god of old. "Captured, tortured, and left to suffer until their time of judgment." His voice reverberates, the sound of it causing my flesh to chill.

If I took this situation any less personally, I'd almost feel bad for those men. But, I don't, so let them fucking burn.

I push myself up then, groaning as I do so. Everything—and I mean ev-ery-thing—hurts like a bitch.

And it's only once the sheets slip off my torso that I realize I'm still wearing my shirt from last night—my ruined shirt. It gapes open and nothing but the grace of God prevents my nipples from popping out to say hello.

War and I are now sitting side-by-side, me on a cushioned pallet, him on the ground next to it, and our shoulders and legs touch. I must be doing better than I was last night because even though I'm hurting, I'm still aware of every point of contact between us.

I force myself to note my surroundings.

Today, I'm back in War's tent. He must have carried me here last night, after he rescued me.

Which means the pallet I'm sitting on ... is War's. My stomach drops. I was trying to avoid ending up in this very place.

I try to focus on that, to hold onto the overwhelmingly bad situation I've found myself in with the horseman, but all I can think about was that he stopped those men and spent the night tending to me, and I'm fucking grateful to him.

So fucking grateful.

I wasn't when he spared my life in Jerusalem, nor was I very grateful when he stopped the zombie attacking me, but I now am.

Just then a soldier calls from outside the tent, "My Lord, there's a matter with a new rider that needs—"

"It can wait," War says.

My gaze flicks over him, lingering on the sensual curve of his mouth.

Why am I thinking about his mouth?

"You can go," I say to him. "I'll be fine."

War glances at me, and I see his hesitation.

"Seriously. I'm not going to die—thanks to you," I tack on.

The horseman's eyes deepen at that. His lips part, and I think he might respond, but instead, his gaze moves over my face, pausing here and there, his eyes getting more and more violent.

I must look like royal shit for his mood to darken at the sight of me.

"They will be fine without me," he states.

"I've lived on my own for seven years," I insist, pulling the fabric of my shirt tight over my chest. "I'll be fine while you're gone." I could use a little privacy.

He stares at me for several long seconds. Then reluctantly, he stands, striding over to a chest where a holstered dagger rests. My eyes watch the way his massive body swaggers with each step of his.

Stop it, Miriam.

War picks up the dagger and comes back to me. Kneeling down, he places the weapon on my lap. "Anyone but me enters this tent," he says, nodding to the tent flaps, "you gut them."

Said like a man who knows his way around a good murder.

My hands clasp the weapon. Right now I'm not feeling too pious myself.

"Ten minutes," he vows rising to his feet.

He heads to the tent flaps. He's nearly left when he pauses, glancing over his shoulder at me.

"There's food on the table." Giving me a heavy look, he repeats, "ten minutes."

With that, the horseman leaves, and for the first time since last night, I'm alone again.

I WAS NEARLY raped and beaten to death.

Now that War's gone, I'm sort of just coming to terms with that.

It probably doesn't help that I'm in a tent again, and everything hurts, and I'm alone, and I don't know how well I'd truly be able to defend myself if someone comes at me again.

Not that I was about to tell the horseman that when he was considering staying. It's one thing to feel vulnerable, another thing to showcase it to the world.

I probe my face a little, trying to figure out by the feel of it just how bad off I am. Along with a split lip, my nose is tender and the skin around my eyes is swollen. Never have I been more thankful that there's no mirror in sight. I don't really want to see the pulpy remains of my face.

I sit there for several minutes, bored and restless all at once. My skin throbs like it has a pulse, and you'd think that the pain would push out every other human urge, but it doesn't.

My stomach knots. God, am I hungry.

I look forlornly towards the food War had mentioned. The table might as well be a million kilometers away in the state I'm in.

I grab the dagger War gave me and I force myself to stand anyway—

Holy balls, I'm going to barf. I'm going to barf all over War's bed right now, and that holds none of the appeal it would've a day ago.

I force my sickness back down and stagger over to the table, pushing my dark brown hair out of my eyes. With a heave, I plop down in a chair, setting my weapon on the table.

I don't think I should've gotten up. Things feel ... broken. Or rather, freshly mended, like my bones are brittle twigs set to snap in the wind.

Spread out before me is a platter full of dried Turkish apricots and figs and dates, olives, cured meat—probably goat or sheep because *everything* these days is goat or sheep, cheese cut and arranged, and several loaves of pita bread. Next to it all is a coffee pot and a gawa cup filled with thick Turkish coffee.

The coffee has long since gone cold, the pita is a little hard, and the cheese has dried out some, but it all tastes like motherfucking heaven. Not even bruises and a split lip can stop that.

As I eat, I look around me again. It's weird to be in here, in War's tent, not just as some sort of visitor but as a *guest*—and an injured one at that.

You are not a guest, you are my wife. I can practically hear War's response even now.

I finish shoveling food into my face, and once I'm done, I sit there, putting off the walk back to the bed.

Time to inspect the rest of my injuries.

I glance down at myself. My ripped shirt reveals mottled, discolored skin. I gingerly move the ripped fabric out of the way to get a better look. Ugh. Right now, my flesh looks more akin to that of the zombies I fought yesterday than it does healthy human skin. Everything is swollen and discolored.

I'm about to turn my attention to the lower half of my body when I hear the sound of footfalls heading my way. I pull my shirt together as best I can.

The tent flaps are thrown open, and War strides in, his expression stormy. When he sees me at the table, his step falters, his face turning fierce in a whole different manner.

"Miriam." His voice is raw and gravely.

I find I like the sound of my name on his lips. He makes me sound ... *formidable*. I could use a good helping of formidable today.

War walks over to the table and pulls out a chair. He sits down next to me, surveying the food then my face. Right now the horseman is all purpose and commanding energy, and I feel like squashed fruit.

War reaches for his upper arm, his wavy hair shifting with the action.

I tense when I see him grab the dagger sheathed there.

The warlord extends the weapon to me. "This is yours."

I stare down at the weapon—*his* weapon. The one I took from him when I first arrived. He was carrying it in that upper arm holster then just like he is now.

"It belongs to you," I say.

He sounds maybe a little exasperated when he says, "*Take it.*"

Alright—I mean, I'm not going to fight this demon over a blade.

I take the dagger from him and set it next to the other dagger he gave me.

"How do you feel?" he asks for the second time today.

"Like shit," I answer for the second time today.

He cracks a smile at that.

I glance around us, making sure my eyes land anywhere but him. "Where do I go?"

"You don't go," he says. "You're staying here."

I begin to protest, but then the horseman takes my arm, lifting a sleeve of my shirt to study the bruising. "It looks better." His eyes move to mine. "But you look tired."

I *am* tired. And I don't really want to fight him, not when he's been taking care of me. It's been a while since I've had anyone take care of me, and I forgot how nice it is.

You don't need anyone to take care of you, Miriam, least of all the horseman.

With that thought in mind, I begin to stand, but it hurts so damn much. I plop back down in my seat.

War pushes himself out of his chair, his eyes pained as he takes me in. I couldn't say what exactly he's thinking, but if I had to guess, I'd say he's realizing that he underestimated how hurt I am.

He comes to my side, and wordlessly, he scoops me up and carries me back to his bed.

The horseman lays me down, and my shirt, which was previously behaving, now gapes open—and there are my breasts.

Could this get any fucking worse?

But the horseman doesn't look down, and I want to cry all over again that he of all people is the one with some common decency.

Quickly I rearrange my shirt.

War kneels next to me. "I need to touch you again."

I give him an incredulous look. "*Why?*"

"You're still wounded."

Oh. Right. He's been tending to my injuries.

I nod, chewing the inside of my cheek. Touch is still an iffy thing for me.

His hand closes over my wrist, and he pushes the sleeve of my shirt up, revealing the discolored, swollen skin. My eyes are on the horseman, taking in his deep frown as he stares at my injuries. But then I'm distracted by the feel of his hands on me.

War runs his palm over the tender flesh of my forearm, his tattoos bright against his knuckles. Beneath his touch, my skin warms. And then, something strange happens.

Before my eyes, my bruises morph from plum to a brownish yellow, and some of my skin's sickly pallor recedes, like poison being drawn from a wound.

144

I glance up at War, my eyes wide as the realization hits me. "You've been healing me."

Chapter 19

NOT ONLY CAN the horseman raise the dead, he can apparently heal the injured.

That's why he's had his hands on me almost constantly since last night. I simply thought I was overly aware of his touch, but no, it seems this is how he heals.

War meets my eyes for a moment, looking distinctly *unsettled* by my words. Someone does not like the idea that he's helping a human—wife or not.

The horseman moves his hands to another section of my skin, and he begins to work on it, ignoring what I said. I don't bother pushing him on it. I don't want him to suddenly decide he's too much of a hard-ass motherfucker to play nursemaid.

For a while he works in silence, and I enjoy the view of his head bowed over me. His hair has been gathered—gold adornments and all—into a bun. I stare beneath it, at the sharp angles of his face. I watch his cheek tense and untense.

All the while, my skin heats under his hands as my injuries slowly vanish. That touch that I flinched away from, that touch that still stirs strange emotions in me, that touch is *healing* me. I can't wrap my mind around it.

"I didn't mean for this, wife. I never meant for this," War murmurs. After several seconds, he adds, "When you cried, no one came. No one but me." His voice is raw as he admits this.

I swallow as I remember. I'd been so sure *someone* would come, someone would stop the men. No one did. We live in a city with no real walls. My screams were heard, they just went unheeded.

If he hadn't intervened, I'd probably be dead. Dead and defiled.

"How did you know to come?"

"I heard your cries."

"How did you know they were mine?" I ask. There are hundreds of women in his camp; surely my voice isn't that distinct.

Now his eyes meet mine. "The same way you know my words when I speak them. Wife, we are connected in ways that defy human nature."

It's a ridiculous answer, and I don't know if I believe it. I know I don't want to.

"I still hate you," I say, without any heat. Mostly because I need to remind myself.

I draw those words around me like a cloak.

The corner of his mouth curves up. "I'm aware," he says.

War works in silence for a bit longer, and I watch him and his careful hands, the wonder of it all not wearing off.

"How do you do it?" I finally ask. "Heal me, I mean."

"I will it. It is as simple as that." He pauses, and I think that's the end of his explanation, but then War adds, "My brothers and I can all do the opposite of our powers—Pestilence can spread sickness *and* cure it. Famine can destroy crops *and* grow them. Death can give and take life at will." War pauses. "I can injure ... and I can heal."

I don't know what to say to that. I think my mind is being

blown right now. They were all tasked to end humanity ... but they were also given the tools to save it.

War stares at me for a long moment, then his eyes go to my lips. This time, I can feel the kiss about to happen. War is unconsciously leaning closer, and I am angling my face to better meet his mouth.

War is violent and uncompromising, but he's not pure evil. He's proving it right now while his touch still warms on my skin.

I'm leaning in, and he is too—

At the last moment, I turn my head away.

I can't.

Forgiveness is one thing. This is another. I can't cross that line.

I can't.

I KEEP WAITING for that horrible moment when War's going to want his bed back, but it doesn't come. Not that afternoon, when I drift in and out of sleep, and not that evening, once the sun has gone down and the camp has quieted.

War comes to me several times, either to quietly set food by my bed, or to place his hands on my skin and continue to heal my injuries, his ruby red tattoos glowing in the darkness.

"How are you still awake?" I mumble when I feel his hands on me for what has to be the fifth time tonight.

"I don't need to sleep," he says.

I crack my eyes open at that.

After a pause he adds. "My body doesn't require it. It's a human trait I've simply taken up over the months."

At first, it doesn't really compute. My brain is too foggy from sleep. But then it does.

"You really don't need it?" I sit up a little at that.

"I can heal the injured and raise the dead, but you're shocked by this?" he asks, a wry smile on his face.

Fair point.

I lay back down. "What else can you do?" I ask.

"You already know all my other secrets. I don't need to eat or drink—though I do enjoy it. My body can heal itself. I can speak every language known or once known to man, though I prefer to speak in dead languages when giving orders. And I can raise the dead."

It falls quiet, and I close my eyes again, letting him work. But I can't slip back to sleep. Not when his hands are on me, and I almost kissed him earlier, and I'm still a bit confused that I even briefly wanted his lips on me so soon after I was attacked.

I open my eyes again.

"Why did they do it?" I ask softly. "Why did those men attack me?"

I gaze at the horseman, and maybe the darkness is playing tricks on me, but in the dim light of the tent, his eyes look so sad, so very, very sad. I've never noticed that before. I've been too stuck on how frightening he was. But now his expression doesn't look so battle hungry, and that changes the horseman's entire face.

"Men's hearts are full of evil, wife," he admits.

I don't have it in me to disagree. I hate the horsemen—I *do*—but right now I think I might hate my own kind more. Were we always this way? This cruel? Or did the four devils that rode onto earth make us like this?

War's hands leave my skin. "Sleep, Miriam. And don't worry about those men or their motives. You will have your justice."

That's oddly foreboding.

With that, War retreats, and I'm left to drift off into uneasy sleep.

THE NEXT DAY, I wake up to a cold breakfast and a pile of my things laid out next to War's pallet.

Oh, and no sign of the horseman.

Off making war, no doubt ...

At least he feels more comfortable leaving me alone today than he did yesterday.

I grab the plate of food and pick at the breakfast, thinking that I have myself a pretty sweet deal: I'm being waited on hand and foot by one of the horsemen of the apocalypse, and he hasn't asked for anything in return.

Yet.

I can hear my earlier warning to Zara ringing in my ears. I can only get away with so much for so long. That's the way this world works.

Of course, that's not nearly so distracting as the fact that now I'm starting to wonder what it would feel like to be with someone like War. Someone who's more a force of nature than an actual man. And I'm not altogether put off by the idea ...

After breakfast, I pick through my things. There's my wood for arrow shafts, my shoes, my woodworking tools, my inherited coffee set, and most titillating of all, the tattered bodice ripper I was bequeathed.

There's also a pile of new clothing sitting among my items, along with a note.

There's a bath waiting for you. It might be cold by now. Enjoy anyway.

I glance up from the slip of paper, and immediately, my eyes land on the metal basin at the back of the room.

I have the oddest urge to cry. Most water is pumped from wells these days, so a bath is a production. Especially a warm one.

I glance back down at the note, running my thumb over the sure, sweeping grace of War's writing. Just like everything else about him, there's a commanding certainty to his penmanship; you'd think he'd been jotting down notes for decades.

Setting the paper aside, I grab the clothes and head over to the basin.

ONE OF THE things I've learned about myself since joining War's army: baths are an anxiety-inducing experience. The sound of every passerby has me ready to leap out of the tub. Which is a shame, because the water—while not warm—still feels amazing.

God, I miss indoor plumbing. I miss it so, so much.

At least I get a chance to inspect my wounds. The bruises across my skin are fainter and smaller than they were yesterday. The cut on my lip is completely gone, and my chest doesn't hurt so much when I breathe anymore.

All that being said, I feel tired and weak, like I've been remade in the last two days—which isn't terribly far from the truth. So in spite of the conversations that drift by and have me tensing in the tub, I let myself linger in the water for a while.

Also, I just really miss good soaks. Sponge baths aren't the same.

I'm just about to get out when I hear someone walking towards the tent. I hold my breath, waiting for them to pass by.

Instead, the tent flaps are thrown open and War stalks inside.

I freeze at the sight of him, naked as the day I was born.

The horseman's face and armor are speckled with blood and a thin coat of dust. Some of it sticks to his hair. My stomach drops at the sight.

War's eyes find mine, and they *heat*.

This is awkward.

So, so awkward.

I sink a little lower into the tub. "Hi."

Hi? The fuck, Miriam?

Also, unrelated, but can he see my nipples? That's a pretty large concern of mine.

"*Wife.*" His voice is gruffer than usual, and my core clenches at the sound. "You found my note."

I did. A little too late judging from the fact that *he's already back*. How freaking long did I sleep?

Better question: how long was War even *gone*?

"Aren't you still supposed to be out ..." I can't bring myself to say it. *Killing people.* "*raiding?*"

My eyes drop to his armor. The last time I saw him wearing his gear, it was riddled with bullet holes from Zara's gun. Now, despite the dirt and blood splatter, the leather armor is smooth and whole once more.

How is that possible?

War strides inside his tent, distracting me. He begins to take off his regalia, starting with his big-ass sword. "I grew ... anxious leaving you alone," he says.

Him anxious? It's *me* who's the anxious one.

He removes his vambraces, then his leather shoulder guards. Next, he unlaces his chest armor, letting it all fall to the floor. Lastly, he removes his shirt.

I suck in a breath at the sight of him shirtless. Beneath all that armor is sweat-slick muscle. The tattoos on his chest burn crimson against his skin.

And that skin! It's just as anomalous as his armor. I've seen bullets enter his flesh and swords slice it, yet his flesh carries no traces of those wounds. He told me he could heal himself, but only now am I seeing actual evidence of that.

War sits down heavily in one of his seats, the wood creaking at his weight. Leaning back, he folds his arms over his massive chest.

"Has anyone bothered you since I've been gone?" he asks.

When I meet his eyes, there's still heat in them.

"No."

To be honest, I'm pretty sure War stationed several of his men around the tent. There were way too many close footfalls for me to believe otherwise. And if there's one thing this guy is good at, it's overkill.

"And how are you feeling?"

Exposed. Vulnerable. Like my tits are on display. "*Better*."

War unlaces his greaves and nods. "Good." His eyes study my skin, and I know he's checking to see how my injuries are healing, but all I can think is that he's getting an eyeful of boob. And now it's become too much of a thing in my mind to actually cover myself like a sane person.

"Close your eyes," I say abruptly.

"Why?" he asks, raising an eyebrow. He's still unlacing his shin guards.

"Because I'm naked and I want to get out and I don't want you to keep looking at me."

The heat in those eyes seems to deepen. "I will see that pretty flesh eventually, *wife*."

Again my core clenches at his voice.

I'm about to protest when his eyes do close. Letting out a breath, I slip out of the bath and wrap a nearby towel around myself. As quickly as I can, I shove on the new clothes War left for me, surprised that they actually fit mildly well. To be fair, a T-shirt and standard issue cargo pants are hard to mess up.

Still.

"Thank you for the clothes," I say. Because civilization might be dead but manners aren't.

"Can I open my eyes?" he says in response.

"Uh, yeah," I say, tugging my shirt to keep it from sticking to my still damp flesh.

War finishes removing his armor, then stands. I don't know what I'm expecting him to do next, but I am definitely *not* expecting him to drop his pants.

Which is precisely what he does.

"*HOLY CRAP!*" I shield my eyes. At least, I shield them a *little*—I mean, *be brave* is my mantra ...

Technically, I should've seen this coming. He was undressing after all. I just expected him to wait until I wasn't looking to change.

Also, two words: no underwear. And now I know for sure that if War ever wanted sex, he'd break me.

Holy balls—or maybe holy *dick* is more appropriate.

Clearly the nudity is a *me* thing, because War seems unfazed by it. He's not even looking at me as he walks across the room, towards the basin. There's just zero awareness that's he's naked and I am ~~perversely intrigued~~ massively uncomfortable.

My eyes slide back to the tub of water I was just in. The one he's now stepping into. There's something literally and figuratively dirty as fuck about the fact that he's reusing my water. And it's making me feel strange and self-aware.

"Do you want me to leave?" I say. I don't even know why I ask it. I *should* just leave. Even though my knees are shaking with fatigue, I should.

War's kohl-lined eyes find mine as he steps in the basin. "And miss your reaction, wife? Never."

"So you *do* know it's inappropriate to flash people?" I say, mustering up some righteous indignation.

The horseman lounges back in the basin. "It's just nudity. It's not supposed to be offensive."

Somehow War, the asshole that's killing everyone off, just managed to sound like the innocent one.

"It's not *offensive*," I say. "It's just ... not done."

"Is it now?" he says. "So husbands don't see their wives naked and wives don't see their husbands naked? They somehow just enjoy each other fully clothed?"

I want to rake my hands through my hair. "We *are not married.*"

War gives me a look that states plainly, *we are.*

"I shouldn't be staying in your tent anymore," I say, backing up. I clearly hadn't thought through the logistics of sleeping here, where War lives and bathes and sleeps.

"You should have *always* been staying in my tent with me. I have let you enjoy your own space because it pleased you, and I enjoy pleasing you and your ridiculous, human whims."

My ridicu—?

"You want to please me?" I say, now officially peeved. "How about you stop killing people?"

War gives me a piercing look. "There's another who I seek to please too, Miriam. And unfortunately for you, He wishes differently."

I SURVIVED THE bath ordeal.

Barely.

Now War is fully clothed and diligently healing my wounds. This time when he touches me, I'm very aware of his closeness. There's a peculiar sort of intimacy to seeing the warlord with the kohl scrubbed from his eyes.

I want to reach out and touch him, and if I look too closely into his eyes, I'm sure I'll see that he wants it too.

So I keep my eyes down.

Once he's done with his ministrations, he ... sticks around.

This is new.

I mean, I'm used to him being in the tent—it *is* his after all—but up until now, I was mostly passed out. I glance at him as he sharpens a blade and flips through some book that looks way less fun than my own romance novel.

This feels ... domestic. Like War is getting that marriage that he keeps harping on about.

I need to get the fuck out of here, *stat*.

Seriously though, what am I going to do about this situation? I can't stay here forever. And the longer I'm here, the more the two of us will get used to these accommodations.

That really can't happen. War's already too attractive for his own good, and now I know that he's capable of being disarmingly kind. I have no resistance to any of it.

It doesn't really matter, regardless. I'm not leaving tonight, when my bones feel like rickety stilts and my skin is still painful to the touch. I'll stay here, I'll endure this a little while longer, and then, when I'm physically ready to leave, I will.

Until then—

I grab my woodworking kit and a piece of wood and begin to whittle the branch down, shaving off the bark like the skin of an apple.

Got to make the time freaking pass *somehow*.

I work in silence, and eventually, my worries fall away and it becomes just me, the grain of the wood, and the steady scrape of my tools. Every so often I smooth my work over with sandpaper, rubbing the arrow shaft until the surface becomes relatively smooth.

"Where did you learn to do that?"

I glance up, only to realize that War's steady gaze is on me—that his gaze might have been on me for some time. I've been so lost in my work I didn't notice.

"It's a long story," I say.

"We've got time."

Damn him and his deep voice. I can't help but think about his mouth every time he speaks.

I might as well tell him the story. Anything to keep my mind from wandering down the path it wants to take.

I set the piece of wood aside. Around me, wood shavings lay scattered like confetti.

"My mother was a history professor at the Hebrew University," I say. "One of the courses she taught was on ancient weaponry. She had a lot of books on old weapons and weapon-making."

Before my mother and sister and I had tried to escape war-torn Israel, I'd already been flipping through those books, my naïve heart set on survival. I foolishly figured that if I could learn how to make weapons, then I could use them to hunt, like some modern day Amazonian.

It was a childish desire that drove an honest interest.

"It took a long time to even make sense of the books, and an even longer time to get just one thing right." But eventually I did. Then one thing became two, and so on. Once I lost my mother and sister and returned to Jerusalem alone and without any sort of income to live off of, I threw myself into my work.

"I made wooden daggers first." Even that was a process of trial and error. Wood can be rotted, it can be too soft, it can be too brittle. But once I understood a bit more about the nature of it and ways of tempering and fire-hardening, that's when I was truly able to manipulate the material. "Then I moved onto other weapons."

I made bows and arrows, testing out softer and harder wood. I learned when to apply heat, how much, and for how long. And I discovered I could repurpose broken glass into arrowheads and thin plastic into fletching. Houses and junkyards were full of these things, as well as string and glue and the odd tool.

My mother's books had most of the answers, I just had to get creative in how I applied them.

"So you're self-taught," War says. He looks impressed, and I'm uncomfortable at how good that makes me feel.

I nod.

"And your fighting skills? Also self-taught?"

I shake my head. "There were some older soldiers who taught me a few basic skills." Soldiers like my mother. It used to be that most Israelis joined the army for at least two years. But by the time I was of age, there was a new political regime, one that didn't believe in training women for war. So I had to work with what my mother had taught me, and what a few other, older Israelis were willing to teach.

"They taught you how to shoot a bow?" War says, incredulous.

"Well, no. *That* was self-taught." Before the Arrival, guns were the weapon of choice. It was only when firearms stopped working properly that bows and arrows, swords and daggers, maces and axes all came back into fashion. "Why do you want to know?" I ask, self-conscious.

"You are a curious creature, that is all." He flashes me a sly smile. "A curious, dangerous creature."

Chapter 20

BY THE THIRD day, I'm moving up and about again. After another night of War's warm hands on my skin, I feel nearly back to normal. There are still aches and pains—like if I twist my torso a certain way, my rib injuries flare to life—but if I tread carefully, I can pretend I'm healed.

Which is exactly what I do once I wake up and find War gone—undoubtedly off hacking away at more doomed people. I get up and move about the horseman's tent, and I'm not going to lie, I snoop the *shit* out of the place.

I lift pillows and flip through the stack of books piled on a side table. I peer at oil lamps and open some of the horseman's chests, disappointed when I end up staring down at weapons and more weapons.

Honestly, War's innermost life is not *that* intriguing. I was hoping to find that he secretly likes to cross dress or collects Russian nesting dolls or some other weird shit like that.

Instead, I find old maps with cities crossed out. I swallow when I see them.

I throw open the last of his chests, and I exhale when I see what's inside.

His blood red armor sits at the bottom of it.

His sword, I notice, is absent.

I pull out a vambrace, turning the arm guard over in my hand. The leather is once again in pristine condition, despite the fact that I swear there were bloodstains on it yesterday. I guess at the end of the day, God washes away all sins.

Why isn't War wearing his gear?

The answer comes a second too late.

"It's light, isn't it?"

I jolt at the sound of War's voice. When I glance over my shoulder, he's in the doorway of his tent, staring at me, his expression inscrutable.

God, how guilty I look, crouched in front of his chest, holding a piece of his armor.

"You don't expect that from armor," he says, heading towards me. "My brothers all wear metal armor, but on the battlefield metal is heavy and cumbersome."

I set the arm guard back inside the chest and close it. Then I turn to face War. He wears a black shirt, the hilt of his sword peeking out from over his shoulder.

"What about that?" I ask, my chin jutting to his weapon. "Isn't that ... cumbersome?"

"Quite. But I'm fond of it."

Behind him, the tent flaps rustle open, and a soldier walks in, carrying a tray of food and coffee. He sets the items down on the table, then leaves.

Once we're alone again, War walks over to the table and pulls out a chair for me.

"Who taught you to offer a woman a seat?" I ask, following him over. I sit down, my eyes on the table setting.

He hasn't released the back of my chair, and he leans in to whisper in my ear, "The same people who taught you how to poke through people's things."

War straightens, and as he does so, I catch sight of a familiar hilt strapped to his arm holster.

160

"My *dagger*," I say as recognition sparks. It was one of the weapons I fought with in Jerusalem. "You kept it." I'd been sure it was long gone. Seeing it sparks some old emotion.

Without thinking, I reach for it, only to have War catch my wrist.

I give him an incredulous look. "It's *mine*."

"Consider it a trade—you get my dagger, I get yours."

"That's not a trade," I complain, standing. "You kept my weapon without telling me and simply gave me yours. I want mine back."

My dagger is duller than War's and the balance is off. I still want it back.

"No." Just by the tone of his voice I can tell it's non-negotiable. Ugh.

I glower at him.

"Why do you even *want* my dagger?" I ask.

There are dozens of weapons in this room alone. There are thousands more throughout camp, and with every city we raid, there are countless more for War to acquire. My humble blade is no match for those.

"I'm ... fond of it."

Just like he's fond of his sword.

He gestures to the chair again. "Sit down."

I do so, eyeing the assortment of food and the thick, steaming coffee alongside it.

Rather than taking his own seat, War kneels, pressing his hands to my wounds. By now I've gotten used to this routine. It's still startlingly intimate to have him this close and to feel his flesh pressed to mine, but I've come to expect it—even *anticipate* it.

I'm not right in the head.

"Are you just healing me because you want to fuck me?"

Holy mother of God. Did those words really come out of my mouth?

What is wrong *with you, Miriam?*

The horseman's head snaps up to me. He stares for several seconds, his eyes dropping to my mouth. "I healed you for my own reasons. Fucking you is another matter altogether."

War finishes his work and sits down in the seat next to mine.

And now I've got to deal with the twelve tons of sexual tension I've introduced into the room.

To distract myself, I force out the words I've been meaning to say to him.

"I'm going back."

War's eyes move casually to me, but I sense deep tension at my words. "Back where?" His mouth actually lifts a little, like *going back* in any sense of the phrase is ridiculous and impossible.

"Back to my tent."

Now War straightens in his seat. He wears a terrible, frightening face, one that causes men to quake before he's laid a hand on them.

"Why?" It's a demand more than a question.

"We're not lovers."

The deep look the warlord gives me has my core heating.

That will change, his eyes say.

"Not to mention that you're destroying the entire world," I say. "It was kind of you to heal me—"

"*Kind*," he repeats, like he's never heard anything so distasteful in his life.

"—but I'm better now, and I want my tent back."

Had I really ever thought the warlord's eyes were sad? There's only violence in them. Soul-devouring, terrible violence.

He leans forward, and that single action has me wanting to recoil.

"What if I told you no?" he says, his voice low. "What if I told you that you couldn't leave?"

I raise my eyebrows. "Are you going to try to stop me when

you've worked so hard to give me space?"

"Make no mistake, Miriam," he says, his voice deceptively soft. "I can do whatever I please. I plucked you from your first home. I can pluck you from your second one too."

"Don't ruin this," I say softly.

His face flickers, and for a moment I think he's remembering how I told him I hated him.

"And if I give you your own tent again, who's to say that you won't be attacked the moment you're alone?"

"You let me ride into battle," I say. "There's a part of you that clearly trusts your god to protect me."

"He's your god too."

Um, agree to disagree.

"If you force me to stay here," I say, "you're no better than those men who attacked me."

Alright, so that's a bit of a stretch.

It seems to make logical sense to War, however.

His jaw clenches and he looks away, his nostrils flaring.

"Fine," he grits out after a moment, his eyes still full of violence. "You can have your tent back—for a time."

War stands and leans in. "But I *will* decide when time's up, and none of your pretty human arguments will change that."

WAR IS A man of his word. He does indeed give me back my tent later that very day ... he just happens to move it right next to his own.

"What is this bullshit?" I demand, staring at the two of our tents sitting side by side. Mine looks laughably tiny next to his.

The horseman stands next to me, surveying the view. I had to all but drag him from his tent to hear me out, and I'm pretty sure he was lapping up my reaction like it was Baklava.

Now he leans in close to me. "You're welcome."

You're *welcome*? What in the actual fuck?

"This is *not* what we agreed to," I say heatedly.

"It's exactly what we agreed to. Just be glad I didn't move it inside my own tent. I was tempted, wife." War eyes me up and down. "How do you feel?"

Like a bloody mess.

I lift a shoulder. "Better," I say begrudgingly. Very, very begrudgingly.

His gaze sweeps over me. He gives a short nod. "Then we will pack up and ride out tomorrow—after your attackers face their judgement, of course."

With that ominous final line, he leaves.

Chapter 21

THE NEXT MORNING, War wakes me from my new tent.

I know it's him from the moment his warm, firm touch meets my skin. I still jolt at the sensation. It's going to take a while to completely erase the attack from my memory.

"Rise, Miriam," he says, already retreating from my tent. "The day has come."

I frown, rubbing my eyes. "What day?"

But then his words from yesterday rush back in.

I'm going to have to face my attackers. That thought makes me both hot and cold at once.

I sit up, running my hands through my hair. I take a deep breath, wishing for a cup of Turkish coffee. I'd drink it, sludge and all, if it could ready me for this day.

Pulling on my boots, I step outside, squinting against the brutal glare of the sun. War is several meters ahead of me, and he's walking like he knows I'll follow. The bastard. I hate being predictable.

The horseman leads me to the clearing at the center of camp, where most of the horde has already gathered. The crowd parts like the sea to let War and me through, closing seamlessly behind us.

It's only once we get past them that I get a clear view of the three men who stand bound and beaten, several armed phobos riders spread out behind them.

The wind is nearly knocked out of me.

My *attackers.*

I can still feel their hands on me and hear the rip of fabric as they tore through my shirt. I was so helpless then.

But now the tables have turned.

My gaze moves from one bound man to the next. I recognize one of my attackers as the man from the first day, the one who called dibs on me. The others are strangers.

Looking at their faces in broad daylight makes them far less frightening. Maybe it's that they're the ones who look terrified, or maybe it's the fact that they can't be much older than me. In a different world, they could've been the men I went to school with.

But that's not *this* world.

A phobos rider breaks away from his comrades, coming forward to hand me a weapon. I take the sword he gives me, then stare dumbly at it.

"What is this?" I ask War.

His upper lip curls in distaste as he stares at the men. "*Wedāv.*"

Justice.

It takes several seconds for realization to dawn on me.

"You want me to *kill* these men?" I ask the horseman.

In response, War folds his arms, saying nothing. Whatever gentleness he showed me over the last few days, it's gone. This is uncompromising War, whose will reigns absolute.

I glance back at the men.

They'll try it again. If not on me, then on another woman. They probably already have before. They are an open threat, and they will continue to be as long as they live.

But isn't that what War believes about all of us? That we're all evil and unchanging? It's just not true. Even though we are all capable of wickedness, it doesn't mean we're doomed to it. We're also capable of goodness.

I stare down at the weapon in my hand, and take a deep breath.

"I won't kill them," I say.

Not now, and not like this.

After a long and heavy pause, the horseman says, "*Ovun obē tūp̄āemi āremeꞇavi teri, obevi pūṣꞇavi teri epevitri tirīmeṭi utsāꞇe teꞁa eteri, obeṭi vuttive iṭuvennēnæppe?*"

They invaded your tent, they sought to rape you and defile you, and you will not mete out justice?

"This is *revenge*," I say.

He narrows his eyes. "*Kēkahatē peꞁivænīki sehi vuttive eke sā sekāꞇevi.*"

Right now, revenge and justice are one and the same.

"I won't kill them," I repeat.

I know I must seem like a hypocrite. I've killed before, and these are no innocent men. If we were out on the battlefield, I would easily fight them to the death. If they cornered me on a dark night in Jerusalem, I would've shot them dead then too. But seeing these men lined up, their wrists bound—this would be an execution.

I am no executioner.

War stares at me for a long time. Eventually he makes a sound low in his throat and gives a shake of his head, like I'm the damnedest thing.

"*Abi abēvuttive eṭu naterennēnek, keki evi abi saukuven genneki, aššatu.*"

If you will not take your justice, then I will take it for you, wife.

The horseman prowls towards the men. Seeing him move I remember that this is who War is. And unlike humans, I'm not entirely sure the horseman can change. He certainly doesn't want to.

My attackers shrink back from him, but there's nowhere

for them to go. They're hemmed in by the crowd and the phobos riders.

As War approaches the three men, he withdraws a sword from its sheath at his hip. It's not the massive sword he wears on his back. This one looks lighter and narrower.

"Avākegēepirisipu selevi menni."

You get my unclean blade, War says, his voice building on itself.

"Gīvisevēpī abi egeurevevesṭi pæt qūeteri, etækin abejēkereñ pe egeurevenīsvi senu æti."

In life you were dishonorable, and so your deaths too will be dishonorable.

The guttural sounds of his words make him all the more terrifying.

"Please," one of the men begins to beg. "We didn't mean it."

The one on the left is noticeably trembling.

But it's the man I recognize who lifts his chin defiantly, his eyes on me. He doesn't look repentant, he looks angry. "Whatever that bitch told you, it's a lie. She wanted it."

War closes in on the man, and he grabs his jaw. "She *wanted* it?" This time when he speaks, he doesn't bother speaking in tongues. We all hear the words perfectly enunciated.

The man glares daggers at the horseman, but he doesn't respond.

After a moment, War lets the man go, and begins to rotate away.

In a flash of speed, the horsemen turns back on the man, and with one vicious stroke, he sinks his blade into the man's stomach, impaling him with it.

I jolt at the sudden violence.

My former attacker lets out a choked cry, and his two co-conspirators shout in surprise.

War releases his grip on the sword, letting the hilt jut out from the man's abdomen.

The man sways for a few moments, then falls to the ground, a growing patch of blood blooming from the wound.

"Does that feel good?" War asks, again making himself understood. He looms over the man, the blade still sticking out of his victim. "I *hope* it does. I bet you wanted my sword shoved inside you just as much as Miriam wanted yours shoved in her."

Dear God.

I'd forgotten about the horseman's savagery.

The man's mouth moves, but all that comes out is a strangled moan.

The warlord's attention turns to the two remaining men. As soon as his ferocious gaze fixes on them, they both visibly wither.

War grabs the hilt of his sword from the dying man's abdomen, and jerks the blade out, the action making a wet, sloshing sound.

The horseman steps up to the most frightened of the remaining two, and without ceremony, stabs him in the stomach. Almost mechanically, he withdraws his sword and moves to the next, repeating the action until all three of my attackers lay dying in a pool of their own blood.

I gaze down at them in horror as they writhe and moan on the ground. The horseman mortally wounded them, but he didn't instantly kill them, leaving them instead to suffer.

War casts his violent eyes on the crowd. "Anyone who lays a dishonest finger on another woman will suffer the same fate."

He turns to me and gives me a nod.

Revenge and justice are one and the same, he said.

Perhaps this is the very reason the world is burning. After all, if this is War being just, then his God's justice makes sense too.

I DON'T IMMEDIATELY return to my tent. Instead, I make the familiar journey back to my original quarters. Call it morbid curiosity or call it closure, but I want to see the place where I was attacked. I want to see if the earth is stained red with the blood that was spilled, or if the ground has already returned to normal.

I don't know why, but the urge presses on me.

About ten meters from my tent I notice something is off. The tents in this area flap forlornly in the breeze. No one is around, and it's silent. So silent.

A chill runs over me, despite the heat of the day.

I continue toward the original location of my own tent, acutely aware that the usual noise and bustle of this area is now gone.

My old neighbors might just be lingering in the center of camp. There were still some people left ...

When I get to where my tent should be, all that's left is an empty patch of earth and some faint bloodstains. As soon as I see those stains, the night once again comes back to me in all its vivid terror. The men's hands on me, pinning me down, *beating* me.

I take a deep breath, trying to unmake those memories. I don't want to feel frail and afraid.

I take a step back, and that unnerving silence swarms in again. I look around at all the empty tents, their flaps snapping in the wind. There are a few overturned baskets scattered about, but there's no life, not even a whisper of it.

When you cried, no one came. No one but me.

War's justice touched more than three men, I realize with a shiver. The people that once lived around me are now gone.

I'M RESTING NEXT to my broken down tent, whittling another arrow shaft when I hear commotion nearby.

I glance up just in time to see phobos riders closing in on someone.

"Let me through!"

I knit my brows at the vaguely familiar voice.

"No one passes by without War's approval."

"His wife *would* approve!"

I set my work aside and head over to the phobos riders, one who now has his hand on his weapon. Beyond the two men is Zara.

As soon as I recognize her, I call out, "Let her through!"

One of the men frowns at me and spits.

Apparently he's super fond of me. The other one, however, the one who brought me the sword at the execution this morning, gestures for Zara to pass by. His comrade immediately starts arguing with him, but he ignores the other man.

My new friend slips by, two heaping plates of food in her hands.

"I've been trying to see you for *days*," she complains when she meets up with me. "And for days those assholes kept sending me away."

"I'm so sorry," I say. "I didn't know."

I lead her back to the packed remains of my tent, aware of the many sets of eyes on us. Apparently the phobos riders don't take kindly to just anyone entering their section of camp—even when their section of camp is getting packed up for traveling.

"It's fine," she says. "I knew I'd get through eventually."

When we get to my things, she hands one of the plates to me. "I wanted to return your earlier kindness."

That ... that hits me harder than it should.

"Thank you," I say, taking the plate from her, a lump in my throat.

"How have you been doing?" she asks, her eyes moving over me. Most of my visible injuries have healed up; I don't know if she can see what's left of them.

"I'm okay," I say.

Today, I feel like our roles have utterly reversed. Zara seems to be in good spirits, and I'm the remote one.

"That night," Zara says, "I heard so many screams. To think one of them was yours ..." she shakes her head. "I thought they belonged to the other people, the ones who had killed ..." she shakes her head.

She listened to those screams and she thought it was some sort of perverse justice.

Zara picks at her food. "I didn't find out it was you until word got around that a woman had been harmed, one the horseman was fond of. I put two and two together ... "Her eyes meet mine. "I'm sorry I didn't come."

"It was your first night. I wouldn't have." Not to mention that she didn't live anywhere close to my tent.

We're quiet for a few minutes, and I pick at the food Zara brought over.

"What's that?" she asks out of the blue, nodding to the carving knife and the piece of wood I was working on.

I pick it up and inspect it. "The beginnings of an arrow."

"You're *making* one?" I'm not sure if it's judgment or awe in her voice. She takes the piece of wood from me and looks at it. "I never learned how to shoot a bow," she admits. "I'm okay with short blades, but that skill doesn't much help me here since I don't actually *own* a blade."

"You don't have a weapon?" I ask, shocked. But of course she doesn't. Zara was stripped of her weapons when she arrived, and she won't be offered another one until the next battle.

If the same men who attacked me had chosen Zara's tent instead, she would have been utterly defenseless.

The thought sickens me.

"Wait right here." I get up and go into War's tent, which is still standing. The horseman isn't inside at the moment, which is probably for the best.

Easier to ask for forgiveness than permission.

I grab one of the sheathed daggers War has scattered about, then leave his tent, returning to Zara. Several nearby phobos riders track my every movement.

"What's that?" my friend asks when I extend the weapon to her.

"Put it on."

"It's not going to fit," she says, unwinding the leather belt that's wrapped around the sheath; it was clearly made to fit a much larger waist. She loops the belt around her, doing the best she can to make it fit.

Zara stares down at it. "Is War going to kill me for this?" she asks, glancing warily at the phobos riders who watch the two of us. They're undoubtedly going to report that I've lifted a dagger from the horseman's collection.

"I'll talk to him. It'll be fine."

She raises her eyebrows. "You're going to *talk* to him?" She says skeptically. "And that'll work?"

"It has so far."

She huffs out a laugh. "What sort of talking will you two be doing? The horizontal kind?"

I make a face even as I laugh a little. "*No.* The normal kind of talking."

She shakes her head. "Either you're the world's most convincing woman, Miriam, or these favors are going to eventually cost you."

You are my wife, you will surrender to me, and you will be mine in every sense of the word before I've destroyed the last of this world.

Zara's right. Nothing these days comes without a price, favors especially. And War has done me *many* favors.

At some point, he's going to make me pay.

Chapter 22

I'VE BROKEN RULE Three.

Avoid notice.

To be fair, War seems to have always taken notice of me. It's now the rest of camp who is very, very aware of who I am.

I feel their stares as I mount Lady Godiva, a new horse that is way less interested in kicking me than Thunder was. The camp's collective gaze makes my skin itch. It's impossible to blend in, and I hate it.

Just like the horseman promised, today the army packed up. Ashdod has been eradicated, as has all the satellite communities that surround it. There's nothing left for War to kill, so it's time for us to go.

Like before, War and I ride at the head of the horde, putting enough distance between us that I can forget for a time that there's a murderous army following in our wake.

The horseman drives us south along Highway 4. The land is too flat for me to see the ocean from here, but I swear I can smell it. It's mere kilometers from the road. And by the conversations I overheard back at camp, we'll be sticking close to the coastline over the next couple of days.

I try to keep my thoughts preoccupied on the journey itself, but inevitably they swing back to my travel companion, just as they have ever since we left camp.

For absolutely no logical reason whatsoever, today I'm unable to ignore him. Or maybe there is a reason; maybe War's barbaric justice earlier today broke something in me.

Whatever the reason, now I can't help but notice the sharp cut of his jaw; his dark, almost black hair; and those curving lips. I take in his red leather armor and his powerful thighs.

I'm having thigh fantasies. About my enemy.

I'm a fucking moron.

Naturally, of course, that doesn't stop me from continuing to glance at War, and the longer I look, the more certain I am that I want to run my fingers over his strange, glowing markings and smear the kohl that lines his eyes. I want to taste those lips again.

I want it all, and I'm not supposed to, which makes me want it all the more.

"Why haven't you been with any other women since we met?" The question just slips out, but as soon as it does, I want to die.

People who are into each other ask these sorts of questions. I'm flagrantly making him believe that this matters to me. And it doesn't, it really doesn't. I'm just curious. I mean, doesn't everyone want to know about a horseman's sex life?

No? Just me?

Shit.

War glances over. "Who told you I'd been with other women?"

"People talk."

I remember when I first came to camp the women made it sound like War had a revolving door of women entering and exiting his tent.

"Ah," the horseman says. "Humans and their foibles." There's a long stretch of silence.

"So?" I press. I've already embarrassed myself. I might as well see this question through. "Why haven't you?"

War fully turns to me, his brown eyes glittering in the sun. "I am committed to you, wife, and you alone."

I want to shrug the statement off. I might've even a few days ago. But for whatever reason, today, that explanation hits me low in the gut.

"Wow, I'm flattered." I try to sound mocking and irreverent, but I don't quite pull it off.

War gives me a pained smile, like the effort of abstinence hasn't been without its challenges. The poor wittle horseman and his neglected dick. What *ever* will he do?

"What if I never sleep with you?" I ask.

"I have been inhuman for a long time, Miriam. I can manage my body well enough until I am inhuman once more."

Shivers. I knew he wasn't truly human, but hearing him say it is a whole lot more sobering than just generally being aware of it.

"You, on the other hand," he continues, "have only ever been human, and you are bound to your most basic nature. We will see how long *you* last, wife."

Today of all days, that statement finds its mark.

OUT ON THE open road, there's no mistaking that I am living in a terrible time. The most obvious sign of it are the bodies. Just like the first time I traveled with War, we pass by several of them. They're bloated and stinking, and scavengers have already mutilated them. They lay out in the street, or half in, half out of residences. I'm sure there are more dead cooped up in houses, rotting away amongst all their worldly possessions.

Scattered near the bodies are piles of bones, and I know that War's zombies are responsible for this.

But it's not just the bodies.

We pass by Ashkelon, the city south of Ashdod. This place, too, has been sacked. Some of the buildings still smolder in the distance, and there's a stillness to the air that feels utterly devoid of human life.

Even once we pass by the city, there are still strange sights that I would never have seen a decade ago. Out here, in between towns, our surroundings are speckled with junkyards and scrap metal. The carcasses of old cars and electronics and other useless technology sit abandoned along the side of the road.

I don't know if the sight of all this old decadence and waste will ever stop being jarring to me. I've sifted through so many junkyards over the years, but even after visiting *hundreds* of times, I am still not immune to the prickling sensation up my back, like there are old ghosts about.

"Can you tell me about your brothers?" I ask, my eyes lingering on a rusted out dryer and a stained fridge we pass by.

"They are lethal and terrible just like me," War says.

Even in the sweltering midday heat, the hairs on my arms rise.

"Where are they?" I ask.

"Where they need to be," he replies cryptically.

"Even Pestilence?" I press. War had mentioned that the first horseman had been stopped.

The horseman curls his upper lip a little. His silence has my heart speeding up. "Where he is, is no concern of mine. His purpose has been served."

I think ... I think that's War's evasive way of saying his brothers really can be stopped.

Now I need to figure out *how*.

"When will Famine come?" I ask.

"When it is his time."

"And ... when is that?"

War shakes his head, squinting off in the distance. "After I have made my final judgment."

"Your final judgment?" I say. "Of what? *Humans?*" I raise my eyebrows.

War turns his head and gives me a long look.

Yes, of humans.

"Why do you think we're here?" War says.

I stare back at him. "Why don't you tell me?" He's the one with all the answers.

"Your kind has not been made wrong," War says cryptically, "but you have all collectively *chosen* wrong."

I'm trying to follow War's words and how they tie into judgment, but I don't really know what he's trying to say. That human nature itself is fine, we just turned evil somewhere along the way? And now he has to punish us for it?

"And so we're all to die?" I say.

"You're being called home."

What he means is that humankind is being swept up into God's trashcan like bad leftovers.

"And there's nothing you can do about it?" I ask. I don't know why I bother. War hasn't shown one iota of interest in actually *saving* humankind. He's completely fine annihilating us.

"Miriam, it isn't for me *to* do anything. Men are the ones who must change. I merely judge their hearts along the way."

I run a hand through my dark brown hair. "How can you even judge us if you're too busy hacking away at us all?"

War's face is grim. "There's an order to what I and my brothers do."

"What does that even *mean?*" He's dancing around my questions.

"Four calamities, four chances."

An unwelcome tingle of fear slips down my spine. "Four chances for *what?*"

His eyes fall heavily on me. "Redemption."

Chapter 23

REDEMPTION. THAT WORD weighs heavy on me that night as I stare up at the sky. Humankind has been so dead-set on stopping the horsemen that we've overlooked one simple truth: maybe it's not the horsemen that need to be stopped.

Maybe it's *us.*

Not our lives—though War would insist differently—but our *actions.* Technology was stopped in its tracks the day the horsemen arrived. But if it was the things we created that were wrong, that single, obliterating act should've been it.

And it wasn't.

Pestilence surfaced five years after that. Five *years.* And now it's been well over a decade since the horseman's initial arrival. Why the wait? What are we missing?

I remember the sight of my three surviving attackers, all waiting to die. I remember looking at those men, being so sure they would hurt someone again if they were freed. I didn't *want* to believe it—I still don't—but I thought it all the same.

Somehow we're all supposed to redeem ourselves. I'm just not sure we're all willing to.

And so we're slated to die.

WE PASS THROUGH Gaza, the entire strip of it. No one remains. It's just as abandoned as Ashdod and Ashkelon. Bodies rot under the summer sun, and the deep, foreboding hum of swarming flies raises the hair on the back of my neck.

Jabalia, Khan Yunis—all the cities within the strip look the same.

Dead.

"What have you done?" I whisper as I take it all in.

"I couldn't leave you," War says.

I glance over at him.

"When you were injured," he clarifies.

Horror dawns on me. While he stayed at my side and mended me, he was still killing.

War meets my gaze, and there's no remorse in his pitiless expression. He'll have it all—me and the end of the world. It's his birthright *to* take it all.

I look away. To think I was fantasizing about him only a day ago ...

My attention returns to the ruins of this civilization. I didn't even know the army raided this far from their basecamp.

Only, the more I look at the carnage and the more I think about it, the more I come to believe that War's army *didn't* move this far south. There are no smoldering buildings, there are no fallen soldiers. There's nothing to indicate man met man on the battlefield and each fought the other to the death.

But there are piles of bones. Lots and lots of bones.

"You used the dead?" I ask.

His only response is to meet my eyes and say again, "I couldn't leave you."

I DON'T SPEAK to War after that. Not for hours and hours.

Unfortunately, he seems perfectly fine with that

arrangement.

It's not until the sun is setting and War is steering his steed off the road and towards a deserted outpost that he says, "I know you're angry with me."

I shake my head. "I'm not angry with you," I say. I can feel his gaze on me. "I'm angry at myself."

War swings himself off Deimos and takes the reins of my own horse, leading the creature to a set of troughs filled with old feed and murky water.

I glance around. We're in the middle of nowhere. Truly. Outpost aside, there's nothing here but road and barren, sun-bleached earth.

"A week ago, your people brutalized you," he says, "and still you think they should be spared?"

I ignore him, sliding off Lady Godiva and wincing at my aching legs.

He ties my horse's reins and returns to my side.

"Answer me," he demands. For once his eyes are angry, and I get the impression he's remembering the night I was attacked.

"Why?" I say. "Reasoning with you accomplishes *nothing*."

War steps in close. "And if it did?" he asks softly. "If I listened to you and tried to change, what then?"

I search his face. Everything about him is brutal—brutal beauty, brutal power, brutal personality.

"I think you know what would happen if you tried to change," I say, lifting my chin a little.

I'm having a difficult enough time keeping my hands off War as it is. If he did give me a reason to believe he was capable of changing for the better, I might be tempted to sully his good name right here, right now.

The horseman's gaze drops to my lips and his eyes noticeably heat. "And if I did this, if I ... *changed*—would that make you less ashamed of the fact that the world hates me yet you are mine?"

"I am *not* yours." There's a very big difference between wanting to fuck a pretty man versus being *his*.

The corners of War's sinful lips curve upwards. "You *are* mine. You knew it the moment you stared up at my face that day in Jerusalem. Just as I knew you were mine then too." His gaze drops to the hollow of my throat, where my scar is.

War steps in closer, drawn by my old wound. "Mine by violence. Mine by might. Mine by divine proclamation."

I think he might kiss me. He has that intense look on his face like he wants to, and he's made it perfectly clear that he believes I am his in every sense of the word.

But instead of leaning down and pressing his lips to mine, he brushes past me and begins to set up camp.

I stare at his back as he works. Why doesn't he just seal the deal? He's strong enough, and he has no problem overpowering innocent humans on the battlefield. Why draw the line when it comes to his unwilling "wife"?

"What would you change about me?" he asks over his shoulder, interrupting my thoughts.

Whatever it is that drives you.

"Stop killing people," I say.

He pauses in his work. "You would have me surrender my purpose?"

Yes. But that's clearly too much to ask of him.

I walk over to him, grabbing the other end of the pallet he's unfolding and help him spread it out.

"At least save the children," I say.

War brushes my hands away, and for a guy that isn't really a guy at all, he sure seems to know a bit about chivalry or whatever it is he thinks he's doing for me.

"Children grow up," he says, "and tragic childhoods make the most vengeful of men."

Men who would try to stop War ... if he could be stopped at all.

I think of my own childhood. Of sitting on my father's lap

and listening to him tell stories of faraway places and people he'd known. I remember being in the kitchen, making challah with my mom, the family recipe supposedly passed down over hundreds of years before I came to learn of it. I remember how peaceful, how loving, my childhood was.

At least, that was how it was *before*.

After ...

I close my eyes and I can hear the grinding smash of metal the day the horsemen arrived. The day my father died. And then, years later—

The water rushes in—

I can feel its icy chill, squeezing the life out of those memories.

The horseman is right. It's hard to remember what you loved without also remembering what you hated.

"Besides," War continues, unaware of my own thoughts, "children become adults, who then beget *more* children."

Problematic when you're trying to kill off a species.

War finishes setting up the pallet, then pulls out a few logs of wood from my horse's pack, along with a weathered packet of matches and some kindling.

"Doesn't that bother you? That children are dying?" I ask, taking a seat on one of the pallets. "Surely there's some part of you—maybe the part that saved me—that's bothered by that."

The horseman begins stacking the dry wood. "Famine takes no issue with children—and Death," a mirthless smile flashes along War's face for a second, and then it's gone. "Death would love nothing more than to hold the entire world in his cold embrace.

"So, no, Miriam, I am not concerned with my leniency."

"What about Pestilence?" I press, slinging my arms over my knees.

"What of him?" War finally says, adding the kindling to the logs.

My heart pounds harder and harder. There's something here. Something to this first brother that War decidedly doesn't want me to know.

"You didn't include him in your list," I say.

War takes his time lighting a match, then bringing it to the kindling.

"Did I need to?" he says, snuffing the match out. "You and I both know that the plague doesn't discriminate its victims."

I narrow my eyes on War, sure that he's being clever with his words. "Whatever it is you're keeping from me, I will find out."

LATE THAT EVENING, after I have eaten and drunk my fill (War abstaining in the name of rationing resources), I watch the horseman over the dying fire. He has his sword across his lap and a whetstone to sharpen its blade. I can hear the rhythmic zing of it as he slides the stone along the metal.

"Tomorrow we will set up camp here," he says, shattering the quiet.

"Here?" I ask, glancing around. We're in the middle of nowhere. "Where even are we?" I ask.

"Egypt," War replies.

Egypt.

I've never been out of the country before. It feels weird, traveling farther than I ever have before. For years I've wanted to travel; go figure that when I finally get the opportunity, it's in the wrong direction.

My gaze sweeps over our barren surroundings again. So this will be the end of our travels. Not that it means anything. The horseman will erect my tent right next to his and we'll continue right on with this *thing* we have between us.

But this *is* the end of something, at least for now. Out on the road it's easier to like a man like War. He's not focused on killing people, and honestly, when you remove that from the equation, he's not nearly so horrible.

The low flames flicker over his olive skin and dance in his eyes. They glint across the blade of his sword and lovingly illuminate his thick arm. War doesn't look like a modern man right now.

"Before you arrived on Earth, who were you?" I ask.

His eyes meet mine. "Not who, Miriam," he says, "but *what*."

I don't say anything, and eventually he continues.

"I have lived along the Somme, rested Normandy, and scattered myself on the ancient shores of Troy; I have tasted most parts of this earth, and my dead have sowed countless fields with their bodies. Even now I can feel those bodies deep beneath me in the soil."

Goosebumps break out along my skin. Half of what he's saying doesn't make sense, but I can feel the truth of it. Every last word.

"I'm old and new and it is a terrible, burdensome experience." *Zing.* He passes the whetstone over his sword again.

"But unlike my brothers, I am unique in one single, fundamental way." He pauses, his gaze heavy on mine.

"What way is that?" I ask, even though I'm not sure I want to know the answer.

His eyes go to the fire. "I exist solely in the hearts of men." War gazes at the flames. Now that I've opened him up, it seems as though his entire story is tumbling out. "All creatures can experience pestilence, famine, and death—but war, true war, that is a singularly human experience."

As I stare at him, his face mostly eclipsed in shadow, realization dawns.

"*That's* why you judge men's hearts," I say. Because War, borne of human strife, is the only one of the horseman to truly understand our hearts and our hearts alone.

War laughs, setting the whetstone and his sword aside. "*All* my brothers judge men's hearts," he leans forward, "it's just that I happen to *know* their hearts. I have resided in them for a long, long time, wife."

Again, a chill slides over me. War's gaze is far too intense, and what he's saying is making me feel like reality and the unknowable are actually separated by a thin curtain, and right now, the horseman is drawing that curtain aside.

On a whim, I move closer to him.

He doesn't know anything beyond war. That's been the entirety of his existence up until now.

Reaching out, I capture his hand between mine. I don't know what I'm doing, only that the glow of his knuckle tattoos look like fireflies caught between my hands.

Immediately, War's gaze moves to mine, and his fingers tighten.

"If you know men's hearts," I say, threading my fingers between his. *What am I doing?* "then you must also know that most men don't want to fight."

It's countries and causes and kings that want war, and soldiers who pay the price for it.

"Are you really so sure of that, Miriam?" But for once, War is the one who sounds like he doesn't want to fight.

I run my finger over his knuckles, tracing each glyph. "I am."

I still have no idea what in God's name I'm doing, but I know that War won't stop me.

He's been wanting us to touch for a lot longer than I have.

He stares at the action, his eyes deep, his body unusually still.

My finger slips over the back of his hand and up his tan forearm, beginning to touch all the skin I've told myself not to touch. Beneath my fingertip, I can feel the thick bands of his muscles. Muscles that, to the best of my knowledge, formed into existence a little over a decade ago.

"*Wife.*" War's voice has gone rough with want, and there are a thousand desires in his eyes. He's starting to lean forward, and he looks like he's going to pounce on me at any second.

Fuck, I think I want to find out what that feels like, just as I want to know what it would feel like to have War's hips nestled between my thighs, his massive body pressed against mine ...

I'm leaning forward too.

I almost manage to forget everything else.

But then, there's a lot to forget. Too much.

I can hear the screams from battle, and I can see the way the birds circled those conquered cities. I remember the corpses—all those corpses—littering so many kilometers of road, and War's armor covered in blood.

I release his hand. He's handsome and kind and he saved my life, but as he said—

I am not like you, and you should never forget that.

Abruptly, I stand. "I think I need to go to bed."

You idiot, Miriam. To think that you almost initiated something with the horseman.

Loneliness is clearly getting the better of me.

I can feel the horseman's gaze on my back as I move over to my pallet. Just like the first time we traveled, mine is heaped with blankets. I'd take War's instead, just to make a point that I can stand to sleep like a miser, but considering the way we were eye-fucking each other only a moment ago, he might get the wrong impression.

And I don't think I'd have it in me to turn him down twice.

As I take off my boots, War puts out the last of the fire. I expect him to say something about what just happened—some promise for more, some frustration that I slipped from his grasp (literally) once again, but he doesn't.

It's unnerving as hell, mostly because I'm reminded that as brutal as War is, he's a strategist. And I think he knows how to play me.

Shortly after I lay down on my pallet, he does the same, removing his shirt as he does so. I can see his tattoos glowing in the night.

"You don't need to go to bed just because I am," I say.

"I don't want to be awake when you're asleep. Talking with you reminds me of how lonely it is to exist."

Those words tighten my chest. I hadn't imagined that the horseman might feel that way when he lives among a horde of humans. To be honest, I hadn't considered that he was even *capable* of feeling lonely. Loneliness is a very vulnerable, very human feeling. It doesn't fit my notion of War.

Maybe your notion is wrong.

He's right there. It's not too late to be a little less lonely for an evening.

"Miriam," he says, interrupting my thoughts.

"Mm?" I say.

"Tell me something beautiful."

I'm not sure I heard the horseman correctly. *He* wants to hear about something beautiful? I didn't think a man like War had room in him for something like beauty.

My notion of him is most *definitely* wrong.

I turn on my pallet so that I can look at the horseman. He lays on his own bed, staring up at the stars. He must feel my gaze on him, but he doesn't turn to me.

Something beautiful ...

The story comes to me almost immediately. "My father was Muslim. My mother was Jewish."

He's quiet.

I run my fingers over the cloth of my blankets as I speak. "They met at Oxford while they were both getting their doctorates. My dad told me he heard my mother's laugh before he saw her face. Supposedly that's when he knew he was going to love her."

My fingers still. "They weren't supposed to love each other."

"Why?" War's voice comes from the darkness.

My eyes move to him. "Their families didn't want them to be together—because they were from two different cultures and two different religions." My father, Turkish-American, and my mother, Israeli.

The horseman doesn't say anything to that, so I continue.

"In the end, it didn't matter to them what their families thought. They knew that love was love. That it can bridge all gaps."

I exhale. Now my parents are gone and this great love story I believed in as a kid came to a shit ending.

So maybe it's not beautiful, after all. The world takes away everything, in the end.

Now he turns his head to face me. "So, you find love beautiful, Miriam?" he asks.

"No," I say, my eyes meeting his in the near-darkness. "Not love itself." Everything I've ever loved I've lost. There's no beauty in that. "It's the power of love that I find beautiful."

It can change so many things—

For better, or worse.

Chapter 24

I WAKE AGAINST War.

Just like the last time this happened, I've left my pallet, my body gravitating towards the horseman's like a magnet.

I lift my head a little and see that at least this morning, War has left his own pallet as well, the two of us meeting somewhere in the middle.

That only makes me feel a smidgen better.

My eyes move to the horseman. He's still asleep, his long lashes fanned out against his cheeks. I feel my skin heat even as I slowly allow myself to settle back into him.

Is it wrong to reimagine this situation? Because I want to. So badly.

The longer I'm pressed to him, the more my body awakes to his. I'm aware that he's made of muscle and perhaps nothing else, and that all of that muscle feels so very *good* against me. There's also a perverse part of me that enjoys feeling small and protected right here in the cocoon of his arms. It's been a long time since I've felt protected.

My gaze moves to his chest, where his pectorals are wrapped in those glowing tattoos. Before I can think better of it, I lift a hand and trace one. Beneath my touch, the horseman's skin pebbles.

War's arm tightens on me, and he wakes with a slow, devil-may-care grin. I wonder how many more of those I'll get today. I'm horrified to realize that I've started to anticipate those smiles. The horseman doesn't do much smiling, so each one I win gives me perverse pleasure. Emphasis on *perverse*.

"Wife, you're making a habit of finding your way into my arms."

A habit that, judging from his face, he's going to do nothing to deter.

"You met me in the middle," I say a little defensively because I'm feeling an awful lot like I'm pursuing him right now when it's been the other way around.

War gives me another sleepy smile, which heats my core.

"How could I not?" he says. "In sleep I don't have nearly so much restraint."

He still hasn't let me go, and I haven't tried to move out of his arms. I think neither one of us is all that eager to end this moment.

The horseman reaches out and traces the scar at the base of my throat. "How did you get this?"

The question shatters my mood.

The explosion roars through my ears, the force of it knocking me into the water.

Darkness. Nothing. Then–

I gasp in a breath. There's water and fire and ... and ... and God the pain–the pain, the pain, the pain.

I squeeze my eyes shut against the memory. When I open them, it's carefully tucked away again.

"Why does it matter?" I ask.

War's deep eyes rise to mine. "It matters."

I frown. "I was in an accident. I have other scars in other places."

This, of course, is the wrong thing to say. War's eyes grow

avid; he looks like he wants to peel my clothes away and read my skin like it's a roadmap.

His gaze moves up the column of my throat. Past my mouth and nose. I lock eyes with him, and neither of us looks away. I can see those flecks of gold in his irises. I can even see that right now, his eyes have been stripped of violence.

What's left in them is pure desire.

My breathing speeds up and my core begins to throb, and I want him, I want him, I want him. I thought sleeping it off would change things, but it hasn't.

His face is so close. Too close.

It's me that closes the distance between us. Me who presses my lips to his. This is pure, unadulterated impulse.

So much for not pursuing him ...

He tastes just as I remember. Like smoke and steel. And unlike the rest of his body, War's mouth is pliant.

The kiss is supposed to be gentle, but the horseman hijacks it, crushing his lips against mine. He's devouring me with the same intensity he has in battle.

He rolls us over so that I'm on my back and he's above me, pinning me to the ground. He keeps his weight off me, but even still, he feels as solid and heavy as those tanks rotting in Jerusalem's junkyards. Shamelessly, I grind against him, biting back a moan.

In the distance, I hear the slow clop of hooves, but my attention is intensely focused on War as his hand moves down to my chest and cups a breast.

I don't mean to, but a breathy gasp slips out.

War breaks away from the kiss long enough to say, "Wife, I have not been living until this moment. You must make that sound again."

Fuck, he noticed that?

Clop, clop, clop, clop.

The horseman's lips return to mine, and his hand is back on my breast, and I am rubbing my pelvis against his like it's a professional sport.

Clop, clop, clop, clop.

This is going to happen right here, right now. My dry spell will officially be *over*. I'll deal with the fallout of this bad decision later.

A shadow rolls over us, and when I bother looking up, I notice War's horse leaning over, snuffling the horseman's hair.

Unlike Lady Godiva, War didn't bother to tie up his steed out here. And now his horse just cock-blocked the shit out of this situation.

War breaks away from me. "*Deimos*," he groans, sounding exasperated as he pushes the horse's muzzle away.

Giving me an apologetic look, War rolls off of me to deal with his steed.

I sit up, dusting the dirt off my hair and clothes, feeling only a little chagrined at what I just did. I watch War interact with Deimos, petting the beast along his cheek and neck.

I've always thought the war horse, with his massive frame and blood red coat, was a frightening creature, but right now he seems more like a needy little kid, eager for his father's attention.

Alright, horses might have a thing or two over bikes. Even if they poop everywhere.

I'm just about to wander over to where horse and rider stand when I hear some low sound. I squint at the road and see indistinct shapes right at that point where land meets sky.

Deimos wasn't cock-blocking us after all. He was sounding the alarm.

War's army is on the horizon.

Chapter 25

I STEP OUT of my newly erected tent that evening, armed with purpose.

Outside, the forlorn little spot War and I camped out in is now covered with tents as far as the eye can see. The private moments we had here only hours ago have been replaced with people and industry.

I feel a brief pang of loss, but it quickly fades, replaced by my growing nerves.

I bite the inside of my cheek, my eyes going to the horseman's tent. I've come up with a plan of sorts. A cringe-y, half-baked plan, but a plan nonetheless. One that makes my stomach drop a little every time I think about it.

At least it will stop making you feel so torn—if it works.

War is going to invade the next big city in another day or two. I need to make this happen before then.

I take a single step towards his tent, then hesitate.

My plan *could* wait until tomorrow ...

Then again if I put it off, it might never find the courage to do this again.

I begin to head towards War's tent, my heart in my throat.

The night is warm and still, and the sounds of camp surround me—the dull purr of torches, the distant bellows of laughter, the soft flutter of canvas. If our circumstances were different, these noises would be comforting.

God, am I really going to do this?

The phobos riders who are normally standing guard around the area are gone. I approach the tent, and from inside I hear several voices talking.

I hesitate, twisting my clammy fingers together, my breath coming too fast.

Now might really be a bad time for this.

The low murmur of the horseman's voice drifts out from inside, and my stomach clenches.

I can still turn around. He would never know.

Be brave.

I pull the canvas flap aside just the smallest amount.

Inside, the horseman listens to his men as they strategize how to best invade Arish, the next city on his list apparently.

"The ocean blocks the city from the north, the desert from the south," a phobos rider says. "We're coming from the east, leaving civilians only true escape to the west. It might be best to split the army and come at it from both ends."

I frown at the man talking. He's speaking of how to best annihilate an entire city.

War studies the topography, his chest bare, his tattoos glowing like rubies.

"There's also Highway 55 to think about," a female soldier says, moving her finger over a section of the map. "It does lead to the desert, but if people are desperate enough, they will use it to flee south—"

A hand wraps roughly around my upper arm.

"Spying on the warlord?" a man growls from behind me.

I turn and catch sight of yet another one of the horseman's phobos riders. Uzair I think his name is. He's got an especially mean look about him.

He shoves me inside War's tent. The horseman and the other soldiers look up at the commotion.

"I found your woman lingering outside the tent. She was listening to your plans," Uzair says.

War's eyes flick over me before moving to the man. "Go."

The rider hesitates. Clearly, he thought he was going to get a pat on the shoulder for ratting me out.

He gives War a stiff bow and leaves.

The remaining soldiers are watching the horseman, waiting on his cue before they act.

War jerks his head towards the flaps of the tent. Wordlessly, the lot of them file out. As they go, most of them give me hard looks.

I haven't earned any allies amongst his men.

The horseman stares at the tent flaps for several seconds even after everyone has left.

"If you wish to know my plans," he finally says, "you only have to ask."

War and I both know I'd only use the information to sabotage his efforts.

"That's not why I'm here," I say.

"Then why *are* you here?" he asks, moving away from his map. His eyes are alight with interest.

Be brave. Be brave. Be brave.

He strides closer, and I take him in—*really* take him in. From his imposing frame, to his dark eyes and sharp cheekbones, his cutting jaw and the vast expanse of his bare torso. Everything about him was made to end lives.

I open my mouth—

Bail.

"You know what, forget about it." The words rush out.

Another time, I promise myself.

Just as I turn to go, War catches my arm, and I twist back to look at him.

He searches my face. "You have a look in your eye ..."

I have a look in my eye?

"Tell me why you're here," he commands.

My gaze moves from the hand on my arm to his face.

Just woman up say it already.

I exhale. "I have a proposition for you."

"A proposition," he repeats. His voice carries weight to it, weight that heats my cheeks.

If anyone would understand trades, it would be War. Opposing sides meet, exchange one thing for another, and then resume conflict in the morning.

He continues scrutinizing me with growing intensity. "What is it, wife, that you propose?"

While I stare up at him, I step in close. Very deliberately, I place my palm against his chest.

"I think you want *this*," I say softly, unable to spell out exactly what I'm offering. "And more."

So much more.

War breathes deeply, and his eyes burn. He doesn't deny it.

"This is your proposition?" he asks.

My dreaded plan.

I nod.

"What do you want?" His voice is deep and resonate.

He wants to make a deal.

I release a shaky breath. This is exactly what I've been hoping for. The misgivings I have pale in comparison.

"Stop raising the dead," I say.

I'm not asking War to end his damnable crusade; I'm simply asking that he not completely eradicate us all. Maybe then some people would survive War's raids. At this point, *some* is better than *none*.

War closes his eyes and moves a hand over mine, pinning my palm to his chest.

"It's a good offer." The horseman opens his eyes. "I'm as tempted as I'll ever be—"

I feel my hope expanding ...

"—but no, Miriam, I will not agree to this."

... then plummeting.

My cheeks flush at the rejection.

I was a fool to think I could persuade him so easily. Or to think that my body has that high of a price tag on it. And then there's also the petty humiliation I feel. It was debasing enough to offer up my *services*—but to then have them turned down anyway?

All at once I'm angry—mostly at myself, but at War as well.

I begin to pull my hand away, but he holds it prisoner.

"So quick to leave?" he says.

I openly glare at the horseman, and the look causes him to laugh menacingly.

"Yes, hate me, savage woman; your anger makes you come alive."

He still has my hand pinned.

"This is where we bargain," he says.

"This is non-negotiable," I say. "You can take my offer or leave it and let me go."

War ignores my words. "What if we camped a little longer between cities?" he says. "I could buy your people some extra time."

A few days? If I'm going to screw this horseman when and how he asks for it, I want to be buying years—decades even—of someone's life. Not *days*.

"That's not good enough."

He flashes me a cruel smile. "You're quick to jump from trades to demands."

"And you're quick to shoot them down," I snap.

The horseman releases my hand, but only so he can run his thumb across my lower lip.

The warlord leans in. "You will give yourself to me anyway. You are marked for me, my war prize."

Now it's my turn to give him a cruel smile. "Maybe," I say. "Maybe you'll get me, maybe you won't. But it won't be tonight—*and it could've been.*"

War's eyes seem to darken.

Oh, touched on something he wanted now, didn't I?

Too bad.

I turn and head for the door.

I'm nearly to the tent flaps when he says, "The aviaries."

My brows furrow, and I glance over my shoulder at him. "What?"

He takes a step forward. "I won't burn the aviaries."

I can hear my heartbeat begin to pick up.

The aviaries. That was a city's most efficient system of communication. If they were left intact, then other cities could be warned about War. People might then have time to flee before the horseman ever entered their city.

I scrutinize the horseman, swiveling more fully to face him. "Is this some sort of trick? You aren't just planning on giving me your word only to kill the birds off in some other manner?"

War looks almost pleased at my question. Perhaps his strategic mind likes being tested. Meanwhile, here I am, just finding the whole thing tedious.

"I won't stop my men from killing the birds," he says, "but I will not explicitly order them to destroy the aviaries."

This is the best I'm going to get. And it's damn well better than his first counteroffer.

Slowly, I nod. I nod before I can truly think through the other ramifications of this deal. The ramifications that are going to cost *me.*

"Alright," I say softly. "I agree to your terms."

The horseman's uncompromising gaze is fixed on mine. Finally, he gives a small nod. "Good. Then we have ourselves a trade."

His eyes move over me, heating as they go.

"Now, come to me," he says. His voice has gone rougher, deeper. "Show me what I've bought myself."

Chapter 26

THIS IS REALLY happening.

God, I hadn't expected it to happen this fast. Maybe I hadn't truly expected it to happen at all. I think I might still be in shock.

I take a shaky breath. Anxiety and trepidation and perverse excitement all churn in my stomach as I take those halting steps back to him.

One of his hands cups my cheek, and I jolt at the sensation. Now that I know what the two of us will be doing—what I've *agreed* to do—his touch feels particularly electric.

"The things I have imagined, wife," he murmurs, his thumb stroking my skin. Leisurely he drinks in every facet of my face—my nose, my lips, my cheeks, my eyes.

A shiver courses through me.

War leans in, his mouth the barest breath from mine. Just when I think his lips are going to close over mine, he says, "Touch me."

I swallow.

Raising my hand, I touch his face softly, so softly. I don't think this is what War had in mind when he gave me the order, but he's not objecting. He continues to stare at me, his gaze searing.

What sort of mind lies beneath this handsome face? I'd call him evil and yet I've seen the human brand of evil. It thrives on cruelty and torture. I don't think War is depraved, even though his brutality is astounding.

I trail my fingers over his high cheekbone, down his jaw and the column of his throat. I continue to move my hand lower and lower until my palm returns to that spot just beneath his pecs.

War closes his eyes, exhaling through his nose.

He has a warrior's build, which isn't surprising—and it's nothing I haven't already seen. But tonight, when I know it's going to be pressed against my own skin, tonight I *notice*.

Now I'm staring at his chest and those glowing markings. Why am I so nervous? And why am I making this weird? Should I just kiss him?

"Have you done this before?" he asks, opening his eyes.

I nod, not meeting his gaze. I don't tell him that I haven't done it *much*. Too tricky with pregnancy.

"Have *you*?" Like an idiot the question escapes my lips before I can stop myself.

War tilts my head up, forcing me to meet his eyes.

"Mmm," he says, which I guess is his way of saying *yes*.

Before he can do anything else, and before I have a chance to make this feel truly uncomfortable, I bring my hands to his chest again. Ignoring the way they tremble, I smooth my palms over his flesh.

Beneath my touch, I feel War's skin pucker, and it's a shock, knowing I can do that to him.

I move my hands down, reaching for his trousers, ready to get this whole thing going, but then War catches one of my wrists.

"Wait."

Wait?

My knees are nearly knocking together with nerves. I don't think I *can* wait.

Holding my arm, War draws me over to a side table, where a decanter and glasses rest. Uncorking the container, he pours out two drinks and hands one to me. The other he keeps for himself.

I take it, wrapping both my hands around it. At least this will take the edge off. My senses could stand to be dulled.

I take a tentative drink of the alcohol. It's spicy, and I honestly couldn't say what particular type of distilled spirits I'm drinking, but it warms me instantly, so I take another drink.

Maybe I can simply do this drunk …

In the spirit of that thought, I tip back my glass and swallow the rest of the drink down, grimacing at the sting of it.

War watches me closely. After a moment, he sits down in his chair, his gaze never leaving me. I think he's going to point out that I look nervous. Instead he takes a long swallow of his drink, then sets the glass aside. After a moment, he takes my drink from me and sets it, too, aside.

Reaching out he grabs me by the hips and reels me in so that my legs are caught between his. My heart is hammering away in my chest.

Staring up at me, the horseman begins to rub his thumbs over my skin. Slowly, his palms skim up my sides, lifting my top along with them. His touch is electric. I've never been so aware of myself in my entire life.

Bit by bit he lifts my shirt, revealing a tattered bra beneath. I finish removing the shirt, casting the garment aside.

I feel like I'm about to leap out of my own skin, which is alarming, considering how little we've done.

Need to spearhead this.

With that thought, I lean in and kiss him.

Sweet relief.

The moment my lips press against his, all my anxious energy turns into intensity. I clasp my hands on either side of his face, directing his mouth to mine.

He groans against me, and whatever agonizingly slow pace he set out for us earlier, it vanishes in an instant. His hands are in my hair as he devours my mouth.

My knees are still weak, and I practically have to crawl onto War's lap to keep myself from collapsing on the floor. The skin of my chest presses against his, and I shudder against him.

The warlord grinds his hips against me, and I can feel his hardness straining against the material.

"The feel of you against me ..." he growls out, "*all the saints*, it's like a memory of heaven."

I don't know what to say to that; the horseman just likened me to heaven—and he'd know all about the place. On a more personal note, no one has ever cherished any part of me the way War is doing right now. And it's heady. It's so goddamn heady.

War breaks away from my mouth. "I want to see your pretty breasts," he says, his voice gravelly.

I stare back at him, dazed from his lips.

Before his words fully process, he's removing my bra. A moment later, my breasts spill free.

Automatically, my arms come up to my chest, and my earlier nervousness comes back in full force.

Still, it's War who pulls my arms away from my chest, revealing my dusky nipples. His smoldering gaze dips to meet mine. "You have no reason to be nervous, wife."

Wife. The sentiment makes my stomach drop.

"Please don't call me that right now." I thought I'd gotten used to the term, but I was wrong. Right now it sounds far too intimate. I can trivialize what I do with the horseman so long as I remain emotionally distant.

"That's one thing I will not agree to. Wife."

I narrow my eyes at him.

His hand skims over my skin, then cups a breast. It's almost laughable, how big his hands are. They engulf my breast—and then some.

He brings his other hand up, so that he's cupping them both. His thumb scrapes over a nipple.

"I want to be in you, Miriam," he breathes. "It's all I've been able to think about lately."

His words set my core on fire. Need is growing in me to take this farther, *faster*.

War lifts me easily, giving himself access to the breast. I feel his hot breath exhale against my nipple, and then he takes it into his mouth.

My reaction is instant.

I moan, arching against him, pressing myself against his chest. His lips are like sin, and I can feel myself getting wet with every stroke of his tongue.

He groans against me. "Wife. That sound."

I need more.

"What do you want me to do?" I say instead.

"Touch me wherever it pleases you."

Now *that* is a tricky command. It implies that *any* part of him pleases me, and even though my lips are already swollen from his kiss, and even though I'm straddled in his lap and my panties are soaked, I still don't *want* any part of him to please me.

And I definitely don't want him to know it.

But desire wins out. I run my hands over his pecs, his shoulders, his back and arms. I'm touching him everywhere, *everywhere*. His body is enormous, his massive torso dwarfing mine.

The horseman groans again, and again he grinds against me. His lips begin to skim over my chest, getting more demanding, and his hands are getting greedier. Reflexively, I run my fingers through his dark hair.

His violent, kohl-lined eyes lock on mine, and they sharpen with purpose.

War picks me up and carries me over to his pallet, setting me down on the bed I slept in not so long ago. It feels familiar and foreign all at the same time, the sheets smelling faintly like the horseman.

I lay there and look up at War, who looks larger than life from this angle.

Minutes ago I would've been all jittery nerves. Now I just want him.

He kneels down next to me, his gaze pinned to mine. His hands go to my boots, removing them and my socks one by one. He moves up the bed, his fingers going to my waistband.

My throat bobs a little as he unbuttons my pants. The sound of the zipper dragging down ratchets up my excitement. He hooks his fingers around my pants and underwear, and then he drags it all down, bit by bit, unveiling me as he goes.

I hear his sharp intake of air, and his eyes are transfixed on my core, even as he pulls my clothes down my calves then off my feet. He looks mesmerized by the sight of me laid bare on his bed.

After a moment, War straightens, his own hands going to the black boots he wears, his muscles rippling with the movement.

He begins stripping for me, and it's so damn sexy. The horseman is shirtless, so there's not much to remove once his shoes are off. His hands move to his own black trousers. He doesn't look away from me as he draws them—and whatever he wears beneath them—down, down, down.

My gaze dips, and—*oh*. A little tendril of nerves come back.

His cock is enormous. Big enough to intimidate me, and big enough to hurt, if we're not careful.

I suddenly feel my inexperience. I'm in over my head, and War has probably been with enough women to see just how unpracticed I am.

Before my insecurities can rush in, the horseman kneels on the pallet, and then his body settles heavily over me. His hips fit themselves between mine, just like I once imagined they would, and his chest presses against every bit of my exposed skin. The sensation is better than what my sick fantasies could dream up.

Around us, the lamps flicker, their glittering light dancing along War's body.

The horseman gazes down at me for several seconds. "Now, wife, I can breathe easy. All is as it should be."

His mouth meets mine, and it feels like I'm being brought to life.

War doesn't ask me again to touch him. He doesn't need to. His mouth lights a fire within me, and I'm filled with wild, reckless need.

I slip my hands around his torso, my palms skimming up his back. I don't need to hear him speak to feel how pleased he is. Maybe it's having my hands on his skin, maybe it's the proprietary nature of the touch. All I know is that he deepens the kiss, his tongue lashing against mine.

His cock is trapped between us, and having him inside me is a physical need.

Burning up. I'm burning up from the inside out, my breath coming quicker and quicker.

My hands slide back down the slope of his spine and over the sculpted roll of his ass.

Need him in me.

He smiles against my lips as he kisses me, like he heard my thoughts.

"For millennia I've craved this." His low voice seems to vibrate against my skin. "For millennia I've been denied."

I release a breath, caught between how frightening his words are and how sexy the sentiment is.

I reach between us, wrapping a hand around his cock.

War hisses through his teeth. "God's will, *Miriam*, your

touch ..."

He descends on my lips, thrusting forward into my hand.

I lift my hips, positioning him at my entrance. I'm panting, ready to feel—

"*No.*" War says, his body tensing against mine.

No?

He moves a little off me then, and my hand slips from him. I want to weep that the ache inside me hasn't been abated. I'm three deft thrusts away from completion, and he's denying me?

"Not until you surrender," War says.

"What?" I can barely focus on his words. I have no idea what he's talking about, only that he's mentioned me surrendering to him once before.

"I want more than your body, wife, and I won't fully have you until you surrender yourself to me."

What? I put a hand to my head. What does that even mean?

For several seconds, the only sound in the room is my shallow breath. "So we're not having sex?"

Please. Take my vagina. She wants you.

War's eyes gleam. He grabs my knees and spreads my thighs, exposing my most intimate parts.

"Well now, that depends on your definition of sex."

And then he descends on me.

Chapter 27

OH MY GOD, oh my God, oh my God.

"What are you doing?" My voice sounds breathless, but those damn nerves have come back.

War's only response is a slow kiss on my inner thigh.

My mouth goes dry. I've never done this, I've never ever done this and I think I might be panicking. War has me wholly and completely at his mercy.

And he doesn't have all that much fucking mercy to begin with.

I try to move my legs, but War has them pinned in their current, uncompromising position. He glances up at me, steadily trailing those kisses inward, towards my core.

"Relax, wife, you're going to enjoy this."

Why is he doing this? The sexual favors were supposed to be to *his* benefit, not mine.

War is a good kisser, but I don't find out just *how* good until his mouth makes its way to the end of my thighs.

He pauses, and I can't stand this long, drawn out moment.

Then his mouth meets my pussy, and it is like *nothing* I have ever felt before. Reflexively, I buck against his kiss, and I don't think I like this. I'm too exposed, and it feels overwhelming. His lips and tongue move over every section of my core, and nerve endings I didn't even know I had are now going off.

I try to shrug him off, but it's like trying to knock over a building. "It's too much, War. *Please.*"

I feel him smile against me. "Steady, wife, I haven't even gotten to the best part."

The best part?

I'm breathless with sensation, and he's unrelenting. The horseman licks and nips and sucks and torments me until I'm gasping and moaning and helplessly shifting my hips up to meet his mouth.

And then he finds my clit.

"Oh my *God.*" It's like a bomb goes off. I almost come right there and then.

My hands find their way into his hair, and he makes a deep, approving noise low in his throat.

"Please, War, *please.*" I don't even know what I'm begging for, only that the horseman can fix it.

He inserts a finger into me, and that's all it takes.

I cry out as an almost violent orgasm rips through me.

"*War.*" My fingers tighten into his hair as wave after wave of it radiates through me. I'm making embarrassing, desperate noises, and *I am not okay.* I move against him over and over, his mouth dragging the sensation out for as long as he can.

It's only after I come down that War moves away from my pussy. I stare at him like I've never seen him before.

The horseman moves up my body and gives me a carnal kiss. I can taste myself in the kiss, and I'm embarrassed and aroused and I don't know what to do about the fact that that was so much *more* than I intended it to be.

He lays down next to me, gathering me into his arms.

And he cuddles.

Shit. A lonely girl like me has no defense against this,

especially right now, when I feel particularly vulnerable.

I've only just caught my breath when I realize that now it's my turn.

I don't think War is going to ask, but I also really want those aviaries intact. That's why I made this trade in the first place.

The horseman is drawing circles on my back when I reach down between us and wrap my hand around him.

He's still painfully hard. His cock jerks, and his body tenses.

I start to move down his body, past his glowing tattoos, past his abs, past the tantalizing triangle of muscle that makes up his pelvis, until I'm kneeling between his thighs, my hand still fisted around him.

War props himself up on his forearms. "*Wife.*" His eyes glitter.

"A deal's a deal," I say. I move my hand up and down his shaft to emphasize my point. In response, his hips jerk.

"God's wrath," he swears beneath his breath. "What, exactly, do you intend to do—?"

His words cut off sharply as my lips wrap around the head of his cock. He groans, his hips bucking up to meet my mouth.

He's huge, and I'm clumsy and not at all sure what I'm doing, but he's groaning and shuddering, so I must be doing at least *something* right.

"Mercy to the fallen, I've never ... never felt sensation like this ..." His words taper into a groan.

Alright, either he's laying it on thick, or I totally missed a career as an expert prostitute because War seems to *really* be enjoying this.

At some point I find a rhythm, and then it's his hands that delve into my hair, holding me to him.

"Your mouth against me—it's the most exquisite pain, wife."

I'm happy he thinks that because my God, this man's dick is going to break my jaw.

Once I gain enough confidence, my hand moves to his balls.

"*Miriam—*"

That's all the warning I get.

War thickens inside my mouth, and then he's coming and coming and coming. I taste him against my tongue for a moment—am I supposed to swallow? But then it doesn't matter because I am swallowing, and he's making sexy, satisfied sounds as he continues to piston in and out from between my lips.

I feel oddly proud of my oral game for a hot five seconds before I realize I just gave a horseman of the apocalypse a blowjob, and I have superhuman cum inside me and I'm pretty sure none of this is good.

War pulls me up to him, distracting me from that disturbing line of thoughts.

"I may know every language, wife," he says, his sex-roughened voice extra deep, "but I have no words for what I feel right now."

I search his kohl-lined gaze, then give him a soft kiss on the lips.

The horseman is painfully kind. Much kinder than I ever imagined him to be.

It doesn't change who he is, the cynical part of me says. And then the guilt creeps in at what I did and what I will continue to do with the horseman. Worse, I truly wanted it for my own selfish reasons.

At least the aviaries will be saved. I can rest easy knowing that.

I lay there in the horseman's arms for a long time. Long enough for our breathing to return to normal and our bodies to cool. I even spend a few minutes tracing War's glowing tattoos.

Just like last night, I want to reimagine us, if only to alleviate my guilt. I want to pretend I get to have him and a decent life and no more battles and everything else that I know I don't get.

The daydream only lasts for a few minutes. Once I can hold reality at bay for no longer, I begin to get up.

I've only just begun to step out of War's bed when he hooks an arm around my torso and drags me back to his pallet.

"Where are you going?" he asks, his breath hot against my ear.

I flash him a surprised look. Isn't it obvious? "Back to my tent."

"No," he says simply.

I lay there, my back against his chest, for a second. "This is not what we agreed on," I say.

"Your touches," War replies. "That's what we agreed on. And I'm claiming them all, even the ones that happen when I'm *not* taking you in my mouth."

My face heats. I don't know what to say to that. I don't really have an argument. I just hadn't planned on continuing to cuddle with this monster.

He leans over me and begins trailing kisses down my torso.

Not that he plans on cuddling ...

His lips pass my belly button.

"Things will be different now," he murmurs against my skin.

I feel hot and cold, wrong and right, all at the same time.

His lips move lower, lower ...

"Again?" I say breathlessly. "But I'm not ready—"

He kisses my clit and I buck against him.

Oh God, what have I agreed to?

"Yes, Miriam, we're doing this again. And again. And again." He pulls away long enough to look up the line of my body. "My wife," he says, "I look forward to this trade."

THE SUN HAS only just risen when I wake. I'm caught in a tangle of War's limbs, and my body feels raw and tired from everything we did throughout the night.

Next to me, the horseman sleeps soundly. My eyes drift to his mouth, and my cheeks flame all over again. My core is extra sensitive and my thigh muscles hurt as I sneak out of War's bed and slip the scattered bits of my clothes back on. Once I'm dressed, I head for the exit.

I pause, glancing back to take the horseman in one last time.

The sharp angles of his face have softened in sleep; he looks almost happy. I feel my stomach flutter in response, the sensation quickly followed by horror.

This is just a physical relationship. Anything else only promises heartbreak.

Chapter 28

I SIT IN my tent, my forearms resting on my gathered knees, my thumb pressed to my lips as I think. Today I can't even concentrate on making bows and arrows.

Every time I close my eyes, I swear I can feel the glide of War's hands and the press of his lips. And every time a set of footfalls near my tent, I tense, sure they're his. But so far today, he's given me my space.

"Miriam! Are you in your tent?" Zara's voice rings out.

Fuck. She's the *last* person I want to see right now. And the one time that I need the phobos riders to keep her out, they let her through.

"Yeah," I say weakly, "I'm in here."

Several seconds later, the flaps pull back and she peers inside at me. "What are you doing in there? It's hot."

I'm hiding.

Instead of answering her, I step out of the tent.

As soon as I do so, Zara looks me over, a frown growing on her face. "Are you okay? You look like shit."

I wince. "Thanks for your honesty."

"Never mind about that." She clasps my hand between

hers. "Are you riding out tomorrow?" she asks, a note of urgency in her voice.

Oh God, the invasion. A wave of nausea rolls through me at the prospect.

"Yeah, I think so," I say.

Just because I've gotten used to this place doesn't mean I won't try to stop these soldiers at every opportunity I get.

"Miriam," she squeezes my hand fiercely, "They put me on cooking duty for tomorrow, but I need to ride out with the rest of you."

"Why?" I ask her quizzically. Being a soldier means you have to kill your own kind ... and it means that you yourself might be killed. Neither are desirable options.

"My *sister*." Her voice breaks. "She lives in Arish with her husband and son. I need to get them out."

My stomach bottoms out.

"You're sure they live there?" It's a dumb question; of course she's sure.

Zara nods anyway. "My brother-in-law, Aazim, is a fisherman."

A fisherman ...

The ocean blocks the city from the north.

I squeeze her hand. "Does he have a boat?"

"He shares one with some other men, I think ..."

Behind Zara, a phobos rider heads towards us.

I glance back at my friend, my mind racing.

"Please," she says, "if there's any way you can help—

The phobos rider steps up to us, his eyes moving between me and Zara.

"The warlord wants to see you," he says to me.

My focus is still on Zara. I squeeze her hand again and make a decision.

"I'll help," I say, nodding. I pull her in for a hug, and whisper into her ear. "I'll meet you at your tent first thing tomorrow. Be ready—and bring whatever weapons you can with you."

She nods as she pulls away. "Thank you," she says softly, even as the phobos rider ushers me away.

I wave to Zara, then follow the rider. After a long stretch of silence, I take the man in. It's the same soldier who handed me the sword the day I was to kill my attackers.

"What's your name?" I ask. He has gentle eyes, and the few other times I've interacted with him, he hasn't been as hostile as some of the other phobos riders.

"Hussain," he says.

War's tent looms ahead. The sight of it causes me to flush.

"I'm Miriam," I say distractedly.

The horseman wants more. I can sense it.

My body thrums at the thought.

Hussain gives a small laugh. "I know who you are," he says. He sounds kind and not at all like he despises me.

I'm not used to kindness here—to be honest, even back in Jerusalem, kindness was a rare thing. Life is a series of debts, loans, and obligations. Kindness is just something to muddy the waters.

The two of us get to the tent flaps. Hussain bows and steps away, leaving me to enter alone.

When I step inside War's tent, everything feels different. In this enclosed space, nothing else besides me and the horseman exists. Not the death and grief and violence and horror of the outside world.

In here, with the smell of leather and perfumed oil in the air, I'm reminded of other, more intimate things.

Across the room the man himself lounges in a chair, a glass of wine dangling from his hand.

"*Miriam.*" His eyes heat when they meet mine, and I can practically see last night playing out in his mind.

He stands, setting his wine aside.

I take a deep breath and move to him, my hand trailing over the table as I pass it by. I glance idly at it, but then what I

216

see catches my attention.

A map of Arish is spread out, various notes and arrows scribbled across it. This was the map War and his phobos riders were looking at yesterday when they were talking strategy. Despite all his supernatural abilities, the horseman still relies on us, the natives, to help him out.

War steps in close behind me.

"I still can't believe there are people who are loyal to you," I say, my fingers moving over the writing. Different hands have penned different notes.

"My riders aren't loyal to me, Miriam." His breath fans along my neck. "They are loyal to the art of breathing."

My skin puckers at his nearness, and it takes several seconds to ignore my body's response to him.

I turn from the map, the table jutting into my back. I have to crane my head to look up at War.

"Why *are* you doing this?" I ask.

"Doing what?" His eyes are fixed on my mouth.

"Fighting. Killing."

War gives me a strange look, like I'm asking him why birds fly or hearts beat. Something that needs no answer.

"Why *wouldn't* I be doing this? It's why I'm here. It's what I am."

It's what I am.

I keep thinking of him as a person, not as an entity, but I guess that's what he is—*war*. He just happens to wear a human face.

"Could you stop fighting and raiding?" I ask.

"I won't."

"That's not what I'm asking."

War stares at me for a long time, his eyes narrowing. "Yes, wife, I suppose I *could* stop."

If, of course, he wanted to. That makes this a little worse; I wasn't positive until now that the horseman might have a choice in the matter.

I take a shuddering breath. "Do you have a bow and arrow?" I ask, changing the subject.

War studies me. "I do," he says carefully.

"Can I use it tomorrow?"

"Tomorrow?" he repeats. "You mean for the battle?" The horseman narrows his eyes. "And here you had me convinced that you were trying to push for peace."

I don't respond to that. I'm afraid anything else I say might make War decide that keeping me out of the fight is the smarter option. It's definitely the safer one.

But I doubt War's mind even goes there. Not since I convinced him last time that his god would protect me.

He leans in close, resting his knuckles on the table, pinning me in. "Who, sweet wife of mine, do you plan on shooting with my bow and arrows?"

My jaw tenses. "Whoever crosses me."

The corner of his lips curves up. "I knew you were going to be trouble." His gaze drops to my lips. "But never mind that. That's not why I called you here."

My abs tighten. "I know why you called me here."

"Good. Then no more talking."

War doesn't wait for me to respond. In an instant, his hand is cradling the back of my head and his mouth is on mine.

Embarrassingly, my knees weaken, and I grab onto the horseman's forearm to keep myself upright.

War is a demanding kisser, his hands in my hair, his tongue insistent against my lips until I part my mouth and let him in.

He lifts me up and onto the table, setting me on its edge. "This morning, you left before we'd begun."

Roughly, the horseman removes one of my boots, then the other.

"There's no rush," I say a bit breathlessly.

War's hands go to my pants, unbuttoning them, and then

pulling them over my hips and down my legs.

He gives a low laugh. "Oh, I don't plan on rushing this."

My panties come off next. The horseman kneels, pulling my hips towards him.

God, we're doing this again.

"War—"

But then my words give way to gasps.

IT'S A LONG time before the two of us do much more talking. Hours and hours later. By then, we're back in War's bed, my body draped along his.

He runs his fingers down my spine. "Your skin is softer than I imagined," he says, his eyes following his hand. "So soft, my mortal bride."

I prop my chin on his chest. This close to him, I'm struck again by how ... *off* he is. He's just a little too large, a little too ferocious, a little too captivating.

He doesn't shine like I always imagined an angel might, and he's obviously not pure and clean in the way that angels are depicted, but there's something about him, something alien and *other*. Something decidedly not demonic, though I want to demonize him—or I used to want that anyway.

War sees me staring, and he smiles at me, his eyes amused. "If I didn't know better, I'd think you enjoyed gazing at me just as much as I enjoy gazing at you."

I take one of his hands and thread our fingers together.

"I do like gazing at you," I admit. I bring his hand to my mouth, kissing his tattoos one by one. "And I like touching you."

I shouldn't tell him things like this, especially when they ring true to my own ears.

War's face changes, subtly. Or maybe it's simply his eyes. He wraps an arm around me and flips the two of us so that I'm beneath him. "Touch me all you like, wife."

I trace his markings, suddenly feeling proprietary and

unsure all at once.

"How many times have you done this?" I ask, deliberately keeping my tone light.

It doesn't fool the horseman.

He searches my face, settling against me, his forearms on either side of my head. "What does it matter?"

It *shouldn't* matter.

I swallow, and he notices, his eyes honing in on the small action. It causes his brows to furrow. "I don't know what I'm supposed to say. You look frightened, wife."

Frightened?

"I'm not *frightened*," I say, offended.

You'd have to be emotionally invested to be frightened.

Again, his brows draw together. "This is a human thing I don't understand, but if you really want to know, then I have done this countless times before today."

I groan and cover my eyes with my hand. *Countless?* I've been with four men, and only one of them was memorable in any way, shape, or form. And he's now laying on top of me.

The horseman pulls my hand away from my face. "Miriam, you're being strange. Does it matter?"

I guffaw. "You *have* to know it matters," I say. Shame makes my face heat. I mean, come on, I know this guy isn't human, but he's been on earth long enough to bed *countless* women—and maybe some men too. Surely he should know that people care about these things.

"You want to know about the other women I've been with?" he asks.

Of course I do. I'm luridly curious about shit like that. I'm also ashamed of that fact.

I don't even need to respond; whatever he sees on my face must be clue enough.

"Ah," he says, "you do but you don't. How perplexing, wife."

War gazes down at me, and it's alarming how handsome he

is with his dark hair and princely features.

He lets out a breath. "I have been with dozens upon dozens of people, Miriam. Their faces bleed together—I cannot recall any of their names."

"Are there still some in your army?" This is such a barbed question.

"Some."

Ick. I make a face. For some reason, that makes him feel a little less like mine.

He isn't yours, Miriam.

"How do they feel about that?" I force out the question.

"How do they feel about what?" War asks, baffled.

"Having sex with you only to see you with another woman?"

War gives me a look like he's trying to make sense of the nonsensical. "Why should that concern me?"

It's my turn to give him the strange look. But of course, why *should* that concern him? The horseman didn't grow up acutely aware of social etiquette and taboos amongst humans.

He doesn't say anything more. I guess that's all the answer I'm going to get.

"Now, how about you?" he says.

"What about me?" I ask suspiciously.

"I want to know about the other men you've been with."

"*No.*" The answer comes to my lips so fast.

War smiles, running a finger over my mouth. "That few."

"Why does it matter?" I ask him essentially the same question he asked me only minutes ago.

The horseman's gaze shifts to my eyes, and that one look cuts through all my bullshit. "I have feasted on you. I am going to be inside you. I want to know who else has."

Strange, strange man. He didn't seem to understand my motives for bringing this subject up when it was me grilling him, but now that he wants to know my sexual history ... suddenly, he's acting *very* human. Human and possessive.

I shake my head. "I've fooled around with three men. I've only ..." I take a deep breath and force the words out. "I've only had sex with one of them." And even that was only a two-time thing. Getting off is tricky business in an age of limited contraceptives. It's not usually worth it.

"Who was he?" War's expression has gotten decidedly more bloodthirsty.

"Who were they?" I throw back at him.

If War expects me to tell him about my sexual exploits, then I expect the same from him.

He gives me a chilling smile. "So many humans are drawn to power, regardless of the cost. It's tempting, like eating dessert before dinner. My previous partners all came to me and offered themselves, and there is nothing so satisfying as a fight followed by a fuck."

I don't know if War is deliberately trying to put me off, or if he's just lost in his own twisted head.

"But in the end," he continues, "that's all they were—a good lay and nothing more. I haven't tried to dabble in any sort of emotional entanglements until now."

With me, he means.

"Why start now?"

"Because you are here. Had you been here the day I awoke, I would've started then. It was never the *when*, but the *who* that prevented my heart from getting involved."

I was ready to be put off by War, but I find I'm not ready for this. His unapologetic words get under my skin, and I feel a little off kilter.

"How do you feel about your heart getting involved?" I ask carefully, staring up at him.

"Exhilarated." Another unapologetic answer I'm not ready for.

He leans in close. "It is as thrilling as war."

LATE THAT NIGHT, long after the camp has gone to bed, I slip

222

out of War's arms and exit his tent. The horseman mentioned earlier that he wanted to wake for battle with me at his side, but ... that's just not happening. Sexual favors are one thing; spending the night is another.

War must've known I was going to sneak out, however, because when I enter my tent, there's already a bow and a quiver waiting for me, along with a note: *For your soft heart.*

Chapter 29

LONG BEFORE THE sun has risen I meet Zara in her tent. Though most of the camp is still asleep, she's already up.

"I was worried you'd forgotten," my friend says when she sees me. She's already dressed and jumpy with nerves.

"I couldn't possibly," I say. Not when she has her family to save. What I would *give* for that opportunity.

I adjust the bow thrown over my shoulder. "This is what's going to happen," I tell her without much preamble. "I'm going to be given a horse, and you're going to take it."

There's no way that she would receive a horse otherwise.

"You'll ride with the other mounted soldiers, that way you'll get a head start."

She would still enter the city behind the phobos riders, but at least she wouldn't be at the end of the army, where the foot soldiers are. Where I'll be.

"Once you find your sister and her family, give them no more than ten minutes to pack up the essentials—think food and water and blankets. Then get them to the docks." I take a deep breath. "They'll need to take your brother-in-law's boat and sail as far away from here as they can—and they'll need to stay away." Even once the battle is over, there will be zombies prowling about for who knows how long—maybe indefinitely. If Zara's family returns, they will die.

"Oh," I add, "and don't give anyone reason to attack you."

In Ashdod, I saw soldiers turn on each other for no reason at all. There's no true loyalty out there, and the horseman doesn't much care if his ranks are culled; there are always more people willing to be recruited.

Zara nods, pulling me in for another hug. "Thank you, Miriam. Thank you so much."

"Don't die," I warn her, hugging her back.

"I don't plan on it."

I PICK UP my horse, and just as planned, I covertly hand the reins over to Zara. If this were a normal army, I would never be able to get away with this half-baked plan. But in War's ever changing army, we're used to not recognizing the soldiers that fight alongside us.

"Is there a place I should meet you?" I ask Zara. "You know, if you need help or things don't go according to plan?"

She hesitates, I'm sure because she doesn't want to think about things not going according to plan. But then she nods. "My family lives on the west end of the city, near the docks. There's a cluster of palm trees near the beach ..." Her voice trails away and I can tell that she herself is having trouble remembering what the place looked like.

"I'll try to find you, though we'll probably miss each other."

A nearby soldier whistles in our direction, motioning with his hand for Zara to join the other mounted soldiers.

With a parting smile, she pulls herself onto the horse and steers the creature near the others.

Adrenaline spikes in my system. I hope this works.

"There you are," a voice says behind me.

I turn around and meet the gaze of Hussain, one of War's

phobos riders. He's laden with weaponry.

"War is looking for you; you weren't in your tent this morning." It stops just short of an accusation, so I don't bother explaining myself. Hussain nods back towards camp. "This way. The warlord will want to see you before he rides."

He leads me back towards the horseman's tent. Just outside of it, the torchlight illuminates War as he checks his steed's bridle.

Deimos, I've learned, doesn't stay with the other horses. He's far too temperamental for that. He's either stabled separately, or he roams freely.

The horseman glances up, and the moment his eyes lock on mine, he seems to relax. He leaves his horse, closing the distance between us and taking my mouth in his.

I raise my eyebrows, even as I return the kiss. This is what we agreed to—intimacy—I just hadn't expected it to move to public displays, but of course it does. The horseman is fine with people knowing what I mean to him. It's me that takes issue.

After he breaks away, he touches my bow. "I see you found my gift."

Gifts and kisses. What the fuck am I doing with this man?

"And your horse?" he asks, glancing over my shoulder.

"I'm going to enter the city on foot."

War narrows his eyes, and for one nerve-wracking moment, I'm sure he knows I claimed a horse earlier.

Instead, he clasps the back of my neck. "Stay safe, wife—and try not to be too meddlesome."

He gives me another quick kiss, and then he's striding back to his blood-red horse.

I watch him mount, the horseman looking like some savage conqueror from a bygone era, his giant sword strapped to his back, his leather armor groaning with his movements.

Giving me a final, long look, he kicks Deimos's sides and rides away, towards the waiting procession of soldiers. I follow

226

slower, and by the time I get to the group, they're already starting to move.

And so begins my second invasion.

I HEAD INTO Arish with the foot soldiers, so I'm one of the last to arrive. As I enter, I can already see the great plumes of smoke billowing into the sky. The fighting has moved inward, the streets I pass through already littered with bodies.

Farther in, I see the first aviary. The buildings surrounding it are on fire, but this one remains untouched. War made good on his word.

Out of curiosity, I peer inside. There's a man lying dead on the ground, but the cages themselves are empty. No dead birds. No living ones either.

Maybe they were set free—and maybe they flew away with warnings attached to their bodies.

I stare at those empty cages, and for a second I feel a breath of pride. But then I step away from the building, back onto the street, and the whole city seems to be burning and people are screaming or lying dead in the road. In an instant, my trade with the horseman feels like foolishness. Like too little too late.

I move inward, passing a burning mosque and a café whose outdoor tables have all been overturned. I run past shops and apartment buildings, past the dead who will be cruelly re-animated before the day is done.

Three blocks up the battle is raging. Many of the soldiers around me rush forward, heading directly into the fray. I move a little slower, trying to remember the directions Zara gave me. I need to eventually find my way to the west end of the city, in case she needs some help.

I'm not even halfway there when I hit the thick of the fighting. Soldiers on horses are cutting down everyone. People are screaming, fleeing—it's all becoming horribly repetitive.

I notice a soldier grab a woman in a burka, a knife at her

throat. He fumbles at her clothing, trying to lift it up. All that modest clothing, all her piety—it hasn't saved her from this. War made it forbidden to rape in his camp, but he hasn't forbidden this.

In the next instant, my bow is in my hand. I reach behind me, pulling an arrow from my quiver, nocking it in place.

I remember those demanding hands on me. I remember what it felt like to get pawed at. To feel my clothing ripped open. The fear and humiliation that this was happening to me and that I was helpless to stop it.

I don't even realize I've aimed and fired until the arrow cleaves through the soldier's back, the tip of it bursting through his chest. The woman, who'd been sobbing and begging, now screams at the sight. The soldier stumbles to the ground, and the woman manages to get away.

I lower my bow, my breathing hoarse. Sweat is beginning to bead on my face. For a moment, I can't seem to remember myself.

Find Zara.

I blink several times. Right. I sling my bow over my shoulder and run.

Chapter 30

IT TAKES FAR longer to cross the city than I anticipated. The streets are utterly congested with fighting—if you can call it that. It's more like seek and destroy; Arish's civilians run, and War's army chases them down.

I make it to the ocean, and my heart stops at the sight of it. All that crystalline blue water looks like something from a dream.

Or a memory.

My lungs pound. The sunlight above me grows dim even as I struggle.

I open my mouth to cry for help.

The water rushes in—

I shake the memory off and continue on, following a street that runs alongside the beach. As I move, I see people swimming in the sea ... and I see that some soldiers have headed out after them. There are a few boats that speckle the water, a disappointing number of them capsized, likely by the very people who are currently bobbing out there with the waves. Everyone wants to be saved.

"Miriam! Miriam!"

I turn at the panicked sound of my name, and there's Zara.

We're nowhere near the westernmost end of the city. That in and of itself is enough for my unease to grow. But it's the sight of her slumped against a beachside building, her headscarf in tatters around her shoulders, that truly has me concerned.

I sprint over to her.

It's only as I get close that I see the limp little boy cradled in her arms, an arrow jutting from his chest.

Oh no.

I slide on my knees to her side.

"I couldn't save them," she weeps, bowing her head over the toddler's body. "I couldn't save any of them."

My stomach turns at the sight of the wounded toddler in her arms; he must be her nephew. Someone did this to a little boy. They shot him in the chest like his life meant nothing.

"They'd already come through by the time I arrived," she sobs.

We're coming from the east, leaving civilians only true escape to the west, one of War's soldiers said when they were strategizing their attack *It might be best to split the army and come at it from both ends.*

War's soldiers must've done exactly that.

"I'm so sorry, Zara." I hadn't even thought to warn her of this—not that it would've done much good. I'm sure she rode as fast as she could to get to her family. If she was too late, there was never a chance for them to begin with.

I feel tears well in my eyes as I glance down at the toddler. I slept with the horseman, and for what gain? It didn't save Zara's sister, or her brother-in-law, or her nephew.

I place a hand on the boy. I almost jolt at the warmth of his skin. I stare down at him, and I see his chest rise and fall just the slightest.

"He's still alive," I say, shocked.

She's openly weeping as she shakes her head. "He's not

going to make it—how can he possibly make it?"

I glance down at where the arrow is embedded in his chest. Already, the clothing around it is coated in slick blood. It surely is a mortal wound, and yet ...

Maybe there still is something to gain from this.

"There's a chance—a small chance ..."

What am I even thinking, saying these words and giving Zara hope? It's such a doomed idea.

Zara blinks up at me, and I can tell she doesn't believe me—that she has been disappointed too many times *to* believe me.

I glance around. Where would the horseman be right about now?

"War!" I shout uselessly. "War!"

"What are you doing?" my friend says, looking aghast that I'd call for the horseman.

"He can help."

Zara stares at me like I've gone mad. "He's the one *responsible* for this," she snaps.

"Do you want his help or not?" I snap back.

She presses her lips together.

I stand. "I need to find him. It's a longshot ..." I say, backing away.

It's more than a long shot, Miriam.

I don't let the insidious thought creep any deeper than that.

"I'll be back." I run the way I came, feeling the futility of the situation. I'm not possibly going to find him in time. And even if I do, convincing him to help another human is even less likely. That doesn't stop me from tearing down street after street, shouting War's name, asking anyone I can if they've seen him.

I run up two blocks then hook a right, then a left, and there he is, charging down the road, his sword brandished, his body strewn with blood.

He's not going to help.

It's so laughably obvious. I mean, why would he?

And just when I managed the first impossible task too—finding him.

"War!" I shout.

His head whips to me. This far away, I can't tell what expression the horseman wears, only that after a moment, he sheathes his sword behind his back and gallops towards me.

War closes the distance in less than a minute, pulling up to my side.

"Wife," he says, grinning, his eyes a little mad. "Enjoying that gift?" He nods at my bow.

"I need your help," I rush out.

This isn't going to work.

His expression changes in an instant from crazed to serious. "And you shall have it."

We'll see about that ...

He reaches out for my hand. I grasp his palm and let him pull me onto his saddle.

"What is it?" he asks, once I'm settled in front of him.

I wet my lips, turning my head half towards him. Now the tricky part.

"I'll tell you, but first, we need to get there," I say.

It's a testament to War's own belief in me that he goes along with this, letting me direct him back to the beachside building without protest.

Zara is where I left her, her nephew still cradled in her arms. Even from here I can see that she's murmuring soft things to him.

I know the instant War sees Zara. Behind me, his body stiffens.

The horseman pulls back on Deimos. "What is this?" he demands. All gentleness has drained from his voice.

I turn to him in the saddle and place a hand on his cheek. "Please," I say.

Beneath my touch I feel a muscle in his jaw jump.

For a moment, the two of us simply stare at one another. I'm hoping against hope that he feels enough for me to help. But I'm not positive he does.

Before he responds one way or another, I hop off his steed and head back to Zara's side.

War is slower to join us, though to give him credit, he *does* dismount his horse and follow me. I wasn't sure he would.

"You pull me from battle to save one of *them*?" he says behind me. "Is that what this is?" His voice is rising with his anger.

I crouch next to Zara. She's shaking, either from fear or grief or both. Her nephew has gone even paler, though his eyes flutter a little.

"If you don't do anything, he will die."

"*Have you gone mad, wife?*" he all but bellows. "That is the exact point! And you tear me from battle *for this?*" His eyes are inflamed with his fury.

This is the first time I've ever truly seen War in a rage. Even when he kills, he isn't like this.

I think he might actually be experiencing regret for the first time, right here, right now. All at the hands of his human wife.

I take a deep breath, trying to ignore how my own body has begun to quake with fear. He's terrifying enough when his emotions are under control. But seeing him angry makes me feel like my insides have liquefied.

War takes a step closer. "Have I not sacrificed enough for you already?"

I rise to my full height, despite my terror. I've seen another side of this man. I just have to coax it out. So, going against my instincts, I walk back towards him.

God is he angry, the violence isn't just in his eyes anymore. It's spilling all over his face, from his tight jaw to his flared nostrils. But he stares at me as I come closer as though he's never encountered someone like me—and he might be willing to hear me out.

I take War's hand. "What do you want from me?" I ask.

He grimaces. "I will not make another bargain with you."

"I'm not talking about bargains," I say. "Back in your tent you told me that you wanted more than just my body. Do you still want that?"

War's upper lip is twitching in anger and distaste. Probably not the best moment to ask him *this* kind of question. I think right now, he'd like nothing more than to annul our fake little marriage.

I squeeze his hand. "This is how you get everything," I say softly.

His concessions, his kindness, his altruism and mercy—those are the things that will win me over.

"I will get what I want from you either way."

"*You won't*," I say, steel in my voice.

The horseman's gaze thins.

"You want me to stop hating you?" I say. "You want me to love you absolutely?"

At the word *love*, War straightens, like I'm finally speaking his language.

"This is how you get me to love you," I say. It feels wrong promising the horseman things I don't intend to give. And maybe he knows that because he looks at me for a long time.

He judges men's hearts. What's he finding inside mine?

The warlord turns from me and looks at the child. He grimaces.

His gaze flicks back to mine, and he gives me a final, long look, his upper lip still twitching with anger. "For your soft heart," he says bitterly.

Dear God, did that actually ... *work?*

War leaves my side, heading for Zara and her nephew. As he gets closer, Zara clutches the boy tight to her chest.

"No," she begs.

"It's alright, Zara. Truly," I say. At least I hope it's alright.

234

The horseman kneels down next to her, studying the boy's injury. Reaching out, he rips the toddler's shirt apart, causing Zara to jolt.

"What are you doing?" she demands.

Ignoring her, War reaches out, his hand hovering right above the wound. I can see his fierce frown. After a long moment, he presses his hand to the boy's skin, and I see the toddler's body shudder.

I move towards them, drawn in by War.

The horseman's other hand moves to the arrow shaft.

"Brace him," War instructs Zara as he fits his fingers around the weapon. "I'm going to take this out, and he's not going to like it."

Nodding, Zara wraps her arms more tightly around her nephew.

With a single, deft jerk, War rips the arrow from the toddler's body.

The boy wakes with a shrill scream, beginning to kick and thrash. In a very real sense he's fighting for his life.

Just as soon as the arrow is out, War's hand is back on the injury, despite the boy's bucking. The horseman stays there for a long time, even as the toddler continues to thrash and wail against his hold. War's grip is unyielding, and eventually, the little boy loses his fight. He whimpers, then falls to exhausted silence.

Silent tears track down Zara's face, and I can see her body visibly shaking. This is tearing her apart.

After what feels like an unending amount of time, War pulls his hand away from the wound.

"It's not completely healed," War says, "but it's beyond the risk of serious infection now."

He levels his eyes on Zara. "Twice I have helped you now. I expect some loyalty in return for it."

My friend frowns but gives War a slight nod.

The horseman stands, turning from the two of them. His

violent eyes lock on mine.

He steps in close to me. "Don't ask this of me again, wife," he says darkly. "You will be denied."

With that, War brushes past me. He mounts Deimos, and then he's gone.

Chapter 31

I KNEEL DOWN next to Zara, who's holding her nephew tightly to her, tears tracking down her face.

Her hands go to the wound. There's still blood covering the area, but once she smears it away, it's clear there's nothing beneath the blood except a fresh scab. At the sight of it, a choked sob slips out of Zara.

"He saved Mamoon's life." She glances up at me. "How did he do that? And how did you know he *could* do that?"

I sit down heavily next to her. "He saved my life once before."

He's saved your life more than once.

Zara takes my hand and squeezes it. "I can't repay you, Miriam. Thank you. I am forever in your debt."

"You are *not* in my debt. Besides," I reach over and pull Zara's headscarf back over her hair. "You and your nephew are not safe yet." I glance out at the ocean, where people paw at several of the capsized boats. Our earlier plan—to have Zara's family escape to sea—has vanished like smoke in the wind. "Let me find you a horse so the two of you can return to camp safely—and remember, if anyone comes at you, *kill them.*"

There's so much ferocity in Zara's eyes. "Gladly."

I leave them there, scanning the streets for any riderless horses. Inevitably, there's always some spooked steed riding about. They don't make for great transportation, but at least it will lessen the odds of Zara and her nephew getting attacked. War's army doesn't tend to target mounted men and women.

A block away, I see a horse tethered to a lamppost. I jog down the street towards it. It's definitely some soldier's ride, judging by the weapons and kitsch shoved into its saddle bags—the items clearly lifted from some poor soul's house.

Too bad for that soldier, his stolen goods are about to get stolen from him.

As soon as I get to the horse, I begin to untie the creature's reins.

"Hey!" a man shouts from above me.

Three stories up a soldier leans out the window. Apparently, this is the horse's rider, busy pillaging another house.

"What the fuck are you doing?" he yells at me.

Ignoring him, I finish untying the reins and haul myself onto the steed.

There's something undeniably satisfying about stealing from a thief.

Tapping the horse's sides, I take off, smiling at the string of colorful curses the soldier shouts at my back.

It takes barely any time at all to ride back to Zara and her nephew.

I swing off the horse, dust billowing in my wake. "Alright, you get on first, then I'll lift your nephew—"

"Mamoon," she interjects. She gives me a small smile. "His name is Mamoon."

"—I'll lift Mamoon to you."

She hesitates, not wanting to be away from him for even a moment. But eventually she stands, lifting her exhausted nephew in her arms. She hands him to me, then pulls herself onto the steed.

I look down at the toddler in my arms, and my heart swells.

He's alive when he might've died. War spared him.

War spared him.

Zara reaches out and I lift her nephew up and into her arms. Together the two of us settle him onto the saddle in front of Zara.

The moment Mamoon realizes he's on a horse, he begins to cry. It's not the burning houses or the screaming people, or even my weapons that ends up terrifying him. It's the horse.

"Sssh. Mamoon," my friend says. "Zaza's got you."

"Hey!" That same male voice from earlier shouts. I glance over, and I see the soldier stalking towards us.

I turn back to Zara. "Time to go."

Zara glances over at the man.

"Will you be—?"

"I'll be fine." I'm already sliding my bow off my shoulder. "Go. I'll see you later."

Zara nods and gives the horse a swift tap to its sides, and her mount takes off.

"*Hey!*" the man says again. "That was my *horse!*"

"Get another one," I say, turning to him as I pull an arrow from my quiver.

"I'm not going to fucking get another one," he says, storming towards me, a sword on his hand. "You're going to get my horse back, or you're going to regret it."

I nock the arrow and aim it at his chest. "Come any closer, and I will shoot."

The soldier doesn't so much as falter.

I release the arrow, and he sidesteps it. I aim and fire another and another—both he evades without even looking concerned.

"Is that the best you fucking got?" he shouts.

It's about then that I notice the red sash around his arm.

A phobos rider.

"I don't care how much the warlord likes your pussy; I'm going to carve you from limb to limb and leave you to rot."

And he knows who I am—along with how to threaten the crap out of someone.

I grab two arrows and nock them at the same time, training them on the rider. I have only ever practiced this and always with shit results, but if I don't hit the man soon, I'll be forced to draw my blade, and against his sword ... he will have the upper hand.

I pull back hard on the bowstring and release the two arrows. Both miss, one veering wildly off. But the shot distracts the rider, and the next arrow I release ... that one hits the man square in the chest.

The phobos rider staggers, glancing down at his pierced flesh, his eyes wide.

Before he can do much else, I fire off two more arrows, one which hits him directly in the heart. The rider's body recoils at the impact. Now his eyes aren't wide so much as they're unfocused.

He stumbles forward, then falls to his knees.

I'm just lowering my bow when I feel the tip of the sword at my back.

"The only reason you are not dead, girl," says the voice behind me, "is because I want our warlord to know your crimes."

Well, shit.

Chapter 32

BACK AT CAMP, under the rays of the setting sun, the soldiers line the traitors up.

I'm one of them.

The new captives have already sworn their allegiance—or they're dead. Now it's our turn for judgment.

I'm shoved forward, towards the clearing, my hands bound. People are yelling at me, putting their hands on me; their hate is a palpable thing. They do this to every traitor, and yet I'm singled out amongst the crowd, undoubtedly because by now everyone knows of my relationship with War.

The horseman sits in his throne at the head of the clearing. I'd almost forgotten about that throne. He's a different person up there, different from how he is on the battlefield—bloodthirsty and calculating—and different from how he usually is with me—gentle and kind. Sitting on that throne, still clad in his bloody regalia, he's haughty and aloof. Although, today, I'll admit he does look more agitated than usual.

As I walk into the clearing, I keep my chin held high, despite the fact that the ground is soaked in fresh blood and the bodies of the newly dead prisoners are lying in a pile off to the side.

The crowd is screaming and spitting and raging, raging, raging. More than one person is literally throwing horse manure at us.

Dear God, is this really what you intended? To make men into demons and let hell reign on earth?

The line of us are forced to face War.

He looks the lot of us over, his bored gaze moving from traitor to traitor until his eyes land on me. For an instant, there's a spark of relief. Then his face hardens.

I'm not positive, but I get the impression that none of his riders told him my whereabouts. I guess they wanted to take a more dramatic, more public approach to the entire thing.

War stands, and the crowd goes quiet. I don't know what he's thinking, what's going on behind those turbulent eyes of his. It's probably regret that for a second time today, I'm undermining all his carefully laid plans.

"*Miriam.*" His voice ripples across the camp, and no one is immune to it.

People pause in their dung-throwing so they can stare at the horseman, then me.

His gaze drops to my throat, then my bound hands. When he looks at me again, there's an edge to his eyes.

"Release her." He doesn't attempt to speak in tongues.

"My Lord," one of the phobos riders objects, stepping away from the other riders. "She killed one of your riders."

I don't recognize the man speaking, but I do know he isn't the soldier who captured me today. That ended up being Uzair, the same phobos rider who also caught me loitering outside War's tent when the horseman was discussing battle strategies with his men. Right now, Uzair stands with the other riders, his jaw hard.

"Why are you keeping her around?" demands this new phobos rider, stepping into the clearing.

War looks bored as he stares down at his man.

Several soldiers are approaching me, presumably on War's order to release me, but their expressions are hard. It's clear they believe I should die today.

They come up to my side and take me by my upper arms, leading me away from the lineup.

"She kills our men, sabotages your plans, and yet you spare her? *Her?*" the phobos rider says, incensed. "Never have you made exceptions before. Why now, and for what? A whore?"

War's eyes narrow.

"*Kikle vležŏš di je rizvoroš maeto vlegeve ika no ja rizberiš Vlegi?*" the horseman says, now reverting to one of his dead languages.

How could you understand my motives if you don't understand God?

"Has she made your mind weak, horseman?" At this point, the phobos rider just seems to be openly baiting War, which is never a good idea when dealing with a dude who happens to relish bloodshed.

The horseman takes an ominous step forward, and the crowd ripples with unease. He takes another and another, descending down his dais and entering the clearing.

He strides over to the man until he looms over his rider.

It happens so fast I barely have time to register. War pulls out a dagger from his hip and shoves it through the soldier's heart. The rider's lips part, and his eyes are just as wide as the phobos rider I killed earlier, like death comes as a surprise to him.

War withdraws his blade, and blood cascades out of the open wound.

The phobos rider chokes a little, his gaze swinging around at all the quiet people. He sways for a moment, then falls to the ground, dead.

THE PHOBOS RIDER'S blood hasn't cooled before War muscles

his way between the soldiers and scoops me up.

He's quiet as he carries me back to his tent. I don't bother telling him I can walk. I'm not too interested in opposing him right now, when he's defied his own conventions twice in one day for me.

Behind us, the crowd is quiet, but once we're well out of eyesight, I hear the noise ratchet up again, and then, all at once, the crowd seems to roar—undoubtedly as a result of the rest of the traitors' executions.

I close my eyes against the thought of all those people I stood with minutes ago. They dared to stop the army, and they died for it.

The horseman carries me into his tent. It's only once we're inside that he sets me down.

He pulls out one of his blades and saws through my bindings, freeing my wrists before tossing aside the thick rope.

"War—" I begin.

"*Don't.*"

One look at his expression, and it's clear he isn't fucking around.

Agitatedly he begins to remove the rest of his weapons.

"God didn't send me a wife," he says under his breath. "He sent me my reckoning."

I stand there, rubbing my wrists, unsure where my feelings lie. On the one hand, I saw so much gruesome death today—and this man is responsible for it all. On the other hand, he saved a child, then spared me. I'm disgusted by his world, but I'm also strangely indebted to him.

"You shouldn't be attacking my army," he says roughly.

"Why not?"

"*Because I said so!*" he bellows. War turns on me now, his face enflamed in anger. "I saved a life for you—I went against my very nature to do so—and you thank me by *killing* my men in return?"

"That man was going to kill me!"

His face sharpens. "Don't lie and pretend it was just one man who you killed."

"Why does it suddenly matter?" I say, my own voice heating. "You gave me the bow and arrow knowing full well what I intended to do with it."

"You've created dissention in my ranks," he says.

I undoubtedly have. And people will hate us both for it.

"There's already dissention in your ranks, or have you forgotten that you destroyed all these people's cities and killed their families before you took them prisoner?"

A muscle in his jaw jumps.

War steps up to me, coming in so close our chests touch. "I have been lenient with you. I won't make that mistake again."

My heart drops at that. It was his leniency that spared Mamoon. That's the one part of him I *don't* want changing.

He begins to brush past me when I catch his arm.

The horseman pauses, glancing at me. His eyes are still furious.

"Thank you," I say. "For saving the boy."

War leans away, looking a little disgusted, like I've managed to offend his delicate sensibilities.

I grip his arm a little tighter. "Seriously. You cannot know what that means to me." He spared a stranger's life. It's almost inconsequential next to the heaps of people he killed, but he's never saved someone outside of his own self-interest. Not until today.

War searches my eyes, maybe looking for validation that he did something right, even though to him it felt wrong.

My throat bobs, and I realize that there are things I am going to have to do if I want War to ever consider saving another life.

I move my hand from his arm to the back of his neck, and I draw him down towards me. When he is within reach, I lift myself on my tiptoes and I kiss away any last regrets he may harbor.

He doesn't fall into it—not right away. But once he does give himself over to the kiss, he gives himself wholly. His hands are suddenly in my hair and his pent up anger is turning itself into passion.

There is nothing so satisfying as a fight followed by a fuck, he'd said.

Show him how grateful you are for the lives spared today. Maybe then War will again consider being lenient in the future.

Heart pounding fast, I begin to touch the horseman's body. He's still wearing armor, bloodied, dirty armor. I begin to pull at it.

"Take this off," I command.

"First you get me to break my rules, now you give me commands?" He says this even as he begins to undress us both. "You're playing a delicate, dangerous game."

"Aren't dangerous games your favorite?" I say.

War reels me in close. "Savage woman, *I don't play games.*" With that he rips away the last of my clothes.

We're still bloody from battle, but that doesn't stop the two of us from coming together. I pull him down to the carpet-covered floor, his large body engulfing me.

I take one of his hands, threading it between mine. The markings on his knuckles glow, and I kiss them one by one. These hands have caused so much death, but now they've saved me and another.

Perhaps one day these hands will stop the killing altogether. It's insane to wish for something so farfetched, but I'm addicted to the possibility. It's all the hope I have left.

War's cock is hot and hard against me, and I can sense that battle hungry buzz still burning through his system. He's practically shaking with the need to bury himself in me.

The idea of having sex with the horseman is utterly terrifying and completely exhilarating. I shift beneath him, until the head of his cock is pressed against my entrance.

For an instant, War's hips press forward, and oh my God

this is going to happen. But then he groans and pulls away from me, his entire body trembling with his restraint. "Heavenly creature, you were created to tempt me." War is breathing heavily. "But you haven't surrendered. Not yet. I'll have you wholly only then."

The horseman reaches out, cupping my pussy. Very deliberately, he dips a finger in. "But for now, this will do."

Chapter 33

WHILE THE REST of the camp—War included—is at the revelries later that evening, I head over to Zara's tent, food in hand. It's become our thing, bringing each other food when we've had a rough day.

I enter the tent without knocking. Inside, Mamoon is asleep on Zara's pallet, and my friend sits next to him, stroking his hair.

She jolts when I enter, her hand reaching for her dagger. She relaxes when she sees me.

"Sorry, I should've announced myself," I say.

In response, she pulls me to her and gives me a tight hug. She doesn't let go after several seconds, and pretty soon I hear her muffled sobs as she cries into my shoulder. Today was an awful day for her. She lost her sister and her brother-in-law, and she nearly lost her nephew.

I rub her back and hold her, letting her spill out all of her grief. It goes on for a long time, and her sobs are mostly silent, probably due to the fact that she's trying to let Mamoon sleep.

"What do I tell him?" she whispers.

I shake my head against her. "I don't know." This is such

an unnatural situation. There are no easy words for it.

Eventually, her sobs become sniffles, and then she pulls away, wiping at her eyes.

"How's he doing?" I ask.

"Okay," she says, her voice shaky. "I mean, he's traumatized, but he's *alive*." Her voice breaks a little over the word. "That's more than I can say about—"

About the rest of her family.

"What happened to them?"

Zara gathers her legs to her chest. "War's riders got to them first. They weren't even in their home when I got there. I think they'd tried to flee—I found their bodies lying in the street ..."

Mamoon stirs, and Zara lets the story trail away.

"What does he know?" I ask, nodding to her nephew.

Her features crumble and she shakes her head. "I'm not sure. He hasn't spoken much."

"At least he has you—and you have him."

Zara takes a deep, shuddering breath and nods.

She wipes her eyes again and looks me over. "How are you?" she asks, pulling herself together. Alarm rushes into her eyes. "Oh my God, this *afternoon*," she says, like she's realizing what happened for the first time. "You did so much for my nephew, and then you were caught for it—I'm so sorry." She begins to cry again, and I catch her hand.

"Hey, hey—*hey*," I say. "I got myself into that mess. Not you. Don't be sorry for it. Besides, War won't let me die, so ..." So I get to be the little asshole that wrecks his plans. Kind of. I then have to make up for it in sexual favors that I enjoy more than I should.

"I don't want you to suffer for my situation," Zara says.

Suffer might not be the word I'd use ...

"I'm not," I assure her.

"Be careful with the horseman," she says to me. "What he did today ... he's more than just enamored with you."

I swallow a little. I assumed War liked me solely because he believed his god made me for him. To think that there might actually be real feelings ...

No, Zara must be mistaken. War feels passion and possession towards me but nothing more.

Absolutely nothing more.

"THE WARLORD WANTS to see you," Hussain calls out from the other side of my tent late that same night.

By then I've long since returned from seeing Zara and her nephew. I've even managed to finish making two arrows.

I set the book I'm reading aside, blow out my oil lamp, and leave the tent, following the phobos rider towards War's quarters.

Out of nowhere Hussain says, "You better watch your back, Miriam."

I glance at him sharply. Is he *threatening* me?

He meets my gaze, then sighs. "The men have been talking about you, and they haven't been saying anything good."

It's not a threat, I realize, it's insider information he's passing along.

"Listen, Miriam, just ... be on your guard," he continues. "War doesn't pick his phobos riders for their honor."

Meaning that I'm a marked woman. My arms break out in goosebumps at that.

The two of us arrive at War's tent. Hussain bows his head, then backs away into the darkness, leaving me alone.

I take a breath and force myself to set aside that worry for another time. I have more immediate matters to deal with. I pull back the flaps of the horseman's tent and step inside.

Only ... the horseman is nowhere to be seen.

Panic.

This was a setup. Whatever Hussain was alluding to, it's not going to happen at some point in the future; it's about to happen *right now*.

I pull my dagger from its sheath just as the tent flaps are pulled back.

War walks in bare-chested and he's drunk. Very drunk.

"Wife." His eyes alight when he sees me. He crosses the room, wholly ignoring the dagger in my hand. Sweeping my hair back from my ears, he takes my face in his hands.

His eyes are bleary. "Lay with me."

For a moment, I don't breathe. I don't move at all, even though those three words have pulled all sorts of inappropriate responses from my body.

A minute ago I was sure I was about to be ambushed; instead I'm getting propositioned. By a drunken horseman.

"I thought you wanted me to surrender first," I say.

"I changed my mind." His thumbs stroke my cheeks, and it's so damn tempting. So, so tempting.

He must see how weak I am because he leans in and kisses me ferociously. The second he does, I taste the spirits on his tongue.

I pull away. "How much *did* you drink?" I ask him suspiciously. War's a big man; he'd likely need to drink an entire trough of alcohol to get to this point.

"Enough to cast aside my reservations."

Lay with me.

I lean my forehead against his shoulder as a thought comes to me. "Even if I wanted to—

"You want to," he says, his voice sure.

My stomach clenches at his voice. It's low and certain, and he sounds like a lover—like *my* lover.

"What about protection?" I say. Something I distinctly *haven't* thought about until now, though I definitely should've.

He pulls my face away from his shoulder, his bleary eyes sharpening.

"Protection?" he says. "From *what*? I am the embodiment of war. Whoever attempts to cross me will find themselves dead."

I want to laugh. I want to melt into the floor.

"Not *that* sort of protection," I say.

Oh boy. I didn't expect to have this conversation today.

The horseman's eyebrows pull together.

"I could get pregnant," I say slowly.

I can't tell by his expression whether or not he's following.

Maybe I've gotten this all wrong. Maybe War can't have kids. I mean, he's no ordinary human.

I take one look at his muscle-packed body. I'll be damned if I've ever seen a more virile man. I feel like one long look from him could knock me up.

My next question just spills out of me.

"Have you ever gotten a woman pregnant?"

Those glowing tattoos shine from the darkness. The horseman stares at me, looking like he's poised to strike. In fact, the longer I stare, the more menacing he appears.

"Why would you ask such a question?" he says.

Curiosity mostly.

"Have you?" I press.

Whatever state of inebriation War was in when he entered his tent, it's gone.

"What do you think, Miriam?" Those violent eyes are locked on mine, and he sounds particularly dangerous. "Do you think I impregnated a woman while I moved across your land? Do you think I then killed my child, along with its mother?

"Or do you believe that they are both here somewhere in camp, hidden from view?"

I don't know. I wouldn't put any of it past him, despite the fact that he sounds offended. So offended, in fact, that I'm now pretty sure that despite the sex fest he's had since coming to earth, he has no children.

That thought should relieve me. Instead, the whole conversation is reminding me of all the reasons why sleeping with War is a bad idea. Fooling around with him is only fun when I don't have to think too much about it.

"Coming here was a mistake," I say. I begin to walk past him, towards the exit.

He catches my arm and spins me to face him. "This was *not* a mistake."

"Sleep it off, War," I say. "You'll feel better once you do."

"So you're fleeing then?" he accuses.

"Isn't that what all us humans do?" I ask.

"Not you, savage woman," he says, his expression dark and cunning as he grips my arm. "You fight even when it's unwise to do so."

"What *would* you do, if you got a woman pregnant?" I ask.

War just stares at me.

He has absolutely no idea, and that is terrifying in its own right.

"Goodnight, War," I say.

I jerk my arm from his hold, and I leave his tent.

I DON'T SEE War again until the next day. By the time he comes to me, he's already returned from raiding all the satellite communities around Arish. From what I've seen of Egypt so far, there aren't many of these. Out here, there's desert and ocean and sky and nothing else.

"Did you have a hangover?" I ask him. I sit outside my tent, busy fitting a glass arrowhead to a finished wooden shaft.

"A hangover?" He smiles a bit. "There was a brief flash of pain and some fleeting nausea, but I wouldn't call that a hangover."

Part of me is belatedly surprised that he knows what a hangover is, but he's lived among soldiers for a year now. He was bound to learn about them eventually.

"Do you remember our talk?" I ask him. "From last night?"

His face changes, but I can't say exactly what his expression is. Brooding? Curious? Right now it's impossible to tell.

"Every last bit."

Awesome.

He takes my hand. "Come, I want to have you alone to myself."

I take his hand, even as my eyebrows furrow. "Where are we going?"

He whistles. "You'll see."

A minute later, Deimos comes galloping towards us, his deep red coat shining in the sun. He still has his saddle and bridle on from the morning raid.

The horse comes to a stop next to us.

"How do you get him to do that?" I ask. He doesn't need to be stabled, and he comes at his master's call. I haven't met that many horses, but I don't think this is normal.

War leans towards me. "He is no more a horse than I am a man."

Point taken.

The horseman gestures for me to mount Deimos. For a moment, I hesitate, not sure that I want to spend more time with War than is absolutely necessary. But in the end, I get on.

War swings into the saddle behind me, so close his thighs encase mine, and his chest presses against my back. This isn't the first time I've shared a saddle with the horseman, but it is the first time I've *noticed* him.

His hair tickles against the skin of my neck, and I can feel his breath against my cheek. An arm comes around my waist, pressing me deeper into him, and I should not be so affected by this.

I mean, for fuck's sake, I've had the man's dick in my mouth.

"Stay with me in my tent," War says against me, his breath fanning across my ear.

"What will be left of me if I do?" I don't mean to say it out loud, but the words come out anyway.

"Wife, I'm not going to eat you if you move in—well, I *will* eat you, but I know you enjoy that sort of thing."

I feel my cheeks heat, remembering the feel of his mouth between my thighs.

I half turn my head to him. "Can you not say stuff like that?"

War's hand tightens against my stomach. "Stay with me, Miriam."

"No—unless you want to make another trade."

The horseman is quiet. "You do realize I could simply *make* you stay with me."

So he's threatened before.

"Then do it," I say, knowing he won't.

It must be odd for him, a man of action, to make empty threats. He's never had to before me. When you want the world dead, it's easy to make real threats—or, more War's style, simply kill without ever threatening someone at all.

"You will fall to me, wife, just as everyone and everything else has."

That is exactly what I'm afraid of.

THE HORSEMAN STEERS us south, into the desert. There's nothing out here except rolling expanses of dry earth. It's beautiful in a very austere sort of way.

We've only ridden for maybe five or ten minutes when War stops his horse.

"Where are we?" I ask, glancing around as I hop off Deimos.

"I don't exactly know," he says, dismounting, his kohl-lined gaze squinting at the sun.

I glance around. "So there's no particular reason why you brought me here?" I ask.

"Oh, there's a reason," he says, "it just has nothing to do with our surroundings."

I've taken a few steps away from him, but now I glance

back. "What's the reason?" I ask.

"I want to hear what you sound like when no one but me is listening."

Chapter 34

WHEN IT COMES to intimacy, War gives more than he takes. Which is a lot. It's *all* a lot. He has the appetite of a deity, and I can barely keep up on either end.

He's making me *work* for those aviaries.

I lay on a blanket with him, our clothes cast aside.

"I like it when you're like this," he says, trailing a finger over my bare abdomen.

I glance over at him. "I bet you do."

"Not just in *that* way, wife," he says, giving a low laugh. "You are more open with me in these moments."

I am? Alarm bells are going off.

"And you like that?" I say.

"Of course I do."

I study the horseman's face. "Why?"

His gaze searches mine. The gold in his eyes glitters in the light.

He's more than just enamored with you. Zara's words ring in my ears.

Before War says anything, something moves in the distance, causing me to jolt in surprise. My entire body is exposed. I desperately gather my clothes to me, trying to cover myself.

"What is it?" War says, his voice sharp. His gaze follows mine.

It's a person, one I've now doomed to death.

But when the horseman sees him, the tension in his body eases. "Relax, wife. He's one of mine."

"One of yours?" Does he mean one of his soldiers? Because I really wouldn't want one of them seeing me naked.

"The re-animated dead," War explains.

The hairs on my arm stand up. I'd almost forgotten about that ghoulish ability of his.

I take the distant figure in again. "What is it doing out here?"

"Miriam, my undead linger everywhere I am or have been. They patrol every piece of earth I've touched."

I figured as much after encountering his zombies back in Ashdod.

"How long do they patrol a city?"

"Forever. Once I've claimed a territory, I do not give it up."

Chills.

Every single place that War has been, his undead are there still, never sleeping, never ceasing, but always, always hunting.

Tucking a strand of hair behind my ear, I scoot away from the horseman, an action he notices. I keep letting myself forget about War's true nature.

"You have seen me kill many times, Miriam, and yet this bothers you?"

"Of *course* it bothers me," I say. "It makes me not want to touch you."

War's face ... that violence is back in his eyes, but for a single instant—a single, brief instant—I see his hurt.

It's almost preposterous to think a force of nature like War is even *capable* of feeling hurt. But maybe I'm not the only one who gets vulnerable when you strip them down.

"But you *will* keep touching me," he says. "So long as you want your aviaries to remain intact, you will—and I don't need to remind you how easily I can undo all of the progress you've bought your kind."

"Bought," I repeat. Now it's me who feels hurt—hurt and used and dirty. Forget that this situation was my idea, or that that's exactly what I did—I bought my fellow humans the barest possibility of survival—it still burns me raw to hear War talk about it like it's some cold, emotionless transaction.

I get up, completely naked, not really giving a fuck what War sees. "I'm glad we both know that's all this is." I begin to pull on my clothes. "I would hate for you to get the impression that I actually want you."

"Oh, you want me." The horseman sounds almost smug.

I shove my feet back into my pants. "Fuck. You."

"Not until you surrender everything."

Done, done, *done* with this. I finish getting dressed and begin to walk away.

"You will be riding back with me," War commands from behind me.

I give him the finger in response.

I've barely walked twenty meters when I see movement out of the corner of my eye. I turn just in time to see the zombie from earlier loping towards me.

I manage not to scream, but I'm not going to lie, I pee myself a little at the sight of the creature sprinting towards me.

Behind me, War stands on our blanket, pulling his pants back on as he watches the scene.

"What are you doing?" I yell at War, never fully managing to rip my eyes from the zombie.

The dead man—pretty sure it's a man at least—is hurtling towards me.

Fuck it—I begin to run.

I make it half a kilometer before the creature tackles me.

The two of us go tumbling into the sandy earth.

Dear God, the smell. Like someone is raping my nostrils. I gag a little on it. And now when I do see the creature, I really do scream. This one isn't as freshly dead as the men I fought a city ago. His skin is a greyish hue and it's rotting away in areas, revealing his decomposing innards.

The zombie drags me to my feet just as the horseman rides over on Deimos.

He stops at my side, reaching out a hand. "Come, Miriam."

I glare up at War. "*No.*"

"Then my man will be forced to escort you home."

I think I have bits of that decomposing man in my hair. I definitely have them smeared across my shirt and pants.

Going to have to burn these clothes. Damnit.

"At least he'll be better company," I say.

War frowns at me, looking frustrated and bothered all at the same time. "So be it. Enjoy the walk, wife."

And then he rides off.

Bastard.

It takes nearly an hour to make it back to camp, and the entire way the dead man has a grip on my upper arm. The stench of him is too much, and I vomit four separate times. Eventually I simply plug my nose and breathe in and out of my mouth.

In spite of this, I don't regret my decision to walk back. Not even a little.

Right now the dead man is still better company than War.

I DON'T SEE the horseman again for days. He doesn't call on me, and I stay the hell away from his tent, spending my time reading, making weapons, and visiting with Zara and her frightened nephew.

So I'm surprised when, on the day we pack up camp, I'm given a horse and instructed to wait for War.

I almost don't.

I'm no longer upset about the revelation that War's dead haunt all the fallen cities of the world. It's terrible and shocking and it makes the horseman even more barbaric than I already imagined him to be, but it is what it is, and now I know.

I'm not even upset about the nauseating walk back to camp—though I had been for a while after I returned.

At this point I'm just pissed off because I've *been* pissed off, and I don't know, the emotion has developed some inertia of its own.

But then War comes riding through camp, looking like a red sun rising on the horizon, and I feel eager to see him—eager to be angry with him, eager to hear his deep voice and to gaze at that face. And maybe to even touch him. I may not like the guy, but I think I'm addicted to him.

The horseman stops when he gets to my side. He stares at me for several seconds.

"Wife," he says. I cannot tell what he's thinking.

"War."

He gives me a slight nod and takes off again. I follow him to the front of the procession, feeling the eyes of the entire army on us. And then they're behind us and it's just me and War and the endless road ahead of us.

The horseman is the first one to speak.

"If we're to be married, we have to get along."

"We're *not* married," I say for the five billionth time.

"We are."

Exasperating man!

"You had a dead man tackle me!" Okay, maybe I am still a little ticked about my walk back to camp. I have a fucking right to be. I smelled like a corpse for two entire *days*.

"You wouldn't listen," he says.

"No, it was *you* who wouldn't listen!" I say, my voice rising. Oh yeah, I am so ready to jump back into the arena and fight this man. "You're so used to commanding people that you think you can command me too."

"Of course I can."

I'd throttle War if I could get away with it.

"That's *not* how marriage works," I say, trying to simmer my emotions back down. "At least, not a good marriage—and you want this to be a good marriage, don't you?"

Why am I even trying to reason with him?

He gives me a long look. "Of course I do, wife."

"Then you need to *listen to me* and you need to *respect my opinions*." It's the two most obvious rules of marriage, and yet War is completely unaware of them.

"And you need to respect my will," he fires back. "As my wife, you should be obedient the few times I demand it of you."

Obedient?

I'm seeing red.

"Fuck it. I want a divorce."

"No."

"I'm not going to be obedient—hell, you don't even *want* me to be obedient. I know you don't." He's clearly been around too many misogynists.

War runs a hand down his face, one of the rings he wears catching the light. "Feel like I'm being beaten with my own blade," he mutters. "Fine. I will try to be more ... *respectful*. To your *opinions* ... even when they are absurd."

I glare at him.

"And I will listen to your soft mortal wants. But in exchange, you must listen to *my* will when I give it."

"I will listen to it," I say.

I just might not go along with it.

"Good." He looks pleased.

I just give him a look.

This is going to be a long ride.

I'VE ABANDONED MY rules. The ones for surviving the

apocalypse. I don't know when it happened—whether I left them back in Ashdod, or if they traveled all the way to Arish before I forsook them.

I only know that each one no longer applies to surviving the apocalypse now that I'm stuck with one of the horsemen orchestrating it.

The only rule I still fall back on is Rule Five: Be brave. Every single waking second of my day consists of me trying to be brave when all I really want to do is shit myself and hide.

Unfortunately, out here in the barren desert, there's nowhere to hide.

It's a long, lonely ride. The road we take is surrounded by uninterrupted desert. And even though I know that the ocean lingers off to my right, the highway is inland enough that I don't usually catch glimpses of that blue water.

The summer sun cruelly beats down on the two of us, and for all the time we've been riding, we might've gone two kilometers ... or two hundred. It's impossible to say.

The only real way I can tell we're making progress is by the few landmarks we pass—an abandoned house, a barren outpost, a trough of water next to a hand-pump well. Oh, and of course, the few fishing villages we pass by, a cluster of carrion birds circling above them.

Eventually, the sun dips down ahead of us, and War chooses a place for us and our horses to rest.

After the two of us get a fire going, I begin to fry up dinner. This trip, War's packed a skillet and some salted meat to cook. I stare at the strips of meat after I lay them out. The sight of them twists my stomach. It looks too much like all those humans whose bodies were ripped open during battle.

Next to me, the horseman sits on his haunches, staring at the fire.

"Why do you have an army if you could simply use your dead to kill off humans?" I ask him while I work.

It seems to me that, with the sweep of his hand, War could

annihilate us all, and it would be a whole lot faster and more thorough.

"Why don't you sing all the time if you have the ability to?" he responds, his eyes flashing. "Why not run everywhere if you can? Just because I have the power doesn't mean I always *want* to wield it."

So he doesn't want to kill us off that efficiently? I don't know whether that's merciful of him or just cruel.

"Besides," he says, "I rather enjoy camp. It reminds me of who I am and who I have always been."

Battle brought to life, he means.

"That's a bit odd, don't you think?" I say. "You want to remember who you are by gathering humans around you and enjoying their company."

"No, I don't think it's odd at all," War says, getting up to grab a bottle of wine he's packed. He comes back with it and two glasses. Sitting back down, he says, "I am borne of men, and I am here to judge them. Naturally I want to be amongst them."

"So there's a part of you that likes humans," I say.

"Of course I like humans." War uncorks the wine and begins to pour us each a glass. "Just not enough to spare them."

That is so twisted.

He hands me one of the glasses, and I take a deep drink from it.

"I am a commander of men," he continues. "Not even death can stop my reach."

Not even death can stop my reach.

War is right. Even in death he can weaponize us. I remember the revenant who led me back to camp. His eyes were mostly gone, his skin was mottled and sloughing off, and yet he moved as though he were alive.

"How do you control the dead?" I say.

The horseman levels his gaze at me. "We are talking about

the powers of God, Miriam. There is no human explanation I can give you."

"Could you do it, right now, if you wanted to?"

War raises his eyebrows. "You want me to raise the dead?"

That's not exactly what I asked, and yet now that he's broached the subject, I'm perversely curious. I don't know why. It's ghoulish and frightening.

I nod anyway.

The horseman reaches out, and I feel the ground around me shiver, like it's ticklish. Several meters away the arid earth shifts, and the partial skeleton of a horse pulls itself from the sandy soil. The creature is missing many of its bones, but it stands as best it can.

It's hard to say that this is anything other than magic.

The skeletal horse begins to move as though it were alive, even though it looks long dead.

"It's ... not human," I say.

"I can re-animate both people and creatures."

The horse ambles up to me, and instinct is telling me to get up and flee. But damnit, I've faced worse. So I sit there and let it get close.

The horse bumps its muzzle against my shoulder, and part of me is disarmed by this poor thing that moves like a horse and acts like a horse even though it's long since breathed its last.

"Are you satisfied?" War asks.

I nod, maybe a little too quickly.

The horse takes several steps away from me, then all at once, it falls to the earth, nothing more than a scattered pile of bones.

Chapter 35

THE NIGHT SWEEPS in and the fire burns itself down. Just when the evening air is starting to get a chill to it, the horseman gets up from the fire. I can hear him at my back, removing his weaponry. I still hold my empty glass, and all that wine in my stomach is churning.

This is the first time I've traveled with the horseman since our agreement, and out here, without an army around us, my universe feels very small. It's only big enough to hold me, War, and this uncomfortable feeling that rises in me every time we're together.

The horseman comes back to me and reaches out a hand. "Come, wife. It's late and I want to feel your warm flesh against mine."

That same uncomfortable feeling rises in me. Right now it's giddiness and a thrill that comes with giving in to the horseman. We're either all or nothing, enemies or lovers. It's dizzying. Our bodies get along much better than our mouths.

I take War's hand and let him lead me to the pallet he made us. There's just one bed tonight. My abs clench at the sight.

The horseman reels me in close, his hands going to my dark hair as he leans in and kisses me. And the kiss is all it takes to break me wide open.

I've shored up all my desire for him during the long day, but now I gasp as his heavy hand moves down my neck and along my collar bone. My own hands find his abs, and God was *clearly* biased when he made this man because War is perfect. Every hard ridge, every sloping muscle and lean edge— perfect, perfect, perfect.

As he strips me down, I try not to think about the fact that I'm so very obviously *not* perfect. I have scars from that long ago accident, I have scars from all the skirmishes I've fought in since, and I have scars from all the nicks and cuts I've given myself for my job. And then there are all the imperfections that I was simply born with.

I'm crudely fashioned compared to this horseman.

But as War lowers me down, removing the last of my clothing, his hands and lips move over me like I am perfect. The horseman slips between my thighs, and as I stare up at the stars, a stupid, awful tear slips out. Because I feel so cherished. So cherished and so goddamned *perfect.*

It shouldn't be this way. It *shouldn't.*

But it is.

AFTER THE TWO of us have exhausted ourselves, I lay with War on his pallet. Our pallet, I guess—if I'm being honest with myself.

I don't bother telling the horseman that this feels right. That his ridiculous body somehow fits mine like a puzzle piece.

War runs his fingers through my hair. "Tell me about yourself," he says.

"What do you want to know?" I ask, glancing over at him. I wish I could see his face in the darkness.

"What makes you love being a human? What are your

favorite things? I want to know it all."

"I like art," I say carefully, turning back to gaze at the sky. "I like repurposing junk into beautiful objects."

"You mean your weapons," he says.

I stretch myself out along his body. In response, War pulls me in close to him.

"That's just how I was able to make money off of my art," I say. "But yeah, my weapons are part of it."

"And why do you enjoy art?" War asks.

I lift a shoulder. "It's cathartic for me. I don't know."

"Tell me something else," War says.

"I miss the taste of my mother's Shakshuka," I admit. I never learned how to cook her exact version of the spicy breakfast dish. There are so many small, simple things like that, that I lost when I lost her.

"What else?"

"My sister Lia wanted to be a singer." I know War is asking me about myself, but this is who I am—a lonely girl carrying around the ghosts of her family. "I don't know where she even got her voice from," I continue. "The rest of us couldn't carry a tune, but she could. She used to sing when she couldn't fall asleep at night, and I used to hate it—we shared a room," I add. "But then at some point, it became soothing, and I'd often drift off to her songs."

That might've been the worst part of all of it when I came back. The silence. There were so many nights where I'd lay there, on my old mattress, my sister's bed across from mine, and I'd wait for the song that never came.

After a while, I started sleeping in her bed, like I could somehow suck out the marrow of her from her old sheets. It never worked. Not even when I then moved to my mother's bed to try to draw some small comfort there.

"Sometimes I carve music notes into my bows and arrows," I admit to War. "I don't even know what the notes stand for, or if they're even accurately drawn, but they remind me of

Lia."

The horseman runs an idle hand down my arm, and I'm reminded about how intimate this whole situation is.

"Do you carve anything else onto your weapons?" he asks.

I glance at him again. "Why do you want to know?" I ask.

"I want to know everything about you, wife," he says, just as he did earlier.

I take a deep breath. "I draw hamsas for my father." I can't even say how many weapons I've decorated with the image of an evil eye fitted into the palm of a hand.

"Why hamsas?" War asks.

Unconsciously, I reach for my bracelet, fingering the small metal charm as I focus back up at the sky.

"Hamsas are known among Jews as the 'Hand of Miriam,'" I explain. "Any time my father would see a piece of jewelry with a hamsa on it, he'd buy it for me—because it was my namesake." The hamsa I wear is the last bit of jewelry I have from him. Everything else I've lost over the last decade. I'm petrified of the day I'll lose this, too.

"And in honor of my mother," I continue, "I'd sometimes carve a sword—or sometimes a sword piercing a heart—into my bows. The sword is in honor of what I learned from her books on weaponry, and the heart ... well, that one's for self-explanatory reasons." My own heart aches now, revisiting all the reasons why I so fondly cherished my family and why I so desperately missed them.

The horseman is quiet. He doesn't do very well, I've come to find, with difficult emotions like grief and sadness.

"It's strange being a human," War finally says. "For the longest time, I watched what it was like to be a human, but I never felt it. I didn't understand the true bliss of touching a woman or tasting food or feeling the sun on my skin. I knew of it, but I didn't *understand* it until I became a man.

"There are things I *still* don't understand," he says, almost to himself.

War might not know it, but he's captivating when he talks like this, as though he has one foot in this world and one foot in another.

"What sorts of things?" I ask.

"Loss," he says. He's quiet for a moment. "It's one of the most common aspects of war, and yet I've never experienced it."

"You better hope you never do," I say, thinking of my family all over again.

Loss is a wound that never heals. Never never never. It scabs over, and for a time you can almost forget it's there, but then something—a smell, a sound, a memory—will split that wound right open, and you'll be reminded again that you're not whole. That you'll never fully *be* whole again.

"Tell me more about them," War says. "Your family."

My throat works. I don't know if I have it in me to keep talking about them. But then my lips part and the words come pouring out.

"My father was the wisest man I knew," I say. "But to be fair, I only knew him as a child, and when you're a kid, adults in general seem very wise." I search the sky, trying to remember more. "My dad was funny—really, really funny." I smile as I say it. "He could make you laugh, usually at your own expense. It was okay, though, because he made fun of himself all the time too. He was good at celebrating everyone's rough edges.

"And he was so ... *real*." There were many times when he'd talk to me as though I were an equal. "With some people, you can never get beneath the surface, you know?" I say, even though the horseman probably doesn't know. "With my father, you always could."

I try to hold onto his memory.

"I've forgotten his voice," I admit. "That's the most terrifying part of it all. I can't remember the way he sounded. I can remember things he's said, but not that."

It's quiet for several seconds. The horseman doesn't say anything, he just strokes my hair.

"My mother was quiet but strong. I learned that after my father died when she suddenly had to singlehandedly take care of me and my sister. Her love was a fierce thing."

I fall to silence.

"What happened to them?" War says.

I've already told him about how my father died. As for my mother and sister ...

"There was an accident."

The water rushes in—

I touch my throat. "That's where I got this scar." I can't bring myself to share the rest of the story.

War's hand stops stroking my hair. After a moment, his fingers move down the column of my throat. They pause when they get to the scar. His thumb smooths over the raised skin between my collarbones.

My own hand falls away from my throat, and I close my eyes against the feel of his fingertip.

"I'm sorry, wife," the horseman says. "Your misfortune is my gain."

My brows knit. That's such an odd thing to say.

"What do you mean?" I ask, opening my eyes.

War's lips brush my skin as he pulls me in close. "The day you received this scar is the day you became mine."

NOT ALL PLACES look like they've been touched by the apocalypse.

There are the remote villages like the one we enter two days later that the modern world clearly swept past. These are the places where farmers still herd their livestock through the streets and the dogs are wild and the buildings use the same mudbrick architecture they have for the last thousand years.

These towns seem to have hardly felt the hit of the apocalypse, and they weathered it much more gracefully than my city did.

War and I enter the fishing village, which is hardly more than a few streets perched next to the Mediterranean Sea. As we pass through, a couple men sit outside of their homes, sipping Turkish coffee and smoking hand-rolled cigarettes.

I stare at them in wonder. War and I pass through many towns, but almost all of them have already been visited by death.

Not this village. The people here are enjoying this day just as they would any other.

"What are you going to do with them?" I ask, my question punctuated by the *clop* of my horse's footfalls.

"What I always do, wife."

My stomach clenches at that. Riding next to War is suddenly, distinctly uncomfortable.

We're drawing eyes to us the farther into town we get. I realized who War was shortly after I first saw him; I wonder now, as people stare, whether they are having the same realization I once did.

Or it could simply be that these days, no one trusts strangers, particularly strangers with giant fucking swords strapped to their backs.

"You don't have to kill them, you know," I say under my breath. "You could just skip this place. Just for the hell of it."

"My wife and her soft heart," War says. It sounds like a genuine compliment. "Would you really like that? For me to spare these people?"

Is he being serious?

I take in his merciless features.

Yes, I think he might actually be.

"I would," I say, barely daring to believe it.

War stares at me for several seconds, and I hold his gaze, ignoring our growing audience.

Eventually he makes a sound at the back of his throat and focuses on the road again.

I don't know what to make of that.

My hands clench the reins. I'm so tense—so, so tense. I keep waiting for War to withdraw his sword, to tell me that it was all a clever trick, but he doesn't.

We pass through the village, then leave it behind us altogether. Only then do I fully release my breath. It's not until the village is entirely out of sight, however, that I speak.

"You didn't kill them," I say, disbelieving.

"No," War agrees. "I didn't. I have dead for that."

Beneath our feet, the ground quakes. It takes about a minute, but eventually I hear screams start up at our backs, and now I know exactly what's become of that village.

Chapter 36

THIS TIME, WHEN camp is established and the tents go up, mine is missing, along with the rest of my things.

I know who's behind this.

I storm into War's tent. "Where is it?" I demand.

The room is full of phobos riders, all of them pouring over yet another map of yet another town they're going to ravage. They glance over at me.

Uzair, the one who caught me killing his comrade in Arish, frowns at me while Hussain, the only phobos rider who has been kind to me, gives me an unreadable look.

But it's War's ominous form that manages to eclipse everyone else. Today he looks particularly savage, with his arm guards on and his chest bare, his crimson tattoos glowing from where they wrap around his pecs.

"Wife." The kohl lining his eyes is especially thick, and it makes him look very *other*.

"Where is my tent?" I demand.

"You're standing in it."

I narrow my gaze. "That is *not* what we agreed to."

"I do not negotiate with humans," War says.

My gaze sweeps across the room again, and I take in all the faces of War's riders. Suddenly I understand.

In Arish, I made the horsemen look weak among his men. Now he's reclaiming his authority—at my expense.

Right now nothing I say will derail him. That's obvious from his expression alone. Anything else I say now will only serve to make me look weak and whiny, and already these riders seem to have a pretty low opinion of me.

Giving War a final, lingering look, I turn to leave.

The horseman can make me live with him, but he can't force me to stick around during the day.

"Oh, Miriam," the horseman calls out to me just as I reach the tent flaps. "One last thing: tomorrow, when we head into battle, you will be riding with me."

THE NEXT MORNING I wake to the feel of War's mouth trailing kisses over my shoulder. The room is dimly lit by oil lamps. The two of us are naked, and I feel him hard against me.

His kisses move down my arm.

This is what I've feared about living with the horseman. How is a lonely girl like me supposed to fight this? It's everything I've craved, and the devil next to me knows it.

"Surrender," he whispers against my skin.

I stretch back against him. "You surrender."

He groans, a hand gripping my hip. For a moment, he grinds into me. I feel him lean his forehead against my back, his breathing heavy. "I'm going to be damn near distracted today, imagining you right here, against me."

Reluctantly, he gets up, and while I might hate who he is and the fact that he's forced me to live with him, right now, I'm most upset that he's left my side. How's that for having your heart and your head at war with one another?

I really need my own fucking tent back.

"Come, wife," War says. "It's time to prepare for battle."

The reminder sobers me up. More people are going to die today. First it was Jerusalem, then Ashdod, then Arish. Now, from the whispers in the air, it sounds like we're attacking Port Said. I scrub my face, not ready to face another day of carnage.

Across the tent, War pulls on his black pants, and then his black shirt. This outfit of War's is always the same, and it's always in pristine condition in the morning, regardless of how mangled and bloody it might be the day before.

I grab my own shirt and pants, which aren't nearly so clean, and I pull them on. I sit back down to lace up my boots, then I start donning my weaponry, starting with my bow and quiver.

"Why do you keep letting me ride into battle?" I ask him as I finish securing my quiver.

From his perspective, I can't see any reason to let me keep joining the fight.

The horseman glances over at me from where he's lacing up one of his leather greaves. "Why indeed?" he muses. "Would you prefer I chain you to our bed like the doting husband I am?"

"Only if you stayed with me," I say, not missing a beat. I'm being half serious. If I could keep War from battle ... but no, his army and his dead would just do the killing for him.

His eyes heat at that.

"You were made to tempt me, wife," he says.

The horseman finishes lacing one greave and moves to the other. "You told me we're to respect one another in a marriage."

I ... did. I'm surprised he remembers.

"You want to fight. This is me respecting your wishes."

This is War's version of respect? I almost laugh at the absurdity of it. He's forced me to sleep in his tent—I mean, fuck respect right there—but he's still going to allow me to fight in a battle that could get me killed because that's the husbandly thing to do?

To be honest, it sounds very much like horseman logic.

"Besides," War adds, unaware of my own thoughts, "you're killing humans."

"Not the ones you want dead," I argue, securing my dagger to my side.

"I want them *all* dead," he says. "You're making my job easier."

I stare at him for several seconds, and it's like a grenade explodes in my mind.

I'm helping his cause.

Every single person I kill is one less person living on earth.

All thoughts of respect dissolve away as an acute sort of devastation sinks in. I sway a little on my feet, and for a moment, I think I'm going to be sick.

I assumed I was actually doing something useful.

War finishes putting on his armor and comes towards me. Outside the tent I can hear a few muffled footsteps as soldiers quietly leave their homes, readying themselves for a day of fighting.

"Ready?" he asks.

I almost say no. I'm still reeling from that revelation. The last thing I want right now is to play into the horseman's hand by killing more people.

But then I remember those soldiers who liked to use raids as an opportunity to rape women or commit other atrocities. Someone still needs to keep them in line—War's words be damned.

I nod to the horseman, and together we leave the tent.

THIS TIME, RIDING with War doesn't feel comforting in the least. The horseman holds me close, but he feels remote. I have a horrible suspicion he's taking his mind to that place where he kills.

The city comes into existence in stages—first with a few

decrepit buildings, then several more, then rapidly the city fills itself out. Port Said butts right up against the Mediterranean Sea, every square kilometer of it tightly packed with building after building. At this early hour, the city is quiet, so terribly quiet.

My chest constricts. Only now am I beginning to realize what it truly means to be at the front of War's army. I've only seen battle once it's been raging for a time. I've never seen what ignites it. And now I'm having visions of War storming into homes and killing people right in their own beds.

"I need to get off," I whisper.

If anything, War's arm tightens on me.

"I need to get off," I say louder.

The horseman utterly ignores me, but when I start to struggle, his grip becomes unyielding. I might as well be pinned in by a steel band.

War makes a clicking noise with his tongue, and Deimos begins to speed up until we're hurtling forward at a gallop. My dark brown hair is whipping behind me, and the dagger holstered at my hip is bumping into my thigh over and over again.

"What are you doing—?" I've no sooner asked it then I start to see a couple figures come out of the darkness, weapons gripped in their hands as they stare at us. It takes a little longer to notice the uniforms in the darkness.

The Egyptian military.

One of them nocks an arrow into his bow, pointing it at us. "Stop and state your business," he orders. The other soldier beside him likewise raises his bow.

War reaches behind his back, and I hear the ominous zing as he pulls his sword from its scabbard.

"Don't, War," I say, staring at the men as they begin to shout. "Please don't."

He ignores me.

In the next instant, an arrow comes whizzing by my face, so

close I hear the hiss of it cutting through air.

All the while, War keeps galloping onward, heading straight towards the uniformed men. He leans to the side of his saddle, his enormous sword gripped in his hand. Another arrow whizzes by, this one hitting the horseman in the chest. I hiss in a breath.

And then War's upon the men. He swings his sword, cutting a soldier down like he was swatting away a fly. I swallow my scream, even as I feel a few droplets of blood hit me.

The other Egyptian soldier turns on his heel and runs, shouting at the top of his lungs, "The horseman is here! War is here!"

I struggle against the warlord all over again, trying to get away.

"Stop it, Miriam," he orders.

Um, *fuck that.*

"If I let you down now, the civilians will attack you—so might my riders if they don't recognize you."

That makes a certain amount of sense. I mean, when you're at the front of the army entering a town to raid, the only person you have to avoid killing is the horseman himself. Everyone else is fair game.

War runs down another soldier, cleaving his head from his shoulders.

He's not going to stop. He won't ever stop.

I start fighting him in earnest, even as the shouts carry down the city and more uniformed men come running in our direction.

"*Miriam.*"

"Let me *go.*"

He doesn't want to, I can feel it in his stubborn grip. Especially not now when people are starting to wander out of their houses and the Egyptian military unit is mobilizing.

"Damnit, Miriam." He sheaths his sword. "I cannot

protect you if you're fighting me."

I swivel around. "You can't protect me at all right now." As if to enunciate my point, another arrow whizzes by.

His eyes widen a little as he realizes probably for the first time that yeah, I might be right.

"You don't get both me and your precious battle," I say.

His jaw clenches, his eyes stormy.

Behind us, I hear an otherworldly sort of howling rise up.

I glance over War's shoulder in time to see his phobos riders storming into the city, whooping and howling like animals as they descend.

The horseman looks behind him, following my gaze, and I use the distraction to shove off him.

"Wife!" he shouts after me. I slip off of Deimos and dart away, weaving into the darkness.

I don't glance behind me, but I can hear the clatter of arrows and then the sound of War unsheathing his sword again.

"*Miriam!*"

Now people are beginning to leave their houses, and the screams are starting to catch on. The phobos riders thunder down the street, their howls becoming almost deafening, and I have to duck to avoid getting gouged by an axe-wielding rider.

"Miriam!" War's voice rings out again, but I don't dare tear my gaze away from the fighting to look at him.

Another phobos rider singles me out, breaking away from the group to hunt me down. Rapidly I grab an arrow and nock it. I release the string, letting the arrow fly. It misses the rider, but pierces the flesh of his mount. As I watch, the horse rears back, and the man falls off.

My hand itches to grab another arrow and finish the soldier off.

You're making my job easier.

I curse under my breath and run.

Chapter 37

FIND THE AVIARIES.

If I can get there, maybe I can at least do some good.

Around me, dozens of flaming arrows are arcing through the sky. I never thought cities like Jerusalem or this one could burn. There's nothing so obviously flammable about them. But now that this city is catching fire right before me, I notice that there are canvas awnings and lines of clothes and curtains and shrubbery and wooden carts and stalls and so many other flammable things that can catch fire. And as I run, they do.

People are beginning to swarm the streets as they try to escape. Children are crying—hell, grown men and women are crying—families are fleeing and it's all so, so hopeless.

I almost miss the aviary. The birds aren't making much noise and everything on the streets is drowning out whatever sounds they *are* making.

I rush inside, and nearly get beheaded by a middle-aged man with an axe.

I jerk back just in time to miss the blade, but only just.

"I'm not here to hurt you!" I say.

He grips his weapon tighter. "You look like it to me."

I hadn't thought through the fact that I might look like the enemy. "I want to send out a message."

The man brings his arm back, the axe blade gleaming. "I bet you do, you filthy liar. Get out of my building. *Now.*"

"War can raise the dead," I rush out. "Did you know that?"

"Get out," the man says again.

"He has an army, but he uses his dead to kill off everyone," I rush out. "That's why no one knew he was coming."

Behind the man, I see a shaking older woman still in her night clothes. Probably his wife.

"Please," I beg, looking at her. Already, the sounds are getting louder as the army encroaches outside, and the caged birds are beginning to look a little agitated, fluttering then resettling their wings. "I need to warn other cities. There's not much time."

"Why should I believe you?" the man says, drawing my attention back to him.

"Because I've seen it."

He still doesn't appear convinced.

"Look, if I wanted to do you harm, I wouldn't try to reason with you. If we can get a message out, we can alert other cities." And just maybe they'll have time to evacuate before War's army arrives.

The woman at the back of the building steps up to her husband. "Listen to the girl."

The man looks harried. "She's fighting with the horseman," he objects.

"If you don't write down her message, I will," his wife says, a fire in her eyes.

I feel my throat thicken. This is the piece of humanity that I've been missing for so long. Bravery in the face of death.

Huffing, the man heads over to a desk pushed beneath the storefront's main window. "What would you have me write?" he asks, disgruntled.

I turn to face the door, drawing an arrow, prepared to

defend this place while I can.

I take a deep breath. "'War is coming,'" I begin. "'The horseman has an army at least 5,000 strong, and he's been traveling down the coast from Israel.'" I continue. "'He can raise the dead, and his dead patrol every city he's raided, looking to kill any who survive—'"

The door to the aviary bangs open, and instinctively I release my arrow. I hit the soldier right between the eyes. The woman screams, recoiling back a little.

I grimace, but nock my bow again, pointing the weapon at the ground while I reach out and lock the door.

I call over to the man. "'—Port Said is already falling as I write this,'" I say, continuing to direct the note. "'Warn all you can of what I've told you.'"

A stone crashes through the window, just missing the aviary owner. He shouts, dropping his pen as the rock slams into the giant cage behind him, startling the birds.

His wife rushes over to him, grabbing some of the thin sheets of paper and pulling him away from the window. As I watch, she grabs a pen and begins scribbling down the same message.

My heart is beating so loudly I can hear it.

This isn't going to work.

The fighting is right outside. I can hear other houses being raided, other families screaming for their lives. Worst of all are those cries that suddenly cut out. So many innocent people are being butchered, and behind all this carnage is War.

The door rattles as someone tries to get inside. It stops jiggling a second later, but then I see a man's face in the window, a sword in his hand.

I level my arrow at his face. "Move along unless you want to die."

Without another word, the soldier leaves the way he came.

I release a breath. So far, I've been fortunate, but it's only a matter of time before my luck runs out.

The man steps into the communal bird cage behind his desk. Rolling up the note, he slips it into a tiny cylinder on the back of one of the pigeons. Once he's finished attaching the message, he carries the bird to the back of the building and opens the door.

A soldier is waiting for him.

All I hear is a flutter of wings and a choking sound. Then the man is falling and the spooked bird is flapping into the sky.

His wife screams, dropping her pen and paper to rush over to him.

No, no, no.

I lift my bow and arrow, but before I can get a clean shot on the soldier, I hear the thump of an arrow and I see her body recoil. Another arrow follows.

The woman ran to her husband when she saw him killed. She *ran* to him. War thinks humans are the scourge of the earth, but is there anything so powerful as the way we love?

As soon as she falls, I see the woman who shot her.

I release my own arrow, and it clips the soldier in the shoulder. With a cry, she stumbles out of the back doorway, and now I'm stalking through the aviary, reloading.

I can't look at the fallen couple who spent their final minutes trying to relay my message.

Outside, the soldier is trying to yank my arrow out of her flesh. I shoot her again, this time in the leg.

She screams, half in pain and half in anger. "What the fuck are you doing?" she accuses, clearly recognizing me.

I lean over her and grab the arrows from her quiver, adding them to my own supply. Just in case I run low.

"I'm trying to save humanity, asshole."

With that I stalk back inside and kick the door shut.

I'm going to die today.

That thought has crossed my mind during pretty much

every battle, but today it settles on me with cold certainty. A macabre part of me wants to know what War would think about that. He seems to care a great deal about my wellbeing, but he doesn't love me, and he doesn't mind death, and he's brought me into battle once again despite how dangerous it is.

Would he mourn me?

He might, I think.

I head back over to the desk and grab the scribbled messages from where they lay. Between the husband and wife, they managed to get two more notes written. I take them both and fold them up, cramming them into tubes attached to the back of the first two pigeons I reach. Clutching the birds close, I rush back outside.

The soldier I shot is still there, leaning against the wall, trying to remove my arrows.

"What you're doing is pointless," she huffs, watching me as she works.

"Yeah, right back atcha," I say, eyeing her futile efforts to remove the arrowheads.

I release the birds, watching them rise into the morning air. I don't linger long enough to see whether or not they make it out of the city. I think it might crush the last bit of my hope if I saw them fall.

I head back inside. There are five more birds in the cage. Between three people, we've only managed to release three birds.

I grab the pen and paper from where the woman dropped them, and I begin to scribble out the same message I instructed the couple to write.

It's an odd sensation, fighting against the horseman—fighting against God Himself, apparently. This is about the time that people pray. Instead, I'm trying to sabotage War's efforts. I don't know where that puts me on the scale from good to evil. I always assumed good was synonymous with God. I don't know now. But this feels right. I have to assume that's worth something.

I miraculously manage to get two more birds out with messages before a phobos rider hops through the window.

Our eyes lock and a bolt of recognition shoots through me.

Uzair, the man who caught me spying on War and who caught me killing another phobos rider.

"*You*," he says. He stalks towards me.

My bow is resting over my shoulder and my dagger is still holstered. Before I can reach for either, Uzair grabs me by the hair and yanks me forward. I stumble, yelping when a clump of hair rips free. My hands go to my head, my eyes pricking at the blinding pressure on my scalp.

"What are you doing?" I demand. But I already know.

This is about the phobos rider I killed back in Arish. It might also be about the second rider that War killed, the one who challenged the horseman when he removed me from the lineup of traitors.

Without answering me, Uzair drags me outside, where smoke from several burning buildings now obscures the morning light.

I knew I had a rocky relationship with War's phobos riders, but I didn't realize it was this bad. They are, after all, relentlessly devoted to their leader.

I guess that devotion doesn't extend to me.

Hussain had warned me to watch my back. I just hadn't listened carefully enough.

Uzair throws me into the street. As I hit the ground, I hear an ominous wooden crack come from one of my weapons.

Please let that be one of my arrows. Anything but the bow.

"Get up, you filthy *bitch*," Uzair demands.

Gritting my teeth, I push myself to my feet.

"Eating our food, sleeping in our camp," he says, prowling towards me. "Sucking the warlord's cock."

He closes in on me and, pulling a fist back, he swings. I stumble out of the way, just barely managing to avoid the hit.

"Just because War won't let you suck it himself doesn't mean you have to get jealous." I'm goading him. I don't care.

The phobos rider comes at me again. Swinging once, twice, three times. I evade the hits—each by a hair's breadth.

"I was hoping I'd come across you," he says. "I thought you'd be smart enough to stay away from the fighting. It's so easy to die out here."

His meaning is clear: *it's so easy to make you disappear.*

And it really is. People don't pay that much attention. Everyone else is busy killing or saving themselves. It was sheer bad luck that this man caught me killing his comrade during the last battle.

I grab War's dagger and unsheathe it.

Uzair smirks at the sight. He pulls his own sword out, which is much bigger and longer.

Fuck me.

In fighting as in sex, bigger tends to be better.

Never going to win this way.

My eyes sweep over the street—over the combatants and the carnage. Far in the distance, I see War. He's hard to miss on his red steed. But this far away he can't possibly recognize me in my black pants and dusty shirt. I'm just another civilian about to die.

My attention returns to Uzair, who's closing in on me again.

Screw it.

I turn on my heel and take off in the opposite direction.

"Fucking coward!" I hear him shout, followed by the sound of him sheathing his sword. "Come back!"

It's too good to hope that Uzair will just let me go. I mean, I *do* hope it, but I'm not surprised when I hear the pound of his heavy footfalls behind me.

If he gets ahold of me, it's game over. He's a better fighter and he has a better weapon and a longer striking range. And he's undoubtedly had much more practice than me at killing.

I pump my arms and legs, running towards War, even though he's far away. Too far away.

To my right are several burning buildings. Making a quick decision, I dart for the nearest one, dashing through the gaping doorway.

Inside, the air is hazy with smoke, but I catch sight of stairs just as I hear Uzair closing in behind me. I sprint for the staircase, coughing as I breathe in lungfuls of smoke.

"You're not getting away!" Uzair calls after me. "Not today. Our warlord can't save you out here!"

I take the stairs two at a time. When will this asshole give up?

As soon as I reach the second floor, I stagger a little at the sight I'm met with. The hallway stretches out in front of me, and the far end of it is blazing, thick plumes of smoke rolling away from the flames.

This was a bad idea.

I charge forward anyway. So long as Uzair hasn't given up the chase, I need to keep running.

I squint against the thickening smoke and the blistering heat; I can barely see where I'm going.

Behind me I hear the phobos rider's persistent footfalls.

Fuck.

Run, run, run!

I flee down the hall, where the fire is worst. I don't know what I'm doing. By the time I realize that I might be able to jump out of a window, I've passed the rooms still intact enough to do so.

I don't hear the metallic hiss of Uzair's sword when he unsheathes it behind me, but I feel the tip of it catch the back of my neck when he swings, the blade slicing open my skin and loping off a chunk of my hair.

I trip, sprawling out across the ground, the arrows in my quiver scattering. The floor is hot to the touch.

He tried to behead me!

I can feel my blood dripping down the back of my neck, the heat evaporating most of it. The rooms to my left, my right, and ahead of me are all engulfed in flame.

Trapped.

I flip onto my back as Uzair looms over me, swallowing down my rising fear. I still have my dagger gripped tightly in my hand, but it's next to useless at this point.

This is my end.

Wife. I can almost hear the horseman's voice in my head. *Don't die on me now.*

"War won't forgive you for this," I say. This might be the first time I've openly acknowledged what I think I mean to the horseman.

"He's not going to know it was me," Uzair replies.

I suppose he won't. War might not find my body at all. The thought sends my pulse thundering. I'm not sure why it bothers me, only that it does.

I take a deep breath and stare up at the phobos rider, my forearms braced against the scorching ground.

Uzair pulls his sword back, the blade already caked with blood.

He swings downward, aiming for my neck, his attack controlled. I watch that blade fall, and I almost let him get me.

I'm not ready.

There are things I haven't said to War, things I haven't done and things I still haven't even admitted to myself.

I roll away, barely missing the blow.

The phobos rider swings again at me, and this time, the edge of his blade opens my arm and trails across my chest. And Goddamn, it hurts like a bitch.

I bring my boot up and kick Uzair's wrist. The impact jars his weapon from his hand, and the sword clatters to the ground.

He reaches for it, bending down within striking range. And

that's when I lunge.

I plunge my dagger into the rider's neck, grimacing when his blood spurts out like a fountain.

He stares at me, furious, like that wasn't supposed to happen. I was just a helpless, defeated woman.

Uzair tumbles forward, next to me. By the time his body hits the ground, he's all but dead. I pull my dagger from his throat and stagger to my feet.

Need to move. The walls are on fire and the ground is becoming unbearably hot, even through the soles of my boots.

Now that the fight is over, however, I move slowly, my muscles leaden. I heave in several deep breaths, but I can't seem to pull in enough air. Instead, smoke burns my lungs.

I've only taken a few steps forward when, ahead of me, part of the ceiling caves in, barricading me in and turning my only exit into a thick wall of fire.

My stomach bottoms out.

Should've let Uzair kill me. It would be a better death than the one I'm going to get. I walked myself into my own grave, coming into this building.

The flames stream up the walls like some savage orange river. I cover my mouth with my shirt and squint against the smoky darkness.

Can't see, can't breathe.

I stumble towards the obstruction, even as more of the ceiling crashes down around me. I'm starting to feel faint from all the smoke inhalation.

This is the end.

BOOM!

A shadow bursts through the debris, the flames licking its sides. From the darkness, I see a blood red shape take form—*War's horse*, I realize. Deimos gallops towards me.

My eyes move up, and I meet the violent, turbulent gaze of the horseman himself.

His eyes burn brighter than the fire—and his expression!

Like heaven itself couldn't stop him.

War swings himself off his horse and runs towards me. When he gets to my side, the horseman cups my face, his hands cool against my burning skin.

"*What were you thinking?*" His shout resonates above the roar of the fire.

I touch his face, my breath labored. My lungs are on fire, and I can't seem to stay grounded. The only thing that's keeping me present is War's panicked expression and his grip on me.

"*You could've died!*" he says.

And then he kisses me.

He ravages my mouth like it's a city he's set to destroy. His lips part mine, and then the taste of him fills my mouth.

It's like savoring heaven and hell and earth and death and all the things there aren't names for.

This doesn't feel like all our other touches, the ones where we owed each other something. War's massive body trembles with anger and need and want. Want and want and want and want—

I think I'm faint with relief and lust—that and the darkening air must be to blame for the black dots that cloud my vision. But then I feel my legs buckle, and then I feel nothing at all.

Chapter 38

I DON'T REMEMBER War catching me, and I don't remember us mounting his steed. But I do wake in time to see us charge through the burning building.

The horseman's hand is under my shirt, his palm nestled between my breasts. Even now, when we're still in danger, he's dead set on healing me.

The ceiling and walls are falling around us like tears, and yet Deimos remains steady through it all, even as embers drop onto his dark mane. I swipe them away, though even that small action causes my vision to darken.

We clamor down the stairwell, the jostling ride causing me to cough until I'm breathless.

There's no gradual shift from darkness to light. One moment we're inside the smoky building, and the next, we're outside, daylight blazing about us. I can barely see the sun through the burning haze of the city, but still the sight of it—bright and bloody—causes a sob to slip out of me.

The horseman pulls me tighter against him.

"I thought I was going to die," I tell him, my voice hoarse. I was certain of it.

War glances down at me with his terrible eyes. "Not today, wife," he vows. "Not ever."

THOUGH THE BATTLE rages on, War flees the city, clutching me to his chest.

I'm not sure what to make of the situation, only that something has shifted between us.

My body is still shaking from battle, and I'm so tired.

I sway a little in the saddle, just remembering that final fight. The bite of steel, the breath of fire, the smoke filling my lungs—I cough at the memory, and once I start, I can't seem to stop. I cough and cough. My entire body shakes with the effort and my vision clouds.

"Stay with me, wife," War commands. There's such authority in his voice that I force my eyes to flutter open. I hadn't realized I'd closed them ...

Another bout of coughing racks my chest. The air is dry and my throat is dry and I'm not taking in enough oxygen.

I feel more than see War's eyes on me this time. He curses beneath his breath, then moves his hand out from under my shirt—only to wrap it around my throat.

For a moment, I panic. I've just been in battle after all. Having a hand at your throat should mean you're going to get choked out. But this is War, War who insisted only moments ago that I wasn't going to die.

And his touch is so gentle—almost comforting. My eyes close and I release a shaky breath, leaning back into him. He brushes a kiss along my temple, and the two of us ride like that.

Whatever power the horseman wields, it's so subtle that I don't feel it at first. But the longer we ride and the longer his calloused hand presses against my throat, the less I need to cough.

When we arrive at camp, people watch us with startled expressions. War and I aren't supposed to be back. The horseman cuts through our settlement, charging forward until we arrive at his tent.

War hops off his steed, then grabs me by the waist. He pulls me down and into his arms.

And then his sinful lips are back on mine, heated and demanding. I lose myself in the taste of him as he scoops me up and begins carrying me. I hear the rustle of canvas, and then War is setting me on my feet inside his tent.

He looks at me and things are different.

He's different. The violence he carries around like a cloak is gone. My horseman seems ... *human.*

Not looking away from me, War removes all of his armor, then all of his clothes, his expression serious.

He comes over to me and now it's my turn. His hands are deft as he pulls off my shirt, then my pants. I just sort of stand there. We've undressed dozens of times, but not like this. Not with the horseman looking at me with so much *life* in his eyes.

Once I'm naked, he lowers us both to his bed. I'm dirty and bloody and weak with fatigue. This doesn't ring of romance.

But when he presses my body to his, there's nothing about it that feels sexual. Intimate—yes—but not sexual.

I take a ragged breath, my eyes going to War's. "What are we doing?"

"You almost *died*," he responds. There's a wild edge to the horseman's features. He lifts a shaky hand and tucks a strand of my brown hair behind my ear. "If I hadn't rode in when I had ..." Rather than finishing the sentence, he pulls me towards him, pressing a kiss to my lips, as if to make sure that I am still indeed, alive.

"Isn't that why you're here?" I say softly, when the kiss ends. "We're all supposed to die." My throat burns as I speak.

"Not everyone—not you."

My eyelids are heavy.

I'm so tired. So, so tired. Whether it's exhaustion from

battle, smoke inhalation, blood loss, or War's healing magic, my body is demanding sleep.

"I'm still human," I murmur. I'm always going to be part of the problem in the horseman's eyes.

"Yes," War says. "You are painfully human. Your bones want to break, your skin wants to bleed, your heart wants to stop. And for the first time ever, I am *desperate* for none of those things to happen. I have never known true fear until now."

The admission is so raw, so cutting, that I pull back from him a little, just to drink his expression in.

The horseman healed me once before, right after I was attacked. I was just as close to death then. But for all of War's concern then, he hadn't acted like this. Whatever icy heart he was given when he came to earth, it's beginning to thaw bit by bit. And now I'm catching a glimpse of the true man beneath it.

I reach out and trace his lips. "You're not as you seem," I breathe, already drifting off.

War kisses the tip of my finger. "You never were."

With those final words ringing in my ears, I slip off to sleep.

I WAKE TO the press of fingertips. They trail down my back, each one feeling sure and steady. The touch is so pleasant, so unexpected, that I arch into it.

There's a language to gestures. This one conveys a single emotion—

Beloved.

I squeeze my eyes tightly together, something thick lodging in my throat.

It's been ... a long time since I felt that way. And with a man, *never* like this.

I drag in a ragged breath when I remember the man behind the touch.

War.

But even with him, this is new. When I was attacked in my tent, he touched me with care, and since the deal we made, he's touched me with desire and affection. This, however, this feels a lot like—

I can't even think the word. The entire idea of it is too scary—and too impossible.

The horseman's fingertips leave my flesh. A moment later, I feel the warm press of his lips against my back.

Too much. My heart feels like it's going to burst.

I flip over, and my gaze meets War's. His eyes have gone soft and deep.

He strokes my hair. "For millennia I've craved this." *Human connection*, he means. "For millennia it's been just out of my reach."

Until now.

My pulse is picking up. I'm still naked underneath War's sheets, and with the horseman this close, I'm *so* aware of that fact. Excitement and fear are mixing together.

I place a hand against his chiseled cheek. War turns his head, his lips brushing a kiss against my palm.

Now it's my turn to go soft on him. I've seen the horseman lustful, angry, determined, vicious. Seeing this doting side of him completely changes each one of my responses.

"*You* undo me," War says hoarsely.

My stomach flutters at his words.

A putrid smell outside briefly cuts through my soft thoughts.

God, what is that stench? It's not *me* is it?

"What happened, Miriam?" War asks, drawing my attention back to him.

His features have sharpened, and he's back to looking like a creature who hunts humans.

He wants to know about today. About why I was in a burning building, a dead phobos rider at my feet.

I swallow a little. My throat still hurts and talking only makes it worse. "Uzair tried to kill me."

The horseman swears under his breath. "My riders are the worst of your kind. Effective, but utterly devoid of compassion."

Who is this man who speaks of compassion, and what has he done with War?

"And you bested one of them in close combat," the horseman continues. He sounds almost ... impressed. War bows his head to kiss my neck again. "I hope you made Uzair's death slow and painful."

I thread my fingers through his black hair. "That's an awfully petty thing for a messenger of God to say."

He presses his lips against my skin, and my hand tightens on his thick locks, holding him close to me.

"Even we horsemen have our moments."

I actually laugh at that. In response, he smiles against my neck. I feel that smile *everywhere*. I arch into him, my core aching.

Need him. Need him so badly it hurts.

War kisses my throat again, and this still isn't normal between us. It's too raw, too outside of simple want.

"Touch me," I whisper.

"I *am* touching you," he says, and damn him, that smile is pressed against my flesh again, and it's making my body come alive.

Do I have to spell it out?

I take his hand and move it down my stomach, towards my—

"You're still healing," he says, drawing his hand away.

And now he cares more about tending to me than he does enjoying me? Who *is* this man?

"I feel fine." Or at least fine enough for what I have in mind.

"You think I don't want to?" War takes my hand and

places it over his crotch. Since I fell asleep, he's donned a pair of pants; that's the only reason I'm not holding his cock in my hand at this very moment. As it is, it strains against the material.

War leans in close. "It is taking everything in me not to peel off my pants and fuck that sweet pussy of yours, wife. *Everything.*"

Dear God, if that little speech was supposed to dissuade me, it *way* missed its mark.

"I have been *crazed* with emotions I have never felt today," War continues. He has a wild edge to his eyes. "I am a man of action. I want nothing more than to feel you alive and wrapped around me. And I'm trying to resist, so I'd kindly ask for you to not try to break my limited willpower."

I release a shaky breath. A part of me wants to push the horseman to the edge, just to see what breaking him would be like, but a bigger part of me is hypnotized by this new side of War.

He *can* change. He's working on changing. For me and because of me. I hadn't been sure before, but I am now. This is a seed I want to cultivate.

So I back off, despite my raging hormones. (I mean, hey, I almost died. I think my survival should be rewarded with an orgasm or three, but that's just my opinion.)

I settle deeper into his bed. I'm still bloody, and I smell like smoke, and I'm sure I'm ruining the horseman's sheets.

"How did you know that I was trapped in the burning building?" I ask War. My voice comes out with a croak.

Maybe I'm not as fine as I thought I was ...

It's the thought that's lurked in the back of my mind since he saved me.

"I saw you running in the distance," he says.

I remember seeing War's striking figure so far away. Too far away to believe he could see me, but apparently he had.

"And I saw a man chase you inside," he adds.

Oh. Well then.

A few women enter the tent just then, interrupting our conversation. With their entrance comes another gust of that putrid smell. I crinkle my nose, even as I clutch War's blankets tightly to me. God, how I miss doors. And knocking. And privacy in general. It's a distant dream now that I live in a city of tents.

Between the women, they carry a basin filled with steaming water. They set the tub down, along with several towels, and step away. Their eyes look spooked, and they keep glancing behind them at something outside the tent.

"Do you need anything else?" one of them asks, turning her attention from the tent flaps to me and War. Her eyes move curiously over me, taking in my bare shoulders and my dirty appearance and the fact that I'm in the horseman's bed. A blush creeps across her cheeks.

"That's all." War waves them away.

Once we're alone again, he nods at the tub. "Would you like a bath?"

I would give my left *tit* for a bath.

My blankets are off in an instant. It's only as I get up, naked from head to foot, that I truly feel my fatigue. I sway a little from it. My throat burns, my lungs rattle, the sword wounds on my arm, neck, and torso sting, and my legs want to fold under me.

I take a few shaky steps forward before the horseman comes over and scoops me up.

"I can walk," I protest.

"Let me do this, wife," he says, his lips close to my ear.

Reluctantly, I let him carry me across the room to the bath. He sets me in the water, which is scalding.

I melt into it.

Swear nothing has felt this good in a long time.

That's not true though, is it? I've had many, many experiences with War that outshine this one. Just the thought has my cheeks flushing and my abdomen clenching.

I really could use a happy-to-be-alive orgasm right about now, despite my fatigue.

Leaning forward, I wrap my arms around my legs and turn my head so I can rest my cheek against my knees. My eyes flutter closed at the pleasant feel of it.

I hear War settle down beside the tub then dip something into the water. A moment later, I feel the press of wet cloth against my back.

My eyes open. "What are you doing?"

"Washing my wife."

My back stiffens. We're venturing into unfamiliar territory. There's the sexual touches and the healing touches—those I've gotten used to. But allowing the horseman to bathe me is a new sort of intimacy.

Up until now, I'd fought this off. Maybe I'm just too tired or maybe it was the revelation that there is still so much unsaid and undone between me and War. Whatever the reason, I don't fight it this time.

"Okay," I say.

War doesn't respond to that, but I feel him drag the cloth up and down my back, carefully tracing around the wound at the back of my neck. The washcloth slips into the water, turning the warm liquid a little redder.

Once he's done with my back, he moves around to the front of the tub and begins to wash my arms, once again being careful to clean my sword wounds.

"I have been a fool," he admits.

My eyes snap to his.

"You're not going to fight in any more battles, Miriam," he says. It's not a question.

I pause at his words. No more battles?

How to spread the word then?

His eyes meet mine. "I won't lose you," he says vehemently.

My throat thickens.

"I can't believe I ever allowed myself the luxury of thinking it couldn't happen," he adds, his gaze dropping back to my wounds. "Especially after you were attacked. I simply never thought He would allow—"

Just then a soldier enters the tent. "War—" he begins.

God Almighty! Is privacy dead?

I cover what I can of myself.

The horseman doesn't look up from where he's washing me. "Get out."

"But you haven't raised the dead—"

Awareness sharpens in War's eyes. They lift from my skin, meeting mine once more. The horseman is a man of habit, and his most consistent habit is that at the end of every battle he raises his dead.

I think of those few birds I released. How paltry my efforts were in the face of the horseman's undead.

War starts to stand, pulling away from me, his expression turning serious, calculating. I got the barest glimpse of this new man, one who has heart and compassion. I'm not ready to lose him so soon.

I catch War's hand.

"Please don't." It comes out as a whisper. "Please War. All those people who survived—please don't kill them." I squeeze his hand tightly.

He stares down at me, searching my face.

Beyond him, the soldier shifts a bit impatiently at the entrance.

War has no reason to listen to me now. I have nothing new and compelling to tell him that I haven't already tried to, and I have nothing else to offer him that I haven't already offered.

But something about today has changed the horseman. I see it even now as he stares at me.

"It will make no difference in the end," he says, his eyes so brilliantly alive.

I give him a meaningful look. "It will make a difference to

me."

This is how you get me to love you, I told him in Arish. I have a feeling he's remembering those words right now.

The horseman stares at me some more, then says over my shoulder to the man waiting, "Call the men in. Tonight, the dead will not rise."

The dead will not rise.

I can hear my heart thundering.

The soldier leaves, and we're alone again.

I try to take in a deep breath, but I'm breathless.

I thought it was an easy promise to make, telling War that mercy was the key to my love. I hadn't realized there was any truth to those words.

Not until this moment.

I stand, the water sloughing off of me. War gazes at my body, his eyes hungry. He's still holding himself in check, but he was right earlier—he has limited willpower. And right now, I *am* going to break it.

I step out of the tub and into the horseman's arms, plastering my wet body against his. Immediately, his hand comes around my waist, the washcloth falling, forgotten, to the ground.

He's still kneeling, and for once I'm taller than him. His hands skim either side of my waist, and he dips his head, pressing a kiss to my stomach.

I run my fingers through the horseman's hair and tilt his head back, forcing him to look at me. I spend only a moment glancing down at War's lips—and then I kiss him.

The instant our mouths meet, I melt. He's decadent, sinful, saintly.

He breaks away from the kiss. "What have you done to me?" he whispers. "What have you done? Wife, wife, wife," he murmurs against my skin, his lips moving lower. Down my throat and across my collarbones. He trails his mouth over my chest wound, which has now scabbed over, thanks to him.

302

After a minute, his mouth continues on to my breasts.

His hands tighten as he presses my arched back deeper into him. War's mouth closes over a nipple, and a moan slips from my lips. I've never been this way with other men. I've never been able to let my guard down so much.

"*Ve lethohivaš,*" he says.

You intoxicate me.

His tongue lashes over the tip of my breast, toying with me. I press myself deeper against him, needing more, so much more.

All the touching, the kissing, the oral—none of it has been enough. Especially not now that War makes me feel beloved, and not when he looks at me with something like humanity in his eyes.

Not when he's given up raising the dead because I asked.

War's mouth moves from one nipple to the other, and his hand slips between us, his thumb running down the length of my slit.

I'm breathing hard, gasping as I arch into him.

Not enough. Not enough. Not enough.

"*War,*" I breathe.

I need him inside me. Screw my remaining injuries, they'll heal—*he* will heal them.

The horseman stills. I'm sure he hears something in my voice. He breaks away from my nipple, his gaze rising to mine.

My breath is caught in my throat, and my body is beginning to tremble with nerves and excitement. I'm not sure I can force out the words I want to say.

I hesitate, unsure of everything except my own foolishness.

There can be no going back from this.

I hold his gaze. "*I surrender.*"

Chapter 39

WAR IS COLD steel and dark intent, and for a second after my declaration, that's all I see on his face.

But then he smiles, looking far, far too handsome for his own good. He pulls my head down to his lips and kisses me all over again, and I feel his lust and excitement and, and— and something else. Something I'm not at all comfortable with.

The horseman breaks away, and that grin still pulls at his lips, but it's dimming.

"I meant what I said earlier," he says. "Your body needs to heal."

I want to growl in frustration. He chooses *now* to be noble?

But War hasn't moved away from me. He might want to do the right thing, but he's no idealist. I can practically feel his need to be inside me, just so that he can be sure I'm truly alive.

"I almost died today," I finally say to him, "and when I thought it was the end, do you know what I regretted most?"

He stares up at me, waiting for me to continue.

"I hadn't said and done everything I wanted to with you.

Show me what I've been missing."

With that, I kiss the horseman again.

I feel it in his lips, the moment his resistance gives away. He groans into my mouth, and then his arms tighten around me. His lips go from entertaining mine to demanding more, more, more. There's a fervor to his touch that wasn't there before, and it feels like I'm falling headfirst into uncharted waters.

Just being in his arms has me forgetting about my last aches and pains. I don't know if that has to do with his healing abilities, or if his presence is overwhelming the rest of my senses.

He strokes my slit again, and I hiss in a breath.

Oh God, I really did manage to convince him to do this. That becomes clear when his hand continues to stroke my core, his thumb rubbing languorous circles around my clit.

I give a frustrated moan.

Still need more.

The horseman breaks off the kiss, flashing me a devilish grin. "Did you think I'd ease your discomfort with one small declaration, wife?" he says, his voice especially low and gravelly. "I want you *undone.*" He punctuates his words by dipping a finger inside me. Instinctively, I move against him. I can feel wetness between my legs, wetness that has nothing to do with the bath.

My eyes narrow. Two can play that game.

I begin to reach between us when he catches my wrist. "Ah ah." His fingers are still moving in and out of me.

I'm beginning to pant. "Please, War."

"Please what?"

Is he really going to make me spell it out? "I want you inside me."

I am lit on fire.

His kohl-lined eyes are heated, and I can feel his erection straining against his pants.

All at once his fingers leave me, and he picks me up, carrying me back to his bed. It's still soiled from when I laid there earlier, and the scent of smoke and ash clings to it.

He lays me down, only pausing to remove his pants. His cock springs free, and my God, I forgot how terrifyingly large his dick is. Large enough to make my jaw ache when my mouth is wrapped around it. And the rest of the horseman is so big and violent that for a moment, my desire abates.

Maybe this was a bad idea.

War kneels at the foot of the bed, running his hands up my legs as he surveys my body. He leans forward, until his chest, with his strange, shining tattoos, presses against mine.

Whatever his earlier reservations against sex were, they're long gone now.

Leaning down, he kisses me, the movements of his mouth more carnal than they were just moments ago. My heart is starting to pound faster and faster. This doesn't feel like a little innocent experimentation, or a bad decision fueled by too much booze. This doesn't even feel like regular sex. (Not that I have a ton of experience in that department.) Maybe it's the way War is looking at me, but what we're about to do feels heavy with meaning.

It's just a simple, physical act, I reassure myself. Plenty of people do this. It's *no big deal.*

The horseman's hand goes back to my clit, maybe to tease me some more, but I'm already drenched.

He flashes a wicked smile when he feels how ready I am.

"Wife, how I have anticipated this day. And now to see your sweet body aching for mine. I find I am more eager for this than even battle." He says this like he's surprised himself a little.

Whatever. I'm past the point of caring. All I know is that I need the horseman in me in a way I haven't needed anything in a long time.

He strokes me again and again, even though he doesn't

need to. Even though I'm already mad with desire.

I arch into each touch, desperate for more.

Suddenly, his hand is gone. His hips shift, and a moment later, I feel the tip of him press against my opening.

I tense, remembering how big he is. After holding him in my hand and on my tongue, I thought I understood his size. But I didn't. I'm only realizing that now.

With one slow stroke of his hips, I feel War begin to enter.

He hisses as he meets resistance. "Relax, wife. We were meant to fit together."

Um, only a woman with a vagina as big as a crater was meant to fit War's cock.

The horseman waits until he feels me begin to relax, my legs spreading a little wider. He begins to push in again.

Dear God. It seems impossible, and yet I feel my flesh give way, making room for his seemingly unbearable size. My fingers dig into his back when the stretching becomes too much.

He pauses, staring down at me. "Miriam?"

"Just ... give me a moment. It's a lot ..." *Of dick.* So much dick.

I can feel beads of sweat forming on my forehead. After several seconds, I nod. "Okay. I'm okay."

War continues his slow sink into me, his gaze searching mine. "Wife," he says, looking gobsmacked, "you feel *incredible*."

War's face is nothing short of rapturous. I know he's seasoned at this, so I'm surprised to see how much it's affecting him.

His eyes are intensely focused on me. I'd have assumed that they'd be drifting far, far away as sensation overwhelmed him, but he's so present.

Disconcertingly present.

He's sweating with his need to move slow, to be gentle. I can tell a driving force in him wants to thrust his cock inside me as fast as possible and then to fuck me with abandon. I can practically feel him vibrating with the need. And maybe he'll eventually do that, but I don't think that will happen today.

It takes ages, but finally, his hips meet mine as he seats himself fully inside me, stretching me to my limits.

I release a breath. I don't know if I've ever felt anything so exquisite in my life. And he hasn't even started moving yet.

"I have waited ages for this moment," he says. "Cannot believe it's finally upon me." War smiles again, and I can't get over how unbearably handsome he is.

I'm shaking with need, my legs splayed on either side of him, feeling more vulnerable than I ever have. I didn't expect that. This was supposed to just be sex. But the way War is staring down at me, it feels like everything I've worked so hard to brick away is being exposed all at once.

"Finally, my wife, you have *surrendered*."

He begins to move, pulling out of me just enough to rock back in. My breath leaves me all at once. I was expecting it to hurt. Instead, every slight movement feels so cataclysmically good.

"*Wife.*" The warlord gazes down at me, his normally violent eyes now full of some gentle emotion. My stomach bottoms out when I realize the emotion isn't simple desire. "I cannot tell you how I have longed for this. You are mine finally—totally and completely, nothing to separate us."

The horseman thrusts into me again, as if to emphasize his point.

My nails sink into his back at the sensation, and he pauses, maybe to make sure that he's not hurting me.

I can barely form the words over my own heightened desire.

"Don't stop," I breathe. "Please don't."

Again, that roguish smile.

War begins to thrust himself into me, first with slow,

meticulous precision, but then with increasing force. I'm arching into each thrust, and already I feel my orgasm starting to build in the background.

The entire time, War watches me, like he wants to own every look, every moment. Every so often he whispers phrases in other languages that translate to *my beautiful wife* and *never have I known such pleasure* and *this is the closest to heaven I have been in a long time.*

This is ... not at all like my other experiences with sex. This is the kind of sex that ruins you.

As I feel him stroke me deep within, I finally sense the horseman's true nature. He cannot be anything other than battle breathed to life. All this flesh holds the violence of eons; I feel it in each thunderous thrust of his hips. And yet, as his hands slip over my body, there's an unexpected softness to his touch.

He kisses me up the column of my throat, his hips pistoning in and out, in and out.

"So beautiful," he now murmurs. "How long I have yearned for you."

War's pace changes, deepening—and it's as though the last several minutes have been a tease and this is the real thing.

Instantly my body is coiling, my looming orgasm now building rapidly—too rapidly—

All at once I shatter.

I cry out, pulling the horseman tightly to me as I feel my climax rip through me. Over and over I feel it, and just when it begins to end I feel War thicken inside me.

"My wife, my heart." He groans as his own orgasm moves through him, his thrusts becoming stronger and faster as he spills into me.

War gazes down at me, his eyes going a little hazy as he rides the last of his orgasm out. What feels like an eternity later, the horseman's thrusts begin to slow. Eventually, he has no choice but to slip out of me.

I'm sore everywhere; the kind of sore that makes your cheeks flush.

War lays back on his bed and drags me onto his stomach. He cups my core, even as I feel his cum begin to leak out of me.

"To feel that a part of me is inside you still—wife, there is no more thrilling sensation in the world," he states.

My breathing begins to slow, my sweaty flesh cooling. All my aches and pains are flaring back to life.

Now that I'm beginning to come down, War's adoration is starting to—well, I'm having a few misgivings.

The sex—I definitely want second helpings of that—but the horseman is looking at me like things have changed. And yeah, my close brush with death had given me some perspective, and yeah, I did surrender to him and all, but now I'm sensing that my words and actions might mean a smidge more to him than they do to me.

I begin to push away from him. "I should clean myself up ..." There's still a tub full of water, and now I'm sticky—

War pulls me back down, luring me back to him with his heated kisses. "Not so quick, my wife." He brushes my dark hair aside so that he can kiss the nape of my neck.

"But I'm dirty," I protest, desperate to put a little distance between us.

"*Nothing* about what we did was dirty," War says, a bit too fervently. "And I like having myself all over you."

That's exactly what I'm having an issue with.

"It is going to be different now," he adds.

I swallow. Uh oh.

"Um, what do you mean?" I say carefully, keeping my tone light.

"You are mine wholly and completely—and I am yours. For now and always it will be this way."

Oh dear God. That sounded a lot like a vow to me.

What have I done?

Chapter 40

DESPITE MY MISGIVINGS, we spend the rest of the afternoon and evening in War's bed, getting up only to eat and drink.

I don't know if he's aware of my unease, but if he is, he couldn't have devised a better strategy for distracting me from it. I might be troubled by War's feelings for me, but I have zero problems with how he makes love.

Not even nighttime seems to quench whatever thirst drives the horseman. War wakes me up twice more for sex.

By the time morning sunlight is streaming through our tent, War's hand has moved its way down to my clit for the millionth time. He strokes it, and I moan softly in protest. My body feels like it's been wrung of every last orgasm.

Despite that, I feel myself slicken against his hand. Who would've thought I'd have another round in me?

"Cannot keep my hands off of you," War says, moving his other palm to my breast. Against my better judgment, I arch into his touch.

"So receptive," he murmurs.

Something I seriously did not take into account earlier—all this skin on skin action has almost completely healed me.

And my libido is thanking War for it.

The horseman rolls on top of me. I tilt my pelvis up, and for the thousandth time in the last twenty four hours, my horseman slides inside me.

Much, much later I manage to actually pull myself out of bed and clean myself up as best I can (much to War's disappointment). Before I can get reeled back in for more sex, I dress and slip outside.

I nearly scream the moment I do so.

The living dead surround War's quarters.

They stand idly around the tent, weapons held at the ready. Most of them rock slightly, their decomposing features slack. And yet, despite the fact that their eyes are unfocused and their heads don't turn at the sound of my footsteps, there's an awareness to them.

So *that* explains the smell.

I cup my hand over my nose. The stench is much worse out here, and the hot day is doing nothing to help it.

A moment later, War steps out next to me, a smile clinging to his lips. One look at him and the entire camp will know that the horseman got himself some ass last night.

Awesome.

"What is this?" I ask, my gaze sweeping over the corpses.

"They're for your protection." His smile slips away. "It seems I cannot trust even my own men to keep you safe."

Now that my gaze sweeps over my surroundings, I finally notice that the phobos riders that used to stand guard are indeed gone.

In their place are armed zombies, their blades holstered at their sides.

"This really isn't necessary," I state, covering my nose again. Ugh, I can taste the rot on my tongue.

"On the contrary, wife, now it's more important than ever." Even as War says it, his zombies back away, giving me space to breathe. "I warned you already: I won't lose you."

The horseman cups my face, his gaze searching mine. "Death always comes between humans. I won't let it happen to us."

I see his age then, in his eyes. Thousands upon thousands of years of wars. So many lives and so many deaths. It's moments like these when I remember that he was never born and he can never die.

I sense that all those years of battle have worn War down. That beneath his violence, he's held onto a spark of something that doesn't seem very War-like: peace, connection, *love*. I see that longing in his eyes.

And now I've begun to make the mistake I was never supposed to make. I've started to forget that War is a jackal set on devouring the world. I've started to see him as someone worth caring about.

As someone I *do* care about.

THE NEXT WEEK is a blur of touching and sex. War extends our time at camp simply so that he can relegate some days to staying in bed and nothing else. And there's no more mention of raising the dead—my undead guards aside.

And if I thought this brief, sex-filled blip would end the moment we packed up camp, I thought wrong. War stops several times on the road so that he can fit himself inside me, and the nights during our travels are largely sleepless.

Even when we make camp in the next settlement, it doesn't end. He seems more ravenous for me than ever.

War fucks like he fights. He's brutal, deliberate, and full of raw masculine energy. He takes me like it's the one thing he was made for, like this is the last time he'll ever be in me. Like he's reaching, reaching, reaching for something he can't quite grasp.

I was right the first time I felt him in me; he's ruined me. Because the craze isn't one-sided. If it were, I'd relish the fact that at any moment I could just walk away and be alright. But

I don't think I could. Not at this point. So instead, I now have to grapple with the fact that I'm enamored by a man who has committed atrocities.

He's barely slipped out of me when he gathers me against him, holding me close.

Outside, the Egyptian sun is rising, turning the cream walls of our tent a rosy hue. All around me, everything has a hazy, warm glow.

"Two days from now, when battle begins, you will stay here," War says softly, rubbing circles into my back. "My undead will guard you until I return."

My body goes rigid. I almost forgot about the upcoming raid.

After Port Said, we traveled inland, heading through the Nile Delta towards the city of Mansoura. Here, several kilometers outside the city's walls, we made camp.

The land around us is a bit lusher than it was at our earlier stops, but the decaying, rubble-filled state of the towns we passed detracts from its natural beauty. Cars still congest many of the streets, old computers and appliances litter the landscape, burned carcasses of buildings line the road, and many of the recent additions Egypt has made to its cities— such as gas lamps and horse stalls—have already been vandalized.

From everything I've seen of these parts, I'd say the people here were suffering long before War came around. They don't need any more pain.

Seeing my face, War says, "Mansoura must fall, and I will be there."

I feel my heart plummeting, plummeting. War had put off his godly duties over the last week. I had stupidly hoped he might put them off for longer—*much* longer.

"You don't have to," I whisper. "You could stop."

He pulls me in close and steals a kiss before I can push him away. "For you I nearly would."

Nearly.

The last week managed to lure me into a false sense of reality, but the dream is over.

I knew things weren't going to change. What I hadn't realized is that I'm suddenly *not* okay with that.

Be brave, Miriam.

If I want the world to change, I'll have to do something about it.

"There is something I want to know," I say carefully. "If you can judge men's hearts, can you see whether they intend to do evil?"

What are the limits of your abilities, dear horseman?

War's brow furrows at the change of subject. "Not even I can see the future, Miriam—nor can I read men's minds. I can only understand their basic essence. And even that can alter with time and intent."

I trace one of War's crimson tattoos; the markings look like spilled blood on his chest.

"Do you know *my* heart?" I ask carefully.

"I do," he says.

"Is it good?"

"It's good enough." *For me,* the silence seems to add.

It's good enough.

Good enough for the horseman to believe I truly surrendered to him back in Port Said, which is all he ever really wanted from me, anyway.

The thing is, a *good enough* heart is not the same as a *good* one. And that's unfortunate for War, because a good heart might always tell the truth, but a good enough one won't.

When I told him I surrendered, well—I lied.

I've given up *nothing.*

THE EXPLOSION ROARS *through my ears, the force of it knocking me into the water.*

Darkness. Nothing. Then—

I gasp in a breath. There's water and fire and ... and ... and God the pain—the pain, the pain, the pain. The sharp bite of it nearly steals my breath.

"Mom, Mom, Mom!"

Can't see her. Can't see anyone.

"Mom!"

"Miriam!"

I gasp awake, clutching my throat.

War stares down at me, his eyes like onyx. A line forms between his brows. "You were having a nightmare."

I take several deep gulps of air.

A nightmare. Right.

I wet my lips, sitting up, and the horseman moves back a little, giving me space. My skin is damp with sweat, and strands of my hair are plastered to my cheeks.

It's been weeks since I last had this nightmare. I had almost forgotten that before War, this particular memory had all too frequently haunted my dreams. I don't know why it's decided to take a backseat until now. Maybe lately my mind has just been haunted by newer and more grotesque images.

"What were you dreaming of?" War asks. Just the way he says it makes me think that the horseman doesn't dream—or that if he does, it's a very different experience from my own.

My finger traces the scar at my throat. "It wasn't a dream. It was a memory."

The water rushes in—

"Of what?" War's voice is hard as flint, like he wants to do battle with something as insubstantial as a memory.

I swallow.

Might as well tell him.

"Seven years ago Jerusalem was getting overtaken," I say. Rebels and zealots had fronted an attack on my city. "My mother, sister, and I were escaping. No one was safe in the city, particularly not a half-Jewish, half-Muslim family."

Those days of tolerance and progress that my parents once

spoke of had been snuffed out like a candle.

"My family made it to the coast." I can still see the shuffle of bodies on the beach. There were so many other families just like ours, desperate to escape war-torn Israel for another place—any *place*.

"We piled into a motor boat. By then, most engines in Israel had stopped working, and the ones that were still in operation were unreliable at best."

That was seven years ago. Since then, all engines had stopped running.

"My mother knew it was dangerous, that something could go wrong, but it was our only option."

Europe had closed its borders. They didn't want foreigners—particularly not ones from the east and south. In their minds we'd steal their jobs and eat their food and overwhelm their precarious economies.

If we wanted to get through their borders, we were going to have to do it illegally, and this treacherous boat ride was the only way to do that.

"The boats were ... bad. They were narrow and rickety, but worst of all, they relied on motors for propulsion.

"I didn't want to get in ours. I was so afraid the motor was going to give out right in the middle of the open ocean. I was afraid I'd die at sea."

War listens, rapt, his eyes searching my face as I speak.

"In the end, my mother and sister shamed me into stepping into the boat. They knew I didn't really want to leave Israel—or New Palestine as it was starting to be called." That was where my father died, where I grew up. It held all my memories. I knew we needed to leave, but I didn't want to. It seemed cruel that I had to give this up too. We'd already lost everything else.

"We made it off the beach. The engine was making funny noises, but we got away from land at least."

I pause.

Some memories are lost to the sands of time, but others, like this particular one ... I could live to be a hundred and I'd still never forget.

"The explosion was a surprise." I didn't know engines *could* explode. "One moment I was sitting there, alongside my mother and sister, and in the next I felt heat and pain as I was thrown into the water.

"My backpack had been wrapped around my ankle." That bag was full of the last of my earthly possessions. "I remember it dragging me down."

My lungs pound. The sunlight above me grows dim even as I struggle.

"I tried to get it off, but I couldn't. I was sinking, and I couldn't get back to the surface."

I open my mouth to cry for help.

The water rushes in—

I glance down at my fingers. "I don't know how I survived. I really don't. I thought I drowned in those waters."

"But you didn't," War says, his voice soft.

I nod. "When I came to, I was onboard a fishing boat. The fishermen said they saw me floating in the water alone, far from any wreckage."

"I don't know what happened to either my mother or sister. I don't even *know* if they're alive." My voice breaks.

War leans forward, cupping the side of my face. "I vow to you, wife, we will find what's become of your family."

I nearly stop breathing.

It's what I've always wanted. What I could never quite attain when I was just a weapons dealer in Jerusalem.

War couldn't give me a more precious gift.

Does he realize it?

My gaze slips down to his lips. I lean forward and kiss him. "Thank you."

And then I show him I mean it.

318

Chapter 41

IT'S BEEN A while since I stopped in to see Zara. A big part of my hesitancy has been trying to explain to her that I'm now banging the horseman that wiped out her hometown and most of her family. I can't imagine that conversation going over too well. But I've put this visit off for too long.

As soon as I leave War's tent, the dead congregate around me, smelling like a demon's asshole and looking even worse. Death does no one favors.

I frown at them.

I begin to walk, and the zombies fall into formation around me like some sort of undead security force.

I pause. "War!" I call out behind me.

Several seconds pass, then the horseman steps out of his tent, his trousers slung low, his dark hair sex-tousled, his rippling torso highlighted by the morning sun. A cup of coffee is in his hand, and he wears a loose smile on his face, his white teeth stark against his olive skin. It's gross just how gorgeous he is.

"Reconsidering seconds?" he asks, his eyes laughing at me as he takes a small sip. He's not talking about breakfast.

I give him a reproachful look. "I have to be friends with the dead now?" I gesture to the zombies.

His smile widens a little at that, his eyes bright. "Consider it a working relationship."

I huff, walking back to him, the revenants at my heels. "No one's going to kill me."

"I know," he agrees. "Because no one's going to want to come within five meters of those men." He nods to the zombies.

Ugh. "I just want to visit my friend."

War's expression darkens. "The one who tried to kill me? The same one whose boy you forced me to save?"

I look heavenward for patience. "It doesn't matter who I'm visiting. I need your word that the dead won't come into any tents I enter—or hover too close by."

The horseman scrutinizes me. "What is the point of having guards if they cannot be around to protect you?"

I want to tell him that the bodyguards were his idea, not mine, and that I don't give a flying fuck whether I even *have* guards. But knowing War, that kind of logic would land me with twice as many zombie nannies, all of whom would insist on entering Zara's miniscule tent.

I rub my face. "Please War." I drop my hand. "I'll go along with your bodyguards. Just give me a little freedom. I need friends."

He stares at me for a long time, then turns his attention to the undead who've congregated around me. Finally he inclines his head. "For your soft heart."

I release a breath. "Thank you." With that, I turn on my heel.

I feel those violent eyes on me as I walk away, the dead closing ranks around me once more.

The phobos riders that live in War's area of camp stop and stare (somewhat hostilely) at me and my macabre bodyguards as I pass them by. But the real looks come when I enter the main area of camp.

Men and women openly gape at me, their eyes darting from dead man to dead man. And the same children who I've seen handle weapons now scream and flee at the sight of the walking dead.

I'm regretting this trip already.

By the time I get to Zara's tent, she's already standing outside of it, her arms crossed and an eyebrow raised.

"Why is it that I always hear about you before you arrive?" she says by way of greeting.

"I think I'm just unlucky."

She eyes the dead men. "They're not coming in my tent," she warns.

I glance at them, suddenly unsure how I'm supposed to get them to beat it. "I've arrived," I tell them. "You can back off now."

In response, they spread out, flanking the area and causing a nearby woman to scream and drop the clothing she was washing. The rest of the women loitering along this row of tents watch us curiously.

Zara jerks her head towards her home. "Why don't we chat inside?"

I follow her in, and in the dim, warm confines of her tent, I see Mamoon playing with some faded plastic toys and a well-loved teddy bear.

"Mamoon, say hi," Zara says.

"Hi," he replies without looking up.

Zara purses her lips together, and she looks a little like she wants to cry.

"How's—" I jerk my head to her nephew, "it going?"

She sighs. "Hard. It's really, really hard. But I have more than what most people here do, so I'm counting my blessings." She takes a deep breath, her emotional walls coming up. "But that's not what I want to talk about right now." Her eyes move over me. "*Where* have you been for the last week? You disappeared on me."

I don't want to say it, I really, really don't.

Her eyes pass over me again. "You screwed him, didn't you?"

I sit down hard and nod.

"Yeah." I fucked him good.

"Well?" she adds. "Was it worth it?"

I glance at her nephew.

"He has no idea what we're talking about. It's fine."

Not so sure about that ...

"So?" Zara presses. I can't tell if she's angry. She sounds annoyed, and she seems a bit on edge, but then again, ever since I've known her, Zara's always been a bit edgy.

I give a humorless laugh. "You mean did I enjoy it?" I give her a look. "Yes. I did." It's problematic how much I've enjoyed it.

"And now you feel guilty?" she asks.

I level a look at her. "Naw ..."

The corner of her mouth curves into a sardonic smile. "I don't judge you, you know," she says, sitting down next to me.

I chew on my lower lip. "I wouldn't blame you if you did," I say.

She takes my hand, squeezing it tightly. "You convinced that beast to save—" Her voice breaks. Zara nods to her nephew. "War's killed *everyone* I loved—except for one person, and that was only because you got through to him. So no, I don't blame you for screwing the monster, though I'm sorry you're the one forced to do the deed. I'd sooner saw his balls off, myself."

I give Mamoon another desperate look, sure that between me and Zara we're corrupting the poor boy's ears.

"He saw his parents killed, he's walked by executions, and now dead men are standing guard outside his tent," Zara says. "A little sex talk is the least of my worries."

Fair point.

"I made War a promise not to get in his way, and as much as I hate it, I intend to uphold that promise," my friend continues. "So have your way with him and don't think I'm going to cast my judgment on you or walk away from our friendship. I owe you a debt I can *never* repay. And who knows, maybe you'll end up saving someone else's little boy because of your ... relationship."

I give her a tight smile.

"Just don't avoid me," she finishes. "I missed your company."

"Okay," I say softly.

And that's the end of the sex talk—at least for now.

For the next couple hours, Zara and I talk about everything and nothing. I could've sat with her and chatted the entire day away, but eventually my friend drags me and Mamoon out of the tent, towards a group of women gathered several tents down.

Mamoon keeps giving the zombies around us wide-eyed looks as Zara leads him on.

"They won't hurt you," I say. "They're here to protect us."

That's a bit of a lie—they're here to protect me and no one else—but I won't let them hurt Mamoon, so it's nearly the truth. And luckily, my words seem to take the edge off of the toddler's fear.

The loose circle of women sits under a canvas shelter someone's erected. They sit and chat while they mend clothes, weave baskets, and do other odd jobs that don't require much concentration.

When they catch sight of our group, I see one woman slosh a cup of tea she's drinking. Another gasps.

"What's this?" another women demands of Zara. She doesn't bother looking at me.

"War's wife decided to join our group," my friend replies, like it's the most normal thing in the world.

The women grow quiet, each of them eyeing me, some

curiously, others unkindly. One gives me a small smile. I recognize a face here and there from when I lived in this quarter of camp, but no one acts as though I was ever like them.

"Of course you're both welcome," one woman says a little stiffly. Her face warms when she sees Mamoon. "David is playing soccer with Omar if you'd like to join." She points behind her, towards the end of the tents, where two small boys are kicking a weathered ball around.

Mamoon glances up at his aunt, and when she gives a nod of her head, the little boy goes running off towards his new friends.

Zara keeps her eyes on him for several seconds after that, her face pinched with worry. There's always something to worry about here—the soldiers' cruelty, the numerous weapons scattered about camp, the sheer size of our tented city. A child could get swallowed up whole.

"Would either of you like some tea?" one of the women asks.

Zara blinks, moving her attention to the woman. "No thank you."

"I'm good too," I say.

I shoo my undead guards away as the group makes room for us in the circle. After a tense few minutes, conversation returns to normal.

"... I saw Itay go into her tent last night."

Some tittering laughter.

"So that's who was making her find God while the rest of us were trying to sleep."

"Poor Ayesha next door has a child. Try explaining that one!"

Shocked laughter rolls through the group.

I listen to them, strangely fascinated. All around us, people are dying by the thousands, and yet here these women are, gossiping about someone getting laid.

"How's War?" asks a woman, her curious gaze falling on me.

At first the question doesn't even register. It's not until the other women turn their gazes on me that I realize they all want to know about my sex life and oh my God I did not sign up for this when I decided to visit Zara this morning.

"What do you mean?" I say, faking ignorance.

The woman's mouth curves into a smile. "Has he made you find God?"

Someone else chimes in. "Of course he has. Otherwise there wouldn't be dead men guarding her."

It's painful how accurate that statement is.

"What I want to know," another woman says, "is how good the horseman was at giving you a religious experience."

Several of the women laugh; even Zara cracks a smile.

They're trying to include me, I realize. This isn't the Spanish Inquisition, this is how these women connect, despite all their differences. They're all relatively new friends, after all.

"Do you really want to know?" I say.

This is so embarrassing.

A few women nod.

I gather together my confidence. "The horseman is *definitely* better at love than war."

It's not entirely true, but it causes the women around me to titter with good natured laughter.

"That man was *made* to please a woman," someone else adds. More chuckles.

The conversation moves on, and everyone seems to breathe a little easier.

My heart lifts when I realize that I passed whatever test they threw at me. I might've come as War's wife, but I'll be leaving as one of them.

I while away the day there, listening to their gossip and adding in a few tidbits about my own experiences. For the first time in a long while, life feels normal—or at least normal enough.

That all ends when someone mentions the invasion tomorrow. I could pretend away the horrors of this place for a bit, but eventually they push their way back in.

The collective mood of the group dips, the laughter dying away. When I first came to camp, I was so certain I was the only one fighting to stop the horseman. But now it's clear that other people care too. They're just not in a position to do anything about it.

I am.

I've secured the aviaries—and that's something—but I saw firsthand during our last invasion just how little that actually amounts to. Only a handful of birds flew away with my message, and who knows how many of them were shot down by archers.

But the key to surviving the horseman's attack *is* to be forewarned about it. If people have enough time to flee their homes, and if they run in the right direction, then maybe they can cheat death.

Unfortunately, I won't have another chance to send off warnings, not if War is prohibiting me from joining the fight. If I want to do something to help the world, I'll have to work around my violent husband.

The key to surviving his attack is being forewarned about it.

The answer is right there, staring me down.

"Miriam—*Miriam*," Zara says, snapping her fingers in front of my face. "Where did you go?"

My gaze locks with hers. "I just had a thought."

326

Chapter 42

IN THE DEAD of night, I slip out of War's bed, careful not to wake him. He's deep asleep, his breath hissing steadily out of him.

The lamps in the tent are all snuffed out, and I have to feel my way around to the clothes I set out nearby. As quietly as I can, I tug them on, then pull on my boots. Lastly, I strap on my weapons and head outside.

My undead guards are still on duty, their sightless eyes staring out at nothing. But as soon as they sense me, they creep close.

I begin to walk, heading around War's tent, and the zombies fall into formation around me just as they did earlier.

Need to shake them.

At least there are no living soldiers in this area anymore. That's one obstacle I managed to avert.

A short distance away from War's tent, there's a private corral. Inside it is a massive horse with fur the color of spilled blood.

Deimos.

Sometimes War lets his horse wander untethered, and

sometimes, like tonight, he corrals him—separate from the other horses, of course.

At night and without War's comforting presence, Deimos looks a shit-ton scarier than I remember. He stands at the edge of the corral, his head turned in my direction. He looks as though he's been waiting for me.

Before I lose my nerve, I go up to the unearthly steed. He bumps my chin with his muzzle.

"Hey there," I whisper, trying to act brave. I reach out a hand and gently rub the horse up his snout and between his eyes.

He nips at my hair, the action causing me to jolt, but the gesture seems affectionate.

Maybe I'm just imagining things, but I think War's horse might actually *like* me.

I take a deep breath. I don't know much about horses, only that they can be finicky creatures. And since I've been traveling with War, I've seen my fair share of horse kicks and bites. If these little ol' ponies don't like something, they make their displeasure *known*.

We'll discover how much this one truly likes me in the next few minutes ...

I hop the fence, and now I'm caged in with him. Several seconds later, the corpses that surround me amble over the wall of the corral as well.

Dang it. I was kind of hoping the fence would deter the dead.

Only now do I realize that one human girl, six undead creatures, and a savage steed all crammed into a tiny corral is a recipe for disaster.

However, the aggressive reaction I anticipate from War's horse never comes.

He utterly ignores the dead surrounding us, ambling over to me instead.

I pet the side of Deimos's face. "Will you let me ride you?"

I whisper.

When Deimos doesn't stampede me, I decide that I might just be able to do exactly that.

His saddle hangs nearby. I have very little experience saddling a horse, and a lot of trepidation saddling *this* one.

Definitely going to get kicked. Deimos is a mean bastard. I've seen him kick and bite and nearly trample a good dozen men since I joined this camp.

But as I lift the saddle pad and then the saddle, hefting them onto his back, he doesn't try to hurt me. I lean under him to secure the straps, and this is the moment of truth. I hold my breath, waiting for some sort of horsie retaliation. Instead, he tosses his head about impatiently, as though to say, *hurry up.*

Meanwhile, my guards stand passively by. I glance at them, wondering if they're able to communicate with War. My stomach drops at the thought.

He's fast asleep, I reassure myself. That doesn't stop me from throwing a spooked glance in the direction of his tent.

Once I'm done securing the saddle, I open the gate, grab the reins and try to lead Deimos out.

The horse tosses his head about until I release his reins. Then he begins to make his own exit, picking up speed with every footfall.

I end up having to rush to his side and hastily hoist myself onto his back before he outpaces me.

For a split-second Deimos tries to shake me off, and I'm sure this is the end of my half-baked plan. But I cling to the horse, and after a few seconds, he seems to accept the fact that I'm going to be riding him tonight.

His trot increases in speed as we head away from camp. Around us, my undead guards begin to run, trying in vain to keep up. But the human body can only move so fast—even a magically animated one. The corpses begin to fall away from us, and I desperately hope they're not going to immediately report to War.

I've barely shaken my guards when I hear the hiss of an arrow as it whizzes by.

Fuck. I'd forgotten about the soldiers who patrol the perimeter of War's camp. Foolishly I'd assumed that they'd been replaced by the dead. But no, they still stand guard.

Another arrow whizzes by, and I lower my body so that I'm plastered against Deimos.

I hear their distant shouts, but at some point, we travel outside the range of their weapons.

I escaped my guards *and* camp itself.

I release a ragged breath.

Step one complete.

Now onto step two.

IT TAKES OVER an hour to get to Mansoura. The city grows like a weed from the ground, the outskirts nothing more than rubble being reclaimed by nature.

The few gas lamps that are lit reveal more broken shells of homes. The small buildings look like gravestones, their walls riddled with bullet holes.

Clearly there was fighting here, just as there had been in Jerusalem. Maybe religion was at the root of it, like it was for my country, or maybe it was something else. Desperate people are often angry people. And since the Arrival, so many of us have been desperate. That's really all it takes to start a war— anger and desperation.

Once I enter the city proper, I quickly realize two things: One, Mansoura is huge—much larger than some of the cities we've raided so far. And two, in spite of its size, it might already be abandoned. Window panes are missing, buildings are crumbling, and the streets are littered with debris.

However, the gas lamps are lit, and somebody had to light them, which means despite all outward appearances, people still live here.

My eyes scour the sleeping city. In less than twelve hours, an army thousands strong will descend on the place, burning and killing and raiding everything in sight. Even on the wings of my passion and War's kindness, there's still this sick underbelly to our relationship.

Egyptian soldiers manifest out of the darkness, just as they did in Port Said. And just like in Port Said, their weapons are drawn. There's even an archer, leveling his arrow at my chest.

"State your business," one of them demands.

Briefly, I wonder if every stranger entering town this late at night is welcomed this way. Doesn't matter.

"War is stationed less than twenty kilometers from your town," I say. "In a few hours he and his army of five thousand will ride into your city, and they will destroy everything."

The soldiers don't lower their weapons.

"How do you know this?" one of them asks.

"I'm his—" *Wife.* I bite my tongue to keep from voicing that damning title. "I'm one of his soldiers."

I hear the creak of wood as the archer pulls back on his bow. One slip of his fingers, and I'll take an arrow to the chest.

"Why should we trust you?" the archer asks.

"You don't have any reason to," I admit, "but I'm begging you to take a chance and evacuate what you can of your city."

My eyes move to said city. If there's still as many people here as there were before the apocalypse, there's no way all of them will have time to escape. But some of them will, and that's all that matters.

"If you don't want trouble," one of the soldiers says, "I'd suggest you go back the way you came."

Why does no one ever believe me?

"Listen," I say. "The rumors about the east are all true. War has already swept through New Palestine. He will sweep through here too. I've seen it happen to several cities. It happened to mine."

I can't tell in the darkness, but the men seem skeptical.

"Have any of your messengers disappeared recently without a trace?" I ask, trying not to sound exasperated. "Have your aviaries had trouble delivering messages to certain cities to the east?"

I see two of the men exchange a look.

"How about the sky? Have you noticed it's been hazy recently? Have you seen some ash floating in the wind?"

Again, the men exchange a look.

"The horseman likes to burn his cities and kill anything that comes close to them. Your missing messengers are dead, and the cities north and east of you have all burned. Port Said is gone. So is Arish and most—if not all—of New Palestine"

The soldiers look at each other, then murmur softly amongst themselves. The archer still has his weapon trained on me, but even he is listening in on the quiet discussion.

Eventually they come to some sort of decision.

"And if we believe you?" one says, albeit begrudgingly. "What then?"

For a moment the words don't process. I guess I hadn't expected them to come around. Not when they'd seemed so distrustful.

"There isn't much time," I tell the soldiers. "War's men will be waking in an hour, maybe less, and they will begin to mobilize. If the people here hope to escape, they will need to leave immediately."

"If you've lied to us," the archer says still holding his bow and arrow loosely, "you'll pay for it."

Unfortunately—

"I'm telling the truth."

FIFTEEN MINUTES LATER I'm galloping down the streets of Mansoura.

"*Wake up!*" I shout as I go. "You all need to evacuate! War is coming!" I move through the city, shouting various versions of the same thing over and over until my voice grows hoarse.

This was the idea that formed when I sat with Zara and those other women. I might not be able to fight War's army, but I could still warn the cities the horseman was poised to attack, starting with this one.

Slowly, Mansoura rouses. Lamps are being lit inside homes, and I can see people shuffling about, or peering outside curiously. Eventually, I see families flood into the streets, some with their belongings.

I pause briefly to take it all in.

I managed to warn them. I actually did it.

I touch my bracelet, rubbing my thumb over the Hand of Miriam. A part of me swells with pride. I actually *helped* these people. They might truly survive War, all because I dared to slip away and alert them to what was coming.

Amongst the chaos I hear the clop of hooves, and a horse and its rider sidle up next to me.

"This was bold of you."

I jolt at that deep, gravelly voice.

"Bold and reckless."

My head whips to the side, and there's War, sitting astride someone else's horse, staring out at the houses with their fleeing residents. He doesn't look angry, but the sight of his calm, pitiless face chills me to the bone.

"W-what are you doing here?" I say.

"I spared your friend's boy in Arish, and I spared the survivors in Port Said, all for your soft heart," he says conversationally. "I was even willing to find your family for you."

My hands begin to tremble. I know better than to trust his level voice.

He turns his pitiless gaze on me. "And this is how you repay me?"

Being with War has lulled me into a false sense of reality, one where he treats me with benevolence and overlooks my actions.

The back of my neck pricks. I think I misread him.

I force myself to lift my chin. We're beyond apologies or explanations. I'm not sorry for what I did, and nothing on this earth will pry that lie from my lips.

He scrutinizes my face. What he sees there causes the corner of his mouth to curve up.

The chill inside me expands, reaching my arms, then my legs.

"I knew you were going to be trouble," he says. "But now, you must see me for who I really am."

He raises a hand—

"*No.*"

God, no. Anything but that.

War ignores me, stretching his arm out, as if to grasp the dark horizon.

All around us, people are moving into the streets. I want to say I don't see the old and the young and everything in between, but they're all amongst the heaving mass leaving their houses. Some of them glance our way, but no one seems to have any idea that a demon is among them.

"Please, War," I beg, reaching for his hand, "You don't have to sabotage this," I say.

"I'm not sabotaging *anything.* You defied my will, and now *they* will suffer for it."

"*Please,*" I say again. A horrified tear slips down my cheek.

I have held this man naked against me. He has saved me from the brink of death and brought out feelings in me no one else has.

He is capable of kindness, of goodness. I've seen it more than once.

"*Please.*" My voice breaks. "This isn't you."

Isn't it though? Isn't this exactly who and what he is?

War ignores me, and beneath us, the earth begins to shudder. The horse he sits on starts to nervously sidestep.

334

"*No*," I say again, this time more hopeless.

I hop off Deimos and take several staggering steps as the earth rolls beneath my feet. Around me, I hear people shout as they grab one another.

I glance over my shoulder at War, but his eyes have gone unfocused. He's not here, but *elsewhere*. And he looks nothing like the man I've come to care for.

The earth rips around me, and bone-white bodies pull themselves from the ground. People scream as soon as they catch sight of the dead rising. There aren't that many dead in this area of town, but in the distance, I hear rising screams. There must by a nearby cemetery or a mass grave of some sort.

And now the chilling realization sets in: Mansoura was probably hit by war fairly recently, judging from the look of the city. And in war, there are lots of casualties ... casualties whose bodies may have been buried within the city.

The dead around me descend on the living with unnatural agility.

I turn back to War. "Stop!"

Nothing.

I stalk towards him.

His horse is already halfway spooked. I debate scaring the steed into a frenzy before I decide instead to force myself up and onto the horse.

I am mad, I think, especially when War's mount lifts its front legs halfway up in warning. But I claw myself far enough onto the saddle to grab onto War's armor, and then I begin to drag the two of us back down to earth.

The action is enough to fully frighten the horse. The horseman's mount rears back, throwing me and War off its back. A split second later, the horse takes off into the melee.

War lays beneath me. His arm is no longer outstretched, his eyes no longer glassy. Yet still the undead don't fall back to the earth. Whatever powers he drew on, they won't be stopped by distraction alone.

I lean over him, and I cup the side of his face. "Please, War. Please find your compassion. Please stop."

"I will not stop, wife. I will *never* stop. It is you who must *surrender* to my ways."

That damn word.

I push myself away from him, suddenly repulsed at the thought of touching him. Of caring for him. He is a blight and a terror to my world.

Around me the town is descending into full blown chaos. The dead kill the living, and every person cut down only lays still for a moment or two. Then they rise again as the vengeful dead. They turn on the living, attacking the very people they sought to protect only seconds before.

Dead husbands kill their wives, dead parents kill their children, dead neighbors kill their friends. A lifetime of relationships—deep, meaningful relationships—are weaponized in an instant.

I barely register the tears tracking down my face. How did we deserve this? What could we have possibly done to deserve this?

The dead ignore me and War completely. It's almost surreal, and for an instant, I remember what it was like to watch television. To be like a fly on the wall as some great scene unfolded around you. You watched it, like a specter, but you were never touched by it.

I force myself to my feet. In a trance, I pull my bow off my shoulder, and grab an arrow. And I begin to shoot the newly dead.

A mother, a grandfather, a husband, a daughter, a neighbor. They hardly react to the arrows that cut through them. I keep shooting, even as I cry. I shoot until there are no more arrows left to shoot. And still the dead keep killing.

I pull out my dagger from its holster and stride into the fray. The undead don't fight me. They part like the Red Sea, moving around me to hunt down more innocents. I can't seem to even get close enough to them to sink my blade into their flesh.

I want to scream.

"You think I wouldn't know of your treachery?" War calls out behind me.

I turn to face my *heavenly* husband, and I'm shaking with all my anger and anguish.

"You hadn't even left camp when my men told me." He begins to casually close the distance between us, ignoring the carnage around him, even as blood sprays onto his black clothing. "How my wife slipped away—on my horse no less."

There is only one thing in this world he will spare, one thing he can't bear to lose. One way he might stop.

Fear washes through me.

Be brave.

I let him get close. It's only at the last minute that I bring my dagger to my throat.

War stops, still too far away to make a grab for my weapon, but close enough for him to see it pressed to my skin. His eyes widen, just for a fraction of a second. The horseman didn't foresee this coming.

"*Miriam*," War uses his menacing voice, the one that makes you want to piss yourself. And yet there's a spark of fear in his eyes.

Right now I'm too reckless to care about either.

"Stop the attack," I demand.

"I will *not* be threatened," he warns.

I dig the knife a little deeper, until I feel a sharp prick and warm blood spills from the wound and down my neck.

The horseman's eyes follow the line of blood, and now he looks like a man watching sand slip through an hourglass.

But *I'm* the one running out of time. The screams are quieting now; the dead have overwhelmed the living. It's not going to last much longer.

"Let them live," I say. I think I'm back to begging.

He doesn't.

He doesn't, and I feel my heart break. I didn't even know it *could* be broken. Not by War.

I can't sway him. We are all truly lost.

I feel my tears coming faster now, each one dripping down my face. It obscures the horseman's form, which is probably how he manages to close the remaining distance between us.

In an instant, he's looming in front of me. He wraps a hand around the hilt of my knife and tries to pry it from me. He's being too gentle, holding his strength back, and rather than forfeiting the knife, I move with it, stumbling into War's body so that now he's holding both me and the blade. The edge of it still bites my skin.

"Do it," I say, goading him. "It was so easy for you to kill them all off. Kill me too."

Now he *does* use his inhuman strength. War yanks his old dagger away, and I see fury in his eyes.

"You are *mad*, wife!" he says.

"You can't do it," I say, even though I already knew this. "You're so sure of your cause, and yet you can't kill me."

"Of course I can't, Miriam. God gave you to me!" he bellows. "Do not squander your life to make a point! I promise you, you won't get it back."

"You don't think I know that?" I say softly.

The horseman grabs me, too angry for words. Deimos has loitered nearby, and War stalks over to the creature, carting me along with him. He hoists me onto his mount.

Only hours ago this man was inside me. I remember his eyes on mine; he stared at me like I was some strange miracle.

That was the dream. This is the reality.

He hasn't joined me on his horse yet, and I stare down at him as the last of the city falls, their cries going silent, one by one.

"You're only willing to follow your god when you have nothing to lose," I say. "But when you do, *then* you defy him?

You're no tragic savior, you're a weak-willed monster."

Chapter 43

WE RIDE IN silence for a long time, during which War has tried to touch my neck wound twice, only for me to slap his hand away. It feels too much like giving in, letting the horseman heal me.

"I'm not going to stop trying to warn them," I say into the darkness. "You'll have to kill me first."

"I've gathered as much," he says.

I don't know what to make of that. But at least the battle lines have now been officially drawn.

"I could kill them all instantly, you know," War says, out of the blue. "Every town, every nation. Man wouldn't stand a chance."

I don't react. I think I'm numb.

"I used to do such things," War continues.

I stare out at the dark landscape, repulsion rolling through me.

"I woke about two years ago," he begins, "right around the southern tip of Vietnam. Back then I had no army, only the dead I raised from the ground. But it was enough. It was *more* than enough. Every city I came upon was wiped out within hours."

I lock my jaw to keep myself from telling him what a monster he is all over again. He knows. I can hear it in his voice.

"I don't kill like that anymore. Despite my battle-lust, there is a part of me—a growing part of me—that takes issue with such tactics."

So you simply kill us slower, I want to accuse him, but what's the point? I'd rather not waste breath arguing with War over his method of killing people when what I really take issue with is the fact that he *is* killing people.

He falls silent again, and the two of us spend the remainder of the journey brooding.

When we arrive back at camp, it's still dark, still silent as the grave.

I pinch my eyes shut. *Don't think about graves.*

A few soldiers on duty watch us curiously as we ride through.

It feels wrong being back here. Like the entire trip was some dark reverie.

War pulls Deimos to a stop in front of his tent. There the undead wait for us, and I *quake* at the sight of them.

I know what they are truly capable of. I saw it firsthand only hours ago.

War hops off his steed, nearby torchlight making his golden hairpieces glint.

When I don't follow him down, he reaches up for me and pulls me off the steed himself.

For a second, I think he's going to bring me into his arms. There's a look in his eyes, like half an apology, and I almost believe it. But the hug never comes.

He grips my upper arms, his expression fierce. "If you were anyone else, wife," he says, his voice low, "I would kill you myself for your actions."

I raise my chin. "Then kill me and let me be free," I say, my voice hollow.

His hold tightens on me. "Goddamnit, woman," he says, giving me a shake, "do you not feel a single *shred* of what I feel for you? I'm telling you this because I *couldn't*—I couldn't *ever* kill you. I can destroy an entire civilization, but not you, Miriam. Not for a thousand different slights you might visit upon me. I'd sooner *cut off my own hand* than hurt you."

I'm blinking back tears all over again, and I'm angry and sad and frustrated and heartbroken all at once.

"Then cut it off," I snap back at him, feeling the poison of my emotions in my veins. "And while you're at it, make it your sword arm."

I know I'm being cruel. Right now I relish it. It feels good to wound the horsemen when nothing and no one else can.

The words find their mark. War releases me, looking shocked, his eyes more naked than they usually are.

Now that he's let me go, I turn on my heel and stalk away.

I've only made it about five steps when one of the undead lurking nearby trots over, making its way to me. I glare at War over my shoulder.

"You are staying with me tonight, just as you do every other night." His voice is deep, controlled. Right now, he is one hundred percent the horseman, set to destroy my world.

"Like hell I am," I say.

The zombie comes in close enough for me to recoil at its smell, but it's War who closes the distance between us, coming so near his chest brushes mine.

He tilts his head down to me.

"I'm giving you your dignity right now." War leans in. "And something tells me you still have plenty of dignity left in you. Don't force my dead to sling you over his shoulder. Now, get in our tent."

I glare at him for a second or two. My body practically shakes with the need to undermine him. But the horseman's already proven once tonight that I can't get away.

I bolt anyway.

Defiance—even fatalistic defiance—feels good.

I don't get ten meters before one of his undead soldiers runs me down. I'm shoved to the ground, then hauled into the corpse's arms.

I curse at him, at War, at God, at every other useless person in this camp. I'm mindless with rage. The horseman wiped out an entire *city* with his will alone. And it was the most awful sight I've ever seen.

All because I tried to save them first.

My curses become sobs. The zombie carries me all the way to War's tent, where the horseman already waits.

"I hate you, you rat bastard," I say to him as I'm dumped on the ground.

War doesn't respond. Instead, he moves through his tent, removing every weapon he stores inside his home. He hands each of them to his undead soldier. "Store these in a secure location," he tells the creature. "And once you're done, bring hot water for the basin."

I don't move from the ground, even as the soldier leaves with War's things. There are still more weapons in War's tent, and the horseman continues to strip the room of them until every last one lays in a pile.

"What are you doing?" I ask.

"I don't trust you with sharp objects right now."

So he's disposing of them.

"That's smart of you," I say softly, "because the moment you close your eyes, I will try to skewer you."

The horseman appears mildly amused as he walks to his table and pours himself a glass of spirits. At least, his expression *appears* amused. His eyes are serious.

He takes a sip of his drink. "I can rise like my dead. You cannot. Therein lies my problem."

It takes me a moment to put together the meaning behind his words. When I do, I raise my eyebrows. "You think I'm going to kill myself?"

War watches me, his face inscrutable.

The horseman swallows the rest of his drink down, then he pours another and kneels down in front of me to hand me the glass. When I don't take it, he sighs and polishes it off himself.

"Why do you care if I kill myself?" I ask, from where I sit. My temper still burns hot, but right now, curiosity is overpowering my hate.

War rises and returns to the table, pouring himself another drink. Once again, he returns to my side and offers it down to me. I hesitate, then stand and take it from him.

"This isn't a peace offering," I state. He can't buy my forgiveness. Not after what I saw and what he did.

"I didn't intend for it to be one."

I move to the table and sit down. I don't know why I'm playing nice at all. War just did the most godawful thing I've ever seen. But then everything that's come after that event has diverged from the appropriate script. I'm supposed to kill him, and he's supposed to punish me, yet none of that is happening.

War fixes himself another drink, then sits down across from me.

The undead soldier comes back inside the tent, carrying a steaming pitcher of water. Silently, he pours it into the bathtub at the back of the tent, then exits, pausing only to pick up more of the weapons War deposited onto that pile.

"How can you want us all to die?" I ask.

"I don't want you all to die."

"Right, it's your boss who wants us gone."

"Believe it or not," War says, looking tired, "there are other creatures on this planet worth saving—creatures that humans have systematically wiped out. Have you ever considered the fact that even if you're God's favorite child, you're not his only one?"

344

"So you're doing this for the mosquitos then?" It should be funny, but I'm still so angry I want to throw my drink at the tent wall.

"There have been several extinction events on this planet, Miriam. And before my brothers and I appeared, the world was heading for another—all thanks to humans."

So we're being killed off to protect everything else that lives on this rock. I hate that the bastard actually manages to sound altruistic after this evening's events.

"Your very nature is flawed," War continues. "Too inquisitive, too selfish. And too brutal. Far too brutal.

"But no, Miriam, I don't want all humans to die. My very essence was borne of human nature. Without you, there is no me."

A chill runs down my arms. With every swing of his blade, the horseman is killing himself.

"So you're not sorry for tonight," I say.

"I cannot change my task, wife," his kohl-lined eyes hold an age-old heaviness to them.

"You can decide not to do it," I say.

"And why should I?" he challenges.

"Because your wife begs you to."

War stills a little at the word *wife*. It's not often that I acknowledge who I am to him. I know he thinks it means that I believe in this strange marriage of ours, and maybe I was coming around to the possibility. But right now I only say it because I know it gets under his skin in a way few other things can.

"Humans have the luxury of being selfish, Miriam—but I don't."

It doesn't feel selfish, trying to spare countless people from slaughter, but I can also tell from the sharp look in War's eyes that tonight, my words will fall on deaf ears. I'm too emotionally invested, and he's too adamant about his cause to be swayed.

I take another sip of my drink. The dead soldier has come back inside, carting more hot water to the basin and scooping up another handful of weapons on his way out.

The bath is for me, I know it without even asking. So I finish my drink and leave the table, stripping on my way to the tub. I don't care what War sees, nor do I care right now if the corpse comes back in and gets an eyeful of boobs. Some of my anger really has ebbed away, but only so that a terrible kind of numbness can set in.

I step into the shallow bath, and I begin to wash myself because I smell like a corpse. I keep my back to the horseman, not interested in seeing him or talking to him or interacting in any sort of manner. Halfway through cleaning myself off, the zombie does come back in and I don't bother covering myself. It doesn't matter; his sightless eyes stare at absolutely nothing as he completes his task.

"So is that it, wife?" War's voice rings out. "You'll now pretend I don't exist?"

"That would be impossible," I say, so quietly I'm not sure he hears it.

The horseman's chair scrapes back, and I think for an instant he's going to approach me. After a moment's pause, however, his footfalls move in the opposite direction. The tent flaps rustle, and then War is gone.

I towel off in the grim silence of the horseman's tent. I'm exquisitely alone, and yet I can feel the horseman's eyes everywhere. I know his dead lurk just outside the tent, waiting for me to run.

I toss my towel over a chair and slip into some clean clothes—clothes that someone else washed and dried and folded. Clothes that aren't mine and don't feel like mine, just like the rest of this place.

Then I move back to War's table and I pour myself another drink, my eyes going to the flickering lamplight around me.

War's a fool if he thinks blades are the only way to die. All this canvas, all these open flames. Fires break out in camp every week. It would be so easy to start one in here and let these flames finish the work they began in that burning building.

But I don't knock over a lamp or set fire to the walls. I don't want to die, despite my earlier bravado.

I close my eyes, a tear slipping out, and then I take another drink of the liquor. And then some more. I want to forget every unpleasant memory since the horsemen arrived.

I can't. I already know I can't, and getting drunk is only going to make me feel shittier. No amount of alcohol can strip away what I've seen. I push away my glass.

I'm living amidst an extinction.

That's what this is. Only, rather than humans taking the entire world out along with ourselves, the horsemen decided it would just be us who died. Us crappy humans.

Getting up, I slip into War's bed, ignoring the way it smells like him. My body is weary, my heart is weary, and shortly after I close my eyes, I drift off to sleep.

I'm awoken sometime later by the horseman, who joins me in the bed, one of his arms wrapping around my waist.

I stiffen in his arms. *I'm not ready for this.*

I try to wriggle away, but he holds me fast in place. He has to strong-arm everything, apparently.

This fucking endless evening.

"You are in my arms, and yet I sense you are far, far away from me," War says. "I don't like this distance, wife."

At least he feels how remote I am. He can stop me from physically leaving his side, but he cannot prevent me from emotionally retreating.

The two of us stay like that for what feels like hours. I don't think either of us sleep, but we don't get up either.

A chasm has opened up between us—or maybe it was always there, but now it can't be ignored.

When the first sounds of rousing men break the silence outside, War reluctantly withdraws his hand and sits up. I hear him sigh.

According to the rest of camp, they're invading Mansoura today. None of them know that Mansoura has already been taken and purged of its living. All that's left is to raid homes and steal goods from the dead.

I'm curious how War's going to handle this. So curious, in fact, that once the horseman rises from bed, I stop pretending to be asleep and sit up myself.

He lumbers over to his leather armor, which he's arranged near the pallet. His enormous sword is laid out next to it, the monstrous blade sheathed in its crimson scabbard. I'm halfway surprised he brought the blade into the tent after the big production he made about removing all the weapons from this place.

A dark, desperate thought grips me at the sight of that sword.

Caught in the hooks of my own mind, I get up, padding over to the blade, drawn in by it.

War pauses right in the middle of putting on his chest plate, his eyes locked on me. He removed all but one weapon from this room, and now his wife is approaching it. I'm sure last night's worries about me trying to hurt myself are now rearing their ugly heads, but he doesn't take the blade.

I kneel in front of his sword. Grabbing the hilt, I pull the weapon out a little from its scabbard. Emblazoned onto the steel is more of that strange writing that decorates War's knuckles and chest. These characters don't glow, but I can tell the language is the same. The language of God.

"Miriam." It's a warning.

I glance over at War, and there's an edge to his violent, violent eyes.

"I'm not going to kill myself," I say.

He doesn't relax, and I kind of enjoy his unease.

Turning back to the blade, I run my fingers over the alien markings. Then, seemingly of their own accord, my fingers slide to the edge of the blade.

"*Miriam.*" My last warning.

I run my thumb over the sword's edge, then curse when I feel the steel nick my skin. The fucker's *sharp*.

I stick my finger in my mouth just as the horseman snatches the weapon from my grip.

"It likes the taste of blood," War says, like his weapon might suddenly grow teeth and eat me whole.

He finishes putting on his armor, keeping himself between me and his sword. Lastly, he secures his blade to his back.

Outside, the noise is getting louder.

"I need to go." War steps in close. I can tell he wants to kiss me—or at least touch me—but he doesn't. The horseman may not be human, but he understands enough about human drives to know to stay away from me. Still, his eyes look regretful.

He waits a moment or two for me to say something, and I consider it—

I hope you don't come back.

May your enemies cut you down.

Rot in misery, asshole.

But my white hot anger is long gone, and it's hard to muster up the energy to stay mad.

War lingers long enough to realize that I'm not going to give him any sort of happy goodbye. With a final, heavy look at me, he leaves the tent, the canvas rustling behind him.

I never truly got an answer to my burning question: how will War handle today?

I did, however, get an answer to a question I *hadn't* intended to ask.

I glance at the cut on my thumb. A drop of blood still beads there. I smile a little at the sight, then rub the blood away.

Chapter 44

I DON'T SEE War again until that evening. By then the raiding celebration is in full swing, the war drums pounding out a hypnotic sound.

It doesn't matter that today's raid was pointless. Every person out here tonight looks jubilant.

I move along the edges of the crowd, people shifting out of the way as my undead bodyguards push their way through the throng.

My eyes flick up to War, who sits on his throne, a frown on his face. War spots me from his throne, his eyes narrowing. He stands, and the whole crowd seems to react to that single action.

I stare at him. I can't not. And my heart, my stubborn, awful heart seems to stutter. It's always love and war with us.

He won't stop. He won't ever stop.

I cut through the crowd, watching as it parts for me and my grotesque entourage.

War leaves his dais, the two of us meeting halfway.

Before I can say or do anything, he kisses me. It's so, so brazen of him, considering where we left off. And now everything the camp assumed about us has been confirmed. In case it wasn't already super apparent.

"Where have you been?" War asks, breaking off the kiss. But it's not really a question. His dead have been guarding me all day; War must've had some idea where they were—and thus where I was. Which was in the women's quarters.

"Do you love me?" I ask him.

War's brow furrows, his dark eyes moving between mine. He's so severely handsome.

His hand goes to the juncture where my shoulder meets my neck, and gently, he squeezes.

"Do you?" I echo.

"Can you really not tell?" he says, so quietly I almost don't hear him.

I take in a shuddering breath. "Then stop the killing," I say. "Please. That's all I ask of you."

"You are asking me to give up *everything*." War actually looks pained at the thought of ending the killing.

He *is* battle incarnate. I might be asking him to do more than stop a simple habit. I might be asking him to deny the core part of himself.

"Please—"

His expression hardens. "*No.*" His tone is absolute, unbending.

I knew he wouldn't capitulate. I knew it and yet it breaks my heart all over again.

Without another word I leave him, his large hand slipping from my shoulder. I cut through the swarming bodies, my nostrils stinging with the smell of sweat and rot that seem to stifle the area. My guards swarm around me.

I've made a lot of consolations with War. So many.

Too many.

Be brave.

There's nowhere to go. Nowhere to escape these horrors. I don't even have my own tent. I want to scream.

I consider leaving the camp entirely—not that it would work, but I still consider it. I glance at my thumb, where the morning's cut has healed over. Leaving would be foolish anyway; I already made plans for tonight.

I head back to War's tent, the only place my zombie guards won't follow me. When I enter, my eyes sweep over the space. There's still no weapons inside, including my arrows.

Behind me I hear the tent flaps thrown open.

"What was that?" War's voice is low and menacing.

My eyes widen. I didn't actually think he'd leave the revelry early. He never does.

I turn around as he stalks towards me.

"You want to be with me, but you are unwilling to actually make any sacrifices," I say. I'm ready to pick back up right where we left off.

War steps in close. "I am not here to *make sacrifices*, Miriam. I am here to *take*. Whatever human notions you have regarding relationships, cast them aside; they will not apply to us."

My anger from last night is back, and it burns so hot that I'm all but shaking with it. The horseman is still challenging me with his eyes.

Then I leave. I leave and I spend the rest of what will undoubtedly be a short life working to forget you.

I bite back the words.

Instead, I push his chest. His body barely sways.

The horseman smiles darkly at me. "Even defeated, you have such fire in you. I have seen villages that burn less brightly."

I push him again ... and again and again. I don't stop until he catches my wrists.

He reels me in, and then he kisses me, his lips fierce and unforgiving. This is the War I remember. He's all power and possession.

I fall into the kiss, trying not to think about anything

beyond moving my lips. It's hard to kiss him, hard to dance this line between desire and anger.

He's an inferno—his mouth hot on mine, his deft fingers pulling at my clothing.

War tosses me onto the pallet, then kneels between my legs. "There are a few sacrifices I *can* make."

He unbuttons my pants and pulls them and my panties off, taking my shoes and socks along with them. And then his mouth descends on my core.

I thread my fingers into his hair, gripping his dark locks tight enough to hurt. I tilt his head up to face me. "I don't want to see what you can give me," I say, still angry—so very, very angry. "Show me the benefits of *taking*."

With a wicked smile, he does.

I WAIT UNTIL War's asleep.

You'd think an immortal like him—one who supposedly doesn't need rest—would learn to stay awake, living with a woman like me. But he hasn't learned to—yet. To be fair, I did everything in my power to make sure he fell asleep this evening.

Now I carefully disentangle myself from him, getting up to slip on my clothing and shoes.

I head across the room and quietly open one of War's chests. Inside, nestled amongst the horseman's things, is some rope I discovered earlier. Quietly, I remove it and head back across the tent.

My mother's voice rings in my ear.

Miriam, don't do it ... I can't tell you how stupid this idea is.

I set the rope on the table then walk over to the pile of clothing War left behind. Sitting on top of it all is the horseman's sheathed sword. He probably intended to put the blade away, but sex then sleep distracted him.

I pick the weapon up, and—

Holy balls, this weapon is fucking *heavy*. I can't believe he swings this thing around all day.

Carefully, I remove the sword from its scabbard. The blade sings when it leaves its sheath.

On the pallet, War stirs.

Biting my lower lip to keep from making a noise, I watch the horseman resettle himself. His breathing evens out, and I relax.

I quietly approach the horseman, using both hands to carry his mammoth weapon. War's head is turned away from me, and for that I'm especially grateful. I don't want to see his sleep-softened features. I'll definitely lose my nerve.

I approach the bed. The sheets only rise up to War's waist; the rest of his naked body is exposed in the dim lamplight of the tent. The tattoos on his chest glow crimson against his olive skin.

While I watch, he shifts in his sleep, turning back to face me.

I stare down at his face, the sword in my grip feeling impossibly heavy. The kohl lining War's eyes is smeared; I can practically see where my fingers ran through it, and right now his features are so soft. He looks very human.

Too human.

I can't do this.

Of course I can't. It's one thing to fight someone in battle or self-defense. Another to coolly calculate … *this*.

My foot moves back a step, inadvertently kicking over a metal pitcher of water perched near the bed—the one I usually drink from when I get thirsty at night.

The deep, reverberating sound of it is deafening in the quiet room as it tips over and spills across the carpet.

Fuck.

War's eyes snap open, and it's too late to back down now. His sword is in my hand and I'm looming over him. It's too late to unravel my plans like I was about to.

"Miriam," the horseman says, his brow pinching as he

takes in me, then his sword. He looks hopelessly confused.

I would've thought he'd recognize treachery quicker than this. He's plenty familiar with it.

He trusts you, his wife, absolutely.

Using both hands, I point the sword towards the horseman's sternum.

War's grogginess is bleeding away, along with his confusion. "What are you doing, wife?"

"You're going to stop hunting us humans down. No more raiding, no more massacring. Whatever quest you're on, it ends, tonight."

Now he's awake.

"What is this? A threat?" The horseman raises his eyebrows from where he lays. His gaze moves over me, and I can tell he's searching for some reason—*any* reason—to explain away my behavior.

I don't move, just keep the blade steadily pointed at his chest, even though my wrists are straining from the effort.

His mouth curves into a mocking smile, though it doesn't reach his eyes. "And if I say no, then what? You'll *kill* me?"

Yes.

He stares at me, and his expression changes just the slightest. I've seen this look on him before, when men dared to cross him.

War sits up a little, propping himself on his forearms even though that brings the blade perilously close to his skin. He's not concerned. At all. I'd forgotten that from the last time I threatened him with a weapon. Pain doesn't frighten him.

"Have you fully thought this through, wife?" he asks.

I thought I had, but ...

"Because if you have," he continues, "then you'll know that I'll only stay dead for a little while," he says. "And when I'm alive again ..." he gives me a hard look, "my wrath, once stoked, is *unquenchable.*"

I can already feel that fury of his building behind his eyes, rising with every passing second.

My breath hitches and my pulse is like a drumbeat in my ears. His words have me hesitating. But I tighten my grip on the hilt and press the tip of his sword to his skin, my resolve redoubling on itself.

"Agree to it," I demand. A drop of blood wells beneath the blade, marring that perfect skin of his.

There's no going back.

"You would have me *surrender*," War says the word like it's an insult.

"It's what you asked of me."

Those eyes of his look as black as the night right now. "*No.*"

That's the second time this evening he's said *no*.

I knew I'd be working with *no* ... and yet, still it's a surprise. An unpleasant one. Maybe because now this means I have to follow through with my own plan. I wasn't intending on that.

My gaze goes to his flesh, where the tip of his blade presses down on him. I'll have to pierce this skin, I'll have to cause the horseman pain.

I *can't*.

I've killed before—too many times have I taken lives. Lives of far better men than War. But now, at the thought of hurting this terrible immortal, my nausea rises.

I can't, I can't, I can't.

Oh God, I think I might actually care for the monster.

My hands are shaking and I feel bile rising in the back of my throat.

The two of us are staring each other down, and I can tell War is waiting.

I have rope and a plan and fuck, I just need to do this.

I can't–

I pull the sword away from War.

His eyes narrow, but he relaxes. "That was a good decision—"

—I can't fall for this monster.

I lunge, driving the weapon back at the horseman, aiming for his throat.

War catches the sword by the blade, his hands wrapping around it. Blood wells beneath his fingers, slipping down his wrists and along the edges of his weapon.

If War feels any physical discomfort, he shows no signs of it.

Instead, it's his eyes that are wounded.

"You would've hurt me—with my own blade." That last part is tacked on like it's insult to injury.

"It's no less than you deserve." I hate that my throat tightens as I say those words.

"No less than what I deserve," he repeats, his tone inflectionless. "Is that what you think? You kiss me and fuck me and breathe my name like a prayer, but you believe I deserve death?"

I stare down at him unflinchingly. "You deserve *worse*."

The corners of War's eyes tighten infinitesimally, and I can feel the breath of that wrath he spoke of. He was mad before, but now I've truly wounded him in a way that no one else can.

This is where the horseman grabs my head and twists it until my neck snaps. And unlike him, I won't be coming back from the dead.

Now it's a matter of life and death.

Fuck your feelings, Miriam, finish this.

I lean my weight on the blade. "Surrender," I command him.

War's upper lip curls, and his eyes flash with his rage as he holds the blade back. Blood is dripping down his wrist and onto the bed. Our bed.

"I know you're capable of it," I say. He's human enough. I've seen him change his mind and change his rules. Killing is a choice for him, no matter how intrinsic it is to his nature.

"I'll give you one last chance to drop my weapon, *wife*." The title stings like a slap. "I will spare you some of my wrath if you do so."

"*Surrender*," I repeat.

With a deft yank, War jerks the sword from my grip and casts it aside. And then the two of us are left to stare each other down. His blood drips from his hands onto the packed sheets beneath him.

Without his weapon, I feel acutely naked.

I could've planned this situation ... better. Instead I let my emotions carry it out, and *it didn't work*.

I don't know if I truly thought it would, just as I didn't know if warning Mansoura would work, but I had hoped that threatening him—then perhaps incapacitating him—might at least do *something*.

Foolish, foolish girl.

War stands, and even though he's naked, he is excruciatingly menacing.

"You *betrayed* me." In the horseman's eyes, that's one of the worst crimes one can commit.

He takes an ominous step towards me, his massive frame looming.

For the first time since Jerusalem, I catalogue each thick bulge of muscle not as an aspect of his otherworldly beauty, but as proof of all the ways he can hurt me.

I take an uncertain step back. All of my former bravado has left me.

How to get myself out of this situation?

War notices me backing up, and he laughs low, the sound terrible.

"It's too late to run, savage girl."

All at once, he's closing in on me, and God save me, this is it.

The horseman grabs me, his blood smearing onto my skin like war paint.

"Did you really think that I could be so effortlessly dealt with? *I created violence.* You cannot outmatch me at my own game."

My knees go weak with my fear. I was an idiot to ever *not* fear this man.

War's hands move to my hair, his blood smearing against my cheeks, my ears, my scalp.

"This is where you surrender, wife," he says, his voice hushed. "Surrender to me truly, just as you vowed you would."

There are so many things War can take from me, but my word isn't one of them.

"I surrender to *no* one," I say. "And if you once believed otherwise, you are a *fool.*"

The horseman's gaze narrows. He laughs then, that deep, chilling sound raising the hairs along my arm.

He cups my jaw. "The earth is full of so many bones," he whispers.

I don't know what to make of those words, only that I should be frightened by them.

War releases my jaw. I can feel my skin smeared with his blood.

His hand moves to the hollow at the base of my throat. He traces my scar, the shape now smeared with his blood. "This is the Angelic symbol for *surrender.*"

Where is he going with this?

His raging eyes rise to mine. "I am not the only one who can resurrect the dead," War says. "You were brought back to life and marked just as I have been," he says.

The water rushes in—

I *had* thought I died that day. A chill sweeps down my spine.

My eyes drop to War's tattoos, and now that I look for it, the shape of them is eerily like my scar. I never noticed the similarities. Not until now.

War runs a hand over his glowing tattoos. "This is my purpose, written on my flesh." He nods to my scar. "That, is yours."

I shake my head.

"Deny your vow all you want, but it won't change the truth: you were made to surrender to me."

Chapter 45

WAR LEAVES SHORTLY after his final words.

In his place are zombies, lots and lots of zombies. I can sense them outside the tent, but it's the ones who are inside—the ones War sent in—that capture more of my attention.

Most of these ones are a bit more decayed than usual, and their ripeness has me covering my mouth.

I'm sure the horseman picked these corpses on purpose.

Proof that War can be just as petty as the rest of us.

The long hours of the night tick by, and I have nothing to fill them with. Sleep eludes me, and my toolmaking kit and arrows were confiscated with the rest of War's weaponry, leaving me nothing to do with my hands. There's still that well-worn romance novel ...

The thought of reading it twists my gut. I couldn't bear to hear about someone else's great love life when mine is such a mess.

I almost killed him. There was a moment when I was leaning on War's sword where I was putting my full weight into the thrust. Only the horseman's sheer strength prevented that blade from piercing his skin.

I rub my eyes, feeling a thousand years old.

Violence doesn't fix violence. I know that, and I knew it before I devised my plan. Yet nothing else had worked. I had been angry and tired of watching too many innocents die. And in the end, at least War had that same wounded surprise in his eye that so many of these doomed civilians had. If nothing else, my horseman got a taste of his own punishment.

By midmorning, the sounds of camp are in full swing. People are laughing, bickering, shaking out dusty clothing, sharpening their blades, or smoking cigarettes and kicking balls around the tents. I've already heard the war drums herald in one execution, and breakfast has come and gone. In all that time, War hasn't returned.

I'm busy staring at the photo of my family, my thumb rubbing over my father's face when the zombies around me straighten. Then, as one, they approach me.

They close in until it's clear they're going to grab me.

"If you want me to follow you," I say quickly, setting the photo aside, "I will. Just please don't touch me."

The guards stop just short of me, flanking me on all sides. Then, as one, they begin walking towards the door of the tent, and I'm swept along with them. Together, the group of us leave War's quarters and head towards the center of camp.

Somewhere in the distance, the war drums start up again, the sound making my skin prickle. The farther we walk, the louder they get, until it's clear the drums are pounding for *me*.

There are hundreds—maybe thousands—of people who have swarmed around the clearing. They watch the group of us pass with a mixture of curiosity and horror. We cut through the crowd, the people around us giving us plenty of room to walk.

As the morning sun beats down on the clearing and the smell of spilled alcohol and vomit rises up from the earth, this feels like a dream that was left out to rot.

Amongst it all, War sits on his throne. His phobos riders

362

spread out around him, most looking stoic, but a few of them appearing pleased. Only Hussain, the one rider who's been kind to me, appears at all concerned.

I'm brought before War, my guards finally stopping at the foot of his raised dais. I haven't been bound or manhandled, but it is clear enough that I'm a prisoner.

The drums are still going, pounding faster and faster, and it's working the crowd into a frenzy.

Something bad is about to happen.

I gaze up at War, and he looks so remote. The horseman gives me a disparaging look, and I feel like I'm just another woman who's satisfied him for a time. But now I'm a toy that's more work than it's worth.

All at once the drums cut out, and the crowd goes quiet. A breeze blows, stirring my hair in the silence.

"*Devedene ugire denga hamdi mosego meve,*" War begins.

You have discovered my one weakness before I have.

Around me, the crowd listens raptly, as though they understand even an iota of what he's saying.

I stare unflinchingly back at him.

"*Denmoguno varenge odi.*" His voice is loud as thunder.

I cannot punish you.

Judging by my situation, I'm sure War's figured out something.

Beneath my feet, the earth begins to quake.

My heart skips a beat. I know this sensation.

"What are you doing?" I ask.

Around us, people glance about, unsure what's going on. Some look more frightened than others; I'm sure those spooked individuals are familiar with this sensation as well.

Besides War, the only ones who don't look bothered are the phobos riders.

War stares at me, his gaze deep and dark.

"*Denmoguno varenge odi,*" he repeats.

I cannot punish you. There's an emphasis on that final word.

"*Eso ono monugune varenge vemdi nivame vimhusve msinya.*"
But I can punish others for your trespasses.

The first skeletal hand breaks out from the ground.

Oh God.

The earth is full of so many bones, he said last night. I hadn't understood his words then, but now, as I watch the dead claw their way out of their graves, I understand. Anywhere War goes, he has a ready-made army.

Someone gives a surprised scream. Then there's another several screams. I turn around just as a ripple goes through the crowd.

The dead rise, some no more than bones, others desiccated husks, and others still who look freshly dead. It's not just human carcasses that are dragged from the ground, either. Animals, too, are pulled from the earth, their bones clattering and grinding together as they move.

People don't know what to make of it. Not even as those bones begin to approach them.

The horseman has never done this before, never wholly turned on his own army.

I glance back at War. His eyes are stormy, his expression resolute. He's made peace with my punishment.

My punishment.

"Stop."

"*Mevekange vago odi anume vago veki. Odi wevesvooge oyu mossoun yevu.*"

I thought you'd want them dead. You've made it your mission.

He's right; I had made it my mission to pick off his army. But now that he's turning on them just like he has every other city ... I'm reminded of our shared humanity.

"Stop. *Please.*"

But he doesn't.

I don't see the first bit of blood spilled, but I hear the scream. Now a true, blood-curdling cry goes up. It's not fear I hear, but *pain.*

Another scream accompanies it, then another.

Most of these undead creatures are nothing more than brittle bone and a bit of dried sinew. It should be effortless to pulverize them into dust. And I'm sure some people do just that, but there are so many dead, and they care nothing about self-preservation, only carnage.

A skeleton bites a man in the throat so hard blood spurts. Another twists a woman's neck. All around me people fall to the ground dead.

All the while, War watches the massacre impassively.

He's an evil motherfucker.

I don't bother begging again. I tried that tactic before, when War *wasn't* trying to punish me. I begged right up until the very end.

I won't give him the pleasure of my anguish. Not again.

This is what heartbreak looks like on a horseman, and it is terrifying.

Now people are scattering, and the dead are giving chase. Some run towards me.

My guards, who haven't joined the fray, unsheathe their weapons. The moment someone comes too close, they attack.

Another wave of screams come from the tents that ring the clearing.

Zara. Mamoon.

I feel the blood drain from my face.

"War—" I was wrong, I'm willing to beg. "War, please, stop this."

He ignores me, his eyes focused on the fight.

I stride towards him, my hands beginning to shake. My friend, her nephew; I couldn't live with their deaths on my conscience.

"War!"

My guards block my way. I try to shove past them, and they grab me, holding me back.

"Damnit, War, look at me."

"No," the horseman says, not bothering to speak in tongues; the screams drown out most of his words. "Now is when *you* look, wife. They fall because you dared to try to kill me."

I jerk against the zombies' hold, but they don't release me. They turn me around and hold me in place as War's horde is slaughtered.

I'm forced to watch the entire thing, and this time, it takes much longer for the living to die than in Mansoura. They lay in bloody piles on the ground, and I guess it's a small blessing that the dead stay dead.

I thought I had lived and seen it all—the loss of my family, the loss of my home, the loss of so many people. I thought that the pain was some sort of armor; if the worst happens to you, eventually, there will be nothing left to hurt you.

Maybe that's true. But this hollowness has its own frightening ache.

Eventually, the screams die off and the chaos gives way to stillness. Eventually, my guards release my arms, and I take a staggering step forward.

The zombies fall to the ground in the next instant. Their task completed, they can rest once more.

My eyes sweep over the clearing, with its piles of bloody, broken bodies. In one sick wave, the entire settlement is gone.

That hollow ache is still there. It throbs along my skin and sits like a lump in my stomach.

It's quiet. So, unnaturally quiet. The canvas tents flap in the breeze, but there are no sounds of life.

Zara. Mamoon.

I take a sharp breath, and their deaths hit me like a physical blow. My entire body trembles from adrenaline and terror and guilt.

I put a hand to my mouth. I won't cry. Not in front of this beast.

I can sense War behind me, his vengeance settling around

us like ash drifting to ground. How I hate him. How I've never hated anything so deeply in my entire life.

My heart squeezes.

I've never cared for anything so deeply either. If he intended to break my heart as I have his, then between Mansoura's destruction and this, he's succeeded.

Under my feet, the earth begins to shake once more.

I cast War a wild-eyed gaze. Is it my turn to die now?

One by one the dead around me rise, animated once more. But whatever brought that spark of life to their eyes, it's now absent. That woman will never smoke another cigarette and that man will never play cards with his buddies. The people who drank and danced in this very clearing only last night are well and truly gone—either to heaven or hell or someplace else altogether.

"I'm never going to stop," War says.

My gaze moves to him. I'm so remote I feel as if I'm made of stone. "Neither am I."

I turn from the horseman when I hear it. Somewhere in the distance comes a child's cry. Everything in me stills.

But he killed everyone.

I wait to hear the sound again, and sure enough, I do, only now, there are several more cries that join in. I don't want to believe it. This must be another part of my punishment, making his creatures sound like the living.

The zombies suddenly begin to move, separating enough to make an aisle from the edge of the clearing to the dais.

Beyond them, I see movement, and now there's more crying and a few shouts. Several dozen zombies stride forward, looking grisly from their recent deaths. They move down the aisle, coming right up to where my guards and I stand. With them, the human noises get louder.

I'm holding my breath as they step away from the aisle, slipping into the crowd of dead, leaving behind a line of very confused, very frightened, very *living* people. At the head of the line is Zara and Mamoon.

I choke on a sob, nearly falling to my knees.

Behind me, I hear War rise. Then, the ominous sound of his footfalls. He comes right up to me, and he presses his lips to my ear.

"For your soft heart."

Chapter 46

"THAT WAS STUPID of you," Hussain says.

The phobos rider finds me later that day sitting amongst a line of empty tents. I've already embraced my friend and her nephew and I've processed—or at least I've *tried* to process—the horrors of the day.

Now I'm simply hiding from what's left of the world.

And judging from Hussain's presence, I've clearly done a shit job of it.

Hussain might be the only one of War's phobos riders I actually get along with, though I haven't talked to him in a while. Ever since a rider tried to kill me, the horseman has been a little reluctant for his men to get close. Now, apparently, that's no longer the case.

"So many others have already tried to kill him," Hussain says, sitting down next to me. My undead guards don't attempt to stop him from getting close. "You must've known it wouldn't work," he adds.

I don't bother asking him how he knows I tried to stab the horseman. My best guess is that War let his men in on his plan. They, after all, stood passively by as the dead killed their comrades. Only the children and the morally pure were spared from death today—oh, and Zara. She's no innocent, but she was my friend, which apparently saved her in the end.

"I wasn't trying to kill him," I say to Hussain.

At least, not *permanently*. Even I know that's an impossibility. I just wanted the massacring to stop. Coaxing him hadn't worked. I thought violence might get through to him; it was a language War understood.

"Then it was an even stupider idea," Hussain says.

"Did you come here to make me feel bad?" I snap. "Because I already do."

The truth is, I don't know what exactly I feel. I was cutting these people down in battle only a week ago; I shouldn't be sad they're gone, especially considering that War saved the deserving from his wrath.

Still feel like shit.

"There *is* no stopping him, Miriam," Hussain says.

"Pestilence was stopped," I say.

"You don't really know that, though, do you?" he says.

Yes, I want to reply, *War essentially told me so himself.*

But maybe the horseman lied. Maybe Pestilence simply finished his mission before he killed off everyone. How am I supposed to know what each horseman's divine plan is?

"So what's your solution?" I say. "Continue fighting until the world ends?"

Hussain gives me a look. "My world already *has* ended. My wife and children are gone, my friends were slain before my eyes. There is no world for me to go back to."

I glance over at him then, my brows furrowing. I hadn't thought of the phobos riders as victims. Not when they are so good at killing.

"Why do you fight for War if he's done so much to hurt you?" I ask.

Hussain gives me a long look, then squints at the sky. "The only part of War that is human is his memory of every battle that has ever been waged. Has he ever told you about those memories?"

I frown at him.

"War's seen us kill tens of millions of people over the centuries, and many of those deaths have been unnecessarily cruel." Hussain exhales, the sound full of weariness. "He's just projecting back on us our very worst nature."

I give Hussain a skeptical look. "And *that* convinced you to fight for him?" Because what I got out of that was that humans need to do a better job of being kind. Not go on being savages until we've destroyed ourselves completely.

"That convinced me that there is something inherently wrong with us," he says.

I stare out at the empty tents. Some of them are sprayed with blood.

"So you believe we *deserve* this?" I ask.

Hussain kicks a rock with his boot. "Maybe."

He gets up and begins to walk away, but then he stops, half turning back to me. "What you did also took a lot of courage, you know."

I release a shuddering breath. That one statement, that brief spark of approval, makes my heart hurt and gives me life all at once. We are all part of humanity. We all want to live. We should protect each other, and I tried. I failed, but at least I tried.

"I can't stand idly by while he continues to kill," I say, my voice breaking.

The phobos rider turns more fully to face me. "Husband and wife pitted against one another—now that's the true war." He backs away. "I'm interested to see who will win."

I DON'T MOVE back into War's tent.

I can't, not after my punishment. I could barely wrap my mind around being close to the horseman after he wiped out Mansoura. And now, when I tried to gut him with his sword and he killed off most of camp for the offense, it feels like the two of us have finally crossed some hard line.

It's easy enough to move out; I simply choose one of the thousands of abandoned tents. I pick the one next to Zara, even though in her words—

"Your dead stink."

Still, she puts up with my decaying guards who haven't stopped guarding me. They aren't the only dead either of us has to put up with; War's now undead army still lingers along the outskirts of camp, the mass of them waiting for the horseman's next orders.

Eventually I get my things back from War—a zombie drops them off at my tent's entrance and walks away. Amongst the pile, there's my tool kit and my half-finished arrows, the aged picture of my family, my romance novel and the dinged up coffee set that I never use. I even get the horseman's old dagger, the one he gave to me shortly after we met.

I guess he's no longer worried about me harming myself ...

The world moves on. One day turns into two, two into four, then it's a week, then weeks.

What's left of camp packs itself up, moves, then resettles— packs, moves, resettles. Life takes on a kind of predictability to it. I ride with the other humans, and I live alongside them too. There are more children per adult than before, so we take turns watching them, and at night, we have them sleep in several of the larger tents.

We pass through Damanhur, then Alexandria, then Tanta and Banha, slowly making our way south through Egypt. The dead now fight and protect the camp, so the living no longer have to bloody their hands (phobos riders aside).

War never comes to visit.

There are no midnight drop-ins, there are no convincing arguments about why I should be sleeping with him. There's no pissed off make-up sex.

He doesn't even try to get close to my tent. The last time I saw him, he was riding back in from a raid with his phobos riders. His undead army came running in behind him, their bodies sick with decay. A few of them got blown up that day after a mishap with some explosives they'd run into in the city.

War's eyes passed over mine, but there was no pause, no deep look, no spark of familiarity.

It's as though our relationship never was.

The entire thing is crushing.

I'm still angry at War, but then I've *always* been angry at him. It's him who's decided to keep his distance. As crazy as it is, I actually *resent* that he's still mad, even though I understand his anger—I tried to kill him, after all. But still, there were so many times when he crossed a line with me, I assumed it went both ways.

Then again, he's made it clear that I'm not to die, while I made it clear that I *wanted* him dead. That's pretty difficult to come back from.

As the weeks tick by, that numbness I felt in Mansoura begins taking over me. After seeing so many deaths, the faces start to blur together. And then there's that terrible human quality of getting comfortable with a habit. We travel, we camp, we siege, we move on. Over and over again. I might hate my reality, but at some point the abnormal becomes horribly normalized.

Maybe this is how War feels—like this is simply normal. I thought for so long that he was incapable of feeling—that his mind didn't work like that—but I think it does. He may be a heavenly creature, but he seems to love and fight and rage and grieve just like the rest of us humans do.

God, I am so tired. So unbelievably tired. The fatigue is a physical thing, and nothing I do seems to shake it. I go to bed drained, I wake up drained, and I drag myself through the day drained.

That's the first sign that something isn't right. The next is my loss of appetite.

Food no longer tastes right. First it was simply the smell of meat cooking. I'd have to stay away from the center of camp, where meals were served because the smell would make me gag. I chalked it up to seeing and smelling too many dead bodies, but now I've lost my appetite for coffee and alcohol as well.

None of it, however, alarms me. I've endured so much trauma and sadness, something like this was bound to happen.

It's not until this morning that I truly worry.

I wake to a horrible churning in my stomach. I catch a whiff of my undead guards, and immediately, I scramble off my pallet, frantically shoving my way out of the tent.

I press the back of my hand to my mouth.

Going to be sick.

I don't make it more than several meters before I retch. My guards stand idly by, and the smell of them—

I vomit again and again, that fetid scent caught in my nose.

Need the guards to move away.

Behind me, I hear another set of tent flaps thrown open.

"Miriam?" Zara's voice is groggy. "Are you okay?"

I can't answer, not until my stomach is completely empty. Even then I lean on my knees, breathing heavily.

"Stay away from me," I rasp, turning around and heading back to my tent. "I'm sick."

Zara doesn't stay away. She comes over and brings me water and bread and fruit and fresh yogurt. I manage to choke down some of the bread and a bite or two of a dried apricot. The sight of the yogurt makes me gag, so she takes it away.

"Really, Zara, you need to stay away from me. I could get you sick—or Mamoon."

"We'll be fine. I do need to get back to my tent, but I'll come back later," she says. "I expect you to finish off all the water I've left for you." She sounds like my mother. "And try to eat. You haven't been ..." Her brows furrow, and for the first time, I see that she's worried about me.

I wave her off. "I'll be fine."

With a final, worried look at me, she slips out, and I'm left to drift back off to sleep.

I WAKE TO the sound of heavy, familiar footfalls outside. They reach my tent, then stop.

I blink my eyes open just as the tent flaps are thrown back.

War stoops inside, and I have to suck in a breath at the sight of him. I'd forgotten how inhumanly handsome he is, with his olive skin and dark eyes, his black hair hanging wildly about his face.

He takes one look at me. "*Miriam.*"

At the sound of his voice and the concern that furrows his brows, I close my eyes. I thought I had lost whatever it was we had. But it's still right there. *He's* right there.

War kneels at my side. His hand goes to my hair, the tattoos on his knuckles glowing red, and he strokes my dark locks back just as he has so many nights before this.

I open my eyes again. "I missed you."

That was *not* supposed to come out of my lips.

His face softens. War studies my features, like he's trying to memorize them. He frowns, the concern back on his face. "Are you sick?" There's a sharp, almost frantic look to his eyes.

"The dead—" I begin. Just the thought of them has me gagging. "The smell—can you get rid of them?"

I hear footfalls moving away from my tent, and I know without asking again that War sent off his zombies. It takes a little longer for their scent to fade away, but once it does, I relax a bit more.

War is in my tent. And he's just as I remember—gold pieces in his hair, kohl ringing his eyes, vast expanses of muscle. Even his black on black attire is exactly how I remember it.

I try not to stare at his devastating face and his thick arms. I'm feeling too miserable to do anything more than eye-bang the crap out of him.

"Need my brother for this," War comments, still studying my face.

"What?" I ask, alarmed.

"If you're sick," he says, "Pestilence would be able to help."

I don't want *any* of his brothers anywhere near me. But the way War says it, it's more a wish than anything else. Wherever his brother is, he's not going to be coming to my aid.

"I'm fine," I say.

"You're not," War insists. "You look far too pale and tired—and skinny. Have you not been eating?" Worry pinches the edges of War's eyes, and he still has a wild edge to his features.

"Why do you care?" I ask him, not meanly, just curious. He hasn't shown any interest in so long.

"Wife, I have always cared."

That title! I didn't realize how badly I missed hearing it until now.

"It's you," War continues, "who never cared." There's an edge of bitterness to his voice.

He thinks *I* was the one staying away? I mean I *was*, but only because he seemed to have written me off completely. My wounded ego can only take so much bruising.

"If only." I look away from him.

At my side, War stills. He takes my chin and turns my face, forcing me to stare him in the eye. "What do you mean by that?" he demands.

"Isn't it obvious?" I say miserably, half aware that Zara can probably hear every single word. Oh well.

"Speak plainly, Miriam," War says, his features sharp and his gaze intense, hopeful.

Am I really going to do this? Shit, I think I am. I'm too exhausted to pretend away the truth.

"I care about you, War," I admit. "More than I want to—*much* more. It's been hell, not seeing you."

War stares at me for a long minute, and then he smiles so big it seems to reach every corner of his face. It's still a ferocious look on him with his sharp canines—not even happiness makes him look less dangerous—but my heart skips a beat at that smile.

"I've missed you too, wife. More than I have words to express."

I flash him a shy grin of my own. Right now, he's making me forget that I feel like roadkill.

"I'm still angry with you," I admit.

"And I'm furious that you tried to gut me—with my own sword no less."

I think it's that last part that really got to him.

He leans in. "But from *my* wife," he adds, "I expected no less." The horseman leans down then and kisses me.

I'm tired and sick, but there is nothing, *nothing* in the world that could stop me from kissing the shit out of this man. He is the one thing that still manages to taste good. His lips devour mine, and his arms pull me in close.

The two of us make out for a long, long time. Eventually, War breaks away to slide his hands under my body.

"What are you doing?" I ask.

He lifts me up. "I'm taking you home."

Chapter 47

NOW THAT WAR has kept his zombies at bay, I find I'm hungry. Very, very hungry. As soon as I see the platter of fruits, nuts, cheeses and breads laid out, I descend upon it. There's a bowl of hummus nearby, and I'm not sure I've ever tasted anything so good in my life.

"You have an appetite?" War asks, coming to my side.

He looks upsettingly eager at the thought.

I guess it's been more than just meat that I've been turning down lately.

"I don't know, this hummus just tastes really good."

Immediately, War strides out of the tent long enough for me to hear him barking out orders for more hummus.

War comes back inside. Grabbing a nearby pitcher, he fills up a glass of water.

"I'm going to bring a doctor over," he says, handing the water to me.

"No," I say too quickly, grabbing the warlord's forearm. I accidentally smear a little hummus on it in the process. Whoops.

His brows come together as he stares at my grip on his arm.

His eyes rise to mine, and he looks suspicious. "What are you not telling me, wife?"

I shake my head. "I just don't like doctors."

Is that really it though? There's been a ball of worry in the pit of my stomach. Something isn't right, but I don't really want to know what that something is. Not yet. This all might simply resolve itself.

"Sometimes, Miriam, we must endure things we do not enjoy. I'm sending for a doctor."

"Please don't, War," I say. "It's just the flu. Humans get it all the time. It'll be gone in a few days."

Just then, one of the horsemen's men comes in with more hummus.

The rider sets the platter down on War's table, then leaves.

"Your body is sick, wife. Don't pretend otherwise. I should have been more vigilant with you because it's clear you're not eating as you should. And I know you've been more fatigued than usual lately."

He's noticed? I should probably be concerned that he's been somehow keeping tabs on me, but instead I'm oddly touched that he's been so aware of my existence.

I'm fucked in the head.

War continues. "And that's not to mention the fact that only this morning you were physically sick."

"I feel better now." Sort of. I mean, I'm still nauseous, and the sweltering heat today is doing nothing to help it, but still, I feel well enough to eat and move around a little.

The horseman gives me a long-suffering look. "We may have been apart for some time, wife, but make no mistake, I won't let you die. Not by the blade and not by illness either."

I exhale. "A doctor won't be able to do anything other than tell me to rest and drink lots of fluids."

War doesn't look nearly so convinced.

"Please, I promise you, I'm not dying," I insist, drinking down the cup of water he gave me.

Behind me, the tent flaps rustle, and one of his phobos riders steps inside. "My Lord, we need to talk to you about"— the rider's eyes flick to me, and he doesn't quite manage to hide his surprise—"the next raid."

"Not now," War says, refilling my glass of water. He only has eyes for me, and it feels embarrassingly good to be the center of his world.

"Go," I say. "I'm fine."

War's jaw tightens subtly. "You're not."

"I *am*," I insist.

"And the undead?" he asks accusingly.

I get his unspoken meaning. He sent away all of his zombies. If he leaves, there will be no one to guard me.

I'm ashamed at how much my heart soars, hearing his concern. I thought he didn't care. There were days when I was sure of it. Only now am I aware of how much that hurt me.

"You're going to have to have faith that I'll be alright," I say. Even as I speak, I feel my nausea begin to rise once more.

"Faith is for humans," War mutters, but after a moment, he nods to his phobos rider.

The horseman comes over to me and takes my face in his hands and kisses me long and hard. "We will continue to discuss your health when I return. Until then, arm yourself, wife."

War releases my face, and then he leaves.

"So you're back with him." Zara's voice drifts in from outside my tent.

I'm back inside my old quarters, gathering together my things. I left War's tent shortly after he did so that I could pick up my belongings ... and muster the courage to tell Zara I was moving back in with the horseman. That's how easily War swayed me. One visit from him and a single request that I live with him again, and I capitulated to it all.

Apparently, I have shockingly weak willpower when it

380

comes to him.

I make my way out of my tent and face Zara. "You heard my conversation with War?"

She nods, her hijab fluttering in the breeze. "I'm going to miss having you as a neighbor ... even if your zombies stink."

I laugh a little at that before my expression turns serious. I stare off behind her, where Mamoon is playing soccer with several other little boys.

This moment and everyone in it seems so fragile. I'm afraid of my own happiness; it's usually the quiet before the storm.

"Do you love him?" Zara asks me, interrupting my thoughts.

My gaze snaps to her.

I open my mouth, but I don't know what to say. There's so much *not* to love about War.

Zara searches my features. Before I can scrape up some sort of answer, she says, "I gave him updates on you, you know."

My eyes widen. "*What? When?*"

"While you two were apart," she says. "He wanted to hear about how you were doing. If you were safe, happy, healthy."

My heart stutters a little at that. So that's how he learned I wasn't eating. I assumed that he'd somehow gotten the information from my guards, but it was Zara who informed him.

"I'm sorry I kept it from you," she adds—not that she sounds sorry.

"Why didn't you tell me?" I ask her. I don't think I'm hurt, but ... I can't say what I'm feeling, knowing my friend was secretly passing along information to War.

"He asked me not to," she says.

"But I'm your friend."

"He forced my loyalty the day he saved Mamoon."

I remember. I just never assumed he would make use of that loyalty.

Zara's gaze goes to my tent. "Here, let me help you with

your things."

Normally, I'd turn down her offer, but I'm still feeling massively fatigued, and my nausea has returned. I'll take all the help I can get.

The two of us gather up my few items, only leaving the coffee set behind. We fit most of my belongings into my canvas bag, which I then sling over my shoulder.

"You better come visit me," Zara says.

I scoff at her. "Like I have anything better to do."

She gives me a look that says, *I wasn't born yesterday*. "I can think of one activity you *might* prefer over me ..."

The two of us break into laughter, and I give her a playful shove. "Zara!"

"What? Don't act like it's not true."

We snicker a little longer.

Eventually, Zara's face smooths. "Seriously though, Miriam, get better. And one piece of friendly relationship advice: if you truly like the guy, try not to kill him again."

I DON'T END up seeing War until later that evening. He comes striding into the tent, looking just as imposing as he's always been. My heart speeds. I still haven't gotten used to being around him again.

His gaze immediately finds mine. "*Wife*." His eyes heat. "I cannot tell you what it does to me, seeing you in our tent. It drove me mad, living here without you."

I set aside the arrow I've nearly completed, when War closes the distance and captures my face, taking my mouth in his. He kisses me with his usual ferocity, and I melt into the embrace.

His hands skim down my sides, and yes, yes, yes. I've wanted to feel War against me every single day since we've been apart. Even when my anger burned red hot.

My hands go to his shirt, fumbling to get it off. His own hands slide under the hem of mine, his thumbs brushing the underside of my breasts.

It's all happening just as I hoped it would, when suddenly, he stops. His hands withdraw, and I want to cry out.

"You're sick." He says it like he's just now remembering himself. He doesn't, however, mention finding me a doctor again. I'd bet my romance book that there *is* no doctor, at least not here at camp.

I shake my head, even though I *do* feel a little nauseous. With each touch of his, desire is eclipsing my sickness.

"If you aren't inside me in the next five minutes, I'm going to be threatening you with another sword," I say.

War's violent eyes crinkle with mirth, and he kisses me again—albeit, a bit hesitantly.

"There is something you should know, wife," he says, pulling away. "In all my years, there's only one aspect of love—"

My breath catches on that word.

"—that I've ever really known," he continues. "And that's *longing*. That's all that the battlefield has to offer—a longing so deep it has a presence of its own. Love is a hope that carries men through dark nights, but it's nothing more than that."

My brows furrow. "Why are you telling me this?"

"When we were apart, that's what I felt. Longing. It was as familiar a sensation to me as swinging my sword," he says. "I hated my empty bed and my lonely tent, but it's what I've always known. It's being with you that's something new, something I want but don't understand."

I think this is an apology and an explanation for why he stayed away, though I can't be sure. War's words make my stomach churn uncomfortably and my breaths come faster and faster.

"Love is more than longing," I say quietly.

It's far, far more than that.

His hand tightens against me. "I am not a man of words, wife. I am a man of action."

I wait for him to continue, still not sure where he's going with this.

"If you want me to believe you—*then show me.*"

Oh.

Well, shit.

How am I supposed to show War what love is when I don't even know what it is I *do* feel for him?

But then I remember what prompted this entire exchange—the fact that I wanted to get in his pants despite being sick. I'm definitely well enough for a bit of sex, and if showing him love is his one stipulation ...

I can give it a try. You know, all in the name of make-up sex.

Swallowing down my nerves, I take his hand and lead him to his pallet. Outside, I hear the torches hiss and pop, and in the distance, someone laughs. But it all seems so very removed from this moment.

I reach up for War's shoulders and push him down onto the bed. He watches me as he lowers himself, letting me take the lead.

I follow him down, maneuvering myself so I'm straddling his waist. I lean over War and I stare into his eyes and remember every good thing he has ever done—from saving Zara's nephew to not raising the dead that one time. I remember all those instances where he saved my own life, and how today he came for me when I was sick.

I stare into those violent eyes until I see them thaw. And now I run my hands over the planes of his face, my thumbs dragging over his kohl-lined eyes until the black makeup is smudged. Leaning down, I kiss him—softly first, but then gradually harder and deeper.

I don't know if I'm doing this right. I don't really know *how* to show the horseman love when love isn't really sex. But it's the best I got at the moment.

As I move over him, I feel the hard planes of his physique,

each curve still new and wondrous to me. There's a giddy flutter low in my belly, and it scares the shit out of me.

My eyes flick back to War's. He's watching me, enraptured.

I pull my shirt off, then my bra, leaning back down to trail kisses over his bare torso.

"Take off the rest," I whisper to him.

He doesn't even hesitate. Whatever I'm doing has lit a fire in his eyes. He flips us around and pulls the rest of our clothes off before draping himself back over my body.

The horseman's hand slips down between my legs, and he begins to touch me until I'm moaning and grinding against his palm, and he's whispering *wife* over and over again beneath his breath.

This is safe territory. We've done this dozens of times. This isn't love, it's plain and simple desire. And even though I'm supposed to be showing War love, this is much more comfortable and familiar.

He leans over me, his eyes intense, and I touch his cheek, even as his fingers work in and out of me.

The warlord's breathing heavily, and he's rock hard and ready. He looks at me like he's about to ask, *What's next?*

I angle my pelvis and spread my legs, my meaning obvious.

"Don't look away," I say, staring up at him. I think that might be the key to this whole *showing love* business.

War *doesn't* look away. Not as he grasps my hips, his fingers slick against my skin, and not as he fits the head of his cock at my entrance. His eyes are on mine as he thrusts inside me, hard enough to make me gasp.

We've stared plenty at each other when we've had sex, but tonight, it's charged. Maybe it's that we both have simply been missing each other, but just the sight and feel of him leaves me breathless. My heart is galloping in my chest, and it's almost entirely from this *thing* between us.

I can so easily imagine it—loving War. Spending the rest of my life in these arms of his.

His cock throbs inside me, so thick that I can feel every twitch and pulse of it. Gently, he withdraws.

"My wife, you are everything I never knew I wanted," he says, thrusting back into me.

Again that giddy flutter. Again that unease at my runaway emotions.

War leans in and kisses me, and everything about it is tender and so unlike my aggressive horseman.

"Forgive me," he whispers against my lips. "Forgive me, Miriam."

The warlord is achingly gentle, each stroke of his hips a plea. He's making love to me, and he doesn't even know it, so desperate is he for my forgiveness.

"Harder," I say, because I'm suddenly in very real threat of feeling something I had no intention of feeling tonight. *I* was supposed to show *him* love, not the other way around.

And yet War shakes his head and keeps his thrusts soft, *loving*. His eyes are trained on mine, just as I instructed him. Only now, this whole experience has slipped out of my control. My heart is still hammering away, and my stomach is still doing funny things.

No, no, no, no, no.

But I'm pinned under that look, and I'm being lured in by those eyes, which look so kind, so sad right now.

His eyes are telling me what his words haven't.

I love you.

The rest of his body is good at talking too. Every touch feels like worship, every thrust feels like a promise. This is all spinning wildly out of my control, and Goddamnit, his gaze is still pinned on me. Why did I ask him not to look away? I can't escape what's in his eyes. I'm melting to it, and I really, really don't want to.

I can feel myself building ... building ... building ...

"War—"

I come then, staring into his face, my lips parting in

surprise as my orgasm crashes through me.

I see his own expression sharpen as his cock thickens inside me an instant later. And then he's coming on the wings of my own climax, the two of us locked in this strange synchrony.

Our orgasms seem to last an eternity, the two of us staring at each other as we ride them out.

This is something new, something more than cut and dry sex. I can't deny it, even if it startles me.

I made love to the horseman. It's thrilling and terrifying all at once.

He slips out of me and pulls me to him, and for a brief moment, things feel comfortable between us once more.

But the comfortable moment starts to drift away when I realize that War is still staring at me, his gaze caught somewhere between want and wonder.

"I have never felt that way before," he finally admits. "What are you doing to me, wife?"

I shake my head. I don't know what *either* of us is doing.

"I cannot unknow this feeling," War continues. "You were right. Love is far more than longing. It's far more than anything I imagined."

Chapter 48

THE NEXT MORNING I wake to extreme nausea.

I slip out of War's embrace as slyly as I can and shove a shirt and pants on. There's no time for bras, underwear and shoes. I scramble barefoot out of the tent.

Luckily, War's tent is on the edge of camp, and I manage to make it to the outskirts before I sick myself, over and over.

Now that my zombie guards are gone, there's no one to witness this, except for maybe one guard in the distance, but he's too far away to get a good look at me.

Once I'm finished, I stagger a little ways away, then sit down hard on the ground, running my hands through my hair.

My mind is quiet for a long time—so quiet, in fact, that when a thought slips in, it feels very, very loud.

My period should've come by now.

I take several deep breaths, even as my heart begins to race.

I try to count off the weeks since I last bled, and I think I get as far back as six before I become unsure.

We've done a lot of moving. It's hard to keep track of the days here ... but no, I think that even assuming I overcounted, my period should still be here.

My unease now pools low in my gut.

I pinch my temples and breathe slowly in and out.

Don't panic, don't panic. There must be some simple explanation.

Maybe it's the stress of all this traveling and the constant war. Maybe my body is in shock. Maybe that has simply delayed my period.

I almost relax. The explanation is *nearly* plausible.

Just as I'm about to stand up, another loud thought drifts in. I try to shut it out. I try to ignore it, but it's right there, sitting in front of me, unwilling to be overlooked.

How many times has War been in you?

My hands are beginning to shake.

Fuck, I think I *am* starting to panic.

The nausea, the awful way food tastes and smells, the fatigue that's plagued me, and the missed period—none of it is normal.

I cover my eyes with a shaky hand.

How many times has War been in you?

Dozens of times. He's been in me dozens and dozens of times.

Dear God, I-I might be pregnant.

Stress could be an explanation for the fatigue and the late period, but not the food aversions. Not the nausea.

I could simply be sick. I really could, but ...

Pregnancy is a more logical explanation.

I drop my hand from my eyes. For a long time I sit there in the foliage at the edge of camp, caught between horror and laughter.

This is what happens when people have sex, Miriam. Particularly sex with super virile god-men.

I put my head in my hands.

Pregnant. I might actually be pregnant. With War's kid.

Holy balls.

The longer I think about it, the more certain I grow.

A horseman of the apocalypse knocked me up.

A disbelieving laugh slips out of me ... then another little laugh slips out. I begin to laugh in earnest. I don't know when exactly my laughter turns into sobs, only that eventually I can feel tears slipping between my fingers and my body is heaving.

I've been crying for maybe five minutes when I hear those familiar, powerful footfalls approach me from behind.

"Wife," War says, his voice shocked. "What are you doing out here?"

I want to curl in on myself and die. I can't even have a moment alone to process this?

"Miriam," he says, coming around to my front, his voice thick with concern.

He kneels next to me and pulls my hands from my face. His gaze passes over me, like maybe I might be injured.

"What happened?" he says. "Did someone hurt you?"

Now my sobs morph back into laughter—sad laughter. My mournful eyes go to his. What am I supposed to say?

War and I hadn't really talked about children—not except for that one conversation that ended in a fight. We should've discussed this more, that's for damn sure.

I place my hand on my stomach, my fingers drumming along it. The horseman follows the movement, but there's no spark of awareness there. Not like there would be if he were born human. There are cues like this that he wholly misses.

I'm pregnant.

I open my mouth to tell him, when I pause. I don't know how he'll react. That alone accounts for approximately half of my fear. We just got back together.

The other half of my fear comes from *being* pregnant. With a horseman's offspring.

Fuck me and my poor life choices.

I stare at War, then his mouth. He kills *everyone.* Everyone.

And the last time I even came close to discussing whether he'd had children with any of the women he'd previously been with, he got offended. I assumed at the time I'd wounded his pride, but maybe there's something else to the conversation, something dark that would frighten me.

I'm being ridiculous. The horseman *cares* for me. He'd care for a baby if it was ours.

I think.

I mean, he reluctantly saved Mamoon, but how many thousands of other children have died in his battles?

Those aren't good odds.

I shake my head, giving him a wan smile. "I'm just tired, and I hate feeling sick."

The horseman's brow is pinched. He looks legitimately concerned. "Spend the day resting. You need it, wife. I will have someone bring you a basin of water to keep yourself cool. No one but me will bother you."

No one but me.

I nod, biting the inside of my cheeks. Again, he doesn't mention the doctor he threatened me with earlier, and I'm absurdly grateful for it. They would know in an instant what it's taken my dense-ass all this time to figure out.

I stare at War for a beat longer.

I could still tell him. It might be alright. He's promised to keep me from death.

He's made that promise to no one else.

Would he extend it to our kid?

Maybe—probably, but there's a part of me that's not sure, and that's reason enough to keep my mouth shut. I'm unwilling to lose anyone else to the horseman.

War reaches out and helps me up, and I pretend everything is alright when it's not. God, it's not.

I'm motherfucking *pregnant.*

I WAIT FOR War to fall asleep that night, just as I always do when I want to deceive him. I'm painfully predictable, and between that and my jumpy state today, I'm sure War can see right through me.

Late that night, however, he slips into bed beside me, his hands moving over my skin like he's trying to map me out all over again. I squeeze my eyes shut against his touch. It's been hard enough faking high spirits today. It's all I can do to act as though I'm asleep.

Eventually his hands still and his breathing deepens. Only then do I allow myself to really think about my situation again.

Pregnant ...

What am I supposed to do?

Either I tell War, or I don't, but if I don't ... I can't stay here, where he will eventually find out.

What's the worst that could happen if I tell the horseman?

He could lump our child with the rest of humanity, the part he wants to purge the world of.

The thought of a father killing his own child seems so preposterous that I want to laugh, but *is* it? Truly? War is way more comfortable killing people than he is sparing them. It's only my own foolish belief in War's goodness that makes me think he wouldn't hurt our child.

That same foolish belief led me to think I could save the people of Mansoura—but the city still fell. And that same belief caused me to beg War to spare various people. And he *did* spare Mamoon, but what were his parting words then?

Don't ask this of me again, wife. You will be denied.

I turn on my back and stare up at the canvas ceiling.

He didn't raise the dead that one time ...

My argument sounds weak, even to my own ears. Wanting something to be true doesn't make it true.

I blow out a breath.

What would old Miriam have done—the Miriam who never met War?

To save her family from threats?

She would have done whatever was necessary.

I've lost everyone I loved. If all War knows of love is longing, then all I know of it is loss.

Only now, there's a tiny new someone. Someone I could still lose.

I won't let that happen. Not again.

No matter my feelings for War, it would be naïve of me to assume the best of him after everything I've seen him do. War's a good lover—maybe even a good partner—but a good father?

I don't know, and I'm not going to risk finding out.

Taking a shaky breath, I lean over and kiss his lips. His arm comes up around me and he rubs my back. "Mmm ... my wife."

Something thick lodges itself in my throat.

I slip away from him then.

"Where are you going?" he mumbles.

I hesitate. "Just ... going to the bathroom." Not entirely implausible. Everyone at camp goes to the bathroom outside.

Quietly, I grab the things I need, and then I leave the tent.

My heart feels like it's crumbling in on itself.

I don't consider saddling a horse. Not when the corrals are usually guarded.

I'll head out by foot until I get to the nearest town War's army swept through. Surely I can grab a bike there—maybe even one with a small trailer hitched to it. I might have a chance then.

I feel like a fool for planning even this. There's no escaping without War knowing. He's always watching me, guarding me, and I've never managed to escape him.

Still, I don't slow.

I have to try. Regardless of what happens, I have to at least give escape a shot.

It's easy to walk right out of camp. The dead no longer guard the tent, and there's not enough living soldiers to sufficiently guard the perimeter.

That all changes, however, once I get far enough out. War's formerly undead army is now stationed out here, far enough from the camp that the smell isn't overpowering.

The hairs on my arms rise at the sight of all of them standing motionlessly. I can't tell which way they're facing, but it seems like they're all watching me with those dead eyes.

A moment later the smell hits me. I place a hand over my nose, gagging a little. Five thousand dead bodies rotting away under the summer sun creates a *stench*. Even breathing through my mouth, I can still taste the fetid rot of them all, it's so thick in the air.

It only gets worse as I close the distance between us. None of the zombies move; no one steps forward to stop me, and none of them turn their heads to watch me pass. And then I'm right up to the line of them. There's enough space between the dead to walk by without rubbing up against them, but I still wait for someone to grab me. I expect it now after so many encounters with them.

When none of them do, I exhale.

That was too easy. The thought fills me with dread.

Now to find a road, *any* road. So long as it leads away from here, I'll be fine.

It takes what feels like an eternity, but eventually I do come across a road. It's only then that I chance a glance over my shoulder.

To my horror, about ten meters behind me, a zombie has left its comrades to follow me.

That's when I begin to run.

Chapter 49

I DON'T THINK I have much time.

I'm still not sure what bond the horseman shares with his undead soldiers, but I suspect he can sense the world through them. Maybe their bond is strong enough to wake him from sleep, or maybe a zombie is going back to wake him right now. I don't know how they warn him, only that it's inevitable that he will be warned—and sooner rather than later.

The dead soldier is still following behind me. He hasn't closed the distance between us, but I'm not losing him either. I push my legs faster and faster.

I need to find a bike as soon as possible. Then maybe I'd stand a chance of losing the zombie, and thus, War.

Just the thought of the horseman is crushing.

It's all the fault of my *soft heart*, as he would say. It hates this too. With every step I take, it shouts that I'm a fool to run, a fool to leave. It believes in the best of War, which is why I ignore it.

Hearts are proven to be idiots.

I haven't made it a kilometer down the road before I stop running. I thread my fingers together over my head and take several deep breaths.

This was a bad idea. All of it—every single decision that led me here. Running, sleeping with War, allowing him to insert himself into my life. All of it.

I glance over my shoulder.

The zombie has stopped behind me. He seems to be waiting for me to make my next move.

Be brave.

My mantra crashes over me, and for once, I think about it in a whole new way.

I've assumed the entire time I've been with the horseman that I have been brave, but I haven't. I've been denying and running from this terrible, heady feeling I get when I'm around him.

But there is no outrunning him or these feelings.

I need to face the horseman down—in love or in war. Even if it means the worst.

No more deeds done in the dark of the night. Whatever comes, I'll face it head on.

In the distance I swear I can hear the pounding of hooves. Maybe it's just my imagination.

I squint into the darkness, and no—there looks to be a figure on the road.

There's only one other person confident enough to venture along these roads at night.

War and his steed manifest out of the darkness, Deimos's deep red coat looking almost black right now.

The horseman pulls up short.

He looks at me, his eyes wild. "Where are you going?" His face is almost mad with panic.

Be brave.

"I was running from you," I say.

His face crumbles. It's an expression I've never seen on him before.

"Do you truly hate me that much?" he asks, his voice

lowering with his emotion.

"I don't hate you at all, War," I say, the evening breeze tugging at my hair. "And I should, I *really* should."

He stares down at me from Deimos, looking so tragic. The wind tugs at his own hair, and God, even cast in shadow, he's magnificent. He could never pass for a mortal, not ever.

I put a hand over my stomach. For the second time today, the horseman notices the action ... and again, it doesn't register.

"Did you ever think about what would happen?" I say. "A human and an immortal get together, even though he's sworn to kill her kind, and she's determined to defend them? Did you ever think about the ramifications?"

War hops off his mount, moving slowly, like I might run if he makes any sudden movements. "Whatever it is that's bothering you, we can fix it—*I* will fix it." He takes several steps forward, stopping just short of me. "Hate me, curse me, just please come back to me, Miriam," he says. His voice breaks. "Please, come back."

He's begging. And I'm trusting the universe to pull through for me because there are too many forces at work that are bigger than me.

I begin to nod, closing the distance between us.

That's all the confirmation War needs to reel me into his arms. He holds me tightly for a long time, like I might slip away with the evening breeze.

Eventually he pulls away enough to gaze down at me, his eyes intense. "I love you," he confesses.

I don't breathe.

"I love you, Miriam," he repeats. "I hadn't known until last night what this strange happiness I felt around you was. But I do now. Being with you makes me feel as though I have swallowed the sun. Everything is brighter, fuller, *better* because of you."

I have no defense against this. I never have. I can take

War's cruelties, I can take his violence. But his love—it cracks me wide open.

"I love you," he continues, "and yet it has been *destroying* us both." He shakes his head. "I won't let that continue to happen. I have wounded you and wronged you, and I will change—I *vow* I will change." He grips me tightly.

I suck in a breath at that.

War told me once that human oaths were brittle things—bound to break with time. In the same conversation he said that his vows—those were unshakeable. And he was right. I begged and pleaded for him to change, I threatened and betrayed, and I got nearly nowhere with him.

Until now. Because now his vow *is* changing. And I don't know what exactly this one entails, only that I'm stupid enough to be hopeful.

No, not stupid. *Brave.* I'm brave enough to be hopeful.

"Say something," he says.

Have faith. That's what I told War earlier. And that's all religion ever really was for me. Faith. That things will get better, in this world and the next.

It's time for me to remember how to have faith in the universe.

I open my mouth and the words spill out.

"I'm pregnant."

Chapter 50

IT TAKES SEVERAL seconds for the words to percolate through War. His brow furrows and then—

The horseman's eyes widen, and his grip on me tightens just a fraction.

"Truly?" he asks, his eyes searching mine.

Hope this wasn't a mistake.

I nod, sucking in my lower lip. "Yeah. You knocked me up real good."

War's gaze moves down to my stomach. After a moment, he places one of his large hands on my abdomen. "You're carrying my child." His fingers flex against my flesh. "My child."

I see his throat work, and I'm petrified, utterly petrified.

War's gaze moves back to mine, and his eyes shine.

Is he sad? Is he happy?

The horseman takes my face into his. "I have never felt this ... joy."

He lets out a laugh, and his eyes ... his violent, scary eyes *tear up.*

Oh my God. He's happy. Obscenely happy. And now, for

the first time since I found out I was pregnant, I feel a spark of happiness too. More than a spark. I smile a little shyly at him, and he takes my face.

"Is this what you were running from?"

I pause for a moment, then nod.

He presses his forehead to mine. "You will never have to fear me, wife—nor will our children. I swear it before God Himself."

Children? Did he just assume there'd be more?

War kisses me then, and I get swept away by him. I can feel the horseman's excitement and his hope in the press of his lips. My heart races. He wants the whole human package— marriage, children, everything. I'm not sure I entirely believed it until now.

"No more, Miriam," War says. "No more fighting, no more running, no more distrust between us. I understand. Finally, I do. What I have done to you and what I have refused to do for you.

"I *understand*," he repeats, emphasizing the word. "From this moment on, things will be different, wife. I gave you my vow and I intend to uphold it. You have surrendered—I will as well."

A chill slides over me then, which is the absolute wrong response because this is *everything* I wanted.

"Just say you'll be mine. Not just in name, but in all ways. Then it is yours. It is *all* yours."

I search the warlord's face, sure that I misheard him. But this is no trick. All I have to do is give myself over to him. To be War's wholly and completely ... and things will change.

It's hard to trust your heart, but it's easy to give in to it.

"I am yours, War," I say. "Now and forever."

AFTER WE GET back to camp, War pulls me into bed and holds me close, his hand drifting down to my stomach.

"I have a child." He's been saying varying versions of this

400

since he found out. He's still dumbstruck by it.

The horseman leans down and places a kiss against my stomach, and I run a hand through his hair.

His eyes rise to meet mine. "I don't know what it means to have a pregnant wife," he admits. "I'm wholly unfamiliar with the process."

I guess he would be. There's not a whole lot of pregnant women involved in wars.

"I've never done this either." For once, we've found something we're both equally inexperienced at.

"What do you know of it?" he asks.

"Not much—other than the fact that women stay pregnant for nine months before giving birth," I say. "I've probably been pregnant for a month or more already," I add.

"An entire month." War digests that, looking fascinated and pleased. "My child has been in you that entire time. No wonder you've been so bloodthirsty."

Oh God.

"What else?" the horseman asks, moving the conversation along.

I rack my brain for the few things I do know about the subject. "My sickness and the food aversions—I think that's part of pregnancy. They say that some women get physically ill during the first few months of pregnancy."

War frowns. "This is *supposed* to happen?"

I lift a shoulder. "I mean, I think so."

The warlord looks massively displeased by that news, and I realize he's displeased on my behalf.

He doesn't want to see me suffer.

"How long does it last?" War asks.

"I don't know." This was never a topic I looked into with much interest. I hadn't assumed it would apply to me anytime soon. "Hopefully not too much longer." It's a miserable state to be in.

I bite my lower lip. "And then there's childbirth." I guess I should probably go over that one too.

Since the horsemen's Arrival, most advanced medical interventions have become obsolete. There are still doctors, and there are still physical procedures and hospitals and all that knowledge we wrote down in textbooks, but the elaborate technology once used to save wayward pregnancies is mostly gone. Women and babies die during childbirth, just as they have for thousands of years before the modern age.

"What is it?" War says, sensing my mood change.

"Giving birth can be dangerous."

"How dangerous?" he presses.

I look him in the eye. "I could die. And your child could die."

"*Our* child," he amends, his hand still pressing against my belly. For the first time since we began this conversation, he smiles a little. "You forget wife—I can heal all manner of injury. As I said before, you and the baby are safe."

Me and the baby.

I glance at War, and I almost want to laugh at the idea of domestic bliss with this horseman. It seems so preposterous. And yet, he's clearly way into it. *Way* into it.

He kisses me. "All will be well. Trust me on that."

THE CHANGE IN War starts small. So small I almost think I'm imagining it. He had promised me—no, *vowed* to me—that he would surrender. And yet I'm not sure I believed him until the proof starts rolling in.

Over the next several weeks, as we travel down the Nile, War stops attacking the small, satellite communities that speckle the land. Even more staggering, the horseman chooses to spare those few humans who manage to survive his raids.

It's a shock to hear—after all, War takes his undead army into battle with him, and those killing machines leave no one unharmed. I'm having a difficult time believing that there is anyone left *to* spare.

But there *are* in fact survivors, and the proof of it comes the day after we leave Beni Suef.

War and I travel alone on our steeds, the Nile a short distance from us. The rest of the camp—the dead and all—trail far behind us, just as War has always arranged it.

As we come up to the city of Maghaghah, an arrow zings past me, so close I feel the air shift. I glance at War, a bewildered look on my face.

This has never happened before during our travels because people don't know *War* is coming.

Another arrow zings by. Then another and another.

Or at least, they didn't *used to.*

"Miriam, move!" The horseman sounds like a general, and instinctively, I obey him.

I pull on my horse's reins, angling myself away from the line of fire. Another arrow whistles—

My body jerks as the projectile hits me in the shoulder. I grunt, pain and surprise nearly throwing me off my horse.

"*Miriam!*" War shouts. His eyes are locked on the arrow protruding from me.

I stare at my wound, warm blood pooling from it. The pain is there, but it's buried under my shock.

Someone just shot me.

They knew we were coming and they shot me.

War steers Deimos in my direction, putting himself between me and the city ahead of us. There are more arrows coming our way. Most fall short or go wide, but several come right at us.

I have to duck to avoid another one.

The horsemen gets to my side, his flank exposed to the onslaught. His face is calm, but his violent, violent eyes give him away.

In one fluid movement, he grabs me by the waist and drags me onto his horse.

I bite back a cry as the action jostles my shoulder.

And then I'm on Deimos and we're retreating, though I've never known War to retreat, ever.

As we ride away, I see a few arrows sticking out of Deimos's side. The horse doesn't so much as flinch from the pain, though it must hurt him.

This is what happens when you let people live. They pass warnings along to cities that haven't been attacked, and those cities prepare. And then they fight with every last piece of themselves.

My heart beats a little faster, and I feel a thrilling sense of accomplishment, despite being on the wrong end of this fight.

This is because of me and War. Without the trades and the fights and eventually, that vow of his, this never would've happened.

War places his hand under the collar of my shirt, near the wound, trying to heal it.

"I can't remove the arrow until we're safe," he says apologetically.

I nod, distracted by the warm drip of blood down my arm.

I chance a glance over my shoulder. The city is quickly growing small, but in the distance, I notice several riders coming after us.

"War ..."

"I know."

We ride for a minute more before the horseman pulls Deimos up short. We turn, so that we can see the men riding out for us.

War lets them come close. Not close enough to shoot us, but close enough to see that these men are wearing uniforms.

They're not just civilians, which means the outside world officially knows the horseman is on the warpath.

War watches them for several seconds. Calmly, he reaches out a hand.

A shiver moves through me at the sight of it. One of his hands is healing me, while the other ...

The ground between us and our assailants buckles and shifts. And then the dead rise, just as they always do.

The earth is full of so many bones.

The riders' horses rear back, and even from here I can hear the men shouting. They fire arrows at the skeletal bodies, but it doesn't stop the dead. The creatures amble towards them ever so steadily. The men turn their horses around and ride back, the dead trailing along behind them.

Only once they're gone does the horseman reach for my arrow. Faster than I can follow, he grasps the arrowhead and yanks it out.

I scream, more out of surprise than pain. A warning would've been nice.

Immediately, War's hand covers the wound, his touch warm. It only takes a little longer for my flesh to feel tingly. The two of us sit like that on Deimos in the middle of the road as the horseman heals me.

After what feels like an eternity, the horseman releases my shoulder. "The wound has closed, though it will take a bit longer to fully repair itself."

I pull my bloody, torn shirtsleeve aside to glance at the freshly stitched skin. "Thank you."

Behind me, War shakes his head. "You're my wife. It is the least of what I would do for you."

I swallow. The two of us are dipping our toes into a real relationship. Well, for War it's always been real, but for me, this is all new. And I feel those words. The weight of them.

His other hand moves to my stomach.

"The baby?" There's such concern in his voice.

The baby. Fuck, that's right.

I lift my shoulders hopelessly. "I'm sure it's okay," I say, more to reassure myself than anything else.

War gives a slight nod. Apparently if I think it's okay, he thinks it's okay.

With that, the horseman dismounts. As soon as he does so,

I see the arrows in his back.

"War!" This whole time he had his own injuries he was ignoring.

I take in the five projectiles buried in his back. My own wound throbs just staring at them all.

When the horseman sees where I'm looking, he glances over his shoulder at the protruding arrows.

"They're harmless," he says, shrugging off my concern.

Are they though?

I remember how he walked into Zara's gunfire when she faced him off. How he cut up his palms fending my attack off. And supposedly he once took a blade to the gut, just for the hell of it. I guess to him, a few arrows might seem harmless.

Still.

"Can you even feel pain?" I ask as he helps me off Deimos.

"Of course I can."

He says it like it should be obvious.

"Then how are you not hurting?" I ask.

"The arrows hit my armor."

Oh. I guess that makes sense. I begin to walk around to inspect them when War catches me.

His eyes move to all the blood that's dripped down my arm, and a deep frown forms.

Here he is, caring about my pain once again. My throat tightens when I remember that only a short while ago I was attempting to do the exact opposite to him.

My eyes go to the sword at his back. "I'm sorry," I say.

I don't know why it's taken me this long to muster the words, but it's long overdue.

"For what?"

I touch his chest. "For almost killing you with your own sword."

He laughs and takes my hand. "You couldn't have hurt me."

"I *did* hurt you though," I say.

Not all wounds leave marks.

War stares at me for a beat longer, then he brings my knuckles to his lips, his kohl-lined eyes fixed on mine as he kisses my hand. "I appreciate the apology, wife. All is forgiven."

I release my breath, and it feels like a weight has been lifted.

I give him a smile. "My husband ..."

He lifts his eyebrows, his own grin tugging at the corner of his mouth. "To hear that term on your lips ... it is the sweetest music, wife."

We share a moment. An honest to God moment that isn't overly complicated. And I let myself enjoy it in all its mushy gloriousness without overthinking it.

A dull sound off in the distance breaks the spell. War glances back towards the city that seems to rise from the desert itself. In the process, I see the arrows that litter his back, some which *drip blood*.

I hiss in a breath. "You *are* hurt," I say, stepping towards the wounds.

War reaches behind his back, and grasping one, he yanks it out and tosses it aside. After he does this for another, I stop him.

"I can do it."

The horseman stills, eyeing me. After a moment, he nods and lets me go around to his back.

There are three more arrows still embedded in his armor and skin. I start with the one near his shoulder, grabbing it by the base. "This might hurt."

I think I hear him grunt out a laugh, but maybe that's just my imagination.

I wrap my hand around the arrowhead, give it a tug, and ... nothing happens.

Now War *does* laugh. "Very painful, wife, I appreciate the warning—"

This time I throw my weight into the action and, with a wet noise, the arrow comes free.

I drop the bloody thing and place my hand over the wound. "I can't heal it like you can."

"That's alright, wife," War says, his voice disarmingly gentle.

I pull out the next arrow and then the last one, yanking hard on each one. Once I'm finished, the horseman turns around and gives me an odd look.

"What?" I say, wiping my hands off on my jeans.

"No one has ever taken care of me." His voice sounds strange.

I meet his eyes. He looks like something out of a fairytale in his red armor, his black hair adorned with gold pieces.

"I care about you, War. I don't want you to hurt. Ever."

War stares at me for a long time. "That's an odd sentiment for me to hear when part of what I am *is* pain. But I cannot tell you how moved I am by your words, nonetheless.

"You have made me mortal in the worst way, Miriam, and I am forever grateful for it."

AFTER THE INCIDENT in Maghaghah, War's zombies begin to precede us on our travels, and so every city I pass through is scattered with dead bodies from the fighting that must've ensued. Things look worse, not better, than they did weeks ago.

But.

But the horseman's dead are not attacking these towns we move through, they're defending themselves. So there *are* survivors. It's still a lot to take in, and as more people are informed of the horseman's arrival, the attacks on the army become more frequent and brutal, and there are more casualties lost from it.

I have to ride through the corpses with the horseman, their blood still dripping from their wounds. I think this is the way things are going to be.

But then, something drastic changes.

Chapter 51

I SIT WITH Zara near the center of camp we've erected just outside Luxor. The kid in me is desperate to catch sight of ancient Egyptian ruins, but the pragmatist knows that's never going to happen. Not during a battle campaign. So I settle for enjoying the sight of the palm trees that hug the bank of the Nile.

Next to me, my friend is trying—and failing—to weave a basket.

Aside from the distant sound of children's laughter and a few murmured conversations, camp is utterly quiet. War and his army rode out long ago, leaving only a few of us behind.

"Fuck this," Zara finally says, chucking her lumpy basket in front of her. "I can't do it."

It rolls away like a tumbleweed.

"I thought it looked okay," I lie. Because sometimes encouragement is better than the cold hard truth.

Zara snorts. "You'd have to be blind to—"

The sound of hoof beats interrupts us.

I glance towards the edge of camp. I can't see past the few cream colored tents in the way, but the longer I listen, the louder the hoof beats become.

For once, War and his riders don't gallop into camp at full speed. Instead, War appears first, Deimos sauntering almost leisurely into the clearing. Several more riders and their war horses follow, each moving sedately. It's only after the first few of them pass that I see the children.

There are hundreds of them being herded into camp, their faces dirty and tear-streaked. They range in age from young teenagers to infants.

I rise to my feet, staring at them all in shock.

Zara stands up next to me. "What on earth ... ?"

War and his riders came back from battle with captured children.

No, not *captured*.

Spared.

There was a time when it was a miracle to get War to save a *single* child. Now he has nearly a city's worth of them.

My horseman whistles to Zara. "I have more children for you to tend to." War doesn't bother speaking in tongues. He hasn't for the last two cities we've camped nearby. Now his mind and words are as open as they've ever been—much to the shock of the remaining humans that live here.

Zara points to herself, her eyes wide. "*Me?*"

War gives a nod.

I raise my eyebrows at her. "I guess you're now the unofficial caretaker of kids."

She gives me a beseeching look before she approaches the line of children. There are so, so many of them.

Zara corrals them, calling over other individuals to help out. Together they move the kids off to the side of the clearing, where dinner is already prepared.

Let's hope it's enough food.

War comes over to me on Deimos, his form obscuring the sun behind him.

"You saved them," I say.

He stares at me for a long moment, then squints into the distance. "It is ... not so easy to destroy them, knowing that they could've been mine," he says, his eyes dropping to my stomach.

My *child*, he means. He sees his own kid in them.

For a moment, I don't breathe. This might be the first time I've seen true empathy from War.

"Is that why you spared them?"

He glances down at me. "I did it for your soft heart," he says. "But still, they could've been mine."

THIS BECOMES A pattern—sparing children—until there are too many children in camp and not enough adults to attend to all of them. We've had to recruit the older kids to help with the younger, which isn't ideal.

That all changes today. Today War doesn't just bring back children along with his other war prizes. Today, he also returns with adults.

These people are blood-spattered and their eyes are wide from the things they've seen, but they come in with the children and receive meals and shelter all the same. They don't have to kneel in the blood of their former neighbors while they swear allegiance or choose death. They don't have to witness daily executions or face killing and dying in battle.

The worst they'll have to deal with is the culture shock that comes with camp life.

War dismounts Deimos and comes up to me, one of his hands moving to my belly.

"For your soft heart."

"WHO ARE THEY?" I ask later that night.

"You mean the people I saved?" War says. He pulls his pants on over his legs, his hair still wet from his bath. His shoulders look a kilometer wide.

I can hear a few phobos riders belligerently shouting outside, drunk from tonight's revelries. I'm sure if I strain my ears enough, I might even pick up the soft sounds of people weeping. This is the most terrible day of their lives, but they have no idea that it's one of the horsemen's most compassionate ones.

He runs a hand through his hair, looking impossibly sexy. "They are the innocents. I judged their hearts and found them pure—or at least as pure as a human heart can be."

I raise my eyebrows. "What made you decide to spare the innocents?" I ask.

The children I understand; he saw his own child in them. What does he see in these people?

"I vowed to you that I would change," he says. "I'm trying."

My throat constricts at that. "So this is all for me?" I can't say whether that makes me feel impossibly cherished or a little sad.

War narrows his eyes, studying my features for several seconds. "That is a rigged question, wife. I say it's for you, and you fear I am changing my ways without changing my heart. I say it's because I've suddenly grown a conscience, and I risk slighting your own significant involvement in this process."

Him growing a conscience could *never* be a slight against me. It's what I've wanted since I first met him.

"Have you?" I ask. "Have you grown a conscience?"

He saunters towards me then, the tattoos on his chest glittering. War kneels down before me and lifts my fitted grey shirt. It's probably just my imagination, but my stomach looks a little fuller.

Grabbing my hips, the horseman leans in and brushes a kiss along my abdomen.

"My entire world is right here," he says, looking up at me. "Late at night, I tremble at the thought of something befalling either of you. Do you understand how crazed that makes me feel?" He stands, moving a hand to my stomach. "There is the barest tendril of another life in you, and it is so vulnerable." His eyes move to mine. "And that is to say nothing of your own vulnerability. I am impervious to death, but anything can take you—and our child along with you.

"It's hard to be aware of that fact and to not think about all the other fathers whose families I've killed. Whose loves I've killed. I am filled with growing shame at what I've done because losing you is already unfathomable.

"So yes, I believe I've grown a conscience."

The horseman has done so many horrible things. He deserves to lose the only things he's ever cared about. Maybe then he would actually know the price of his war. But I don't want to die, I don't want my baby to die, and most twisted of all, I don't want War to feel pain the way he's made others feel it. Even if it would be just.

He's not the only one who's been softened by this relationship.

"You really want a child?" It comes out as a whisper. I didn't even know it was a question on my mind until the words leave my lips.

Being a father seems so completely at odds with everything War is.

"Before I was ... a man," he says, "I would've told you no."

I get a little spooked, just like I always do, at the reminder of what he actually is.

"Back then I was pain and violence and brotherhood and animosity and loss. I feasted on blood and fear. I couldn't conceive of life when I was so consumed with death.

"But then I was given this form, and suddenly, I existed in an entirely different way. I saw human nature *off* the battlefield for the first time. More than that, I felt what it was like to *live* off the battlefield."

War's face is laid bare, and for once, he looks very young.

"It greatly unnerved me, wife. There was so much about human nature that I didn't know until I lived and walked amongst you all, and I felt stirrings of that nature within myself. I thought giving into those feelings was a weakness only mortals succumbed to.

"However, once I met you, and I began *wanting* things I had never imagined wanting—things I had once rejected. At first I gave into these new feelings I had for you because I believed God had sent you to me. I was *supposed* to feel companionship and compassion because He decreed it. I was *supposed* to take you as my wife because He delivered you to me. It wasn't wrong."

"Somewhere along the way, my reasons for giving into these human emotions changed. I no longer pursued you because I was supposed to. I craved your company, your smiles, your fierce anger and clever tongue because it brought me the same joy battle did. And the world bloomed into color. For the first time, I began to truly feel this body and every emotion within it."

I had no idea. No idea that somewhere along all those winding weeks, when everything felt so hopeless to me, War was changing. Even before the vow he made to me, he was changing.

"I realize now," he says, "this is what living, what being *human*, truly is."

IT'S LATE, AND somehow I'm hungry and nauseous all at once. Which really isn't any surprise because this has happened four other times within the last week.

I fucking hate morning sickness. Hate it, hate it, hate it.

I mean, at the very least it could mind its own damn business and just stick to the mornings.

I stumble out of bed. All the lamps are out but one, which is perched on the table. I stumble over to it.

Resting alongside the lamp is a pitcher of water, a glass, and a platter of fruit, cheese, pita bread, and what looks to be hummus.

Caught beneath the platter is a letter that reads, *For my ferocious wife and child. I am hoping that if I feed you while I sleep, you won't try to stab me again. Consider this a peace offering.*

My lips twist into a smile at the note. Only War could make light of the fact that I kinda sorta tried to kill him.

I pick up the note, and much to my mortification, I can feel myself getting emotional.

It's not even like this is a one-off event. For weeks War has been leaving out trays of food for me at night. He's never commented on it; they've just appeared. I hadn't noticed any notes before, but now I wonder if there were other nights with other midnight notes that went unnoticed. Notes that War cleaned up with the tray in the morning.

I've been so consumed by what was happening around me that I hadn't noticed the single, terrible truth within me.

I love the horseman.

I love his violent eyes and the way he sees me. I love his strength and his humor and his ridiculous body, and that smile. That smile that I wait for. I love his voice and his mind. I love how he leaves me platters of food with little notes and how he stole my dagger all that time ago because it was mine. I love our arguments and our make-up sex and our midnight sex and our morning and afternoon and evening sex. I love War's growing humanity and his otherness.

I love him.

Fuck.

I *love* him.

I run a hand down my face. I want to take it back. I want to undo whatever witchcraft he's set on me.

I glance over at War's sleeping form. I can barely make out his face in the darkness, but what I can see makes my stomach feel light.

This is a familiar story to me. Loving what you're not supposed to. It happened to my parents, and now it's happening to me. At least my parents had the benefit of being decent people. War's decency is buried somewhere beneath his bloody agenda and his thirst for slaughter.

But that's changing—*War* is changing, and the world is changing with him.

Chapter 52

WITH EVERY CITY we pass through, more and more people are spared. First it's the children, then it's the innocents, then it becomes the elderly. Eventually, it's not clear *what* distinguishes the people War saves from those he doesn't. There's so many spared civilians that eventually the horseman stops bringing them back to camp. If they've survived his raid, they get to keep not just their lives, but their homes and possessions too.

Today War and I wander through camp, the horseman's eyes drifting to the people who live here. Camp itself is an altogether different beast than it was only months ago. There's much more laughter and far fewer weapons.

I don't know whether War's aware of the metamorphosis this place has gone through, or that he's the one responsible for this change, but I know that I feel a lightness inside me every time I see how things have improved.

When War and I hit the outskirts of camp, he turns to me.

"I have something for you," he admits.

I stop walking, raising my eyebrows. The horseman has given me a lot of things since we first met—a tent, clothing, food, weapons, heartache, carnage, some zombies, and a baby. I'm not entirely sure I want anything more from him.

The horseman pulls out a ring, and I furrow my brows, not understanding.

It's not until War kneels—on both knees—that I realize what this is.

"Will you be my wife?" War asks.

I stare at him dumbfounded, my heart trying to pound its way out of my chest. "I already promised you I would."

"But now I am *asking* you," the horseman says, staring up at me from where he kneels. "No more deals between us, Miriam. I want this to truly be your choice." He searches my eyes. "Will you be mine?"

I could say no.

For the first time, War is actually giving me an out in this relationship. Of course, it's too late for me and my heart. And now he had to go and make himself a better man, a man worthy of saying *yes* to.

"Yes, War. Yes, I'll be your wife."

He smiles so brightly it crinkles the corners of his eyes, his teeth blindingly white against his olive skin.

The horseman gets up and, grabbing me around the waist, spins me in his arms. Laughing a little, I press a hand to his cheek and lean in to kiss his lips.

Once we stop spinning, War takes my hand and begins to slide the ring onto my finger.

"Where did you learn about proposals?" I ask, remembering how he knelt on both knees. It wasn't quite what human men do, but it was close enough to know he picked it up from someone somewhere.

"I'm not completely ignorant of human ways, wife. Just mostly." He gives me a sly smile.

His response has me grinning back. I can't bear to look away from him. He's enraptured me. But then my curiosity has me glancing down at my ring.

It's gold, with a round ruby at its center. It's the color of War's armor and his glyphs and his steed—well, and blood too, but I'm ignoring that one.

The ring is too loose for my ring finger, so the horseman slips it on my middle finger, but then the ring is also too loose for *that* finger, so War moves it to my pointer finger, where it rests comfortably.

This isn't quite human custom either, and I love it all the more for that fact. The two of us, after all, are not quite a normal couple—but we're close enough.

"I love it," I say.

War squeezes my hand. "I like my ring on your finger. My dagger looked good on you too, but this ... this might be even better."

"TELL ME ABOUT God," I say that night after I slip beneath our sheets. War's ring is a comforting weight on my finger.

"Not 'your God'?" War asks from where he sits sharpening a blade, his eyes heavy on me.

It *had* always been his God. Not mine.

I don't know when that changed—maybe it was when *War* changed. Which is ironic, considering I'm derailing him from the holy commands he's supposed to carry out.

"What do you want to know?" he asks.

I prop my head on my fist. "Everything."

War laughs, setting his blade and whetstone aside. "Why don't we start with your most pressing questions?"

"Only if you get in bed."

The horseman's eyes deepen with interest. He stands, removing his shirt. A minute later he slips into bed next to me, scooping my body over to his.

"Better?" he asks.

"Much." My stomach is finally starting to swell, making it hard for the two of us to line up flush against each other.

"What are your questions?"

420

I reach out and trace the glowing words on his chest. "What does this say?" I've never asked.

The horseman stares at me for a long time, and he seems like he's deciding on something.

His lips part and he begins speaking in tongues. "*Ejo auwep ag hettup ewiap ir eov sui wania ge Eziel. Vud pajivawatani datafakiup, ew kopiriv varitiwuv, wargep gegiwiorep vuap ag pe. Ew teggew kopirup fotagiduv yevawativ vifuw ew nideta eov, ew geirferav.*"

The divine words wash over me like a wave, and I feel them as though they are living, breathing things. *Holy* things. My eyes prick because hearing them, I feel like I've just touched God, whatever and whoever God is.

I will be the blade of God and His judgment too. Under my guiding arm, mankind shall surrender their last breaths to me. I shall weigh men's hearts even as I deliver them onward.

I can't doubt that War is anything other than holy. Not after hearing that.

I'm still breathing shallowly when War reaches out, tracing my own crude marking at the base of my throat.

"I have something for you," War says, interrupting my thoughts. He gets up from the bed and crosses the room, grabbing a small item from his trousers.

"You have something else for me?" I say, raising my eyebrows.

Two gifts in one day? That's a dangerous precedent to set.

He comes back over. "I meant to give it to you earlier, but after I proposed ..."

After he proposed, any additional gift would've gotten lost in the moment.

War gets into bed and opens his fist.

All I see at first is red thread, but that's enough for me to know exactly what this is. A split second later, I notice the silver hand, a tiny turquoise stone embedded at its center.

The Hand of Miriam. A hamsa.

"These were on display in Edfu, and I remembered the one you wear on your wrist."

I touch the one he's speaking of.

"I'm not your father," War continues, "but I thought I might do right by him." By giving me another hamsa bracelet and continuing on my father's tradition.

I take the delicate piece of jewelry from him and hold it in my hand.

I close it in my fist. It's been a decade since my father wrapped my last bracelet around my wrist. Receiving this gift from War ... it feels less like my father's gone.

"Thank you," I say softly. "I love it."

War helps me fit the bracelet on my wrist, right next to my other one.

I stare at the two pieces of jewelry the horseman gave me today, and I almost say it.

I love you.

My eyes move up to War.

I love you.

He would be thrilled to hear those words.

I part my lips. "What will happen to us?" I say instead, chickening out at the last minute.

Lately, I've been thinking about the future. *Our* future. Not just what will happen in the next week or month, but where we'll be years into the future.

"What do you mean?" War asks.

"Where do you see our lives going?" Now that there's a baby and War's ways are changing, the future is one great, looming uncertainty.

"Wife, we will live just as millions of others have—in love until a ripe old age."

There's only one problem with that. "But you're immortal, and I'm not."

"That means nothing." Still, War frowns, and I know he's thinking about it all the same.

"It *will*," I insist.

I'm twenty-two now, but I won't always be. Eventually my youth will bleed away into brittle bones and sagging skin. Meanwhile, what will War look like? Will he remain unchanged, his body still muscular and virile? I can't imagine him any other way.

And if he didn't age, what then? What would happen when I was elderly and my husband was still this raw, masculine force of nature? Would we still be together? *Could* we still be together?

And even if we were—

"Eventually I would die," I say, "and you wouldn't."

What then would happen to War? And what would happen to the world? The horseman's vow might end with my death. Would he then return to his old ways and pick up where he left off?

"You spoke once of faith," War says, interrupting my thoughts. "Perhaps now is the time to have faith in me. All will be alright, Miriam. I vow it."

BY THE TIME I wake the next morning, War is gone.

A chill moves over me. The horseman has left early before, but that was back when he plotted with his men. He doesn't do that so much anymore.

I get dressed and force down a little food—my morning sickness actually seems to be going away—and then I leave the tent. Already the sounds of the living are filling the campsite.

I wander around until I spot War. He stands on the edge of camp, petting Deimos along his muzzle. The horseman's dark hair flutters in the desert wind.

He doesn't notice me until I come right up to his side. When he does eventually see me, he smiles. His expression is so free of violence that he could almost pass for a man.

You rip bits of his otherness away and then he becomes like the rest of us.

I don't know if I want him to become like the rest of us. I like his strangeness.

But maybe I get to still have that strangeness, just without the bloodshed.

War continues to pet Deimos. The horse butts his owner's hand away and takes several steps towards me, until the steed has buried his face in my chest.

The horseman turns and watches the two of us. Just when I think he's going to say something about me and Deimos making a cute couple (we so do), he says, "We're leaving Zara and the rest of camp behind."

The world is quiet for several seconds after that as I continue to pet his horse.

His words aren't computing. I won't let them.

"Everyone but the phobos riders," he adds.

Eventually, I glance up at War. "What do you mean we're leaving them behind?"

"At the next city we will leave them behind. I'm dismantling camp."

Now it's starting to sink in.

"What? Why?" My heart begins to race. "Are you planning on killing them?" Because I won't let that happen. Not to Zara or Mamoon—and not to the others either.

War's eyebrows come together. "I didn't say that. I said I am *leaving* them."

"So, they'll live?" I ask.

"Perhaps, perhaps not. But that will be up to their own fortune and luck."

Now I'm trying to wrap my mind around this—that for the first time ever, War will free his captive army. They may be far from their homes—we're now in Sudan, after all—but at least they'll no longer be under War's yoke.

I can't seem to catch my breath. There are too many warring emotions inside me. Pain, that I'll have to let my friend go; disbelief, that this might actually happen; wonder, that War is actually considering this. And then there's a strange, niggling worry that creeps up on me.

This is a part of war that I've seen only once before. The end. The part where you withdraw your troops, you decommission your weapons, you decrease your standing army. I saw it when my country's civil war ended.

Now it's happening again.

Zara and Mamoon will get to live a real life—somewhere not full of death and sadness. For that matter, the rest of camp will get to live some semblance of a normal life. It won't be the same as it was before, nothing can go back to the way it was, but they'll get another shot at life, which is more than anyone else in this camp has gotten before.

"Why are you doing this?" I ask War.

He gives me a smile. "For your soft heart."

Chapter 53

I DON'T WANT to let my friend go. I haven't ever since War told me the news earlier this week, but now it's really hitting me.

War already released his undead army twenty kilometers up the road, their badly decomposed bodies scattered among the dry earth, all that remains of his original army.

He freed his undead. Now it's time to free the living.

Me, Zara, and the rest of camp stand in the middle of Dongola, a town in northern Sudan that sits along the edge of the Nile. It's a striking, sunbaked place, and I hope it makes my friend happy.

Around us, the city's residents watch us with suspicious eyes. The deal War struck with them was that he wouldn't harm a single soul of theirs so long as they could incorporate War's entire camp into their town.

They didn't look particularly thrilled about it—and I don't blame them, Dongola doesn't look fully equipped to handle thousands more people—but when faced with the alternative, they accepted our lot.

Not that they'll necessarily stick to the deal once we leave.

That's why War's going to leave a zombie or two behind, just to keep tabs on them. After all, we humans make brittle vows.

Already adults and children are breaking away from our procession, carting away livestock and other forms of currency that they'll need to rebuild their lives. I feel my heart ache watching them leave. We've all gone on this unique journey together. It's a horrible sort of feeling to watch them go—and to be left behind.

"Are you going to be okay?" Zara asks. She holds the reins to a stinky, grumbly camel, the beast loaded down with goods. She has plenty of items to keep her and Mamoon comfortable, and yet I am still plagued with worry for them both.

I nod.

She glances down at my belly, which is starting to protrude. "You sure?"

Don't cry. Don't cry.

I take a steadying breath through my nose. "I'll be fine. Are you going to be alright?" I glance around me again, noticing all the inhospitable faces. This is better than outright death, but humans aren't always the most compassionate creatures; I've seen too much evidence of that in the last few months.

Zara lets out a sound halfway between a huff and a snicker. "You know I can take care of myself and Mamoon." The latter of whom is clinging to her leg. "I'll be *fine*."

"And the rest of the children?" I bit my lower lip. There are a lot of parentless kids. I worry for them.

"I'll make sure they're okay."

I step into her arms and give her a big hug. "I'm going to miss you, Zara. More than you know." The two of us have been together for months, and we've both seen and done things that no one else has. It's brought us close. Trying to imagine life without her just hurts my heart.

Her arms tighten around me. "I'm going to miss you too, Miriam. Thank you for being my friend from day one—and for saving my life and Mamoon's."

The two of us hold each other for several long seconds. Finally, I break away so that I can kneel down in front of Zara's nephew.

"Can I have a hug?" I ask him.

Reluctantly, he lets his aunt's leg go and steps into my arms.

"I'm going to miss you, little guy," I say, squeezing him tight. "Take care of your aunt."

He gives me a serious look, which I take is kid for, *I will.* Then he retreats back to Zara's legs.

She backs away from me, keeping her nephew close, the camel grunting a little behind her. "By the way, if you ever need someone to kill your husband," she says, nodding across the way to where War sits on Deimos, "just remember that I'm your girl." She flashes me a wicked grin.

A smile tugs at my lips. "I thought you owed your loyalty to him?"

"I can make an exception for a sister of mine," she says, her eyes shining.

Something thick lodges in my throat.

She backs away a little more. "Write to me, Miriam, if you can. Maybe one day our paths will cross again."

My smile is wavering with my sadness. "I'll do that."

Zara waves a final time, and then she turns around and walks away, the city swallowing her up.

CAMP IS QUIET. Far, far too quiet.

I stand outside War's newly erected tent, watching the breeze kick up dust like ashes. We've moved on, leaving Dongola behind. I feel like I've left a part of myself in that city.

The wind whistles through the few tents left. It keeps unnerving me. You'd think after the loudness of living in a tented city, I'd appreciate the silence. But I miss the place as it was.

How's that for irony? I'm nostalgic for the press of tents and the crowd you could get lost in. It was a festering wound of a community, but it's left a void in its wake.

Our camp now consists of no more than thirty tents, and those include the tents that shield our provisions. I stare at the other canvas structures, the ones that house what's left of War's phobos riders. He hasn't been replacing his riders for a while now, so his inner circle of fighters has been steadily growing smaller.

I don't know what will happen to them, especially now that War has released his undead army. Will he ride into the next city with just his men? Or will he raise more dead?

I can see the same question in the pinched, unhappy expressions of War's riders. None of them know what's going to happen next. Their warlord didn't release them with the rest of camp. What plans could he possibly have for them?

The question is all the more pressing since War has left no one in charge of running the daily tasks of camp. There used to be people who would wash your clothes, people who would cook your meals. Those who would weave containers and mend torn tents and sharpen blades and on and on and on. You name a need, there'd be someone to fill it.

To be fair, the horseman *did* try to recruit some of his dead for these jobs, but no one wants decomposing skin to find its way into soup (if the dead even know how to properly prepare such things), or for some zombie's unmentionable parts to smear onto the clothes they're washing.

That being said, there *are* still a few zombies left around camp; War likes having them patrol the grounds. He won't chance them getting close enough to make me sick, but he clearly still has them around for the camp's protection and—to a larger extent—my own.

As I stare out at the few remaining tents, two phobos riders step out of one, their torsos bare, save for the red sash they always wear around their upper arm. They lean in towards each other, chatting quietly. When they see me, one nods in my direction, and the other takes notice, the two falling silent.

The back of my neck pricks. Whatever they're talking about, it's not for my ears.

A short while later Hussain walks by, lifting a hand to me in greeting before joining up with the two other men. Together, the group of them head off, their heads bent together, their voices hushed.

They're all obviously friends, and the sight of them together brings a sharp ache to my chest. I already miss Zara and the easy friendship we had.

Rolling my hamsa bracelets around my wrist, I head towards the outskirts of camp.

Off in the distance, I see Deimos grazing, and nearby him is War. The sight of the horseman still makes my heart flutter.

Like his riders, War is shirtless, and even this far away, I can see his olive skin ripple with his muscles. Standing there amongst Sudan's barren landscape, he looks ... different. Still fearsome in stature, but burdened somehow. It brings back that prickling, uneasy sensation I felt only minutes ago, though I don't know why.

I make my way to him.

When I get to his side, he doesn't turn to me.

"Wife," War says, staring out at the horizon. Out here the world is all yellow, sandy soil and pale blue sky. "Where do you draw the line between those who are innocent and those who are not?" he asks, his gaze distant.

I shake my head, though I'm not sure the question was meant for me at all.

He turns to me, and his dark eyes unbearably tender. "I have seen it all," he says. "There is no clear demarcation between good and evil. And who is to say that even the worst men can't change?"

I search his face. I'm barely following his musings, and I

certainly don't have any sort of answer for him.

He stares at my lips. "I thought I could have it all—my wife, my war, and my sanctity. Instead, you have forced me to question *everything*—life, death. Right, wrong. God, man—*myself*. And I am not one to question, wife."

He glances beyond me, looking at the horizon again. "I have spent so much time judging men's hearts that I haven't judged my own. Not until now. And wife, ... I have found it wanting."

Chapter 54

THAT NIGHT, WAR holds me close—closer even than usual. I feel his uncertainty and inner conflict in the desperate grip of his arms. He really isn't the type of creature to question himself, and now that he has, it seems his identity is crumbling apart.

What is War without *war*?

The horseman searches my eyes. "I love you." His voice is rough with his own emotion. "More than my sword, more than my task. I love you more than *war* itself." He presses his forehead to mine. "I'm so sorry, Miriam. I'm so goddamn sorry for *everything*. For not listening. For your pain and suffering. For every last thing."

War's face blurs as I stare at him. There *has* been so much suffering.

"Why are you telling me this now?" My voice is hoarse.

He strokes my cheek. "Because I am making the decision to end the fighting."

I love you but it has been destroying us both, the horseman had once said. I hadn't realized that he might've meant that literally when referring to himself. War and apathy go hand in hand. To feel, to empathize, to *love*—that must be the beginning of the end for war itself.

Was he doomed the moment he laid eyes on me in Jerusalem? Or was it when I nearly died—or when I surrendered? I know by the time the horseman looked at me and wiped out the entire camp, it was there. He loved me then, though he had no name for what he felt; it was the burn of betrayal that set him off. But by then, the spark that set everything else into motion had already been lit. Sparing the children, then the righteous.

And now, War is considering stopping the destruction altogether.

It's beyond my wildest hope, so I don't know why I feel fear, but that oily sensation twists my gut.

"Why are you doing this?" I ask.

The horseman gives me a soft smile. "Always questioning my motives. I thought you'd be glad."

"What will happen to you?"

I can't bear to say, *What will God do to you?* But I'm imagining it all the same. The horseman is turning his back on his violent purpose. Surely there are some consequences to that.

War tilts my chin up. "Are you actually worried for me?"

My lower lip is beginning to tremble just the slightest. "Of course I am. I don't want you to—*die*." My voice breaks.

I know he's said it's impossible for him to die, but is it really any less possible than raising the dead or healing the wounded or speaking dead languages? Impossible no longer means the same thing it once has.

The horseman's thumb brushes my lower lip. "And who says I will?"

"Tell me you won't," I say a bit desperately.

"My brother didn't."

I go still. "So Pestilence is still alive?"

War nods. "Do you want to know what happened to him?"

he asks. "What really happened?"

"How he was stopped, you mean?" I say.

War's fingers move to my scar, tracing the symbol. "It wasn't violence that got him in the end. It was love."

I don't breathe.

"My brother fell in love with a human woman, and he gave up his divine mission to be with her.

Which is *exactly* what my horseman seems to be doing.

I try to keep my voice steady. "What happened to him?" *What will happen to you?*

"He and his wife live—they have children too," War says.

I feel myself begin to breathe steadily again.

"So they're alive?" I ask. "And happy?"

"As far as I know," War says.

Relief washes through me. War won't die, just as Pestilence didn't. He can leave the fighting behind, and we can have a good life together. A mundane and happy and hopefully long life.

I study War's expression again. "So you're not worried about leaving your task behind?"

War hesitates. "I wouldn't say that."

Like snapping his fingers, my fear returns.

He must see it because he says, "Miriam, do you believe that I can be redeemed?"

"What do you mean? Are you asking if you can right your wrongs?"

The warlord gives a sharp nod.

He's done so many abominable things. From the very day he arrived, he's brought death with him. But what he's done is a different question from the one he's asking.

"I think you're *already* redeeming yourself," I say. "So, yes, War, I do think that can happen."

The horseman gives me a soft look. "Then surely every man, woman, and child on earth is just as capable of redemption as I am. And if they want redemption, then who am I to cut them down before their true day of judgment?"

I shake my head, at a loss. "So you're going to stop the killing?"

He gives a slight nod. "So I'm going to stop the killing."

I DON'T KNOW when the two of us doze off, locked in each other's embrace, only that I'm pulled from sleep by a phantom voice.

Surrender.

The word whispers along my skin, moving over it like a tender caress.

I sit up in bed, breathing deeply. The memory of the word seems to echo in that tent.

Surrender, surrender, surrender.

I touch my scar. This wound and the word it represents inextricably bound me and War together. He was sure I was supposed to surrender. The proof of it was carved into my flesh.

Like a strike of lightning, realization hits me.

The message wasn't for me.

It never *was* for me. After all, I can't read Angelic.

The message is for someone who can.

War.

Chapter 55

THE NEXT MORNING, I wake to War's hands on my stomach.

"Mmm, what are you doing?" I say groggily, stretching in bed.

I feel the horseman's hair brush my bare skin right before he presses a kiss to my belly. "It's never going to cease fascinating me," he says, "that you're carrying my child."

I blink my eyes open and thread one of my hands through his dark locks, which are mussed from sleep.

"Do you know what it is?" I ask.

I mean, he knows a shitload of other things ... maybe he'll know the baby's sex.

War draws circles on my stomach, his expression soft.

His mouth curves into a small smile. "Human, I imagine. Or close enough to it."

I laugh and push at him, though I'm not entirely sure he meant it as a joke. "Do you know what *gender* the child is?"

He looks at me fondly. "Even my knowledge has its limits. We shall find out together."

I pull him to me, giving him a kiss on the lips. "Trading death for life," I say when I break away. "It's a good look on you."

He takes my face in his hands. "I didn't know I was capable of feeling this way, wife. Happiness is a new emotion—"

The tent flap is thrown open, and a phobos rider steps inside, interrupting us.

I yank the bedsheet up over myself, covering my breasts. Just like War, I've taken to sleeping in the nude. So shoot me, my clothes are becoming too tight.

War sits up, not at all bothered by his own exposed skin. "Get out." He sounds just like his old self. Full of confidence and pent up violence.

The rider, a burly, balding man with a thick beard, looks a little unsteady. He gives a quick bow, then rushes in to say, "With all due respect, My Lord, the residents of Karima are riding out to ambush us. If we want to stop them, we *must* leave now."

I glance at War, alarmed. Yesterday, the horseman was dead-set on laying down his sword, but what happens when the humans are the ones to attack? Does he stand by his words, or does he make an exception?

War stands, utterly naked and completely uncaring, swaggering across the room to grab his pants.

The phobos rider looks away abruptly. Then, muttering some quick excuse, ducks out of the room.

I sit up, the blankets pressed tightly to me, watching as the horseman pulls on his black clothing, then his armor. Lastly, he straps his massive sword to his back.

At the sight of it, my apprehension heightens. I can't say what exactly is bothering me—that War might kill as he's always done ... or that he might do something else entirely, something that could have its own set of consequences.

War must see the terrible possibilities playing themselves out on my face because he strides over to me and kneels down next to the pallet.

He reaches out and strokes my cheek. "There is nothing to

fear, Miriam. Whatever your worries are, banish them."

I nod, trying to believe him.

The horseman gives me a kiss, and then he leaves.

THE ENTIRE CAMP—or what's left of it—empties. War is gone, his riders are gone—even most of the horses are gone.

I'm utterly alone, save for the few skeletal guards War brought back to life to guard me. I feel like I'm the last human on earth, my surroundings abandoned, the living nothing but memories.

My surroundings aren't helping. This part of Sudan is all baked earth and sky. And aside from a few ruins and a handful of buildings I caught sight of during our ride in, there's nothing to indicate that people have ever lived here.

But it's not the loneliness that is painful so much as it's the boredom. I've reread my romance novel so many times I could quote entire sections of the book by now. I've stared at the photo of my family until my eyes have nearly bled. And the idea of working on another arrow makes me want to pull out my hair.

Maybe that's what drives me to start snooping around camp.

I've never been in any of the phobos riders' tents. There's never really been the opportunity or the desire. But now that there's literally no one to stop me, curiosity gets the better of me.

I step out of War's tent and cut across the camp, a hot breeze stirring my hair.

The closest tent to me is roughly ten meters away. I head over to it, pausing for only a split second at the tent flaps.

This is rude and invasive. It's also not the worst thing I've done.

I pull the flaps back and step inside.

The place is an absolute mess. There's already a day's worth of dirty dishes stacked in a corner of the room, and another pile of bloodstained clothing. Flies buzz around inside the tent, and shit, that should be incentive enough to clean the place up.

The next tent couldn't be more different. It's Spartan, and what few possessions its owner has, they are arranged in a nice, orderly fashion. Even the blankets on the rider's pallet are tucked in.

My brows knit at that. They were all in such a mad scramble to meet their foes, I wouldn't have thought there'd be time to make the bed ...

The next rider's tent belongs to a woman, though you wouldn't know it by looking at her things. My only clue is the framed photo next to her bed. I recognize her face immediately. It's hard not to when there are so few female phobos riders. In the photo with her is a man—her husband?

All at once I feel some unwanted emotion towards this woman who's undoubtedly slaughtered dozens of innocents. But I can't help it. She once had a family, just like the rest of us, and somewhere along the way, she lost them—most likely to War himself.

For the millionth time I wonder what motivated these riders to not just fight for the horsemen, but to become his most trusted and lethal soldiers. Was it survival? Was it a love of bloodsport? Something else?

I leave the woman's tent then, slipping out like a ghost.

Snooping is starting to lose its appeal. Reluctantly, I head into a fourth tent.

My last one, I promise myself.

This home looks like it's a shared space; there are two pallets pushed together, the sheets mussed from sleep.

Looks like me and War aren't the only two people in camp who are shacking up.

These riders have the unusual luxury of having a wicker chest in their room. Not many do since furniture is hard to travel with.

I head over to it.

Kneeling in front of the chest, I open the lid. Inside, I notice a hookah, tobacco, a spare set of clothes, and a Turkish coffee set. Amongst it all is a folded piece of paper.

I pull out the piece of paper and unfold it. On it is a hand drawn map of the area we're currently in, right down to the Nile River we've been following, the road we've been traveling on, our temporary settlement, and the city of Karima, the latter which is situated in the top, right corner of the map. Certain areas on the paper have X's on them, alongside the names of various phobos riders.

This is a tactical map, I realize. One that seems to include people and the places they need to defend ... or attack.

But War had told me that he was giving up the fighting.

He wouldn't lie to me—particularly not about this.

Which means the map is wrong. It has to be. My brow wrinkles as I continue to study it. The longer I look at it, the stranger I feel.

And then I realize why.

On the map, the phobos riders are positioned along the road, and judging from the markings, the plan is to lead their assailants towards a specific location, one where they can then ambush them. The only problem is, the map doesn't show the assailants coming from the city.

It shows them coming from camp.

Chapter 56

WAR WAS RIGHT. There is nothing to fear.

Until, of course, there *is*.

I put the map back where I found it, and then I *sprint* to War's tent.

He's going to be ambushed.

At least I think he's going to be.

But ... I must be wrong about what I saw. Not because I have faith in War's riders—I wouldn't trust them farther than I can throw them—but because they know better than anyone the extent of the horseman's power and savagery.

They know he can't be killed.

So why plan an ambush?

Maybe I read the map wrong. I don't have a lot of experience looking at tactical maps. It's possible I misinterpreted this one.

Inside War's tent, I grab my dagger and holster and strap it to my waist. It takes a little while longer for me to find the bow and quiver War once gave me. I feel a little foolish, arming myself when I'm still so unsure of what I saw.

War's riders must know something I don't. Or maybe I've

gotten this whole thing backwards. Maybe they're not going to kill the horseman—why does my mind keep going there anyway? *The man can't die.*

Nevertheless, unease sits like a stone in my stomach.

I stride outside, heading for the corral, where a few horses remain. I pause when I see them, another wave of uncertainty washing through me.

Am I really going to do this? It's one thing to strap on weapons, another to saddle a horse and ride into battle on an assumption I made.

And even if my worst fears are true, what could I possibly do that War himself couldn't?

I never get the chance to answer my own questions.

All at once, the earth comes alive beneath my feet, and *it is angry.* Violently it buckles and rolls, nearly throwing me to the ground. I stumble away as all around me, the tents shake and collapse. The horses shift nervously in the corral.

In the next instant, the dead are bursting forth from the ground, clawing their way to the surface. They move with unnatural agility; I've never seen them rise so quickly.

One of the horses charges, breaking through the brittle wood of its enclosure. The rest follow, galloping away.

I spin around.

In all directions, the dead are surfacing. There are hundreds of them as far as the eye can see. I've never seen War call so many.

Most are simply husks of humans, some with many bones missing. There are other animals too—horses, goats, cattle, and something that might be a dog or a jackal. They rise from the desert earth, dust sloughing off of them.

Once they're topside, they begin to run in a single direction: towards the site of the ambush.

WAR.

Something's happened. I'm certain of it now.

442

And my earlier plan is in shambles—the horses are long gone. If I want to help War, I'll have to go it on foot.

I begin to jog in the same direction as the dead as they rush past me. There are so many of them—so many more than one would assume, given the fact that the land seems to be devoid of life.

The earth is full of so many bones.

Far in the distance, I hear a dull *boom*. The sound sets my teeth on edge.

What in the world?

Less than a minute later I hear two more *booms*, each one ratcheting up my nerves.

In response, I push my legs harder.

I've only covered about four hundred meters when suddenly, the undead fall to the ground all at once.

I glance around me at the countless bodies now littering the landscape, my hackles rising.

I step up to one of the corpses, this one nothing more than a skeleton. I stare down at it as the seconds tick away. One—two—three—four ...

Something isn't right.

Something *really* isn't alright.

I glance to the horizon. My unease is back, but now it's redoubled.

You know what?

Fuck. This.

Rule Four of *Miriam Elmahdy's Guide to Staying the Fuck Alive*: listen to your instincts.

I haven't, not since I came to camp. The past several months have forced me to disregard this rule I lived by, but I won't today.

Instinct is telling me that something terrible is happening to War—that something terrible may have *already* happened.

I grab my bow and pull out an arrow from my quiver. I continue jogging along the road heading towards Karima, sidestepping piles of bones and bodies that litter the ground. It's as I'm running that I realize if War's men mean to dispose of him, then they're going to come back to camp to dispose of me as well.

Shit. They might be coming back for me this very moment.

Part of me wants to continue storming headfirst towards War, but the more calculating, survivalist part of me knows that the only advantage I have on two dozen armed phobos riders is surprise.

I scan my surroundings as I run, until I catch sight of a rusted out car which sits just off the road. I make my way to it, and crouching behind its rough metal frame, I train my weapon on the road coming in.

I don't have to wait long before I hear the pounding of hooves in the distance. Peering over the hood of the car, I see a mounted rider. They're too far away for me to make out their features, but I can already tell it's not War. The steed is black and not red, and the rider's stature is not nearly as staggering as the horseman's.

I keep my arrow trained on the rider and wait until he gets close. Then, I pull the bowstring back.

Inhale. Exhale. Aim. *Release.*

My arrow strikes the rider square in the chest, throwing the rider back in his saddle.

Another arrow is in my hand in an instant. The man is only just righting himself when I step out of my hiding spot and release the bowstring.

The shot clips him in the arm—not where I was intending, but hell, it hit him. That has to count for something.

"Miriam!" he bellows, closing in on me. "What the hell are you doing?"

It's weird to hear my name on his lips when I don't know who this man is. Or to hear him shout his indignation when he must know exactly why I'm shooting him.

The rider slows his horse as he gets close to me, then he

444

hops off it. Only now do I see that it's the burly, bearded man who entered my tent this morning. He now has a sword sheathed at one hip and a battle axe at the other. Roughly, he grabs the arrow embedded in his arm and rips it out, tossing the weapon aside.

I nock another arrow, aiming it at him. "What are *you* doing?" I'm impressed that my voice is as steady as it is.

He walks towards me, giving me a disdainful look. "I've seen you march about camp for the last few months like you're some kind of goddamn queen." His hand touches the top of his battle axe.

"Touch that weapon again, and I'll shoot."

"But you're not a queen," the phobos rider continues, his hand falling to his side. "You're just a cheap whore who got herself pregnant." His eyes meet mine. "You put that weapon down now, and I'll give you a quick, clean death. Otherwise, I'm dragging you back to the rest of the men, and we'll each enjoy fucking you a few—"

My arrow hits him cleanly in the throat, and his words cut off with a choke.

I'm not in the mood to listen to this shit.

He takes an unsteady step back, looking more surprised than actually pained. They always look surprised. I don't know why. I already shot this man twice, and I threatened him a third time.

The rider tries to draw the arrow out as blood cascades down his neck. He sways a little, then staggers to his knees, reaching an arm out to brace himself. More blood spurts onto the ground.

I step up to him, readying another arrow. "Where is my husband?"

The rider does the best he can to look up at me, considering there's an arrow running through his throat. He smiles cruelly as he tries to speak. The sound bubbles out his throat instead.

It doesn't matter. I saw the words form on his lips anyway.

War's dead.

Chapter 57

THE PHOBOS RIDER slumps over shortly after that. I lean down and pry his axe from his hand. I use his pants to wipe the blood from the weapon, and then I thread the wooden handle through my belt loop.

The rider's horse has only ambled away a short distance. Stepping over a pile of bones, I reach the horse and pull myself into the saddle. It only takes another few moments to turn the beast around, towards Karima. And then I ride like demons chase me.

War's dead. The words replay themselves over and over again. Maybe that's why his zombies fell all at once. Maybe he didn't release them, maybe his power over them died with him.

He can't die, I have to keep reminding myself. *Not permanently at least.* But then, with every corpse I pass I feel a little less certain.

What if God turned His back on my horseman now that War's decided to end the fighting? What if He's decided that this time dead means dead?

I can't catch my breath. The thought is absolutely

terrifying.

I don't know how long I ride before I register the wet, thumping noise coming from one of the saddle bags. I reach for it out of irritation. The moment I touch the canvas, my hand comes away wet. I glance at my fingers.

Crimson.

I jerk the horse to the stop, a bad feeling coming over me. Swinging off the horse, I loosen the saddle bag and—

I only catch a glimpse of familiar dark hair and a bloody, golden bead before I turn and retch over the side of the horse.

Whatever my eyes saw, they were mistaken. I shouldn't look again. I shouldn't.

I open the saddle bag further.

"No." The word slips out.

War's face is bloody and it looks all wrong. I have to lean over to vomit again.

"*No*," I sob. My entire body is trembling.

He told me he couldn't permanently die. He *told* me that.

But he never told me what would happen if someone did something this drastic, something like removing his head from his shoulders.

I sit there on the horse for close to a minute, aware that time is slipping by.

I don't much care.

A choked sob slips out of me. I press the back of my hand to my mouth, a tear slipping out, then another.

War's gone.

My husband, my love—the man who awoke *everything* in me.

The man who left a part of himself *inside* of me.

All I can remember now are the nights he held me beneath the stars, and the feel of his lips against my skin as he whispered his love for me.

He's gone, he's gone, he's gone. I wanted that so badly once—to be free of him. It's such a cruel irony that now that I want my horseman, someone's taken him from me.

I never got the chance to tell him I loved him.

Another muffled sob slips out. I can feel myself beginning to tremble. I'm about to lose it completely. I can sense myself standing on that precipice, ready to fall headfirst into my sorrow.

I glance towards the horizon and force myself to pull it together.

There will be time to mourn War—endless, yawning amounts of time. I know that all too well.

But for now, while I can still claim it—

I want my vengeance.

I GALLOP DOWN the road at full speed, anger driving me onwards. My thoughts are one continuous scream in my ears.

I can't think about him or about the corpses that decorate the road like confetti.

I'm being held together by revenge and revenge alone.

Why must everything I love be taken from me?

I push the thought away before I slip down that rabbit hole again.

I spot a crumbling building off to the side of the road, and on a whim, I steer the horse towards the structure. Before the steed has fully stopped, I dismount, stepping over two piles of bones so I can slip inside the abandoned construction. I bring the horse in with me.

The phobos riders have to take this road back if they want to return to camp; it's the only one that leads back there. And they *will* return to camp. They've left their possessions behind, and then there's still me to kill.

I hold my bow in my hands, an arrow loosely fitted against it. It takes every last ounce of sheer, iron will not to slide my gaze back to that saddle bag, which is currently dripping onto the floor. I can hear the terrible sound of it.

Drip ... drip ... drip.

I grind my teeth together and stand at the window that overlooks the street. I pause briefly to knock out the glass pane, before I train my gaze and my weapon to the road.

And then I wait.

It feels like hours have passed by the time the phobos riders come galloping down the road. By then my mind is quiet and my aim is steady.

Quite steady.

I have no fear left in me, and my anger has all burned off, leaving nothing but grim purpose behind.

I count the riders. One, two, three—*four*. Four, when there used to be close to twenty. Which means that aside from this group and the man I shot earlier, there are still fifteen soldiers unaccounted for.

I'll worry about that later.

I aim the arrow at one of the riders, take a breath, then release.

It hits the man in the shoulder. His body recoils from the impact, but he manages to stay on the horse, pulling savagely on the reins.

I'm already nocking my second arrow by the time his comrades notice.

Breathe, then release.

The next arrow hits another rider right in the chest. He slumps in his saddle, his horse veering off from the road.

The two remaining riders turn on their steeds, looking for the source of the arrows.

Nock and release. I hit one of them. Three wounded.

All that's left is—

My eyes meet Hussain just as he looks towards me.

"*Miriam*," he snarls.

I hesitate for a split second. Hussain has always been kind to me. I don't want to believe he could have helped kill War—or that he might've been riding back to camp to deal with me.

The second passes and with it, my shock. I grab another

arrow and aim. Release.

Hussain ducks, the arrow whizzing past where his head would be. He kicks his horse into action, galloping straight for the building.

Of course he would be a part of this conspiracy; it seems as though all the riders were in on it.

Still, my heart breaks a little at the sight of him.

Rather than continue to shoot at him, I train my next arrow on one of the wounded riders who has now righted himself on his horse and is circling back. Aiming for his torso, I release the projectile. It hits him just above the breastbone, and I hear his grunt.

That's all I have time for.

Hussain is right on the other side of the doorway. I hear him dismount his horse, his weapons clinking against him.

I nock another arrow, aiming it at the entryway.

There's a stretch of silence—

With a fierce kick, the door blasts inwards. Standing beyond it is the one rider who was ever kind to me. Sword in hand, he steps inside.

I release my arrow.

It hits Hussain in the side. It can't be more than a flesh wound, but it's enough for him to pause.

He glances down at it, then back up at me. "I never thought you'd try to kill me," he says.

In seconds I withdraw another arrow from my quiver and settle it against the bow. "I could say the same."

Aim, release.

Hussain moves, but he's not quick enough to avoid the hit altogether. The arrow lodges itself near his hip bone.

His teeth clench, but that's all the reaction I get. And still he keeps coming forward, removing the arrow as he does so.

I see blood drip from his wound, but he doesn't look bothered in the least. He yanks the second arrow out a moment later, tossing it aside.

What the fuck is this savagery?

Dropping my bow and quiver, I pull out my dagger and the battle axe, backing up. His gaze goes to the axe in my hand. He lifts his eyebrows.

"You managed to kill Ezra?" he asks, recognizing the axe. "Miriam, I'm impressed."

Hussain's gaze moves to my face, then to the horse beyond me. He must see the blood-soaked saddlebag, which means he knows I know.

"Why are you doing this?" I ask.

His attention returns to me. "War's ending his raids. If he hasn't told you as much, you must have at least seen it."

I shift my weight, sweat from my palms slicking my weapons.

"He left his army of children and innocents back in Dongola," Hussain continues, "but not his trained killers. Why do you think that is?"

Honestly, I don't have any idea.

"Let's be truthful with one another: War might spare the innocents of the world—he might even spare the average man, but his phobos riders? We've seen and done too much." Hussain shakes his head. "We gave him everything—"

"Everything but your loyalty," I say.

"He intended to *kill* us."

"No," I say, something deep within me aching. "War didn't intend on doing that."

None of these fighters must've known War's thoughts on redemption and forgiveness. If they had, they would've known that the horseman would've spared them too. War believed even they were capable of redemption. It's these men in the end who lacked faith.

And so they plotted to kill the horseman.

Hussain brings his sword up, his intentions clear.

"You were kind to me," I say a bit mournfully.

Not that it much matters now. It didn't stop Hussain from

plotting against War, nor did it stop me from firing the first shot at him. And it won't stop the phobos rider from trying to slice me open now.

"And you were kind to me," he replies, acknowledging our strange relationship. He takes a step forward, then another, his sword still raised. "Kind enough for me to consider sparing you. But we both know if I do, you'll try to save him."

I stare back at Hussain. There's no use denying it. He already saw me cut down his men. He knows my intentions, just as I now know his.

"Besides," his eyes move to my stomach, "there's also the matter of his child ..."

Without warning, Hussain brings the weapon down like a hammer, and I barely move out of the way in time. I swipe out at him, but I'm too far away and my weapons are too short to connect with anything.

The last of my emotions take a backseat as I truly engage in battle, dodging Hussain's successive blows even as I swipe at him with my own weapons.

The two of us duck and pivot, sidestep and lunge, moving almost in synchrony. It's a violent dance, and Hussain is my partner.

He swings again at me, and this time I'm too slow. I feel the sensation of skin tearing and warm liquid spilling down my arm.

The next second, the pain sets in. *Fuck*, does it set in. My left upper arm is on fire.

The rider follows the hit with another, this one grazing my other arm, equally deep.

I stare at him, my own attack coming to a grinding halt, and I know he's going to kill me. He's going to kill me, and he won't think twice about it. He's done this a hundred times before. What's another death? It's as easy as breathing to him.

Hussain's gaze has grown a bit excited, as though he relishes this moment where his opponent is caught on the brink between life and death.

"Did you truly think you could become the horseman's wife and things could end well for you?" he says almost pityingly. "He is a monster. We all are. We don't have happy endings."

Hussain swings his sword, intending to slice my torso open, and the only advantage I have at this point is that his weapon is heavy and a bit slow.

I duck under the hit, feeling the air stir above me. Instinct is shouting at me to run, but the only chance I have of stopping him is to do the opposite. So when I rise, I step forward, swinging the battle axe underhanded as I do so.

My wounded arms scream against the weight of the weapon, and I have to grit my teeth against the pain.

The axe catches Hussain in the gut, lodging itself deep in his flesh. For a second I can only stare at the hit dumbly, shocked I actually landed a blow.

A split second later he backhands me, knocking me to the ground. I roll before I get a chance to recover, and an instant later, Hussain's sword strikes the floor where I was an instant ago.

I scramble on all fours, crawling away from him, War's dagger clutched in my hand. My cheek feels like it's on fire.

I can hear Hussain's heavy breathing. "I'm not dying today, Miriam," he huffs out, grabbing my ankle and dragging me back to him.

I'm not either.

I flip onto my back just as he lifts his sword over his head, and I kick a booted foot at the axe handle protruding from his belly.

Hussain lets loose a sound that is half angry half agonized, a sound I've heard so many times on the battlefield as men and women died. His sword slips from his hand, and I have to roll out of its way as it clatters to the ground.

The rider's hold on me loosens, and I manage to tug my

ankle from his grip. I pull myself to my feet, my gaze moving over Hussain.

A curtain of blood cascades from his wound. It's a fatal blow, I can tell that right away.

I think he knows it too. He gives a little laugh, even as he braces an arm against a wall. "Can't believe—you got me," he gasps out.

Neither can I.

"He's not coming back to life, you know," he says. "We've made sure of it."

"I don't believe that," I say. I *can't.*

I stand there for a moment, dagger in hand. I could kill Hussain right now. I'm not sure if that would be the more merciful thing to do.

I remember War's words from last night.

Every man, woman, and child on earth is just as capable of redemption as I am ... who am I to cut them down before their true day of judgment?

At the memory, I holster my weapon.

The rider's knees buckle then, and he slides down the wall.

I begin to walk away from Hussain, but then I pause, glancing over my shoulder at him one last time.

"War really was going to let you live, you know. He told me all men deserved a chance at redemption."

Hussain doesn't react to that.

"I don't know how any of us are supposed to redeem ourselves," I admit, "but you still have a little time left. For the sake of our friendship, try."

I GRAB MY bow and quiver and exit the building.

Outside, one of the two remaining phobos riders has attempted to ride away, but he must've slipped off his horse because I see him laying off to the side of the road, inert amongst all the other corpses that litter the ground.

The other rider has also fallen off his steed, but as I leave the building he's limping towards the creature, who's standing fifty meters away.

Using the bow and arrows I've reclaimed, I shoot him in the spine. His back arches, and then he staggers forward several steps before falling to his knees.

I grab another arrow and nock it as I approach him. The rider glances over his shoulder at me, his eyes full of anger.

The second arrow goes through his ribcage. He cries out, slumping to the ground.

"You bitch!" he chokes out as I step up to him.

"Where is War?" I demand, nocking another arrow and pointing it at him.

He lets out a pained laugh. "You'll die if you try to save him." He's gasping for breath. "But go ahead and try."

Deep foreboding slips down my spine.

The phobos rider coughs, then goes still. I nudge him with my boot, but it's clear that whatever life he possessed, it's gone.

I move from him to the other phobos riders, checking each one for signs of life before I collect what arrows I can.

I might need them for the remaining fifteen riders.

I return to the lookout building I'd left my horse inside.

By the time I enter, Hussain is dead, his eyes half open and staring blankly at something on the floor.

Something inside me aches at the sight of him. He undoubtedly committed many, many horrors. Death was no less than what he deserved. Still, he was kind to me when he had no reason to be. I hope that whatever lays beyond this life weighs his good along with his bad.

I grab my horse's reins and lead the creature back outside. I can't stay here and wait for more phobos riders to come to me. If there are others who are making their way back to camp, I'll simply have to face them head-on.

It's time to find my husband.

I RIDE DOWN the road, following the trail of corpses like breadcrumbs. They litter the ground everywhere. By the looks of it, War called all the dead to him, every single one that he could reach.

At some point, the fallen bodies seem to steer away from the road, cutting west, into the desert. I veer off the road, heading towards what I assume is the site of the attack.

The farther I ride, the denser the corpses become. A hot breeze has kicked up, and a layer of sand sprinkles the bodies like garnish.

It's not until I summit a shallow hill that I see the rest of the phobos riders.

I count nine of them amongst the rest of the corpses, their bodies torn from limb to limb, their throats ripped out. They became zombie food by the looks of it. Even more perverse, some of the phobos riders have bloody mouths themselves, as though the moment they died, they turned on their comrades.

I continue on, aware that half a dozen phobos riders are still MIA.

That all changes when, a short distance away, I see a section of earth bare of corpses. It forms a lopsided circle, and at the edges of that circle I see meaty bits of appendages—an arm here, a leg there, an indeterminate body part across the way.

My earlier nausea rises at the sight.

There's no way to determine how many phobos riders died here, or what caused it, only that—based on the blood splatter—several of them did in fact meet their end here.

Only about ten meters away from that, the bodies become so dense they're nearly lying on top of each other. They seem to come to a focal point, as though they were all closing in on someone at the time they fell inert.

Was it War? His attacker?

My horse refuses to wade through the dead, so I hop off and head over to the location on foot.

I pick my way through the bodies, and right at the center of them all, there are more dead phobos riders and lots of blood—but no War.

It takes a bit more searching to find any more clues to War's location.

I scour the area, sure that his body must be around here somewhere.

After wandering for a small eternity, I catch sight of a bare patch of earth. I hustle closer. It's another circular clearing ringed with gore and mutilated bodies.

This time, I notice the scorch marks against the earth, and I remember the dull *booms* I heard back at camp.

It all comes together then.

These idiots were handling *explosives*.

I shouldn't be so surprised; War's army came across some back in Egypt, so I know they still exist. But anyone with a lick of common sense knows that most explosives stopped working long ago. And obviously, the ones that do still work are touchy and unpredictable.

But it would be an effective way to destroy the horseman.

My hands begin to tremble as I move towards the clearing, my eyes trained on the body parts. Am I going to have to pick through the debris to know what became of War?

Just as I begin to scour the edges of the blast site, I notice that there's another, smaller clearing a short distance away. Next to it is a coffin-sized hole in the earth.

I swallow.

Watching my step, I pick my way between the dead, heading over to it.

Don't want to look.

I take a deep breath and step up to the pit.

I have to look.

I peer over the edge.

"*No.*" The word slips out like a sob.

Lying at the bottom of the pit is War.

Chapter 58

I SIT ON the corpse-littered ground, my fist pressed to my mouth, staring at War's open grave. I can feel hot tears on my cheeks.

He was going to stop. All of the violence, all of the killing. *He was going to stop.* He told me as much last night.

At my back I hear the clomp of hooves. A minute later, I feel a horse snout nudge me in the back.

I turn around to see Deimos, his blood red coat marred by blood and several large gashes.

With a stuttering breath, I press my face against his. "What did they do to you and War?"

He nickers against me, the sound oddly pained; it's the closest thing I've heard to an animal crying.

I hold the steed's head, petting his cheek. And then I begin to sob. I sob for this man that everyone fears. I sob for the man that everyone wants dead. I sob for the man I *love*. The man who I never admitted this to.

He doesn't know.

I've said and done so many ugly things to him, but I haven't told him that he's the best part of my day. I haven't told him that he became a better man, and I didn't mean to, but I fell in love with him. That all I want is him, and he's gone.

He said he couldn't stay dead. He all but *promised* it to me.

And I never pegged him for a liar.

I collect myself and take a deep breath, letting Deimos go as I stand up.

I approach the grave once more.

I step up to it, and it's just as hard to stare down at War's body now as it was the first time I peered over the edge. Only this time, I force myself to stop and actually *look* at him.

The first thing I recognize are the tattoos on his hands. Not even death has diminished their glow. That's how I first knew it was him.

His hands are folded over the hilt of his sword, which lays over his armored chest.

If it weren't for his missing ... missing head, he'd look like some savage, sleeping knight. It's an oddly noble position for the phobos riders to place him in, considering how gruesomely they slaughtered him.

Eventually my eyes make their way up to War's head—or where his head should have been anyway. I have to bite back a sob.

The horseman's lower jaw is still attached to his body, and the skin of it and his upper neck look pristine. It's his chest and shoulders that are doused with blood. Lots and lots of blood. The sight doesn't look quite right, though I can't put my finger on exactly why ...

Before I get a chance to puzzle it out, my attention snags on a dark, egg-shaped device nestled next to War's thigh. There's another on the other side of his body. But now that I'm noticing those, my eyes take in the longer, cylindrical objects that rest around him like grave goods.

A chill courses through me. Those craters I passed on my way here, the mangled bodies scattered along their edges ...

You'll die if you try to save him, the phobos rider had told me.

I've never seen a grenade or an IED with my own eyes, but that must be what these are. Explosives.

I had assumed the phobos riders were using them to kill War. I hadn't realized they were using the explosives to keep the horseman *in* his grave—just in case he really could survive decapitation.

I sit back down on my butt, hard, and breathe through my mouth.

Don't cry, don't cry, don't cry. You can't fall apart, not yet. All isn't lost.

My gaze returns to the explosives. I swallow down a low moan.

But it is, though, isn't it?

War has no head and his body is packed with explosives.

I bite my lower lip hard enough to bleed and press my palms into my eye sockets. Now a cry does slip out, and it's an ugly, broken sound.

I was never supposed to fall in love with him. It wasn't just about the fact that he represented everything I was fighting against. It was also my deep certainty that everything you care for, you'll lose.

I drop my hands, my palms wet with tears, and I stare down into that crudely made pit again.

I can't lose you too, War.

What am I supposed to do?

The answer comes in the horseman's own words.

Have faith.

The trouble is, I'm not sure that I have faith in anything anymore, except maybe for him.

"*Can you?*" I ask.

"Die?" War clarifies. "*Of course I can. I just have a tendency to not stay dead.*"

Have faith. I take a deep breath. *Have faith.*

My eyes go back to his body, and I stare at the blood that

rings his lower neck and chest. I stare and stare at it.

Suddenly it hits me, what looks so odd about the blood splatter. Halfway up the column of his throat, the bloodstain abruptly stops. Not a single drop mars the skin beyond that point. It's as though the wound happened at War's neck, and then everything above it ...

Grew back.

I shouldn't dare to hope for something like that, but I can feel it in every shallow breath I take.

I touch my scar, tracing it as I gaze at War. According to him, I drowned in the Mediterranean, and I was reborn there as well. This might be the horseman's own rebirth I'm witnessing.

I take in the various explosives around him—the grenades and the IEDs. What happens if he survives decapitation? If he's rebuilt and whole once more? What happens if I leave him in that pit to regenerate and he wakes and moves and every single one of those bombs go off? What if he's blown apart, his body incinerated? Can he come back from that?

My breath catches.

A more important question: Am I willing to wait and let him suffer that fate?

No. Not in a thousand years.

I love him and I won't let him face death again, and it's my turn to believe in something bigger than myself.

I do have faith—in him and myself and this moment. Maybe even in God Himself.

I step up to the edge of the grave. "I surrender."

Chapter 59

I'VE LOST MY mind.

I'm sure of it when I lower myself into the grave. One misstep, and it'll be my boat explosion, part two.

Be brave, be brave, be brave.

Just as my feet are about to touch the bottom, I notice a grenade nestled in a deep shadow.

Holy balls, I was about to step on it.

Swallowing my yelp, I reposition my feet and land softly in the grave.

For a moment, I wait for the inevitable explosion. When it doesn't come, I release a shaky breath.

For better or worse, I'm in.

My eyes move over War.

Now, how to get him out?

First I grab his sword, prying it out of the horseman's grip as gently as I can. If I pull too hard, one of his arms might slide off his chest and into an explosive.

I manage to dislodge the hilt from one hand before quickly repositioning that hand back on his chest. Then I manage to dislodge and resettle his other hand.

Already, sweat is beginning to bead along my brow. My hands shake from fear, and right now, I really, really need them steady.

Holding the sword in my grip, I lift it up.

Fuck, this thing is stupid heavy.

Why does he need to have the biggest sword of all? So dumb.

My arms tremble as I raise it up. The top of the grave is right above my head. If I can just get it up there ...

I get the tip of it over the edge of the grave, and I shove the rest out as best I can. It takes several agonizing minutes, and by the end of it, I have sweat dripping down my chest and back, but finally, I get the weapon out of the grave.

My attention returns to War. Now that his sword is off him, all that's left is getting this giant of a man out of this pit without blowing both of us up.

I bite back crazy laughter. It's an impossible task. I don't know why I thought I could do this ...

Deep breath.

I push away my worries and focus on the task at hand. Removing the explosives from the grave is out of the question, which leaves only one other option: getting War and myself out of the pit unscathed.

Only, there's no way I'm going to be able to lug the horseman out with my own two hands.

I'd need something stronger to get him out of this grave ...

Something like a horse.

"Deimos!" I stage whisper, like raising my voice might set off one of these explosives ... which it might. You never know.

Last I saw, War's horse was lingering nearby, but for all I know, it's wandered off again ... probably to eat the bones of the long dead, or whatever immortal war horses do.

Nothing happens.

"Deimos!" I call a little louder.

Still nothing.

Freaking horses.

"*Deimos!*" I shout.

I don't blow up. Praise the heavens.

The horse ambles over, peeking over the edge of the pit at me. His reins slide forward, into the grave, the thin leather strap bumping into the shaft wall. I wince as it causes a little dirt to dislodge and skitter down, some of it dusting a nearby IED.

When nothing else happens, I sigh out a breath. Sweat is beginning to drip down my temples.

My eyes catch on the leather sword holster that wraps around the horseman's torso. If I can loop my own belt around War's holster *and* Deimos's reins, and if I can manage to buckle the reins to the holster, then Deimos could hoist War from his tomb. Hypothetically.

Even if that part of the plan works, there's still the issue of somehow incentivizing a horse to actually drag his master up and out of the grave ... and then, of course, there's the issue of the explosives.

It's disheartening to think that this is the best plan I have.

Damnit.

Be brave.

I remove my belt, tossing my weapons over the edge of the pit, and then I turn back to my horseman.

There's a place near his neck that's bare of any explosives. Carefully, I take a step forward, placing my foot on that open bit of earth.

Sweat drips from my brow and onto War's armor as I lean over him and begin to thread my belt through his leather shoulder straps.

Once I'm finished, I reach for Deimos's reins, which still hang into the grave shaft. I grab hold of them, winding my belt through them as well.

I lean my leg against War's body as I begin to buckle my belt.

I think I've got this.

I nudge the horseman's body a little more as I finish strapping it all together. In response, one of War's arms begins to slide off his chest—

No-no-no-no-no.

I drop the belt and the reins and make a desperate grab for his arm, but I'm not fast enough.

His forearm is about to bump right into—

BOOM!

BOOM–BOOM–BOOM!

Chapter 60

War

I WAKE, AS though from sleep, my eyes wincing open. The mortal sun bears down on me, and the ripe musk of the earth is in my nostrils, along with the scent of spilled blood.

It's the smell of my first memory, the one that formed me. That and anger. Back in my infancy, I was all cunning and anger. I've learned since then some of the finer points of men and war.

For a moment, I cannot place where I am or how I got here. I'm lying in some sort of hole and my skin feels new. This is one of those sensations that I doubt humans have much experience with. New skin.

It all comes back to me then—how I was struck down. My riders lured me into a trap.

I feel my rage, like a spark, catch and grow.

They closed in on me and held me at bay and slit my throat damn near to the bone.

My rage doubles and doubles again. How much time has

passed? How long did it take for my body to reform? That is the trouble with skin and bones and blood and muscle. They can only repair themselves so fast, even on one like me.

I begin to push myself up, my body feeling new and old all at once.

A thick mass of flesh slides off of me.

This too, is a familiar sensation. How many fields have I watered with lifeblood and fertilized with flesh? How many men have clawed their way out from beneath such death?

Countless.

I've given this way of life up, and yet it will always be there as my first memories of existence.

I push away the body as I sit up.

But then my eyes catch on the delicate wrist and the two hamsa bracelets—

Everything within me stills. Everything but fear. Cold rolled fear.

I let out a noise.

No.

"Miriam?" My hands go to the body, but the limbs—the two that are left—are cold.

I don't believe it.

It's not her. She wouldn't be this foolish. She wouldn't. Please God, she wouldn't.

I flip the corpse over, trying to wash away the sight of the soft, feminine limbs. Most of the body has been blown away, but there's some skin remaining around the neck.

My eyes move to the throat, to the holy scar at its base.

Surrender.

"*No,*" it comes out as a plea. "*Miriam.*"

There's not much of her face remaining. There's not much of *anything* remaining.

I don't expect my throat to tighten and my gut to twist at the sight of it all. I am used to dismemberment. I am not used to caring about the creature dismembered. But I always have with her. Her injuries always made me feel odd. Crazed and helpless and human. So very, disturbingly human.

She can't be dead.

"Miriam," I beg, tilting her head back. It flops to the side.

A thousand upon a thousand years and so many countless deaths. None of it had cost me anything.

But this one—

She's *not* dead. She can't be dead. Not her and not ...

My eyes slip down to what remains of her torso. A third of it is simply gone, along with all the hopes and dreams it carried.

"*No*," I sob. "No, no, no ..." I cradle her against me.

Desperate, I press a hand to her skin, willing her wounds to heal. But the flesh won't stitch back together. It won't even *attempt* it. It's stopped functioning altogether.

For one mad moment, I consider raising her like any other undead. But my heart crumples at the thought. It wouldn't be her. I've reanimated enough bodies to know I'm working with a vessel and nothing more. What made Miriam *Miriam* is gone. Long gone.

I begin to weep in earnest, clutching her tightly to me.

Why, wife?

Why?

I glance around us at the sand and dust that coats our bodies. At the partially caved in wall near my feet. It takes a bit longer to see the few bits of metal scattered about and the charred remains of Miriam's clothing.

They obviously buried me with the same damn explosives that kept going off when they were trying to kill me. And Miriam ... Miriam must have seen them as well.

Which means my wife came for me despite their presence. Was it suicide? She had an unhealthy leaning towards death. Or had she tried to retrieve me?

My gaze goes back to her throat.

Surrender. The word mocks me now.

I feel mortal and powerless.

That thought alone pulls me from my grief. I straighten my shoulders.

I was *never* powerless. Not when I first woke and not now.

There is still one path that might be open to me, one possibility left.

I hold Miriam's body to me and I begin to chant in Angelic.

This is my last hope. My *only* hope.

I close my eyes and the world disappears.

When I open them again, I am somewhere else.

Chapter 61

War

THANATOS STANDS IN front of me like he's been waiting. He looks unsurprised but vaguely disappointed.

"No," he says.

Around us, the air shifts and moves. We are everywhere and nowhere all at once. So many voices filter in, so many faces flicker by. The humanity we swore to destroy is still teeming around us.

"Why are you here?" he asks, his dark wings looming behind his back.

"You already know," I growl.

He eyes me up and down. "You should be doing your duty."

"I have." I take a step forward. Men quiver at even this slight show of power. Death doesn't so much as flinch. "I want her back."

He tilts his head, his black hair slipping from behind an ear. "I have never seen you want for a human."

Death wouldn't understand love, not as he currently is. He hasn't roamed the earth like I have. It is a sensation one must live to experience.

My voice drops low. "She's marked," I say instead. This is something he will understand.

And yet Thanatos appears unmoved. "She served her purpose, and now she's been called home."

I feel a part of myself break at his words. *I* am her home. Not the Great Everafter.

Stepping forward, I grab his shoulder and squeeze. We have always been close, he and I. Surely he will work with me the way we have always worked together.

"I beg you," I say, my voice low, "bring her back."

Death's eyes narrow. "When have you *ever* begged?" He appears put off by it. "My sure-footed, vengeful brother, you *take*."

And yet I cannot take *this*.

"*Please*."

Thanatos's wings stretch, then resettle. He's intrigued, which is an improvement from *unmoved*. "You and I both know she cannot live," Death says. "That's not our task."

"You spared Pestilence's woman."

Thanatos had mercy then.

"A curiosity I will not repeat," Death says. "Besides, his woman was ... retrievable. Yours is not."

"She's already crossed?" I ask, that sense of hopelessness flooding me all over again. But of course she's crossed. The moment life released her from its clutches, she must've.

My brother's demeanor softens. "She's fine—as is the child."

The child. My child.

When I first woke as a man, and then when I fought—all that time I thought I had nothing to lose. I thought the end necessitated the means. Humans—*all* humans—were doomed to die. It wasn't personal.

472

I feel like I'm choking on my old beliefs now.

"I will do *anything*," I say.

Death's lips press together. "There is only one thing that can be done."

I don't breathe.

"Surrender your sword, War."

My one purpose. My existence and identity wrapped into one.

Surrender. The single sign written on Miriam.

I suck in a breath.

He'd always known. I was the one who'd been a fool in my certainty. I'd basked in my utter confidence that Miriam was mine by divine right and that nothing could change that.

Nothing *can* change that. This isn't over. It doesn't have to be.

Surrender.

Nothing comes without sacrifice—this least of all. Miriam was right, love and war cannot coexist. I can have one or the other, but not both.

My sword wasn't with me when I left the earth, but it's here with me now, settled in its scabbard like we were never separated. I reach for it. The metal sings as I withdraw the weapon from its sheath.

"So that is your choice," Thanatos says, curiosity and disappointment rolled into his voice.

"It *is* no choice." I will cast my lot with the mortals. The fallible, *complicated* mortals.

I begin to hand my blade over, hilt first. Thanatos reaches to take it from me.

At the last moment, I pull back the sword, withholding it. "The child comes too."

Death's dark eyes study me. "What is the point, brother? She was barely a possibility."

She. A girl then.

"She comes back," I insist.

Death looks at me with his dark eyes. He's judging my heart just as much as I've judged humankind's. Eventually he nods. "Enjoy what time you have left with them," he says honestly. "I hope it is worth it."

With those words, a change overtakes me.

I'm stripped bare of my bloodlust and my immortality. It lifts like a weight from my shoulders.

I'm no longer proud War but a penitent man.

"You are *released*."

Chapter 62

Miriam

I BLINK MY eyes open. It's bright, and my skin tingles. I don't feel quite right.

War leans over me, and my eyes focus.

I gasp in a breath at the sight of him, whole and unmarred.

"*Wife*," he says, his own voice shocked. And then he pulls me against him.

War buries his face in my neck, and his huge body begins to tremble. It takes me a moment to realize he's weeping.

"You're *alive*," I say, amazed, running my fingers through the hair on his head. I'd feared that this death was going to be his last.

But how ... ?

"You shouldn't have come for me," he says, his voice hoarse.

I pull away a little to look at him, and I touch one of his tears. I've never seen the horseman weep.

"I love you," I say. I bottled up those words until it was

nearly too late. They rush out of me now. "I will never not come for you because *I love you.*"

War's face is naked emotion. Disbelief and joy fill his features, chasing away his tears.

His hands clasp my cheeks and he searches my eyes. "I am having one of your human dreams," he says. "This is too wonderful to be real."

"I *think* this is real." Right?

I glance around me. We're not in the grave anymore, but we're nearby, the dead still scattered around us. I remember that—and I remember trying to save War. I'd been so close, but then his hand slipped. I don't remember an explosion, but I don't remember anything else either. My memory simply stops.

"What happened?" I ask.

War's throat works. "When I woke ..." he draws in a shaky breath, "You were *gone.*" His eyes are wild with emotion. "You came to save me and *I couldn't save you.*"

I glance down at my body. My clothes are in charred tatters. Just seeing the state they're in ... there must have been an explosion. One that I don't remember and never felt.

I take in my outfit again. The fabric is almost completely burned away, and yet my skin remains unblemished.

The abrupt end in my memory ... I must've been hurt badly enough to black out. Which could only mean that War somehow healed me.

"You *did* save me," I reply, confused. How could he say he hadn't done so? If he hadn't, there would be wounds, and I would be in pain.

"Not with my own two hands," he admits.

My brows furrow. I don't understand.

"Then how?" I ask.

He strokes my hair back. "I am free, Miriam."

I must've hit my head really hard because I'm not following. "Free of what?"

"My purpose."

It's as much as he's admitted before, but this time, I truly process his words. "You really aren't going to kill anymore?" I say.

He shakes his head. "Not unless it's to protect you—or our daughter."

I raise my eyebrows, then glance down at my stomach. "Our *daughter?*"

He smiles at me, and that smile seems to stretch to every corner of his face. He's so painfully gorgeous. "Sorry to ruin the surprise."

Our *daughter.*

"How did you find out?"

"I told you, I didn't save you. My brother did."

"Your brother?" I say quizzically.

"Death."

With that one word, my light mood vanishes.

There's only one reason why Death himself would save me.

"I ... died?" I can barely force the words out.

War stares at me for a long moment. "For a time."

Oh God ... *I died.*

I touch my stomach again, panic clawing up my throat. "And the baby—she's still alive?"

"I made sure of it."

I begin to weep then—because apparently crying is contagious right now.

I don't understand. I went from dying to living. As did War. As did our child.

"I surrendered," I say nonsensically.

War pulls me tight against him. "So did I."

For a moment, the two of us simply stay like that. His body is as solid as ever; he *feels* unchanged, and yet things must've changed.

"What's the catch?" I ask him.

Everything I love, I lose. Now, when it seems like I have

regained it all, I'm afraid it'll slip away from me again.

"There is no catch," War says, "unless you count the fact that now I am well and truly mortal. I will live and age and die as you will."

When he said he was free of his purpose, he meant it literally.

Whatever happened while I was ... *gone* ... it came at a steep personal cost to War. So steep that he lost his immortality.

My heart breaks a little at that. I've seen enough of death to last me at least twenty-seven lifetimes.

"And Deimos?" I ask.

"He will endure the same fate."

"What about the other horsemen?" The ones who haven't yet walked the earth.

War's expression turns grim. "My brothers will not stop, and they are even stronger than me."

So the world still isn't safe—but it isn't *beyond* saving, either. Pestilence and War laid down their weapons. Not all hope is lost.

Besides, that's a worry for a later time.

I'm alive, War's alive, and my child's alive. Oh—and there will be no more killing.

The corner of my mouth curves up as a thought hits me. "Are all your powers gone, or can you still speak every language that has ever existed?"

"San sani du, seni nüşina ukuvı?"

Can you still understand me when I do?

A laugh slips out. "I can."

War and I stare at each other, and for the first time, it truly sinks in.

It's over. It's really over. The fighting and killing and suffering. I get to have this man and my child and a future too.

My smile slips away. "What do we do now?" I ask him.

"I don't care, wife, so long as I do it with you."

Chapter 63

MY HEART IS in my throat when I knock on the blue door in front of me. The house, like many others in Heraklion, Crete, is picturesque, despite showing some signs of weather damage.

Maybe we got it wrong again. It wouldn't be the first time, unfortunately.

On the other side of the door I can hear muffled voices, then the sound of footfalls approaching.

It's taken me a long time to get to this moment—nearly a decade if I tally up all the time that's passed. If, of course, this *is* in fact the moment I've been waiting for.

The door opens, and I don't breathe as I take in the woman standing on the other side.

I got it right. I know it in an instant.

She looks different—much, much older than I remember— but all the familiar features are still there.

"Mom?" I say.

For a moment, my mother just stands there, her face blank.

She studies my own face, like this might be a joke, and then—
there it is. Recognition flares in her eyes. She covers her mouth
with her hands, her eyes welling up.

"Miriam?"

I draw in what feels like my first breath. I nod, blinking
back my own tears. I've waited so long for this.

Can't believe it's happening.

"It's me," I say, my voice shaky.

She lets out a sob, then opens her arms wide, sweeping me
up into her embrace.

My mom is really still alive. And I'm hugging her.

Years of pain and separation dissolve away in that moment.
I dreamed of this embrace so many times.

Her entire body is shaking. "My baby. My daughter." She's
now openly weeping and rocking me against her, and I can't
see straight through my own tears. She pets my hair back as
she holds me. "For years I prayed to whatever god would
listen," she says, the apology thick in her voice. "I stayed here,
on Crete, because I wanted to be close in case—"

I shake my head against her. I'm not here for explanations.
I understand. Everything I went through had to happen for
me to find War and end up right here, and it all started with
my miraculous survival from that first explosion.

"It's alright, Mom. I found you." *And you're alive.* This is my
wildest hope come true. "It's alright," I repeat again.

Now she clings to me, like I'm the mother and she's the
child. "My daughter, my intelligent, resilient daughter. There
are so many things I want to know about you—so many years
and memories ..."

"Mama?" a woman calls from inside the house.

I stiffen at the familiar voice. I remember that voice singing
me to sleep years and years ago. It's like music, hearing it
again when I thought I might never get to.

I glance over my mother's shoulder and see a young
woman approach the door, her brow pinched with concern.

My sister, Lia, no longer looks like the round-faced girl I remember. And yet, I could never mistake her for another.

There's no moment of confusion with her. My sister gasps when she sees me.

"*Miri*," she says, falling back on her old nickname for me.

My mom lets me go long enough for me to fall into the embrace of my sister. I pull her close to me. Closing my eyes, I relish the feel of holding her again.

I feared I'd never get this, I want to say. *I feared I had lost you forever.*

But I didn't lose either my mother or my sister. Somehow we all survived the Arrival, a civil war, and two horsemen of the apocalypse.

Speaking of horsemen ...

Behind me I hear War's unmistakable stride coming up to the door. Up until now, he'd been waiting a little ways away, letting me have my moment. There's nothing like a muscled giant of a man to set people's nerves on edge.

I can tell the instant my family notices him. My sister's arms tense, and I hear my mother draw in a quick breath.

War comes up next to me, and almost instinctively, my sister releases me, stepping back a little. My mother shrinks back as well. Their earlier friendliness gives way to polite wariness. It takes them both another few seconds to register the small human clinging to him.

I mean, men who hold toddlers always look a pinch less threatening—right?

In War's case, maybe it's a very small pinch.

I reach out to him. "This is—" I pause. I still call my horseman by his given name—*War*—but we've bent the rules when interacting with other people. He's been all sorts of names, none of which really fit him.

"I'm her husband," he says for me. "War."

Welp, there went that smooth introduction.

And cue that uncomfortable moment when your family

realizes their son-in-law is *not normal.*

They stare at him with wide eyes.

"Miriam," my mom says, followed by a long pause, "is this … ?" *A horseman of the apocalypse?*

Only, she can't say it. It's too improbable. Too ridiculous.

I lick my lips. "He doesn't do that anymore," I say.

I'm sure that makes her feel *real* reassured.

My mother worries her lower lip, taking War in. "We heard you disappeared," she says to him. "We didn't know what had happened."

Um, surprise. He knocked up your daughter. And now he's on your doorstep.

War might've relinquished his task, but mortality hasn't made him any less terrifying. Nor has it made the process of trying to explain his existence—and current virtuousness—an easy task. The tattoos on his knuckles still glow crimson, his stature is still as looming and lethal as it ever was, and his eyes still carry the memory of all that violence.

My mother's eyes go to the baby. Now, they soften again. "Is this … ?"

"This is your grandchild, Maya," I say.

"You have a daughter," my mom says, glancing at me, and now her emotion is choking her up once more.

"Do you want to hold her?" I ask.

She nods, looking like she's about to cry all over again.

I glance at my husband. War hesitates, his eyes dropping to our daughter. He takes protectiveness to a whole new level with his daughter. To be fair, Maya looks equally unenthusiastic about leaving his arms. But eventually, he hands our daughter over.

My mom takes my daughter in her arms and stares down at her little, brooding face. A tear slips down my mother's cheek, followed by another. She's trembling, and I use the moment to put my arm around her. A moment later, my sister joins us.

We're all reunited and crying like children.

My mother clears her throat and glances at me and War again. "Where are my manners? Come in, both of you. Would either of you like some coffee?"

I nod, caught between happiness and this painful ache in my chest. "That would be wonderful."

Lia retreats back into the house, heading for what I imagine is the kitchen. Tentatively, I begin to follow her. Looking over my shoulder, I see War handily removing our daughter from my mom's arms.

My mother grasps War's forearm and squeezes. "Welcome to the family, my son."

He gives her one of his unreadable looks, then nods, his eyes looking a little conflicted. War's never known what it means to have a mother ... now he might.

My heart is squeezing, squeezing.

"And—thank you, for bringing my daughter back to us," my mother adds, her eyes moving to me.

War's own gaze slides to mine, and he gives me a gentle look, one that makes me forget he was ever anything besides my soul mate. "That's what you do for those you love," he says. "You bring them back."

Epilogue

Year 16 of the Horsemen

IT BEGINS WITH a tremble. The ground quakes from deep within, each second more violent than the last, until it feels as though the very earth itself were trying to shake off its own skin.

Colossal waves crash along coastlines, buildings fall to the earth, and across the world, people take shelter as they wait for the terrible earthquake to pass.

The first horseman staggers as the truth hits him. *It's happening again.*

The second horseman wakes from sleep with a sharp inhalation. Ancient words are ripped from his lips. "*Ina bubūi imuttu.*"

They will die of hunger.

And in a crypt of his own making, an unearthly creature stirs.

His fingers flex around his scythe. His bronze armor rustles as he stirs.

His green eyes open and he draws in his first breath in many long years.

And then he smiles.

Author's Note

GASPS FOR BREATH

Wait, the book is finished? I thought this day would never come! This was a book that simply wouldn't end. War held me by sword point and demanded I make it twice as long and that I work twice as hard as usual before I release it to you all. (He's a bossy brute!) I hope I did right by him and by you. An extra thank you goes out to all you readers who have been waiting a loooong time for this one. I was supposed to release this book months before I did, so I appreciate your patience!

A word about the gibberish in the book. The dead languages War speaks are mostly made up. The only exceptions to this are the bits of dialogue at the very beginning of the novel, his use of the word *wife* ("*aššatu*"), and his final foreign line. The early dialogue is written in ancient Egyptian, though I'm sure my hieroglyphics professor would die at some of the artistic liberties I took with the words and syntax. The other lines in the novel—namely "*aššatu*" and "*Ina bubūi imuttu*"—are Akkadian, and they translate to "my wife" and "they will die of hunger," respectively. A big thank you goes to assyrianlanguages.org, which provided those Akkadian translations.

Every other instance of War speaking in tongues was based

off of translations I got from Google Translate ... then proceeded to take a hacksaw to. (War is not the only savage here, muahaha!) A huge thank you to Google Translate and the languages that inspired the lines (which include Samoan, Macedonian, Kyrgyz, Sinhala, Basque, Latin, and Shona). And apologies to anyone whose eyes were blighted by my desperate attempts at linguistics (which I nearly failed in college ... eep!).

A huge thank you goes to Amanda Steele for proofing this baby at the last minute! You gave up such a large chunk of your time to polish this book up, and I am so, so grateful for it. Your edits were insightful and totally spot on.

To literally all of the authors and readers out there who showed excitement for this book, you are the reason my head no longer fits through doors. Kidding—I can squeeze it through if I shimmy a little. But in all seriousness, your continued professional and personal support means so much.

My family—both immediate and extended—always deserves a shout out. They are some of my biggest cheerleaders, and I'm incredibly lucky that they are my village. Love you all!

To everyone who took a chance on this book, I am so, so humbled by your continued readership. Truly. It still amazes me that people want to read the crazy stories I write down, and I am forever grateful to you all for taking a chance on my words and worlds.

Hugs and happy reading,
Laura

Keep a lookout for the next book in Laura Thalassa's *The Four Horseman* series:

Famine

Coming soon.

Never want to miss a release?

Visit laurathalassa.com to sign up for Laura Thalassa's mailing list for the latest news on her upcoming novels.

Be sure to check out Laura Thalassa's young adult paranormal romance series

Rhapsodic

Out now!

Be sure to check out Laura Thalassa's new adult post-apocalyptic romance series

The Queen of All that Dies

Out now!

Be sure to check out Laura Thalassa's young adult paranormal romance series

The Unearthly

Out now!

Other books by Laura Thalassa

FOUND IN THE forest when she was young, Laura Thalassa was raised by fairies, kidnapped by werewolves, and given over to vampires as repayment for a hundred year debt. She's been brought back to life twice, and, with a single kiss, she woke her true love from eternal sleep. She now lives happily ever after with her undead prince in a castle in the woods.

... or something like that anyway.

When not writing, Laura can be found scarfing down guacamole, hoarding chocolate for the apocalypse, or curled up on the couch with a good book.

Made in United States
North Haven, CT
07 July 2023

38666442R00300